O9-ABF-792

RaeAnne Thayne

———

A COLD CREEK CHRISTMAS STORY & CHRISTMAS IN COLD CREEK

HARLEQUIN®SPECIAL EDITION®

ISBN-13: 978-0-373-83811-0

A Cold Creek Christmas Story &
Christmas in Cold Creek

Copyright © 2015 by Harlequin Books S.A.

Recycling programs for this product may not exist in your area.

The publisher acknowledges the copyright holder of the individual works as follows:

A Cold Creek Christmas Story
Copyright © 2015 by RaeAnne Thayne

Christmas in Cold Creek
Copyright © 2011 by RaeAnne Thayne

HARLEQUIN®
www.Harlequin.com

Printed in U.S.A.

CONTENTS

Dear Reader,

I am sometimes asked what I would like to do if I hadn't become an author. That's a tough question to answer—I really can't imagine doing anything else! But if I did have to pick another vocation at some point in my life, I think I would like to be either a teacher or a librarian.

In *A Cold Creek Christmas Story*, children's librarian Celeste Nichols has the best of both worlds. She's an author and a librarian! In fifty books, I've never written a character who is a writer before and while Celeste is not at all autobiographical, it was still fun to write about the writing journey through my heroine's eyes.

I wish you and your loved ones the merriest of holidays.

All my very best,

RaeAnne

A COLD CREEK CHRISTMAS STORY

Chapter 1

If she didn't have thirty children showing up in the next half hour, Celeste Nichols would have been tempted to climb into her little SUV, pull out of the Pine Gulch library parking lot and just keep on driving.

She shifted the blasted endlessly ringing cell phone to the crook of her shoulder while she sorted through the books scattered across her cubicle in the offices of the library to find what she would be reading for story hour.

"I told you earlier in the week, I'm not ready to make a decision about this yet."

Joan Manning, her and Hope's long-suffering literary agent, gave a low, frustrated sound of disapproval. "We can't hold them off much longer. We've already stalled for two weeks. They want to start production right after the holidays, and they can't do that without signatures from you and Hope."

Celeste gazed down at a copy of Dr. Seuss's perennial holiday favorite, *How the Grinch Stole Christmas*. She had a feeling she was the one being the Grinch here. Hope was completely on board with the extraordinary offer one of the leading animation companies had made for movie rights to their book, *Sparkle and the Magic Snowball*.

Celeste was the one who couldn't quite be comfortable with the idea of someone else taking control of her words, her creation, and turning *Sparkle* into an animated movie, complete with the attendant merchandising and sublicensing. A fast-food chain was already talking about making a toy for its kids' meals, for crying out loud.

The whole journey of the past twelve months seemed like a bizarre, surreal, completely unbelievable dream.

A year ago she had known exactly who she was—an unassuming children's librarian in the small town of Pine Gulch, Idaho, in the western shadow of the Teton Mountain Range.

Now, to her immense shock, she was a celebrated author about to see the release of her second children's book with several more scheduled in the next few years. Along with that had come things she had never imagined when she'd been writing little stories for her niece and nephew—she had a website, a publicist, a literary agent.

Her quiet, safe world seemed to be spinning out of her control, and this movie deal was the prime example.

"A few more days, Celeste," Joan pushed. "You can't keep stalling. You have to make a decision. Hollywood has a short attention span and an even shorter supply of patience. Do you want your story made into a movie or not?"

She liked Joan very much, as brash and abrupt as the woman could be, but everything with her was an emergency and had to be decided *right now*. Pressure pains stabbed with little forks behind her eyes and her shoulders felt as if someone had jammed them in a vice and was cranking down hard.

"I know. I just need to be sure this is the right choice for Sparkle."

"Sparkle is a fictional character. You need to be sure it's the right choice for *you* and for your sister. We've been going over this for weeks. I don't know what else I can say to convince you this is the best deal you're going to get."

"I know that. You've done a great job with the negotiations. I just need…a little more time."

"A few days," Joan said, her voice clipped with frustration. "That's all, then I have to give them some kind of an answer."

"I know. Thank you. I'll get back with you tomorrow or the day after."

"Just remember, most people would see this as a dream come true."

Apparently, she wasn't *most people*. After they said their goodbyes, Celeste set her cell phone back on the desk, again fighting the urge to climb into her SUV and keep on driving.

That was her sister Hope's way, to wander from place to place as they had done in their itinerant childhood. Celeste was different. She liked security, consistency.

Normalcy.

In the past twelve months her life had been anything

but normal. She had gone from writing only for herself and her niece and nephew to writing for a vast audience she never could have imagined.

It had all started when her sister Hope had come home the previous Christmas for what was supposed to be a brief stay between overseas teaching jobs. Hope had overheard her reading one of her stories to Louisa and Barrett and had put her considerable artistic skills to work illustrating the story to sell in the gift store of their family's holiday-themed attraction, The Christmas Ranch.

The result had been a sweet, charming Christmas story about a brave little reindeer named Sparkle. Neither Hope nor Celeste had ever imagined the book would be touted by a presenter on one of the national morning news program—or that the resulting sales would explode internationally and end up saving the floundering Christmas Ranch *and* the family's cattle operation, the Star N Ranch.

She was beyond gratified that so many people liked her writing and the story—and especially Hope's delightful illustrations—but some part of her wanted to go back to that peaceful time when her biggest decisions revolved around what to read for her weekly story hour at the Pine Gulch Public Library.

With a sigh, she turned back to the job at hand. She was still sorting through the final choices when the head librarian poked her head into the cubicle.

"Looks as if we're going to have a nice crowd." Frankie Vittori, the head librarian, looked positively gleeful. "I hope we have room for everybody."

"Oh, that's terrific!" she exclaimed, mentally shelving her worries about the movie deal for now.

She meant the words. She loved nothing more than introducing children to the wonder and magic to be found inside the pages of a good book.

Books had saved her. During the chaos of her childhood, they had offered solace and safety and *hope* amid fear. She had no idea how she would have survived without friends such as Anne of Green Gables, Bilbo Baggins, Matilda, Harry Potter and Hermione and Ron Weasley.

"I only hope we've got enough of our craft project to go around. It seems as if the crowd increases every month."

Frankie grinned. "That's because everybody in town wants to come hear our local celebrity author read in hopes of catching a sneak peek at the new Sparkle story coming down the pike."

She managed to conceal her instinctive wince. She really didn't like being a celebrity.

On one level, it was immensely gratifying. Who would have ever dreamed that she—quiet, awkward, introverted Celeste Nichols—would be in this position, having people actually *care* what she had to say?

On another, it was terrifying. At some point the naked emperor was always exposed. She feared the day when somebody would finally ask why all the fuss about her simple little tales.

For now, Frankie was simply thrilled to have a crowd at the library for any kind of reason. Celeste's boss and friend vibrated with energy, as she always did, her toe tapping to unheard music and her fingers fidgeting on the edge of the desk. Frankie was as skinny as a flagpole, probably because she never stopped moving.

Her husband, Lou, on the other hand, was the exact opposite—a deep reservoir of calm serenity.

They made the perfect pair and had two adorable kids who fell somewhere in the middle.

"I know it's more work for you," Frankie went on. "But I have to say, it's a brilliant idea to have two story times, one for the younger kids in the morning and one for early and middle readers after school."

Celeste smiled. "If you do say so yourself?"

Frankie beamed. "What can I say? I'm brilliant sometimes."

"That you are." Since Frankie had come to the library from upstate New York two years earlier, patron usage was way up and support had never been higher.

Frankie was bold and impassioned about the need for libraries, especially in the digital age. Celeste was more than a little envious of her overwhelming confidence, which helped the director fight for every penny of funding from the city council and the community in general.

Celeste would never be as outgoing and vivacious as Frankie, even though she was every bit as passionate about her job as the children's librarian. She liked being behind the scenes—except for the weekly story times, her favorite part of the job.

She checked her watch and quickly stood up. "I guess I'd better get out there."

She picked up the box of craft supplies they would use for the activity she had planned and headed for the large meeting room they had found worked best for story times.

"Oh, I almost forgot," Frankie said with a sly grin. "Make sure you check out the major hottie dad out there at ten o'clock."

Despite her amazing husband, Frankie was always locating hot guys, whether at their weekly lunches at one of the restaurants in town or on the few trips they'd taken into Jackson Hole or Idaho Falls. She always said she was only scouting possible dates for Celeste, which made Celeste roll her eyes. Her last date had been months ago.

"Is he anybody I know?"

"*I've* never seen him before. He's either new in town or a tourist. You can't miss him. He's wearing a Patek Philippe watch and a brown leather jacket that probably costs as much as our annual nonfiction budget. He's definitely not your average Cold Creek cowboy with horse pucky on his boots."

Okay, intriguing. She hadn't heard of anybody new moving into the small town, especially not someone who could afford the kind of attire Frankie was talking about. Sometimes well-to-do people bought second or third homes in the area, looking for a mountain getaway. They built beautiful homes in lovely alpine settings and then proceeded to visit them once or twice a year.

"I'll be sure to check him out while I'm trying to keep the kids entertained."

Frankie was right about one thing—the place was packed. Probably thirty children ranging in age from about six to eleven sat on the floor while roughly that same number of parents sat in chairs around the room.

For just an instant she felt a burst of stage fright at the idea of all those people staring at her. She quickly pushed it down. Normally she didn't like being in front of a crowd, but this was her job and she loved it. How could she be nervous about reading stories to children?

She would just pretend their parents weren't there, like she usually did.

When she walked in, she was heartened by the spontaneous round of applause and the anticipation humming in the air.

She spotted a few people she recognized, friends and neighbors. Joey Santiago, nephew to her brother-in-law Rafe, sat beside his father, waving wildly at her.

She grinned and waved back at him. She would have thought Rafe was the hot dad—all that former navy SEAL mojo he had going on—but Frankie knew him well and he wasn't wearing a leather jacket or an expensive watch anyway.

She loved Rafe dearly, for many reasons—most important because he adored her sister Hope—but also because she wasn't sure she would be standing here, ready to entertain a group of thirty children with the magic of literature if not for his role in their lives so many years ago.

She saw a few other hot dads in the crowd—Justin Hartford, who used to be a well-known movie star but who seemed to fit in better now that he had been a rancher in Cold Creek Canyon for years. Ben Caldwell, the local veterinarian, was definitely hot. Then there was the fire chief, Taft Bowman, and his stepchildren. Taft always looked as though he could be the December cover model on a calendar of yummy firefighters.

All of them were locals of long-standing, though, and Frankie knew them well. They couldn't be the man she was talking about.

Ah, well. She would try to figure out the mystery later, maybe while the children were making the snowman ornaments she had planned for them.

"Thank you so much for coming, everybody. We're going to start off with one of my favorite Christmas stories."

"Is it *Sparkle and the Magic Snowball*?" Alex Bowman, Taft's stepson, asked hopefully.

She blushed a little as everyone laughed. "Not today. Today we're focusing on stories about Christmas, snow and snowmen."

Ben's son raised his hand. "Is Sparkle going to be here today, Ms. Nichols?"

Was that why so many people had turned out? Were they all hoping she'd brought along the *actual* Sparkle, who was the celebrity in residence at The Christmas Ranch?

Last year, Hope had talked her into having their family's beloved reindeer—and the inspiration for her eponymously named series of stories—make a quick appearance in the parking lot of the library.

"I'm afraid not. He's pretty busy at The Christmas Ranch right now."

She tried to ignore the small sounds of disappointment from the children and a few of their parents. "I've got tons of other things in store for you, though. To start out, here's one of everyone's favorite holiday stories, *How the Grinch Stole Christmas.*"

She started reading and, as usual, it only took a few pages before a hush fell over the room. The children were completely enthralled—not by her, she was only the vehicle, but by the power of story.

She became lost, too, savoring every word. When she neared the climax, she looked up for dramatic effect and found the children all watching her with eager expressions, ready for more. Her gaze lifted to the parents and she spotted someone she hadn't seen before, a man sitting on the back row of parents with a young girl beside him.

He had brown hair shot through with lighter streaks, a firm jaw and deep blue eyes.

This had to be the hot dad Frankie had meant.

Her heart began to pound fiercely, so loud in her ears she wondered if the children could hear it over the microphone clipped to her collar.

She knew this man, though she hadn't seen him for years.

Flynn Delaney.

She would recognize him *anywhere*. After all, he had been the subject of her daydreams all through her adolescence.

She hadn't heard he was back in Pine Gulch. Why was he here? Was he staying at his grandmother's house just down the road from the Star N? It made sense. His grandmother, Charlotte, had died several months earlier and her house had been empty ever since.

She suddenly remembered everything else that had happened to this man in the past few months and her gaze shifted to the young girl beside him, blonde and ethereal like a Christmas angel herself.

Celeste's heart seemed to melt.

This must be her. His daughter. Oh, the poor, poor dear.

The girl was gazing back at Celeste with her eyes wide and her hands clasped together at her chest as if she couldn't wait another instant to hear the rest of the story.

Everyone was gazing at her with expectation, and

Celeste realized she had stopped in the middle of the story to stare at Flynn and his daughter.

Appalled at herself, she felt heat soak her cheeks. She cleared her throat and forced her attention back to the story, reading the last few pages with rather more heartiness than she had started with.

This was her job, she reminded herself as she closed the book, helping children discover all the delights to be found in good stories.

She wasn't here to ogle Flynn Delaney, for heaven's sake, even when there was plenty about him any woman would consider ogle-worthy.

Flynn didn't think he had ever felt quite so conspicuously out of place—and that included the times he had walked the red carpet with Elise at some Hollywood premiere or other, when he had invariably wanted to fade into the background.

They all seemed to know each other and he felt like the odd man out. Was everybody staring? He didn't want to think so, but he seemed to feel each curious sidelong glance as the residents of Pine Gulch tried to figure out who he was.

At least one person knew. He was pretty sure he hadn't imagined that flicker of recognition in Celeste Nichols's eyes when she'd spotted him. It surprised him, he had to admit. They had only met a few times, all those years ago.

He only remembered her because she had crashed her bike in front of his grandmother's house during one of his visits. Charlotte hadn't been home, so Flynn had been left to tend her scrapes and bruises and help her get back to the Star N up the road.

Things like that stuck in a guy's memory bank. Otherwise he probably never would have made the connection between the author of his daughter's favorite book, *Sparkle and the Magic Snowball*, and the shy girl with long hair and glasses he had once known in another lifetime.

He wouldn't be here at the library if not for Celeste, actually. He had so much work to do clearing out his grandmother's house and really didn't have time to listen to Dr. Seuss, as great as the story might be, but what other choice did he have? Since leaving the hospital, Olivia had been a pale, frightened shadow of the girl she used to be. Once she had faced the world head-on, daring and curious and funny. Now she was afraid of so many things. Loud noises. Strangers. Crowds.

From the moment she'd found out that the author of her favorite book lived here in Pine Gulch where they were staying for a few weeks—and was the children's librarian, who also hosted a weekly story hour—Olivia had been obsessed with coming. She had written the date of the next event on the calendar and had talked of nothing else.

She was finally going to meet the Sparkle lady, and she couldn't have been more excited about it if Celeste Nichols had been Mrs. Santa Claus in the flesh.

For the first time in weeks she showed enthusiasm for something, and he had jumped at the chance to nurture that.

He glanced down at his daughter. She hadn't shifted her gaze away from Celeste, watching the librarian with clear hero worship on her features. She seemed utterly enchanted by the librarian.

The woman was lovely, he would give her that much,

though in a quiet, understated way. She had big green eyes behind her glasses and glossy dark hair that fell in waves around a heart-shaped face.

She was probably about four years younger than his own thirty-two. That didn't seem like much now, but when she had crashed her bike, she had seemed like a little kid, thirteen or so to his seventeen.

As he listened to her read now, he remembered that time, wondering why it seemed so clear to him, especially with everything that had happened to him since.

He'd been out mowing the lawn when she'd fallen and had seen her go down out of the corner of his gaze. Flynn had hurried to help her and found her valiantly trying not to cry even though she had a wide gash in her knee that would definitely need stitches and pebbles imbedded in her palm.

He had helped her into his grandmother's house and called her aunt Mary. While they'd waited for help, he had found first-aid supplies—bandages, ointment, cleansing wipes—and told her lousy jokes to distract her from the pain.

After Mary had taken her to the ER for stitches in her knee and he had finished mowing for his grandmother, he had gone to work fixing her banged-up bike with skills he had picked up from his mother's chauffeur.

Later that day, he had dropped off the bike at the Star N, and she had been almost speechless with gratitude. Or maybe she just had been shy with older guys; he didn't know.

He had stayed with his grandmother for just a few more weeks that summer, but whenever he had seen Celeste in town at the grocery store or the library, she had always blushed fiercely and offered him a shy but sweet smile.

Now he found himself watching her intently, hoping for a sight of that same sweet smile, but she seemed to be focusing with laser-like intensity on the books in front of her.

She read several more holiday stories to the children, then led them all to one side of the large room, where tables had been set up.

"I need all the children to take a seat," she said in a prim voice he found incongruously sexy. "We're going to make snowman ornaments for you to hang on your tree. When you're finished, they'll look like this."

She held up a stuffed white sock with buttons glued on to it for eyes and a mouth, and a piece of felt tied around the neck for a scarf.

"Oh," Olivia breathed. "That's so cute! Can I make one, Dad?"

Again, how could he refuse? "Sure, if there are enough to go around."

She limped to a seat and he propped up the wall along with a few other parents so the children each could have a spot at a table. Celeste and another woman with a library name badge passed out supplies and began issuing instructions.

Olivia looked a little helpless at first and then set to work. She seemed to forget for the moment that she rarely used her left hand. Right now she was holding the sock with that hand while she shoved in pillow fluff stuffing with the other.

While the children were busy crafting, Celeste made her way around the tables, talking softly to each one of them.

Finally she came to them.

"Nice job," she said to his daughter. Ah, there it was. She gave Olivia that sweet, unguarded smile that seemed to bloom across her face like the first violets of springtime.

That smile turned her from a lovely if average-looking woman into a breathtaking creature with luminous skin and vivid green eyes.

He couldn't seem to stop staring at her, though he told himself he was being ridiculous.

"You're the Sparkle lady, aren't you?" Olivia breathed.

Color rose instantly in her cheeks and she gave a surprised laugh. "I suppose that's one way to put it."

"I love that story. It's my favorite book *ever*."

"I'm so happy to hear that." She smiled again, though he thought she looked a little uncomfortable. "Sparkle is pretty close to my heart, too."

"My dad bought a brand-new copy for me when I was in the hospital, even though I had one at home."

She said the words in a matter-of-fact tone as if the stay had been nothing more than a minor inconvenience. He knew better. She had spent two weeks clinging to life in intensive care after an infection had ravaged her system, where he had measured his life by each breath the machines took for her.

Most of the time he did a pretty good job of containing his impotent fury at the senseless violence that had touched his baby girl, but every once in a while the rage swept over him like a brush fire on dry tinder. He let out a breath as he felt a muscle flex in his jaw.

"Is that right?" Celeste said with a quick look at him.

"It's my very favorite book," Olivia said again, just in case Celeste didn't hear. "Whenever I had to do something I didn't want to, like have my blood tested or go to physical therapy, I would look at the picture of Sparkle on the last page with all his friends and it would make me feel better."

At Olivia's words, Celeste's big eyes filled with tears and she rocked back on her heels a little. "Oh. That's… lovely. Thank you so much for letting me know. I can't tell you how much that means to me."

"You're welcome," Olivia said with a solemn smile. "My favorite part is when Sparkle helps the animals with their Christmas celebration. The hedgehog is my favorite."

"He's cute, isn't he?"

The two of them gazed at each other in perfect charity for a moment longer before a boy with blond hair and a prominent widow's peak tried to draw Celeste's attention.

"Ms. Nichols. Hey, Ms. Nichols. How do we glue on the hat?"

"I'll show you. Just a minute." She turned back to Olivia. "It was very nice to meet you. You're doing a great job with your snowman. Thanks for letting me know you enjoy the book."

"You're welcome."

When she left, Olivia turned back to her project with renewed effort. She was busy gluing on the button eyes when the woman beside Flynn finally spoke to him.

"You're new in town. I don't think we've met." She was blonde and pretty in a classic sort of way, with a baby on her hip. "I'm Caroline Dalton. This is my daughter, Lindy. Over there is my son, Cole."

He knew the Daltons. They owned much of the upper

portion of Cold Creek Canyon. Which brother was she married to?

"Hello. I'm Flynn Delaney, and this is my daughter, Olivia. We're not really new in town. That is, we're not staying anyway. We're here just for a few weeks, and then we're going back to California."

"I hope you feel welcome here. This is a lovely place to spend the holidays."

"I'm sure it is, but we're not really tourists, either. I'm cleaning out my grandmother's home so I can put it up for sale."

He could have hired someone to come and clean out the house. There were companies that handled exactly that sort of thing, but as he and Olivia were Charlotte's only surviving descendants, he'd felt obligated to go through the house himself.

"Delaney. Oh, Charlotte! She must have been your grandmother."

"That's right."

Her features turned soft and a little sad. "Oh, everyone adored your grandmother. What a firecracker she was! Pine Gulch just doesn't feel the same without her."

His *life* didn't feel the same, either. He hadn't seen her often the past few years, just quick semiannual visits, but she had been a steady source of affection and warmth in his chaotic life.

He had barely had the chance to grieve her passing. That bothered him more than anything else. He hadn't even been able to attend the memorial service members of her church congregation had held for her here. He had been too busy in the ICU, praying for his daughter's life.

"I miss her, too," he said quietly.

She looked at him with kindness and warmth. "I'm

sure you do. She was an amazing person and I feel blessed to have known her. If you need help sorting through things, please let me know. I'm sure we could find people to give you a hand."

With only a little more than a week to go before Christmas? He doubted that. People were probably too busy to help.

He didn't bother to express his cynicism to Caroline Dalton. "Thanks," he said instead.

"Despite your difficult task, I hope you're able to find a little holiday spirit while you're here."

Yeah, he wasn't a huge Christmas fan for a whole slew of reasons, but he saw no reason to share that with a woman he'd just met.

"Daddy, I can't tie the scarf. Can you help me?" Olivia asked.

She *could* use her left arm and hand. He'd seen her do it at therapy or when she lost herself in an activity, but most of the time she let it hang down uselessly. He didn't know how to force her into using it.

"Try again," he said.

"I can't. It's too hard," she answered plaintively. He sighed, not wanting to push her unnecessarily and ruin her tentative enjoyment of the afternoon.

He leaned down to help her tie the felt scarf just as Celeste made her way back around the table to them.

"I love that snowman!" she exclaimed with a smile. "He looks very friendly."

Olivia's answering smile seemed spontaneous and genuine. Right then Flynn wanted to hug Celeste Nichols on the spot, even though he hadn't talked to her for nearly two decades.

His little girl hadn't had much to smile about over

the past few months. He had to hope this was a turning point, a real chance for her to return to his sweet and happy daughter.

At this point, he was willing to bring Olivia to the library every single day if Celeste could help his daughter begin to heal her battered heart.

Chapter 2

She was late.

By the time she helped the last little boy finish his snowman, ushered them all out of the meeting room and then cleaned up the mess of leftover pillow stuffing and fleece remnants, it was forty minutes past the time she had told her sisters to expect her.

They would understand, she was sure. Hope might tease her a little, but Faith probably wouldn't say anything. Their eldest sister saved her energy for the important things like running the cattle ranch and taking care of her children.

She stopped first at the foreman's little cottage, just down the driveway from the main house. It felt strange to be living on her own again after the past year of being back in her own bedroom there. She had moved back after her brother-in-law Travis died the previous summer so she could help Faith—and Aunt Mary, of course—with the children and the housekeeping.

Hope had lived briefly in the foreman's house until she and Rafe married this fall. After she'd moved into the house they purchased together, Faith and Mary had taken Celeste aside and informed her firmly that she needed her own space to create. She was a bestselling author now. While Faith loved and appreciated her dearly, she didn't want Celeste to think she had to live at the ranch house for the rest of her life.

Rather reluctantly, she had moved to the foreman's cottage, a nice compromise. She did like her own space and the quiet she found necessary to write, but she was close enough to pop into the ranch house several times a day.

As she walked inside, her little Yorkie, Linus, rolled over with glee at the sight of her.

She had to smile, despite her exhaustion from a long day, the lingering stress from the phone call with Joan and the complete shock of seeing Flynn Delaney once more.

"How was your day?" she asked the little dog, taking just a moment to sink onto the sofa and give him a little love. "Mine was *crazy*. Thanks for asking. The weirdest I've had in a long time—and that's saying something, since the entire past year has been surreal."

She hugged him for a moment. As she might have predicted, a sleek black cat peeked her head around the corner to see what all the fuss was about.

Lucy, who had been with her since college, strutted in with a haughty air that only lasted long enough for her to leap onto the sofa and bat her head against Celeste's arm for a little of the same attention.

The two pets were the best of friends, which helped her feel less guilty about leaving them alone during the day. They seemed to have no problem keeping each other company most of the time, but that didn't stop them from exhibiting classic signs of sibling rivalry at random moments.

She felt her tension trickle away as she sat in her quiet living room with her creatures while the Christmas tree lights that came on automatically gleamed in the gathering darkness. Why couldn't she stay here all evening? There were worse ways to spend a December night.

Linus yipped a little, something he didn't do often, but it reminded her of why she had stopped at the house.

"I know. I'm late. I just have to grab Aunt Mary's present. Give me a second."

She found the gift in her bedroom closet, the door firmly shut to keep Lucy from pulling apart the tissue paper inside the gift bag.

"Okay. I'm ready. Let's go."

Linus's tail wagged with excitement, but Lucy curled up on the sofa, making abundantly clear her intent to stay put and not venture out into the cold night.

"Fine. Be that way," she said, opening the door for the dog. The two of them made their way through lightly falling snow to the ranch house, a sprawling log structure with a steep roof and three gables along the front. Linus scampered ahead of her to the front door. When she opened it, the delicious scents of home greeted her—roast beef, potatoes and what smelled very much like cinnamon apple pie.

As she expected, her entire family was there, all the people she loved best in the world. Aunt Mary, the guest of honor, was busy at the stove stirring something that smelled like her heavenly brown gravy. She stepped aside to let Faith pull a pan of rolls out of the oven as Hope helped the children set the table, where her husband, Rafe, sat talking with their neighbor Chase Brannon.

The children spotted Linus first. They all adored each other—in fact, the children helped her out by letting him out when they got home from school and playing with him for a little bit.

"There you are," Faith exclaimed. "I was beginning to worry."

"Sorry. I sent you a text."

Faith made a face. "My phone ran out of juice sometime this afternoon, but I didn't realize it until just now. Is everything okay?"

Not really, though she wasn't sure what bothered her more—the movie decision she would have to make in the next few days or the reappearance of Flynn Delaney in her world. She couldn't seem to shake the weird feeling that her safe, comfortable world was about to change.

"Fine," she said evasively. "I hope you didn't hold dinner for me."

"Not really. I was tied up going over some ranch accounts with Chase this afternoon, and we lost track of time."

"Fine. Blame me. I can take it," Chase said, overhearing.

"We always do," Hope said with a teasing grin.

Chase had been invaluable to their family since Faith's husband died, and Celeste was deeply grateful to him for all his help during the subsequent dark and difficult months.

"I'm happy to blame you, as long as that means I wasn't the cause of any delay in Aunt Mary's birthday celebration," Celeste said with a smile as she headed for her great-aunt.

She kissed the woman's lined cheek as the familiar scent of Mary's favorite White Shoulders perfume washed over her. "Happy birthday, my dear. You are still just as stunning as ever."

Mary's grin lit up her nut-brown eyes. "Ha. Double sevens. That's got to be lucky, right?"

"Absolutely."

"I don't need luck. I've got my family around me, don't I?"

She smiled at them all and Celeste hugged her again, deeply grateful for her great-aunt and her great-uncle Claude, who had opened their hearts to three grieving, traumatized girls and gave them a warm haven and all the love they could need.

"We're the lucky ones," she murmured with another hug before she stepped away.

For all intents and purposes, Mary had been her mother since Celeste turned eleven. She had been a wonderful one. Celeste was all too aware that things could have been much different after their parents died if not for Mary and Claude. She and her sisters probably would have been thrown into the foster care system, likely separated, certainly not nurtured and cared for with such love.

She had a sudden, unexpected wish that their mother could be here, just for a moment, to see how her daughters had turned out—to meet her grandchildren, to see

Hope so happily settled with Rafe, to see the completely unexpected success of their Sparkle book.

December always left her a little maudlin. She supposed that wasn't unexpected, considering it had been the month that had changed everything, when she, her sisters and their parents had been hostages of a rebel group in Colombia. Her father had been killed in the rescue effort by a team of US Navy SEALs that had included Rafe Santiago, who was now her brother-in-law.

She wouldn't think about that now. This was a time of celebration, a time to focus on the joy of being with her family, not the past.

She grabbed a black olive out of a bowl on the counter and popped it in her mouth as she carried the bowl to the table.

"I talked to Joan this afternoon," she told Hope.

"I know. She called me, too. I reminded her that any decision about making a movie had to be made jointly between us, and each of us had veto power. Don't worry, CeCe. I told her firmly that I wouldn't pressure you. You created the Sparkle character. He belongs to you."

That wasn't completely true and both of them knew it. She might have written the words, but it was Hope's illustrations that had brought him to life.

"I don't know what to do," she admitted as Faith and Mary joined them at the table carrying bowls and trays of food.

"Your problem has always been that you analyze everything to death," Mary pointed out. "You know someone is going to make a Sparkle movie at some point. It's as inevitable as Christmas coming every year. People love the story and the characters too much. If you like this production company and think they'll do a good job with it based on their reputation, I don't know why you're dragging your feet."

Mary was right, she realized. She was overthinking, probably because she was so concerned with making the right decision.

She hated being afraid all the time. She knew it was a by-product of the trauma she and her sisters had endured at a young age, but neither Hope nor Faith seemed as impacted as she had been.

Hope seemed absolutely fearless, spending years wandering around underdeveloped countries with the Peace Corps, and then on her own teaching English. Faith had plowed all her energy and attention into her family—her marriage, her children, the ranch.

Celeste's life had become her job at the library and the stories she created.

In some ways, she supposed she was still a hostage of Juan Pablo and his crazy group of militants, afraid to take a move and embrace her life.

"Everything's ready and I'm starving," Mary said cheerfully. "What are we waiting for? Let's eat."

Dinner was noisy and chaotic, with several different conversations going at once.

"How did story time go?" Faith asked when there was a lull in the conversation.

She instantly remembered the shock of looking up from Dr. Seuss to see Flynn and his daughter.

"Good." She paused. "Charlotte Delaney's grandson, Flynn, and his daughter were there. I guess he's in town to clean out Charlotte's house."

"Flynn Delaney." Hope made a sound low in her throat. "I used to love it whenever he came to stay with

Charlotte. Remember how he used to mow the lawn with his shirt off?"

Celeste dropped her fork with a loud clatter, earning her a curious look from Hope.

"Really?" Rafe said, eyebrow raised. "So all this time I should have been taking my shirt off to mow the lawn?"

Hope grinned at him. "You don't *need* to take your shirt off. You're gorgeous enough even when you're wearing a parka. Anyway, I was a teenage girl. Now that I'm older and wiser I prefer to use my imagination."

He shook his head with an amused look, but Celeste was certain his ears turned a little red.

"You said Flynn came into the library with his daughter," Faith said, her voice filled with compassion. "That poor girl. How is she?"

Considering Flynn's connection to Charlotte, whom they all had loved, everyone in Pine Gulch had followed the news reports. Celeste thought of Olivia's big, haunted eyes, the sad, nervous air about her.

"Hard to say. She limped a little and didn't use her left arm while we were doing the craft project, but other than that she seemed okay."

"Who is Flynn Delaney and what happened to his daughter?" Rafe asked.

"It was all over the news three or four months ago," Chase said. "Around the time Charlotte died, actually."

"You remember," Hope insisted. "We talked about it. He was married to Elise Chandler."

Understanding spread over Rafe's handsome features. "Elise Chandler. The actress." He paused. "Oh. That poor kid."

"Right?" Hope frowned. "What a tragedy. I saw on

some tabloid in the supermarket that Flynn never left her side through the whole recovery."

Somehow that didn't seem so surprising, especially considering his devotion to his daughter during story time.

"What happened to her?" Louisa asked. At eleven, she was intensely interested in the world around her.

Her mother was the one who answered. "Elise Chandler was a famous actress," Faith said. "She was in that superhero movie you loved so much and a bunch of other films. Anyway, she was involved with someone who turned out to be a pretty messed-up guy. A few months ago after a big fight, he shot Elise and her daughter before shooting and killing himself. Even though she was injured, Olivia managed to crawl to her mother's phone and call 911."

Celeste had heard that 911 call, which had been made public shortly after the shooting, and the sound of that weak, panic-stricken voice calling for help had broken her heart.

"She seems to be doing well now. She didn't smile much, but she did tell me she loves the Sparkle book and that her dad used to read it to her over and over again in the hospital."

"Oh, how lovely!" Hope exclaimed. "You should take her one of the original Sparkle toys I sewed. I've still got a few left."

"That's a lovely idea," Mary exclaimed. "We definitely should do something for that poor, poor girl. It would have broken Charlotte's heart if she'd still been alive to see Flynn's little girl have to go through such a thing."

"You *have* to take it over there," Hope insisted. "And how about a signed copy of the book and the new one that hasn't come out yet?"

Her heart pounded at just the *idea* of seeing the man again. She couldn't imagine knocking on his door out of the blue. "Why don't *you* take it over? You're the illustrator! And you made the stuffed Sparkle, too."

"I don't even know him or his daughter."

"As if that's ever stopped you before," she muttered.

"It would be a really nice thing to do," Faith said.

"I baked an extra pie," Aunt Mary said. "Why don't you take that, too?"

All day long people had been pushing her to do things she didn't want to. She thought longingly of jumping in her SUV again and taking off somewhere, maybe Southern California where she could find a little sunshine. As tempting as the idea might be sometimes, she knew she couldn't just leave her family. She loved them to bits, even when they did pressure her.

She wanted to tell them all no, but then she thought of Olivia and her sad eyes. This was a small expenditure of effort on her part and would probably thrill the girl. "That's a very good idea," she finally said. "I'll go after dinner. Linus can probably use the walk."

"Perfect." Hope beamed at her as if she had just won the Newbery Medal for children's literature. "I'll look for the stuffed Sparkle. I think there's a handful of them left in a box in my old room."

What would Flynn think when she showed up at his house with a stuffed animal and an armful of books? she wondered as she chewed potatoes that suddenly tasted like chalk.

It didn't matter, she told herself. She was doing this for his daughter, a girl who had been through a terrible ordeal—and who reminded her entirely too much of herself.

Chapter 3

"Are you sure you don't want to help? This tinsel isn't going to jump on the tree by itself."

Flynn held a sparkly handful out to his daughter, who sat in the window seat, alternating between watching him and looking out into the darkness at the falling snowflakes.

She shook her head. "I can't," she said in a matter-of-fact tone. "My arm hurts too much."

He tried to conceal his frustrated sigh behind a cough. The physical therapist he had been taking her to since her injury had given him homework during this break while they were in Idaho. His assignment was to find creative activities that would force her to use her arm more.

He had tried a wide variety of things, like having Olivia push the grocery cart and help him pick out items in the store, and asking her help in the kitchen with slicing vegetables. The inconsistency of it made him crazy. Sometimes she was fine; other times she refused to use her arm at all.

After their trip to the library, he'd realized his grandmother's house was severely lacking in holiday cheer. She had made a snowman ornament and they had nowhere to hang it.

Any hope he might have harbored that she would show a little enthusiasm for the idea of decking their temporary halls was quickly dashed. She showed the same listless apathy toward Christmas decorations as she had for just about everything else except Celeste Nichols and her little reindeer story.

Other than hanging her own snowman ornament, she wasn't interested in helping him hang anything else on the small artificial tree he had unearthed in the basement. As a result, he had done most of the work while she sat and watched, not budging from her claim of being in too much pain.

He knew using her arm caused discomfort. He hadn't yet figured out how to convince an almost-seven-year-old she needed to work through the pain if she ever wanted to regain full mobility in her arm.

"Come on. Just take a handful and help me. It will be fun."

She shook her head and continued staring out at the falling snow.

Since the shooting, these moods had come over her out of nowhere. She would seem to be handling things fine and then a few moments later would become fearful, withdrawn and just want him to leave her alone.

The counselor she had seen regularly assured him it

was a natural result of the trauma Olivia had endured. He hated that each step in her recovery—physical and emotional—had become such a struggle for her.

After hanging a few more strands, he finally gave up. What was the point when she didn't seem inclined to help him, especially since he'd never much liked tinsel on trees anyway?

His father hadn't, either, he remembered. He had a stray memory of one of his parents' epic fights over it one year. Diane had loved tinsel, naturally. Anything with glitz had been right down her alley. Her favorite nights of the year had been red carpet events, either for her own movie premieres or those of her friends.

His father, on the other hand, had thought tinsel was stupid and only made a mess.

One night when he was about seven or eight, a few years before they'd finally divorced, his mother had spent hours hanging pink tinsel on their tree over his father's objections, carefully arranging each piece over a bough.

When they'd woken up, the tinsel had been mysteriously gone. As it turned out, Tom had arisen hours before anyone else and had pulled off every last shiny strand.

After a dramatic screaming fight—all on his mother's side—she had stormed out of their Bel Air house and hadn't been back for several days, as he recalled.

Ah, memories.

He pushed away the bitterness of his past and turned back to his daughter. "If you don't want to hang any more tinsel, I guess we're done. Do you want to do the honors and turn out the lights so we can take a look at it?"

She didn't answer him, her gaze suddenly focused on something through the window.

"Someone's coming," Olivia announced, her voice tight. She jumped up from the window seat. "I'm going to my room."

He was never sure which she disliked more: large, unruly crowds or unexpected visitors showing up at the door. Nor was he certain she would ever be able to move past either fear.

With effort he forced his voice to be calm and comforting. "There's no reason to go to your room. Everything is fine. I'm right here. You're okay."

She darted longing little glances down the hall to the relative safety of her bedroom, but to her credit she sat down again in the window seat. When the doorbell rang through the house, Flynn didn't miss her instinctive flinch or the tense set of her shoulders.

He hoped whoever it was had a darn good excuse for showing up out of the blue like this and frightening his little girl half to death.

To his shock, the pretty librarian and author stood on the porch with a bag in her hand and a black-and-brown dog at the end of a leash. In the glow from the porch light he could see her nose and cheeks were pink from the cold, and those long, luscious dark curls were tucked under a beanie. She also wasn't wearing her glasses. Without the thick dark frames, her eyes were a lovely green.

"Hello." She gave him a fleeting, tentative smile that appeared and disappeared as quickly as a little bird hunting for berries on a winter-bare shrub.

"Celeste. Ms. Nichols. Hello."

She gave him another of those brief smiles, then tried

to look behind him to where Olivia had approached. At least his daughter now looked more surprised and delighted than fearful.

"And hello, Miss Olivia," the librarian said. "How are you tonight?"

Her voice was soft, calm, with a gentleness he couldn't help but appreciate.

"Hi. I'm fine, thank you," she said shyly. "Is that your dog?"

Celeste smiled as the dog sniffed at Olivia's feet. "This is Linus. He's a Yorkshire terrier and his best friend is a black cat named Lucy."

"Like in *Charlie Brown's Christmas*!" She looked delighted at making the connection.

"Just like that, except Linus and Lucy are brother and sister. My Linus and Lucy are just friends."

Olivia slanted her head to look closer at the little dog. "Will he bite?"

Celeste smiled. "He's a very sweet dog and loves everybody, but especially blonde girls with pretty red sweaters."

Olivia giggled at this, and after another moment during which she gathered her courage, she held out her hand. The little furball licked it three times in quick succession, which earned another giggle from his daughter.

"Hi, Linus," she said in a soft voice. "Hi. I'm Olivia."

The dog wagged his tail but didn't bark, which Flynn had to appreciate given how skittish Olivia had been all evening.

She knelt down and started petting the dog—using her injured left arm, he saw with great surprise.

"He likes me!" Olivia exclaimed after a moment, her

features alight with a pleasure and excitement he hadn't seen in a long time.

"Of course he does." Celeste smiled down at her with a soft light in her eyes that touched something deep inside him.

"I'm sorry to just drop in like this, but I couldn't help thinking tonight about what you told me earlier, how the Sparkle book helped you in the hospital."

"It's my favorite book. I still read it all the time."

"I'm so happy to hear that. I told my sister, who drew all the pictures, and she was happy, too. We wanted to give you something."

"Is it for my birthday in three days? I'm going to be seven years old."

"I had no idea it was your birthday in three days!" Celeste exclaimed. "We can certainly consider this an early birthday present. That would be perfect!"

She reached into the bag and pulled out a small stuffed animal.

"That's Sparkle from the book!" Olivia rose to see it more closely.

"That's right. My sister made this while she was drawing the pictures for the first Sparkle book last Christmas. We have just a few of them left over from the original hundred or so she made, and I wondered if you might like one."

Olivia's eyes went huge. "Really? I can *keep* it?"

"If you want to."

"Oh, I do!" Almost warily, she reached for the stuffed animal Celeste held out. When it was in her hands, she hugged it to her chest as if afraid someone would yank it away.

For just a moment she looked like any other young

girl, thrilled to be receiving a present. The sheer normalcy made his throat suddenly ache with emotions.

"He's *sooo* cute. I love it! Thank you!"

Olivia threw her arms around Celeste in a quick hug. Flynn wasn't sure if he was more shocked at her use of her injured arm or at the impulsive gesture. Like a puppy that had been kicked one too many times, Olivia shied away from physical touch right now from anyone but him.

Her therapist said it was one more reaction to the trauma she had endured and that eventually she would be able to relax around others and return to the sweet, warm little girl she once had been. He wondered if Dr. Ross ever would have guessed a stuffed reindeer might help speed that process.

Celeste probably had no idea what a rare gift she had just been given as she hugged Olivia back. Still, she looked delighted. "You're very welcome," she said. "You will have to come up to The Christmas Ranch sometime. That's where the real Sparkle lives."

Olivia stepped away, eyes wide. "The real Sparkle lives near here?"

"Just up the road." Celeste gestured vaguely in the direction of her family's place. "We've got a herd of about a dozen reindeer. Sparkle happens to be a favorite of my niece and nephew—of all of us, really. That's where I got the inspiration for the stories."

"Can we go see them, Dad? Can we?"

He shrugged. That was the thing about kids. They dragged you to all kinds of places you didn't necessarily want to go. "Don't know why not. We can probably swing that before the holidays."

Christmas was just around the corner and he was

completely unprepared for it. He didn't like celebrating the holidays in the first place. He didn't really feel like hanging out at some cheesy Christmas moneymaking venture aimed at pouring holiday spirit down his throat like cheap bourbon.

But he loved his daughter, and if she wanted to go to the moon right now, he would figure out a way to take her.

"I like your tree," Celeste said, gazing around his grandmother's cluttered living room. "I especially like the tinsel. Did you help your dad put it up?"

A small spasm of guilt crossed her features. "Not really," she admitted. "My dad did most of it. I have a bad arm."

She lifted her shoulder and the arm in question dangled a little as if it were an overcooked lasagna noodle.

To her credit, Celeste didn't question how she could use that same arm to pet the dog or hold a stuffed reindeer.

"Too bad," she only said. "You're probably really good at hanging tinsel."

"Pretty good. I can't reach the high parts of the tree, though."

"Your dad helps you get those, right?"

"I guess."

Celeste picked up the bag of tinsel where Flynn had left it on the console table. "Can I help you put the rest of it up on the side you didn't get to yet? I'm kind of a tinsel expert. Growing up on The Christmas Ranch, I had to be."

Olivia looked at the tree, then her father, then back at Celeste holding the tinsel. "Okay," she said with that same wariness.

"It will be fun. You'll see. Sparkle can help. He's good at tinsel, too."

How she possibly could have guessed from a half-tinseled tree that he had been trying to enlist his daughter's help with decorating, he had no idea. But he wasn't about to argue with her insight, especially when Olivia obediently followed her new heroine to the tree and reached for a handful of tinsel.

"Can I take your coat?" he asked.

"Oh. Yes. Thanks." She gave a nervous little laugh as she handed him her coat. At the library, she had been wearing a big, loose sweater that had made him wonder what was beneath it. She had taken that layer off apparently, and now she wore a cheerful red turtleneck that accentuated her luscious curves and made his mouth water.

He had an inkling that she was the sort of woman who had no idea the kind of impact she had on a man. As he went to hang her coat by the front door, he forced himself to set aside the reaction as completely inappropriate under the circumstances, especially when she was only trying to help his kid.

When he returned to the living room, he found her and Olivia standing side by side hanging tinsel around the patches of the tree he had left bare.

Her cute little dog had finished sniffing the corners of the room and planted himself on his haunches in the middle of the floor, where he could watch the proceedings.

Flynn leaned against the doorjamb to do the same thing.

How odd, that Olivia would respond to a quiet children's librarian and author more than she had her counselor, her physical therapist, the caregivers at the hospital. She seemed to bloom in this woman's company, copying her actions on the lower branches she could reach. While she still seemed to be favoring her injured arm, occasionally she seemed to forget it hurt and used it without thinking.

All in all, it wasn't a terrible way to spend a December evening while a gas fire flickered in Grandma Charlotte's fireplace and snowflakes fluttered down outside the window.

After several moments, the two of them used the last of the tinsel and Celeste stepped away to take in the bigger picture.

"That looks perfect!" she exclaimed. "Excellent job."

Olivia's smile was almost back to her normal one. She held up the stuffed animal. "Sparkle helped."

"I told you he would be very good at hanging tinsel."

Whatever worked, he figured. "Let me hit the lights for you," he said. "We can't appreciate the full effects with the lights on."

He turned them off, pitching the room into darkness except for the gleaming tree. The tinsel really did reflect the lights. His mom had been right about that, even if she had gotten so many other things wrong.

"Oh. I love it. It's the prettiest tree *ever*," Olivia declared.

"I have to agree," Flynn said. "Good job, both of you."

"And you," Olivia pointed out. "You did most of it earlier. We only filled in the gaps."

"So I did. We're all apparently excellent at decorating Christmas trees."

Celeste met his gaze and smiled. He gazed back,

struck again by how lovely she was with those big green eyes that contrasted so strikingly with her dark hair.

He was staring, he realized, and jerked his gaze away, but not before he thought he saw color climb her high cheekbones. He told himself it must have been a trick of the Christmas lights.

"Oh, I nearly forget," she exclaimed suddenly. "I have another birthday present for you. Two, actually."

"You do?" Olivia lit up.

"Well, it's not actually your birthday yet, so I completely understand if you want to wait. I can just give them to your dad to hold until the big day."

As he might have predicted, Olivia didn't look all that thrilled at the suggestion. "I should open them now while you're here."

"I guess I should have asked your dad first."

He shrugged, figuring it was too late to stop the cart now. "Go ahead."

With a rueful, apologetic smile, she handed the bag to Olivia. "It's not wrapped, since I didn't know it was your birthday when I came over. I'm sorry."

His daughter apparently didn't care. She reached into the bag and pulled out a book with colorful illustrations on the cover.

"Ohhh," she breathed. "It's another *Sparkle and the Magic Snowball* book!"

"This one is signed by both me and my sister, who did the illustrations. I figured since it's your favorite book, you ought to have a signed copy."

"I love it. Thank you!"

"There's something else," Celeste said when his daughter looked as if she were going to settle in right on the spot to reread the story for the hundredth time.

Olivia reached into the bag and pulled out a second book. While it was obvious the artist had been the same, this had different, more muted colors than the original Sparkle book and hearts instead of Christmas ornaments.

"I haven't seen this one! *Sparkle and the Valentine Surprise*."

"That's because it's brand-new. It's not even in stores yet. It's coming out in a few weeks."

"Dad, look!"

She hurried over to him, barely limping, and held out the book.

"Very nice. We can read it tonight at bedtime."

"I can't wait that long! Can I read it now?"

"Sure. First, do you have something to say to Ms. Nichols?"

Olivia gazed at the woman with absolute adoration. "Thank you *so much*! I just love these books and the stuffed Sparkle." Again, she surprised him by hugging Celeste tightly, then hurried to the window seat that she had claimed as her own when they'd first arrived at Charlotte's house.

He gazed after her for a moment, then turned back to Celeste.

"How did you just do that?" he asked, his voice low so that Olivia couldn't hear.

She blinked, confusion on her features. "Do what?"

"That's the first time I've seen her hug anyone but me in months."

"Oh." Her voice was small, sad, telling him without words that she knew what had happened to Elise and Olivia and about Brandon Lowell.

"I guess you probably know my daughter was shot three months ago and her mother was killed."

Her lovely features tightened and her eyes filled with sorrow. "I do. I followed the case, not because I wanted to read about something so terribly tragic, but because I…knew you, once upon a time."

Color rose on her cheeks again, but he had no idea why.

"She's been very withdrawn because of the post-traumatic stress. I haven't seen her warm up to anyone this quickly since it happened."

"Oh." She gazed at Olivia with a soft look in her eyes. "It's not me," she assured him. "Sparkle is a magic little reindeer. He has a comforting way about him."

He was quite certain Celeste was the one with the comforting way, especially as she had created the fictional version of the reindeer, but he didn't say so.

"Whatever the reason, I appreciate it. I had hoped bringing her here to Idaho where we can be away from the spotlight for a few weeks might help her finally begin to heal. It's good to know I might have been right."

The concern and love in his voice came through loud and clear. Flynn obviously was a devoted father trying his best to help his daughter heal.

Celeste's throat felt tight and achy. This poor little girl had watched her mother's life slip away. "She's been through a horrible ordeal. It might be years before the nightmares fade."

"You sound as if you know a little something about nightmares." He studied her closely.

She didn't want to tell him she *still* had nightmares

from those terrible weeks in captivity and then their miraculous rescue with its tragic consequences. She had cried herself to sleep just about every night for weeks. In a second rapid-fire blow, just as the overwhelming pain of losing their father had begun to ease a little, their mother had lost her short but intense battle with cancer and they had come here to stay with Uncle Claude and Aunt Mary.

She couldn't tell him that. She barely knew the man, and he had demons of his own to fight. He didn't need to share hers.

"Everybody has nightmares," she answered. "To paraphrase John Irving, you don't get to pick them. They pick you."

"True enough."

Her dog made a little whiny sound and started looking anxious, which meant he probably needed to go out.

"I need to take Linus home. Sorry again to drop in on you like this out of the blue."

He smiled a little. "Are you kidding? This has been the best thing to happen to us in a long time. She's completely thrilled. And thanks for helping with the Christmas tree. It looks great."

"You're welcome. If you need anything while you're here, my family is just a short walk away. Oh. I nearly forgot. This is for you."

She reached into the bag and pulled out the pie Aunt Mary had boxed up for easier transport.

"What is it?"

"My aunt makes amazing berry pies. She had an extra and wanted you to have it."

He looked stunned at the gesture. "That's very kind. Please give her my thanks."

"I'll do that." She reached for her coat but he beat her to it, tugging it from the rack so he could help her into it.

She was aware of him behind her again, the heat and strength of him, and her insides jumped and twirled like Linus when he was especially happy.

She was being ridiculous, she told herself. She wasn't a thirteen-year-old girl with a crush anymore.

She quickly shoved her arms through the sleeves and stepped away to tie her scarf.

"Are you sure you're okay walking home?" he asked. "Looks as if it's snowing harder. Let me grab my keys and we'll drive you home."

She shook her head, even as she felt a warm little glow at his concern. "Not necessary. It's not far. I like to walk, even in the snow, and Linus still has a little energy to burn off. Thank you, though."

He still looked uncertain, but she didn't give him a chance to press the matter. She returned to the living room doorway and waved at his daughter.

"Goodbye, Olivia. I hope you enjoy the book."

She looked up with that distracted, lost-in-the-story sort of look Celeste knew she wore frequently herself. "I'm already almost done. It's super good."

It was one thing in the abstract to know people enjoyed her work. It was something else entirely to watch someone reading it—surreal and gratifying and a bit uncomfortable at the same time.

"I'm glad you think so."

Olivia finally seemed to register that she had on her coat. "Do you really have to go?"

"I'm afraid so. I have to take Linus home or Lucy will be lonely."

To her surprise, Olivia set aside the book, climbed

down from the window seat and approached to give her one last hug.

"Thank you again for the books and for the stuffed animal," she said. "It was the best birthday ever—and I haven't even had it yet!"

"I'm so glad."

"Goodbye, Linus," Olivia said. She knelt down to scratch the Yorkie again and Linus obliged by licking her face, which made her giggle.

When Celeste turned to go, she found Flynn shaking his head with astonishment clear on his handsome features. She remembered what he had said about Olivia not warming to many people since her mother's death, and she was deeply grateful she had made the small effort to come visit the girl.

"I hope we see you again," he said.

Oh, how she wished he meant for *his* sake and not for his daughter's. "I'm sure you will. Pine Gulch is a small place. Good night."

She walked out into the snowy December night. Only when she was halfway back to the Star N did she realize she didn't feel the cold at all.

Chapter 4

Over the weekend she tried not to think about Flynn and his sweet, fragile daughter. It wasn't easy, despite how busy she was working an extra shift at the library and helping out in the gift shop of The Christmas Ranch.

Even the multiple calls she and Hope took from Joan about the movie development deal couldn't completely distract her random thoughts of the two of them that intruded at the oddest times.

She knew the basics of what had happened to Elise Chandler and her daughter at the hands of the actress's boyfriend, but she was compelled to do a few internet searches to read more about the case. The details left her in tears for everyone involved, even the perpetrator and his family.

Brandon Lowell obviously had been mentally ill. He had been under treatment for bipolar disease and, according to evidence after the shooting, had stopped taking his medication a month before, claiming it interfered with his acting abilities and the regular television role he was playing.

He never should have had access to a firearm given his mental health but had stolen one from Elise's bodyguard a few days before the shooting.

She found it a tragic irony that the woman used a bodyguard when she went out in public but had been killed by someone close to her using the very tool intended to protect her.

The whole thing made her so very sad, though she was touched again to read numerous reports about Olivia's dedicated father, how Flynn had put his thriving contracting business in the hands of trusted employees so he could dedicate his time to staying with his daughter every moment through her recovery.

None of that information helped distract her from thinking about him. By Monday afternoon, she had *almost* worked the obsession out of her system—or at least forced herself to focus on work as much as possible, until Frankie came in after a morning of online seminars.

"I figured out who he is!" her friend exclaimed before she even said hello.

"Who?"

"You know! The hot dad who came to story time last week. I spent all weekend trying to figure out why he looked so familiar and then this morning it came to me. I was washing my hair and remembered that shower scene in *Forbidden* when the hero washes the heroine's hair and it came to me. Elise Chandler! Sexy dad is her ex-husband. It has to be! That cute little girl must be the one who was all over the news."

Flynn must hate having his daughter be a household name, even though her mother certainly had been.

"Yes. Flynn Delaney. Charlotte Delaney, his grandmother, lived close to The Christmas Ranch and he used to come spend summers with her."

"You knew all this time and you didn't say anything?"

It wasn't her place to spread gossip about the man. Even now, just talking to her dear friend, she felt extremely protective of him and Olivia.

"I'm sure they would appreciate a little privacy and discretion," she said. "Olivia has been through a terrible ordeal and is still trying to heal from her injuries. I don't think they need everybody in town making a fuss over them."

"Oh, of course. That makes sense. That poor kid."

"I know."

"How is she doing?"

She thought of Olivia's excitement the other day when she had taken the books to her and that spontaneous, sweet embrace. "She's still got a long road but she's improving."

"I'm so glad."

"Olivia is apparently a big Sparkle fan, and that was the reason they came to the story time."

She had been touched several times to remember the girl telling her how much her book had helped during her recovery. Who would have guessed when she had been writing little stories for her niece and nephew that an emotionally and physically damaged girl would one day find such comfort in them?

To her relief, Frankie dropped the subject. Celeste tried once more to return to her work, vowing to put this ridiculous obsession out of her head. An hour later her hopes were dashed when Frankie bustled back to the children's section, her eyes as wide as if she'd just caught somebody trying to deface a book.

"He's here again!"

She looked up from the books she was shelving. "Who's here?"

"Hottie Dad and his cute little girl! Elise Chandler's poor daughter. They just walked in."

"Are you sure?"

"He's a hard man to miss," Frankie said.

Celeste's heartbeat kicked up several notches and her stomach seemed tangled with nerves. She told herself that was ridiculous. He wasn't there to see her anyway. Maybe he wouldn't even come back to the children's section.

"I wonder what they're doing here," Frankie said, her dark eyes huge.

It wasn't to see her, Celeste reminded herself sternly. She was a dowdy, shy librarian, and he couldn't possibly have any interest in her beyond her status as his daughter's favorite author.

"Here's a wild guess," she said, her tone dry. "Maybe they're looking for books."

Frankie made a face. "He doesn't have a library card, does he?"

"Probably not," she acknowledged. "They're only here for a few weeks, then they'll be returning to California."

The thought was more depressing than it should have been.

"Well, ask him if he wants a temporary one while he's here."

Why did *she* have to ask him anything? She wanted to hide here in the children's section and not even have to face him. But a moment later Olivia limped in, Sparkle the stuffed reindeer in her hand along with the new book.

"Hi, Ms. Nichols! Hi!"

Celeste smiled at both of them. "Hello. It's lovely to see you today. Happy birthday!" She suddenly remembered.

"Thank you," Olivia said. "I begged and begged my dad to bring me to the library today."

"Did you?"

She held up Sparkle. "I had to tell you how much I liked the new book, just as much as the first one. Sparkle is *so funny*. I've read it about ten times already."

"Wow. That's terrific. Thanks for letting me know."

"And my dad read it to me twice and he laughed both times. He hardly *ever* laughs."

"Not true," he protested. "Okay, it's true that I laughed at the book. It's hilarious. But it's not true that I hardly ever laugh. I don't know where you came up with that. I laugh all the time. I'm a freaking hyena."

Celeste laughed out loud, which earned her a surprised look from Frankie.

"You're so lucky that you had the chance to read the new book," Frankie informed her. "Half the children in town would willingly forgo all their presents under the tree if they could lay their hands on the next Sparkle book."

Even though she was grossly exaggerating, the library director had the perfect tone with Olivia—friendly and polite, but not overly solicitous. She had a feeling Flynn would hate the latter.

"It's really, really good," Olivia said solemnly. "I still like the first one best, but the second one is almost my favorite."

Frankie smiled, but before she could answer, one of the other library volunteers came over with a question about checking out DVDs, and she reluctantly excused herself to deal with the crisis.

"Is there something I can help you with?" Celeste asked after her friend walked away. "Would you like a temporary card so you can check out materials? I'm sure that wouldn't be a problem, considering I know where to find you."

"No. Actually, we have another reason for being here."

If she wasn't mistaken, Flynn looked a little uncomfortable, which made her even more curious.

"Oh? What is it?"

He didn't answer and Olivia didn't say anything, either. Finally Flynn nudged her. "Go ahead."

"It's my birthday," the girl began.

"I know. I think it's great that you decided the library is the perfect place to celebrate a birthday. I completely agree!"

Olivia giggled a little. "No, we're not celebrating my birthday here. I told my dad the only thing I want for my birthday is to have pizza."

"Ooh, pizza. My favorite," she said, though she was still mystified about why they might be at the library and why Flynn still looked uncomfortable. "Are you looking for a book on how to make pizza?"

The girl shook her head. "We're going to the pizza restaurant down the street."

"I can highly recommend it. It's one of my favorite places."

Olivia gave her a shy look. "That's good. Because I want to have pizza with *you* on my birthday."

She blinked, taken by surprise. "With…me?"

"Yes. That would be the best birthday ever. My favorite thing to eat and my new friend and the lady who writes such good Sparkle books." She beamed as if the matter was settled.

"Don't feel obligated," Flynn said quickly. "If you already have plans, we completely understand. Isn't that right, Olivia?"

"Yes," the girl said.

Dinner. With Olivia and Flynn. She thought of a hundred reasons why she should say no. How could she possibly eat with these nervous butterflies racing around in her stomach? And she probably wouldn't be able to think of anything to say and would look even more stupid than she felt.

All those reasons paled into insignificance. Olivia wanted to have pizza with her for her birthday, and Celeste couldn't let her own social awkwardness stand in the way of making that particular wish come true.

"I would be honored to come help you celebrate your birthday. Thank you for inviting me."

Olivia's smile was sweetly thrilled. "She said yes, Dad!"

The sight of this tough-looking man gazing down at his daughter with such love just about broke Celeste's heart. "So I heard. That's great." He turned to her. "What time are you finished with work?"

"Five-thirty."

"Would seven work for pizza? We can pick you up."

"I can meet you at the restaurant."

"We don't mind. Do you still live at the Star N?"

She knew he probably didn't mean for that to sound pitiful, but she still had to wince. That wasn't exactly true. She had gone off to Boise for her undergraduate work, then Seattle for her master's degree. She wasn't *completely* a homebody, even if she had jumped at the chance to return to her hometown library to work.

If she was living on her family's ranch, it wasn't because of any failure to launch, only because of the tragic circumstances of Travis's death.

"I live on the ranch but not in the main house," she told him. "I'm at the foreman's place, the small log house closest to the entrance."

"Perfect. Plan on us at seven."

She was going out to dinner with Flynn Delaney and his daughter. This certainly wasn't the way to get the man out of her head, but she didn't see how she could refuse.

The truth was she didn't want to anyway. She was both touched and flattered that sweet Olivia wanted to spend time with her for her birthday.

"Sounds good. Meanwhile, are you sure you don't want to check out some books on a temporary library card? We still have a great selection of holiday books available. It's the section there against the wall."

"Can we?" Olivia asked her father.

"Just a few," he said with a reluctant nod. "It might be tough to keep track of more than that while we're clearing out Grandma Charlotte's house."

Olivia headed immediately toward the Christmas storybooks, leaving Flynn alone with Celeste—or at least as alone as they could be in a public library.

A few moms she knew were browsing through the children's section with their toddlers, and she was pretty sure she caught more than one appreciative glance in his direction. As Frankie said, he was a hard man to overlook.

"Thanks for agreeing to come with us," Flynn said. "It probably wasn't fair to spring that on you out of the blue. I would have called first, but I didn't have a phone number. I guess I could have found the number for the library, but I didn't think about it until we pulled up."

"It's fine."

"Seriously, you made her day. She has been asking me all afternoon if you could come to her birthday celebration. I didn't want to disappoint her. It's still pretty tough for me to deny her anything these days."

She couldn't imagine almost losing a child. The fear must have been overwhelming.

"I'm touched, if you want the truth. I don't believe I've ever been anyone's birthday wish before."

A strange glint appeared in his gaze, an expression she couldn't quite identify. After a moment he smiled. "Face it. You sealed your fate the other day when you showed up in person with a new book *and* a cute stuffed toy. You're now officially the coolest person in town."

She had to laugh at that ridiculous statement. "If that's the case, you both need to get out and meet more people in Pine Gulch."

Amusement crinkled the corners of his eyes. "We won't be here long enough to move in social circles around here. Anyway, I think Olivia and I are both quite happy with those we have already met in Pine Gulch."

Her heartbeat seemed to accelerate all over again at the teasing note in his voice. Her gaze met his and he was smiling at her with a warm look in his eyes that sucked away any ability she might have had to offer a semi-intelligent response.

To her relief, one of the moms came over to ask her a question about the puppet-book packages they lent out—probably more to get a closer look at Flynn, she suspected, than out of any genuine quest for information.

He moved away to join his daughter while she picked a few other books and the moment was gone.

He had to finish taking care of things at his grandmother's house and get out of Pine Gulch.

As Flynn drove the short distance from Charlotte's house to the Star N Ranch, he was aware of a low, insistent unease. This town was growing on him, sucking him in.

He had always enjoyed coming here as a kid to spend time with his grandmother. The setting was beautiful, nestled against the Tetons, with pine forests and crystal clear streams.

The pace here seemed so very different from his childhood home in Southern California, quieter, gentler somehow. Almost like a foreign country, without convertibles and palm trees and self-absorbed celebrities.

He always felt a sense of peace settle over him the moment he passed through the city limits into town.

He thought he loved it here because of Charlotte, because she was such a steady source of love and support despite the chaos of the rest of his world. When he came to Pine Gulch, there were no raging fights that could go on for days, no slamming doors, no screaming voices. Only his calm, funny, laughing grandmother, with her colorful aprons and her bright smile and her small, tidy house beside the Cold Creek.

She was gone now, but he was aware of that same peace seeping through him, so very welcome after the terrible past few months.

It didn't make sense, he knew. He was only here to finish taking care of Charlotte's house, not to find some kind of peace.

That was part of the reason he was so drawn to Celeste Nichols, he acknowledged as he neared her family's ranch. She had a calming way about her that drew him to her.

He couldn't imagine any two people more different than Celeste and Elise—the sweet children's librarian and author and the passionate, flamboyant, ambitious actress.

His marriage had been a mistake from the beginning. After growing up with a mother in the entertainment business—and a father who had hated it—and seeing the neuroses and the superficiality of that way of life, he had wanted no part of it.

After high school and college, he had set his business degree aside and obtained a contractor's license instead. After only a few years his construction company had established a reputation for quality and dependability. Then at one of his mother's frequent parties, he had met a stunning—and hungry—young actress.

She had pursued him aggressively, and he—like probably most guys in their early twenties—had been too flattered to use his brain. In his lust-addled state, it had taken him several weeks to realize she was more interested in his connection to his mother and her powerful Hollywood circle than in him.

But by then Elise had become pregnant, despite the precautions they had taken. He had done what he thought was right and married her, but it had been the ultimate exercise in futility. Both of them had known from the beginning it would never last. The two years before she had filed for divorce had been among the toughest of his life, sweetened only by his complete adoration for his baby girl.

Everything he did, then and now, was for Olivia. That was the only reason he was driving to pick up Celeste Nichols right now, not because of this powerful attraction he hadn't been able to shake since that first day in the library.

What was it about her? Yes, she was pretty in a calm, buttoned-down kind of way with those lovely dark-fringed green eyes and dark curls. She had an understated loveliness she seemed to be doing her best to hide from the world.

His entire life he had been surrounded by beautiful women who were empty shells once a guy broke through the surface to the person inside. Despite their short acquaintance, he was certain Celeste wasn't like that.

Her kindness to Olivia touched him. He tried to tell himself that was the reason for this strange reaction to her. It was gratitude; that was all.

Somehow he wasn't buying it as he passed the entrance to The Christmas Ranch on his way to the Star N.

"What is that place?" Olivia asked, gazing out the window at the colorful holiday display they could see from the road.

"It's a place where people pay money to help find the Christmas spirit," he explained. "They have different activities here like sledding, sleigh rides, that kind of thing."

"Look, Dad! That sign says Home of the Real Sparkle," she read. "That must be where he lives! Can we pay the money and see him and maybe do some of the other stuff? The sledding and stuff?"

Her request took him by surprise, especially considering how apathetic she had been about decorating their house for Christmas. She hadn't summoned much energy at all for celebrating this year. He couldn't blame her after what she had endured, but it was one more thing that broke his heart, especially considering how excited she had been about the holiday season in years past.

Maybe Celeste Nichols and her reindeer book were rubbing off on Olivia.

"We'll have to see. I thought you weren't very interested in Christmas this year."

"I guess we could do a *few* Christmas things," she said slowly. "Whether we do them or not, Christmas is coming anyway."

"True enough." For a girl who had just turned seven, she could be remarkably wise sometimes. She was tough and courageous, he told himself. Even if she was struggling now, she would make it through this eventually.

"Is this where Celeste lives?" Olivia asked when he pulled up in front of the little house not far from the bigger Star N ranch house.

"That's what she said. The foreman's house."

"Look. She has a Christmas tree, too."

Since her family ran The Christmas Ranch, he would have been more shocked if she *didn't* have one.

"I wonder if I can see her cute little dog, Linus."

"I wouldn't be a bit surprised," he told her.

Olivia opened the passenger door almost before he had the SUV in Park, and she raced up the driveway without him, only limping a little. While he was still unbuckling his seat belt, she was already at the doorbell, and by the time he reached the door, Celeste had opened it and was greeting his daughter.

"Of course," she was saying. "You can absolutely come in and meet Lucy the cat. She loves new friends."

Apparently his daughter had invited herself inside. He rolled his eyes but followed her when Celeste held open the door for both of them.

The house wasn't large, perhaps only eight or nine hundred square feet. The living room was decorated in a casual, comfortable style, heavy on bright colors, with lots of plump pillows and books. The Christmas tree was about the only holiday decoration, he was surprised to see.

"Nice place," he said.

"Thanks. I just moved over a few months ago from the main house, but so far I've been enjoying it. I'm close enough to help out with my niece and nephew when my sister Faith needs me. At the same time, I'm far enough away from the chaos that I can write. I've even got my own writing space in the second bedroom."

"It's comfortable."

She smiled. "I like it."

Her furry-faced little dog scampered in from the kitchen, followed by an elegant-looking black cat, who watched them carefully from the doorway as if trying to determine whether they were friends or foes.

"Hi, Linus." Olivia sank to the floor to pet the dog. After a moment, the cat sidled over.

"That's Lucy," Celeste said. "She can be a little snooty at first, but once she warms up, she'll be your best friend. Just give her a moment."

Sure enough, while Olivia mostly paid attention to the small dog, the cat moved closer and closer until she rubbed her head against Olivia's leg.

"I think she likes me," she whispered.

"I'm sure of it," Celeste said with a smile.

"Looks as if you need to pick up a pet or two," she said to Flynn in an undertone.

"Don't give her any ideas," he said in the same low voice. Their gaze met and he felt a strange jolt in his gut at the impact of those green eyes behind the glasses.

"You don't want a little dog?"

He shrugged. When he was a kid, the only pets had been his mother's annoying, yippy little purse pooches. He had never really thought seriously about it before, too busy with work and his shared custody of Olivia.

When things settled down for her a little, maybe he would think about it. She did seem to be enjoying Celeste's pets.

Both he and Celeste seemed content to watch her petting the two pets, and he was aware of that elusive sense of peace seeping in again.

"How's the house cleaning going?" she asked him.

He thought of the work still ahead. "I don't think I realized what an undertaking it was to clear out eighty-five years of living. After about three days of work, we got one of the rooms cleared out today."

"Good work." She paused. "If you need help, I'm available most evenings."

She looked embarrassed after she spoke, though he wasn't quite sure why, when he took the offer as nothing but generous and kind, especially in the hustle-bustle of the holidays.

"Thank you," he said sincerely.

She gazed at him for a moment, then shifted her attention back to Olivia, but not before he saw a hint of color climb her cheeks.

"What are you doing with your business in California while you're here?"

"I'm doing as much as I can long-distance, but it hasn't been easy. Since the shooting, I've basically had to trust my second-in-command to take much of the load at the sites. I've been handling the administrative things after Olivia goes to bed. Everyone who works for me has been great. I couldn't ask for better people in my company, but I think we're all ready for things to start getting back to normal after the holidays."

She looked between him and his daughter, her expression soft. "You're a good father, Flynn. Olivia is lucky to have you."

"I don't know about that," he muttered. "A good father would have known what was going on at her mother's house. I should have seen it. It wasn't a stable situation for a young girl. Elise had boyfriend after boyfriend traipsing in and out of their lives, all tabloid fodder. Brandon Lowell at least had stuck around for longer than a few months. I was stupidly grateful for that, but if I had been paying more attention, I would have seen his downward spiral. Maybe I could have stepped in earlier."

"What would you have done?"

"I don't know. Found him the help he needed, at the very least. Maybe filed for an emergency custody order so we could have avoided all this trauma and pain." The nightmare of the shooting was as vivid and stark as if it had happened the day before. "Elise called me right before it all went south."

"She did?"

He checked to be sure Olivia wasn't paying attention to them but to the animals before he continued. "She told me Brandon had been drinking all day and was acting strangely. She was worried about him, but she didn't sound panicked or anything, was just calling to ask my advice. She'd done this before, called me for advice when he was drinking too much or having a manic episode, but something told me this time was different. I was on a job site fifty miles away, so I told her to grab Olivia and take her to my house, and I would deal with the situation when I got back."

He was quiet, regret a harsh companion. "I wish to hell she had listened to me. She was always so stubborn, thinking she knew best. I was about five miles from her place when I got the call from the police. I'll never forget that instant when it felt as if the whole world changed."

Chapter 5

She couldn't imagine what he must have gone through, knowing his daughter had been hurt. She also could tell by the threads of guilt twining through his voice that he blamed himself for not being able to control the situation and keep his daughter safe.

"What happened wasn't your fault," she murmured.

"Wasn't it?" he asked, the words clipped.

Unable to resist the need to offer him comfort, she reached out her hand and rested it softly on his.

She completely understood where he was coming from. She knew all about that crushing weight of responsibility.

In that last panicked rush toward the helicopter and the navy SEALs, she had been terrified as usual. She had hesitated, frozen in fear. Her father had paused to go back for her and shoved her in front of him, pushing her forward with his usual words of encouragement as they had raced to safety.

He had thrust her into the helicopter ahead of him, but her split second of fear had had a terrible cost. Her father had been shot just before he would have been able to make it to safety.

If she hadn't been so afraid, if she had started to run when he had first told her to go, maybe her father would still be with them now.

"Wouldn't it be wonderful if we were all given one do-over in life?" she murmured. "One free pass to go back and change one action, one decision, one thought-less word?"

He gave her a searching look, as if trying to figure out what moment she would alter. Finally he nodded. "One would be a start, I suppose, though I probably could use about a half dozen free passes."

"Instead, we have to do our best to live with the consequences of our choices."

"Not an easy task, is it?"

No. She had been trying for nearly twenty years.

He flexed his hand and she realized with great chagrin that she was still touching him. She pulled her fingers back quickly, her skin still tingling from the heat of him.

After an awkward moment, he turned to his daughter.

"Olivia, we should probably take off or someone else will eat our delicious pizza."

"We haven't ordered it yet," she said with a concerned frown. "Do you think they'll run out?"

"I was just teasing. But we really should go."

"Okay," she said reluctantly. She rubbed noses with Linus and petted Lucy one last time, then stood up.

She might have been mistaken, but Celeste thought she seemed to be moving better, even than a few days before.

Flynn drove a luxury SUV that smelled of expensive leather with hints of his woodsy, intoxicating aftershave. As he drove to the pizza place in town, she and Olivia talked about the books the girl had checked out of the library and about her schoolwork and her home in California.

He seemed content to listen, though once or twice she caught him giving her a sidelong glance, no doubt trying to figure out how he had gotten saddled spending the evening with the boring children's librarian.

Monday night was family night at the Rocky Mountain Pizza Company—The Rock, as they called it in town. From the outside it looked as though the place was hopping.

This was one of the more family-friendly hangouts in Pine Gulch. Though it had a pool table in the back room, it also featured foosball and air hockey tables, as well as a few vintage video games like Ms. PAC-MAN and pinball.

Celeste came here about once a month, either with her sister or with friends. Usually she enjoyed the delicious wood-fired pizza and the comfortable, familiar atmosphere. The scent alone—garlic and yeast and a fabulous red sauce—made her stomach rumble.

On the heels of that first sensory overload, though, Celeste became aware that people were looking with curiosity at her and her companions.

She saw the police chief, Trace Bowman, and his

wife, Becca, at one table with their children. In the next booth were Nate Cavazos and his wife, Emery, one of her good friends. Emery and Becca both looked intrigued.

For a wild moment, she wished she had refused the invitation from Olivia—or that she had persuaded Flynn to take them all the way to Jackson Hole or even Idaho Falls, somewhere far away from Pine Gulch where people didn't know her.

Instead, she squared her shoulders, waved at her friends and did her best to ignore their speculative looks.

"Hi, Celeste," Natalie Dalton, the hostess chirped the greeting while looking at Flynn and Olivia with curiosity.

She used to babysit for Nat and her siblings. "Hi, Natalie. Great to see you. I miss seeing you at the library these days."

"I still come in, though mostly at night for study groups. I just don't have much reason to hit the children's section anymore unless I've got one of the little ones with me."

Her father and stepmother had two children together, in addition to the four Wade Dalton had had with his first wife, who had died tragically in childbirth.

Natalie turned her attention to Olivia and Flynn. "Hi, there. Welcome to The Rock. I don't think we've met. I'm Natalie."

Celeste felt as though she had the manners of a dried-up turnip right now. "Sorry. This is Flynn Delaney and his daughter, Olivia."

She smiled at them both. "Hi, Olivia. Hi, Flynn."

"We're here celebrating a certain young lady's seventh birthday today," Celeste said.

"Happy birthday!" Natalie exclaimed, beaming at her and holding her hand out for a fist bump.

"Thank you," Olivia said. She didn't meet her eye, and though she raised her hand halfheartedly to bump Nat's, she quickly lowered it again and looked at the floor.

What had happened to the animated birthday girl who had chattered in the car about her favorite Jan Brett Christmas book? Now she seemed nervous and uneasy, as if she wanted to be anywhere else in the world than the best pizza place in the entire region.

Celeste placed a comforting hand on her shoulder. When she'd first arrived in Pine Gulch after their Colombian ordeal, it had taken her a long time before she could completely relax in public places like this. She imagined Olivia was feeling the same way.

"I've got the perfect table for a birthday girl," Natalie said, her cheerfulness undeterred by Olivia's reticence. "Follow me, guys."

Indeed, she led them to an excellent table overlooking the Christmas lights on Main Street. From here, they even could see the fun display in the window of the local toy store.

"Thanks," Flynn murmured. Olivia slid into the booth first and Flynn went in after her. Celeste slid across from them.

"What's good here?" Flynn asked, scanning one of the menus Natalie left them.

"Everything," she answered honestly. "The pizza, the pasta, the sandwiches. You can't go wrong."

"I wanted pizza," Olivia said, her voice still small.

"Pizza it is," Flynn said. "Why don't we order three personal size? Then everybody can choose the toppings they like."

"The personal size is usually huge," she told him. "At least enough for two people."

"That's okay. Pizza leftovers are one of the true joys in life, right?"

When he smiled, she thought *he* should have been the movie star in the family instead of his mother and former wife. He would break hearts all over the world with those completely natural good looks.

Her stomach jumped all over the place again. Oh, this crush was *so embarrassing*. She would be lucky if she could eat any pizza at all.

At least she was able to talk casually when he asked her to help him choose between pizza selections. A few moments later the server, Lucy Boyer—Natalie's cousin—headed over to take their order.

She beamed when she spotted Celeste. "Hey, Ms. N. How are things?"

"Great, Lucy. How are you?"

"Can't complain. I'm working on my college essays and it's such a pain. You probably love that kind of thing, since you're a genius author and all. You might not know this, but for some people writing is *hard*."

She didn't want to burst that particular fantasy by telling her the truth, that sometimes every single word was a struggle.

"Hey, what's this I hear about a Sparkle movie in the works?"

How on earth did rumors spread like that? She hadn't made her final decision yet, though she knew she couldn't wait much longer.

"A movie?" Olivia exclaimed. "Really?"

For some reason, Flynn's easy expression had tightened, and he was gazing at her with his brow furrowed.

"I don't know yet. Possibly." Probably.

She still wasn't sure she wanted to see her baby on the big screen, but at this point she didn't know how to stop that particular train.

"That's seriously cool. I'll be the first in line to buy tickets. That's such a great story."

"It's my favorite, too," Olivia said.

"Cool! I heard from a little squirrel that you've got a birthday today."

Olivia nodded. She looked as though she was torn between withdrawing into herself to hide from the attention and any kid's natural excitement about being the star of the day.

"We'll make sure your pizza is perfect, then. What kind do you want?"

Olivia ordered cheese, which Lucy assured them would come with a special birthday surprise. Celeste picked her favorite, margherita, which came with fresh basil and the hand-pulled mozzarella The Rock was famous for, and Flynn went for the meat lover's delight.

After she left, Flynn picked up the conversation.

"A movie?" he asked.

"We're in talks," she answered. "It's a terrifying proposition, to be honest."

"Will the real Sparkle be in the movie?" Olivia asked.

Celeste smiled. "It's going to be animated, so no."

She and the little girl started talking about their favorite holiday films—Olivia's was *Elf*, while Celeste still favored *It's A Wonderful Life*.

In no time, their pizza arrived. Olivia's surprise was that her pizza was shaped like a Christmas tree.

The pizza was every bit as good as usual, cooked just right in the wood-fired oven.

Flynn apparently agreed. "Wow," he said after the first bite. "That's a good pie. If I'd known how good, we would have been eating here every night since we came to town."

"Doug and Jacinda DeMarco, the owners, are big on the artisan pizza scene. They make their own mozzarella and burrata and try to use locally sourced produce and meats wherever they can. They have an extensive greenhouse where they grow their own fresh herbs and vegetables year-round. It's quite an operation."

"Who would have thought I could find such a good pizza in the wilds of eastern Idaho?"

She smiled, proud of her little community. While it might be primarily a ranching town, Pine Gulch was gaining a reputation as a foodie destination and a magnet for artists.

"I understand they get customers from as far away as Jackson Hole who read about the pizza online and want to try a slice."

She was finishing her second slice when she spotted her friend Caidy Caldwell coming in with her husband, the local veterinarian, and their children. Caidy had grown up in Cold Creek Canyon and had been a friend for a long time. Celeste loved seeing her so happy with Ben.

When she spotted Celeste, she waved, said something to Ben and the kids, then headed in her direction.

"Hi, Celeste! I'm so glad I bumped into you. Great story time last week. The kids really enjoyed it."

"Thanks. It was great to see you there."

"I don't know how you always manage to find such absolutely charming stories—old favorites and then so many that no one has ever heard before."

"That's my job," she said with a smile. That was one of her favorite parts about it, seeking out the new and unusual along with the classics everybody expected and loved.

"You do it well," Caidy said. "Almost *too* well. We might have to quit coming to the library. Every time you read a new book the kids have to buy it."

"Because they're all so good." Her stepdaughter, Ava, had joined her.

"Right. But now the shelves of our home library are bulging."

"You can never have too many books," Celeste answered.

"That's what I always say," Ava exclaimed. She turned to Olivia. "Hi. I'm Ava Caldwell."

"Sorry. This is Flynn Delaney and his daughter, Olivia. Flynn, this is my friend Caidy Caldwell and her daughter, Ava. Ava also has a brother about your age named Jack and a new baby brother who is the cutest thing around, Liam."

As her friend smiled at the two of them, Celeste didn't miss the flash of recognition or sympathy in her gaze before she smoothly masked her reaction. Caidy obviously had followed the news stories and knew what had happened to the girl.

"I'm happy to meet you both," her friend said with a smile. "Welcome to Pine Gulch. I hope you're staying around for a while."

He shook his head. "I'm afraid not. Only until after the holidays."

"Well, you picked one of the best times of the whole year to be here. You won't find many prettier winter wonderlands than this part of Idaho."

"It's lovely," he agreed.

"I didn't mean to interrupt your dinner. I just needed to ask you again what time practice is tomorrow. I know you've told me a half dozen times but I swear Christmas makes my brain leak out of my ears."

"Four thirty sharp at the St. Nicholas Lodge at the ranch. We should be done by six thirty."

"Perfect. My kids are so excited about it."

Celeste had no idea how Hope had persuaded her to take on one more thing, in this case organizing a small program to be performed at an inaugural Senior Citizens Christmas dinner a few days before the holiday.

Hope's particular skill was getting Celeste to do things she ordinarily never would attempt—like publish her books and then agree to allow one of those books to be made into a movie.

"Olivia, if you're going to be here through Christmas, you should think about being in the play," Ava suggested.

Flynn tensed up at the idea, his jaw taut. To Celeste's surprise, Olivia only looked intrigued.

"I was in a play in school once. It was fun."

"This isn't a huge production," Celeste assured Flynn. "We're just doing a simple Christmas program. Everybody who wants to participate gets a part. We're mostly singing songs everybody already knows."

"Can I do it, Dad?"

He frowned. "We'll have to talk about that. We're

pretty busy cleaning out the house. I don't know if we'll have time to go to practices and things."

"There are only three practices," Celeste said. "Tomorrow, Thursday night and Saturday morning, and then the show is Tuesday, the day before Christmas Eve. She would be more than welcome to come. The rehearsals and the show are all at the St. Nicholas Lodge at The Christmas Ranch, just five minutes from your place."

A Christmas program. With an audience, applause. The whole bit. He wanted to tell them all absolutely not, to grab his daughter and drag her out of here.

He'd had enough of performers to last him a lifetime. His entire life, he had been forced to wait on the sidelines while the important females in his life sought fame and recognition. His mother had made it clear from the time he was old enough to understand that he could never be the most important thing in her life—not when her adoring public already held that honor.

Elise had pretended otherwise, but when it came down to it, he had been even less important to her, only a stepping-stone on her journey to success.

He didn't want Olivia anywhere near a stage or a movie set. So far she hadn't shown any inclination in that direction, much to his relief. He wanted to keep it that way.

He told himself he was being ridiculous. It was only a Christmas program, not a Broadway production. Still, he didn't want to offer her any opportunity to catch the performing bug.

She was still so fragile. While her physical wounds had mostly healed, emotionally and mentally she was still had a long journey.

Was he being too protective? Probably. Her therapist in California told him he needed to relax and let go a little. He didn't need to watch over her every single moment. Right now he had a tendency to want to keep her close, to tuck her up against him and make sure nothing terrifying or tragic ever touched her again.

That wasn't a healthy approach, either. He couldn't protect her from everything, even though he wanted to.

"Can I do it, Dad?" she asked again.

This was the same girl who freaked out in large crowds, who didn't like loud noises and who tended to panic if strangers tried to talk to her.

Did she seriously think she could handle being on-stage in front of a bunch of strangers?

"We can talk about it later," he said.

"Absolutely," Caidy said with a cheerful smile, though he thought he saw soft compassion in her gaze.

Did she know about what had happened to Olivia? Probably. Most of the damn world knew. It had led media reports around the world for a week, had been on the cover of all the tabloids and celebrity rags.

When an Oscar-nominated actress is gunned down by her equally famous if mentally ill boyfriend—who then shoots her young child before killing himself—people tended to pay attention.

If he thought he could come to this remote corner of Idaho and escape notice, he was delusional. He doubted he could find anywhere on the planet where the news hadn't reached.

Maybe he could have taken Olivia on an African safari or something, but even then he wouldn't have been surprised if people in the veld knew of Elise Chandler.

"It was nice to meet you," Ava said politely. "I hope we see you at rehearsal tomorrow."

His daughter needed friends, he thought again. They had always been important to her. Before everything happened, she always had been begging to have a friend over to use the pool or watch a movie.

Since her release from the hospital, she hadn't been interested in doing the normal things a seven-year-old girl would do. Ava Caldwell was older than his daughter, maybe eleven or twelve, but she seemed very kind. Maybe Celeste knew of some other likely candidates Olivia could hang out with while they were in town.

If it helped her interact with children around her age, would the Christmas program really be that bad?

Being a parent was a tough enough gig under the best of circumstances. Throw in the kind of trauma his daughter had endured and he felt as though he was foundering, trying to stay afloat in thirty-foot swells.

The Caldwells waved and headed for their table, and Flynn returned to his delicious pizza. The people at the Rocky Mountain Pizza Company knew what they were doing when it came to pie, he had to admit. Olivia, he saw, ate two pieces and even some of the family-style tossed salad, which seemed something of a record for her, given her poor appetite these days.

While they ate, they talked about Christmas and books and a couple of movies they had all seen. Three different times, people who came into the restaurant stopped at their booth to say hello to Celeste.

Olivia seemed to find that of great interest. "Do you know everybody who lives here?" she finally asked.

Celeste laughed, a light, musical sound. "Not even close, though it feels like it sometimes. When you live in a place for a long time you get to know lots of people. I've been in Pine Gulch since I was eleven—except for the years I was away in Boise and Seattle for school."

"Where did you live before that?" he asked, suddenly intensely curious about her.

He was even more curious when her cheerful features seemed to go still and closed. She didn't say anything for several long seconds, so long that he wasn't sure she was going to answer him at all.

"It didn't seem like a tough question," he said mildly.

"For you, maybe," she retorted. "You grew up in California with your mother after your parents divorced, and spent your summers here with Charlotte, right?"

How did she know that? he wondered. He only remembered meeting her a few times back when he would come to visit and didn't remember ever sharing that information with her. Maybe Charlotte had told her.

He gave her a close look but she seemed lost in her own thoughts.

"That's right," he answered. "And you?"

"No one specific place," she finally answered. "I lived all over the globe, if you want the truth. I was born in a hut in Ghana, and before I was eleven, I lived in about two dozen countries. My parents were missionaries who started health clinics in underserved places of the world. Before I came to Pine Gulch, we were living in Colombia."

Some kind of vague, unsettling memory poked at him, a whisper he had once heard about Celeste and her sisters. Something to do with a kidnapping, with her parents.

He couldn't put his finger on the details. What was

it? Was that the reason for those secrets in her eyes, for the pain he sensed there?

He opened his mouth to ask her, but before he could a loud clatter echoed through the place as a server busing the table next to them dropped the bin of dishes.

At the sudden, unexpected sound, Olivia gave one terrified gasp and slid from her seat under the table.

Damn, he hated these moments when her PTSD took over. They left him both furious and profoundly sad. He took a breath and leaned down to talk her through it, but Celeste beat him to it. She reached down and gave Olivia's shoulder a comforting squeeze beneath the table.

"It's okay. You're okay. It was only dishes. That's all. I know you were startled, but you're safe, sweetheart."

Olivia was making little whimpering noises that broke his heart all over again.

"I don't like loud noises," she said.

"Especially when you don't expect them and don't have time to prepare. Those are the *worst*, right?"

To his shock, Celeste spoke with a tone of experience. He gazed at her, trying to remember again what he knew about her and her sisters.

"They are," Olivia said. Though she still sounded upset, he could no longer hear the blind panic in her voice.

"Why don't you come up and finish your pizza? If you want, I can ask Lucy about fixing you one of their best desserts. It's a big gooey chocolate-chip cookie they bake in the wood-fired oven and top with hand-churned ice cream. I think you'll love it. I know it's my favorite thing to eat when I've been startled or upset about something."

After another moment, Olivia peeked her head out from under the booth. "They're not going to make that sound again, are they?"

"I don't think so. That was an accident."

"I hope they don't have another accident," she answered in a small voice.

"If they do, your dad and I are right here to make sure nothing hurts you."

That seemed enough to satisfy her. His daughter slid back onto the seat. She still had a wild look in her eyes, and he noticed she edged closer to him and constantly looked toward Celeste for reassurance while they finished their pizza.

He didn't miss the protective expression Celeste wore in return, an expression that turned *his* insides just as gooey as that chocolate-chip cookie she was talking about.

He couldn't let himself develop feelings for this woman, no matter how amazing she was with his child, he reminded himself.

He had to focus on his daughter right now. She was the only thing that mattered.

Chapter 6

"Is she asleep?" Celeste whispered an hour later, when they made the turn onto Cold Creek Road.

He glanced in the rearview mirror and could see Olivia curled into the corner, her eyes closed and her cheek resting on her hand.

"Looks like it." He pitched his voice low. "She's always been a kid who can sleep anywhere, especially when she's had a long day. Driving in the car has always knocked her right out. When she was going through the terrible twos and used to fight going to bed, I would strap her in her car seat and drive her around the block a few times. She always ran so hard that when she finally stopped, she would drop like a rock by the time we hit the first corner."

"Did she stay asleep?"

"Yeah. That was the amazing part. She never seemed

to mind when I unstrapped her from her car seat and carried her into the house to her bed. I was kind of sorry when she outgrew that phase and started sleeping in her own bed without a fuss."

Beside him, he caught a flash of white in the darkness as Celeste smiled a little. "I imagine she was an adorable toddler."

"Oh, she was. Scary smart and curious about everything."

He felt a sharp pang in his heart when he thought again about how much she had changed, how she had become so fearful and hesitant. Would the old Olivia ever return, or was this their new version of normal?

"I wish you could have known her three months ago. Before."

Celeste reached out to touch his arm briefly, like a little bird landing on a branch for only a moment before fluttering away again.

"She's a wonderful girl, Flynn. A terrible thing happened to her, yes, but she's already demonstrated what a survivor she is. Trust me. She'll get through it in time. She may always have those dark memories—nothing can take them away completely—but eventually she'll learn how to replace them with happier thoughts."

He glanced over at her. "Is that how you coped?"

He could sense her sudden fine-edged tension. "I don't know what you mean."

"What happened to you? I vaguely remember my grandmother saying something about you and your sisters enduring a terrible ordeal, but I've been racking my brain and can't remember what. I should. I'm sorry."

She was silent for a long time and he didn't press,

just continued driving through the quiet night through Cold Creek Canyon.

The creek here wound beside the road and through the trees, silvery in the moonlight. Tall pines and firs grew beside cottonwoods along the banks, at times almost forming a tunnel over the road. It was beautiful and mysterious at night with the snow fluttering gently against the windshield and the occasional house or ranchette decorated with Christmas lights.

She finally spoke when they were almost to the Star N. "It's a time of my life I don't like to think about," she murmured.

"Oh?"

She sighed. "I told you my parents moved us around the globe under sometimes difficult circumstances."

He nodded, wondering what her life must have been like without any kind of stable place to call home. Had she thrived there or had she always felt as if something were missing in her life?

She loved to read. Perhaps books had been her one constant friend through all the chaos and uncertainty.

"When I was eleven, we moved to Colombia to open a clinic in a small, undeveloped region. My parents were assured over and over that it was a safe area to bring their daughters."

"It wasn't?"

"The village where we lived might have been safe, but several in the region were not."

With reluctance he pulled up in front of her house, wishing he could keep driving. He shouldn't have worried. She didn't appear to notice where they were, that he had parked the vehicle and turned to face her. She hardly seemed aware he was there as she spoke, her features tight and her eyes focused on some spot through the windshield that he had a feeling wasn't anywhere close to eastern Idaho.

"We had been living in the village about six weeks when the clinic drew the attention of the local rebel leader in one of those unstable villages who happened to be in need of some extra cash to fund his soldiers. I guess Juan Pablo thought he could get a handsome sum in ransom if he kidnapped the crazy American do-gooders. The only trouble with that plan was that my parents weren't associated with any larger organization with deep pockets. They were free agents, I guess you could say. There was no money to pay a ransom and no one to pay it."

"What happened?"

"Juan Pablo didn't believe my parents when they insisted no one could pay a ransom. He thought if he held us long enough, the US government at least would step in, especially with the lives of three young girls at stake. We were held hostage for several weeks in a squalid prison camp."

What the hell had her parents been thinking, to drag three young girls all over the world into these unstable situations? He was all for helping others and admired those selfless people who only wanted to make a difference in the world, but not when it cost the well-being of their own children.

"Did someone eventually pay the ransom?"

She shook her head. "That was never one of the options. Juan Pablo was just too stupid or too blinded by greed to realize it. Instead, after we had been held for several weeks, a team of US Navy SEALs mounted an early-morning rescue."

She paused, her head bowed and her dark curls hiding her features. When she spoke, her voice was low, tight with remembered pain.

"The rescue wasn't a complete success. My father was…shot by Juan Pablo's rebels while we were trying to escape. He died instantly."

"Oh, Celeste. I'm so sorry."

"You can see why I feel great empathy for Olivia and what she's going through. Seeing a parent die violently is a trauma no child should have to endure."

"I completely agree," he said. "Again, I'm so sorry."

She lifted one shoulder. "It happened. I can't change it. For a long time, I struggled to deal with the injustice of it all. My parents were only trying to help others and my father paid the ultimate price for his benevolence. I can't say I've ever really found peace with that or ever will, but I've been able to move forward. For what it's worth, I freaked out at loud noises for a long time, too. Probably a good year or two after the accident."

"You seem to handle them fine now."

She gave a small laugh. "I wouldn't be a very good children's librarian if I couldn't handle a little noise, believe me. I would have run screaming into the night after the very first story time."

"So how did you come to live with your aunt and uncle?" he asked.

She shifted her gaze to his for only a moment before she looked out the windshield again, as if she couldn't quite bear to make eye contact while she told the rest of the story.

"In possibly the cruelest twist of all, our mother was diagnosed with cancer shortly after we were rescued from Colombia. She had been sick for a while but hadn't sought the necessary medical care. She'd apparently suspected something was wrong before we were taken and had made an appointment for tests in Bogota in the days right around our kidnapping—an appointment she couldn't make, for obvious reasons. It was…an aggressive and deadly form of cancer. Largely because she didn't get the treatment she needed in a timely manner, she died four months later, after we came back to the States."

Unable to resist, he reached for her hand and held it in his for a moment, wishing he had the words to tell her how much he admired her.

So many people he knew would have pulled inside themselves and let the tragedy and injustice of it turn them bitter and angry at the world. Instead, she had become a strong, compassionate woman who was helping children learn to love words and stories, while she wrote uplifting, heartwarming tales where good always triumphed.

She looked down at their joined hands, and her lips parted just a little before she closed them and swallowed. "After our mother died, Uncle Claude and Aunt Mary opened their home and their hearts to us, and we've been here ever since."

"And thus you entered the world of Christmas extravaganzas."

This time her laugh sounded more natural—a sweet, spontaneous sound that seemed to slide through his chest and tug at his heart. He liked the sound of her laughter. It made him want to sit in this warm car with her all night while soft Christmas music played on the stereo and snow fluttered against the windshield and his daughter slept soundly in the backseat.

"There was no Christmas Ranch before we came here. Uncle Claude had the idea a year later. My sisters and I share the theory that he did it only to distract us because he knew the holidays would be tough for us without our parents, especially that first anniversary."

"You were kidnapped at Christmastime?" That only seemed to add to the tragedy of it, that people could cruelly and viciously use an innocent family for financial gain during a time that was supposed to be about peace on earth and goodwill toward men.

"Yes." She leaned back against the seat and gazed out at the snowflakes dancing against the windshield. "My mother and father would try to keep up our spirits during our captivity by singing carols with us and encouraging us to make up Christmas stories."

"Ah. And you've carried on their storytelling tradition."

"In my feeble way, I guess you're right."

"Not feeble," he protested. "*Sparkle and the Magic Snowball* is a charming story that has captured the hearts of children and parents alike."

She looked embarrassed. "Mostly because of Hope and her beautiful illustrations."

"And because the story is sweet and hopeful at a time when people desperately need that."

She shifted in the seat, her cheeks slightly pink in the low light.

"I never expected any of this. I only wanted to tell stories to my niece and nephew. I don't know if I would ever have found the courage to submit it to a publisher. I didn't, actually. If not for Hope, all the Sparkle stories would still be in a box under my bed."

He released her fingers, not at all sure he liked this

soft tenderness seeping through him. "Your parents would be so proud of you. Who would have guessed when you were sharing stories with your parents and sisters while you were all hostages during a dark Christmastime that one day you would be a famous author?"

"Not me, certainly."

"Does writing make you feel closer to your parents?"

She stared at him for a long moment, her eyes wide. "I… Yes. Yes, it does. I never realized that until right this moment when you said it. Sometimes when I'm writing, I feel as if they're with me again, whispering words of comfort to me in the darkness."

It would be easy to fall for her. Something about her combination of vulnerability and strength tugged at him, called to him in a way no other woman ever had.

He didn't have *time* for this, he reminded himself sternly. His daughter needed all his attention right now while she tried to heal. He couldn't dilute that attention by finding himself tangled up with a lovely librarian, no matter how much he might want to be.

"I had better go," she said after a moment. Did she also sense the growing attraction between them? Was that the reason for that sudden unease in her expression? "You should get a certain exhausted birthday girl home to her bed. Besides that, Linus and Lucy are probably wondering what in the world I'm doing out here for so long."

"Of course."

With far more reluctance than he knew he should feel, he opened his door and walked around the vehicle through the lightly falling snow to her door.

The December night smelled of pine and smoke from a fireplace somewhere close. The familiar mingle of scents struck deep into his memories, of the happy times he used to spend here with his grandmother. She had been his rock, the one constant support in the midst of his chaotic family life.

He breathed in deeply as he opened her car door. As they walked to her house, he realized with shock that this was the most peaceful he had felt in weeks, since that horrible day when he'd pulled up to Elise's house to find sirens and flashing lights and ambulances.

"You don't have to walk me to the door, Flynn. This isn't a date."

He suddenly *wished* it had been a date, that the two of them had gone to dinner somewhere and shared secrets and stories and long, delicious kisses.

If it had been a date, he possibly could give into this sudden hunger to kiss her at the doorstep, to finally taste that lush mouth that had been tantalizing him all evening.

"I want to make sure you don't slip," he said. It wasn't exactly a lie, just not the entire truth. "Ice can be dangerous."

She said nothing, though he thought her eyes might have narrowed slightly as if she sensed he had more on his mind than merely her safety.

They both made it up the steps without incident, and it only took her a moment to find a key in her purse.

"Good night," she said after she unlocked her door. "Thank you for including me in Olivia's birthday celebration. It was an honor, truly."

"We were the lucky ones that you agreed to come. It was a dream come true for her, sharing delicious pizza with her favorite author."

"I imagine her dreams will become a little more lofty

as she gets older, but I'm happy I could help with this one." She gave him a sidelong look. "I hope I see her at the rehearsal tomorrow for the Christmas program. She really seemed to be interested in participating, and we would love to have her. Don't worry. She'll have fun."

Damn. He had almost forgotten about that. The peace he had been feeling seemed to evaporate like the puffs of air from their breaths.

"Don't plan on her," he warned.

"Why not?" she asked with a frown.

He raked a hand through his hair. "She's been through a brutal experience. Would you have been ready for something like this right after your own trauma?"

"I don't know," she admitted. "But if I expressed any interest at all, my aunt and uncle would have been right in the front row, cheering me on."

"I'm not your aunt and uncle," he said, with more bite in his voice than he intended.

She froze for just a moment, then nodded, her sweet, lovely features turning as wintry as the evening. "I'm sorry. You're right. I overstepped."

Her words and the tight tone made him feel like an ass. She was only trying to help his child.

"I'm sorry," he said. "I just can't see how getting up in front of a bunch of strangers and singing about peace on earth will help a young girl suffering from PTSD."

"I suppose you're right. I will say that my parents firmly believed a person could ease her own troubles while helping others—or at least trying to see them in a different light. Living here with Uncle Claude and Aunt Mary only reinforced that message. They started The Christmas Ranch so my sisters and I could find comfort in the midst of our own pain by bringing the joy of the holidays to others. It worked for us. I guess I was hoping it would do the same for Olivia, but you're her father. It's ultimately your decision."

Talk about backing a guy into a corner. What was he supposed to do?

Olivia *had* expressed a desire to participate, the first time anything had sparked her interest in weeks. He certainly had the right as her father to make decisions about what he thought was best for her, but what if he was wrong? What if she truly did need this? How could he be the one to say no to her?

"Fine," he said reluctantly. "I'll bring her tomorrow. If she enjoys herself, she can come back. But if I believe this is at all stressing her, I'll immediately put an end to it."

She smiled and he was struck again by how lovely she was. Behind her quiet prettiness was a woman of true beauty; she just seemed determined to hide it.

"Oh, that's wonderful. We'll be thrilled to have her. We'll see you tomorrow afternoon, in the main lodge at the ranch. Do you know where it is?"

"I'll figure it out."

"Excellent. I'll see you both tomorrow, then."

He knew that idea shouldn't leave him with this bubbly anticipation.

"Good night. Thanks again for having dinner with us."

"You're welcome. It was truly my pleasure."

He started to leave and then, prompted by the impulse that had been coursing through him all evening, he reached forward and kissed her softly on the cheek, the light sort of kiss people gave to even their casual acquaintances in California.

She smelled delicious—of laundry soap and almonds and some kind of springtime flowers. It took him a moment to place her scent. Violets—sweet and fresh and full of hope.

Instantly, he knew this was a mistake, that he would be dreaming of that scent all night.

Her eyes, wide and shocked behind her glasses, were impossibly green. It would be easy—so very easy—to shift his mouth just a few inches and truly kiss her. For an instant the temptation was overwhelming, but he drew on all his strength and forced himself to step away.

"Good night," he said again. To his dismay, his voice sounded ragged.

"Yes," she answered with a dazed sort of look that he told himself was only surprise.

He didn't give himself the chance to explore if that look in her eyes might have some other source—like a shared attraction, for instance. He just turned around and headed down the steps of her porch and toward his vehicle and his sleeping child.

When she was certain Flynn was in his car, driving back down the lane toward the main road, Celeste moved away from the window and sank into her favorite chair. Lucy—all sleek, sinuous grace—immediately pounced into her lap. She took a moment to pet the cat, her thoughts twirling.

For a moment there she had been almost positive Flynn Delaney had been about to *really* kiss her. That was impossible. Completely irrational. She must have been imagining things, right?

Why on earth would he want to kiss *her*? She was

gawky and awkward and shy, more comfortable with books and her fictional characters than she was with men.

They were from completely different worlds, which was probably one of the reasons she'd had such a crush on him when she was a girl. He represented the unattainable. His mother was a famous movie star, and he was certainly gorgeous enough that *he* could have been one, too, if he'd been inclined in that direction.

He had been married to Elise Chandler, for Pete's sake, one of the most beautiful women on earth. How could he possibly be interested in a frumpy, introverted *children's librarian*?

The absurdity of it completely defied reason.

She must be mistaken. That moment when he'd kissed her cheek and their gazes had met—when she'd thought she'd seen that spark of *something* kindling in his gaze—must have been a trick of the low lighting in her entryway.

What would it have been like to kiss him? *Really* kiss him?

The question buzzed around inside her brain like a particularly determined mosquito. She had no doubt it would have been amazing.

She was destined never to know.

She sighed, gazing at the lights of her little Christmas tree sparkling cheerily in the small space. If she weren't careful, she could end up with a heart as shattered as one of the ornaments Lucy liked to bat off the branches.

It would be so frighteningly easy for her to fall for him. She was already fiercely attracted to him and had been since she was barely a teenager. More than that, she liked and admired him. His devotion to Olivia and his concern for her were even more attractive to Celeste than those vivid blue eyes, the broad shoulders, the rugged slant of his jaw.

If he were to kiss her—truly kiss her—her poor, untested heart wouldn't stand a chance.

After a moment she pushed away the unease. This entire mental side trip was ridiculous and unnecessary. He wasn't interested in her and he wouldn't kiss her, so why spend another moment fretting about it?

Still, she couldn't help wishing she never had encouraged him to allow Olivia to participate in the Christmas program at the ranch. He was only here for a few weeks. The likelihood that she would even *see* the man again would have been very slim if not for Olivia and the program, and then she could have let this hopeless attraction die a natural death.

No worries, she told herself. She would simply do her best to return things to a casual, friendly level for his remaining time in Cold Creek.

How hard could it be?

Chapter 7

Dealing with thirty jacked-up children a week before Christmas was not exactly the best way to unwind after a busy day at work.

Celeste drew in a deep breath, let it out slowly and ordered herself to chill. The noise level inside the two-story St. Nicholas Lodge was at epic levels. In one corner, a group of third-grade boys tossed around a paper airplane one of them had folded. In another, two girls were singing "Let it Go" at the top of their lungs. Three of the younger boys were chasing each other around, coming dangerously close to the huge Christmas tree that was the focal point of the lodge.

All the children were so excited for Christmas they were putting off enough energy to power the entire holiday light displays of three counties.

How she was supposed to whip this frenzy into organized chaos she had no idea.

"Whose crazy idea was this again?" her sister said, taking in the scene.

She sent Hope an arch look. "Go ahead. Raise your hand."

Hope offered up a rueful smile. "Sorry. It seemed like a fun idea at the time, a way to keep the local kids engaged and involved and give their parents a little break for shopping and baking, with the payoff of a cute show for the senior citizens at the end. I suppose I didn't really think it through."

"How very unlike you," Faith said drily from Celeste's other side.

Faith's presence was far more of a shock to Celeste than the wild energy of the children. Their eldest sister was usually so busy working on the cattle-raising side of the business that she didn't participate in many activities at The Christmas Ranch.

Perhaps she had decided to stop by because Louisa and Barrett were participating. Whatever the reason, Celeste was glad to see her there. The past eighteen months had been so difficult for Faith, losing her childhood sweetheart unexpectedly. It was good to see her sister reaching outside her comfort zone a little.

"I guess I didn't expect them all to be so…jacked up." Hope couldn't seem to take her gaze away from the younger children, who were now hopping around the room like bunny rabbits.

"You obviously don't have children," Faith said.

"Or work in a children's library," Celeste added.

"All kids act as if they're on crack cocaine the whole week before Christmas," Faith continued. "How could you not know that?"

"Okay, okay. Lesson learned. Now we just have to

do our best to whip them into shape. We can do this, right?"

At the note of desperation in Hope's voice, Celeste forced a confident smile. "Sure we can."

Though she had her own doubts, she wouldn't voice them to Hope. She was too grateful for her sister for bringing light and joy back to the ranch.

After Travis's death in a ranching accident, Celeste, Mary and Faith had decided to close The Christmas Ranch, which had been losing money steadily for years. It had seemed the logical course of action. The Star N had been all but bankrupt and the Christmas side of things had been steadily losing money for years.

The plan had been to focus on the cattle side of the Star N, until Hope came back from years of traveling. She put her considerable energy and enthusiasm to work and single-handedly brought back the holiday attraction.

Part of that success had come because of the Sparkle books, which still managed to astonish Celeste.

She would always be deeply grateful to Hope for reminding them all of the joy and wonder of the season. Helping her with this Christmas program was a small way to repay her for all her hard work on behalf of the family.

"We've got this," she said to her sisters with a firm smile that contained far more assurance than she really felt.

She stepped forward and started to clap her hands to gather the children around when the door opened and a couple of newcomers came in. She turned with a smile to welcome them and felt an actual physical jolt when she saw Flynn and Olivia.

Despite his agreement the night before, she had been

certain Flynn would end up not bringing Olivia. She had seen the clear reluctance in his eyes and knew he worried the girl wasn't ready for this sort of public appearance.

She was thrilled for Olivia's sake that he had changed his mind, even if it meant she would have to do her best to ignore her own reaction to him—and even though she wouldn't have been nearly as exhausted today if not for him.

Her night had been restless. She couldn't seem to shake the memory of that moment when he had kissed her cheek—the warmth of his mouth, the brush of his evening shadow against her skin, the delicious, outdoorsy scent of him.

She shivered now in remembered reaction.

"Are you cold?" Faith asked in a low voice.

No. Exactly the opposite. "I'm fine." The lie rolled out far more easily than she would have expected. She had never been very good at stretching the truth.

"That must be Flynn," Hope said in an undertone, following her gaze to the newcomers. "Wow. He's really filled out since he was a teenager. Where's a nice lawn to be mowed when we need it?"

Faith laughed aloud, something she did very rarely these days. She had become so much more sober since Travis died.

"Good luck with that, finding a patch of bare lawn in Idaho in December," Faith said. "Too bad you can't talk him into shoveling snow without his shirt."

That was an image Celeste didn't need to add to the others in her head. She felt herself color, then immediately regretted the reaction when her sisters both looked between her and Flynn with renewed interest.

Drat. They were both entirely too perceptive. The last thing she needed was for either Hope or Faith to get any matchmaking ideas where Flynn was concerned.

She quickly left her annoying sisters and moved forward to greet the newcomers.

Olivia looked nervous, half hiding behind her father. She visibly relaxed when Celeste approached.

"Hi, Celeste."

"It's my favorite just-turned-seven-year-old. Hi."

"It's noisy in here," Olivia informed her in an accusing sort of voice, as if it was *Celeste's* fault all the children were so wild.

"I know. Sorry about that. We're just about to get started. Once we focus everybody's attention, things will calm down. How are you today?"

Olivia smiled a little. "Okay, I guess. My dad didn't want to bring me, but I asked him and asked him until he finally said yes."

"I'm so glad," she said.

She shifted her gaze finally to Flynn and found him watching her with an unreadable look. She was suddenly aware that she must look tousled and harried. She had come straight from work, stopping at home only long enough to let Linus out and yank her hair up into a messy bun. She wore jeans and her favorite baggy sweater, and she was pretty sure her makeup had worn off hours ago.

For just a moment, she wished she could be beautiful and sophisticated instead of what she was—boring.

"Hi," she said to him. To her dismay, her voice sounded breathless and nervous. "I wasn't sure you would come."

"Apparently my daughter is relentless. Kind of like someone else I know."

She had to smile at the slightly disgruntled note in his voice.

"This will be fun. You'll see. We're going to practice until about six thirty. If you have shopping to do or want to go back to work on your grandmother's house, you're welcome to return for her then. Actually, I could even drop her off. It's not far."

He looked around at the chaos of the jacked-up children and then back at his nervous daughter.

"I believe I'll stay, if you don't mind."

What if she *did* mind? What if the idea of him watching her for the next two hours made her more nervous than a turkey at Thanksgiving?

She didn't know what else she could do but nod. "Sure. Of course. There are sofas over by the fireplace where you can make yourself comfortable. If you'd rather be closer to the action here, feel free to bring over a chair."

"Thanks."

He then proceeded to take neither of those suggestions. Instead, he leaned against the wall, crossed his arms over his chest and turned his full attention in her direction.

"Right." She swallowed and glanced at her watch. They should have started practicing five minutes ago.

She clapped her hands loudly and firmly three times to grab everyone's attention and said in her most firm librarian voice. "By the count of ten, I need everybody to gather around me and freeze in your best Christmas statue pose. Ready? One. Two. Three…"

By the time she hit four, all thirty children—thirty-one now, including Olivia—had made their way to her and adopted various positions. Destry Bowman, one of the older girls, was stretched out on the floor pretending to be asleep. Cute little Jolie Wheeler looked as if she was trying to do a figure eight on skates. Her niece, Louisa, appeared to be reaching on tiptoes for something, and it took Celeste a moment before she realized she was trying to put ornaments on an invisible Christmas tree.

Olivia looked uncertain, standing nervously with her hands clasped in front of her.

Celeste gave her a reassuring smile and then turned her attention to the other children.

"Perfect. Statues, you can all relax now and sit down."

The children complied instantly and she smiled. They might be a wild bunch but she loved them all. Each was someone whose name she knew, either from being neighbors and friends with their parents or from church or her work at the library.

"Thank you! This is going to be great fun, you'll see. The senior citizens and your families are going to *love* it, trust me, and you'll have fun, too. Are you all ready to put together a great show for your families?"

"Yes!" they shouted as one.

"Let's get to it, then."

He never would have predicted it when he walked into chaos, but somehow the ragtag collection of hyperactive children had calmed down considerably and were working hard together.

Celeste had organized the children into small groups of five or six and assigned one older child to teach them the song or dance they were to perform. She in turn moved between the groups offering words of advice or encouragement, working on a lyric here or a dance move there.

He found it charming to watch, especially seeing her lose her natural reserve with the children.

Was that why she had become a children's librarian, because she was more comfortable interacting with them? He was curious—but then he was curious about *everything* that had to do with Celeste Nichols.

Naturally, he kept a careful eye on his daughter, but she seemed to have relaxed considerably since they'd walked in. Just now she was talking and—yes!—even *laughing* with three children he'd heard call Celeste their aunt, a couple of boys about her age and a girl who appeared to be a few years older.

Had Celeste said something to them, somehow encouraged them to be especially welcoming to Olivia? He wouldn't have been surprised, but maybe they were as naturally compassionate and caring as their aunt. Whatever the reason, the children seemed to have gone out of their way to show kindness and help her feel more comfortable, which went a long way toward alleviating his own concerns.

He doubted anything could make him feel totally enthusiastic about Olivia performing in the little production, but it helped considerably to see her enjoying herself so much and interacting with her peers.

He wasn't sure he was ready to admit it, but Celeste might have been right. This little children's performance in a small community in Idaho might be exactly what Olivia needed to help her begin to heal from the horrors she had endured.

He finally relaxed enough to take a seat on one of the sofas by the fireplace and was reading through email messages from his office on his cell phone when one of the women Celeste had been talking with when he and Olivia arrived took a seat on the sofa across from him.

"Hi, Flynn. You probably don't remember me, but I'm Hope Santiago. Used to be Nichols. I'm Celeste's sister."

Ah. No wonder she had looked familiar, though she only shared green eyes in common with her sister. Instead of Celeste's silky brown hair and quiet, restful loveliness, Hope Santiago was pretty in a Bohemian sort of way, with long, wavy blond hair and a cluster of exotic-looking bracelets at her wrist.

He had met her before, he thought, back when he used to come here for the summers.

"Hello. Sure, I remember you. You're married now. Congratulations."

She gave a pleased-as-punch smile and gestured through the doorway to what looked like an office where a big, tough-looking dude with a couple of tats was speaking on a cell phone.

"That's my husband, Rafe. He and I run The Christmas Ranch together."

"The two of you must just be overflowing with Christmas spirit."

She chuckled. "We do our best. Thanks for letting your daughter participate in the show. It means a lot to Celeste."

He wasn't sure he had exactly "let" Olivia do anything. He'd been steamrollered into it, when all was said and done, but so far things seemed to be working out.

He shrugged. "It's for a good cause, right? Making some older people happy. That can only be a good thing, right?"

"Exactly." She beamed at him.

"You're the artist," he realized suddenly. "The one who took Celeste's Sparkle story and turned it into a book."

She nodded. "That's me," she answered.

"They're charming illustrations that go perfectly with the story," he told her. "I read the second book again to my daughter last night, for about the twentieth time in just a few days. It's every bit as sweet as the first one. The two of you make a great team."

She looked pleased at his words. "Thanks, but Celeste is the creative genius. I just took her fabulous story and drew little pictures to go with it. Any success the Sparkle book has seen is because of her story."

"That's funny. She said almost exactly the same thing about you and your illustrations."

"She would," she said with a laugh. "Don't make the mistake of thinking we're always adoring sisters, so sweet to each other we'll make your teeth hurt. We're not afraid to have it out. I think I've still got a little bald spot in the back of my head where she yanked out some hair during a fight when we were kids. She might look sweet and all, with that quiet librarian thing she has going, but she can fight dirty, even when you're bigger than she is."

He had to laugh. He glanced over at Celeste, who was holding an upset preschooler on her lap and trying to calm him, her face close to his. Flynn did his best to imagine her in a physical fight with one of her sisters. He couldn't quite make the image fit, but had to admit he enjoyed trying.

She must have felt his gaze. She looked up from the little boy and whatever she was saying to him. He saw her swallow and watched her features turn rosy, much to his secret enjoyment. After a moment, she turned back to the child and he shifted his gaze back to Hope, who was watching him with interest.

"Looks as if we're just about wrapping up here," she said casually. "If you haven't had dinner, why don't you and your daughter come up to the ranch house after practice? Aunt Mary is making lasagna and her famous crusty bread sticks. You can celebrate with us."

"What are you celebrating?"

"We just agreed to let a film studio begin work on an animated Sparkle movie. It's going into production immediately, with hopes that it will be out by next Christmas. And with the money we're getting for the film rights, we're paying off the second mortgage our uncle took on the Star N. We'd love to have you celebrate with us."

His stomach rumbled on cue while he was still trying to take in the surprising invitation. "That's very kind of you, but I don't want to intrude."

"Intrude on what?" Another woman who looked enough like Celeste and Hope to make him certain this was their other sister joined them by the fireplace.

"I invited Flynn and his daughter over for lasagna. Aunt Mary won't mind, will she?"

"Are you kidding? She'll be over the moon to have a few more people to fuss over, and you know she always makes enough to feed half the town."

His first inclination was to say no. He even opened his mouth to refuse the invitation, but then he caught sight of Olivia looking more relaxed and animated than he had seen her in a long time. Right next to her was

Celeste, apparently done calming the upset little boy and now smiling at something Olivia had said.

He couldn't seem to look away.

"Sure," he answered before he had a chance to think it through. He had no plans for dinner beyond warming up the pizza they'd had the night before, and he had a feeling Olivia was getting a little tired of his meager culinary abilities. "Thank you for inviting us. Lasagna sounds delicious, and we would be honored to celebrate with you, especially since Olivia is your biggest fan."

"Excellent," Hope said, looking delighted.

"I'd better call Aunt Mary and let her know to set two more places at dinner," Faith said.

The two of them walked away, leaving him wondering what he had just done.

Chapter 8

This was a mistake.

Flynn sat at the big scarred kitchen table at the Star N wondering what on earth he had been thinking to agree to this.

Since the moment he sat down he had been aware of an itch between his shoulders, a feeling that he didn't belong here.

He couldn't quite put his finger on why.

The food was delicious, he had to admit. The lasagna was perfectly cooked, cheesy and flavorful with a red sauce his late mother's Italian chef would definitely have endorsed. The bread sticks were crispy and flavorful, and even the tossed salad seemed fresh and festive.

He couldn't fault the company. It was more than pleasant. He enjoyed listening to Celeste's family— her aunt Mary, who turned out to be a jolly woman with warm eyes and an ample girth, her two sisters as well as Hope's husband, Rafe Santiago, and Chase Brannon, a neighboring rancher who seemed more like part of the family.

More important, Olivia seemed to be more relaxed and comfortable than he had seen her in a long time. She sat at one end of the table with Celeste's niece, Louisa, her nephew, Barrett, and the other boy he had seen them with at the rehearsal. It turned out the boy was Rafe's nephew. From what Flynn could tell, the boy lived with Rafe and Hope, though Flynn didn't completely understand why.

The children were deep in conversation, and every once in a while he heard laughter coming from that end of the table. Olivia even joined in a few times—a total shocker.

So why did he feel so uneasy? He didn't want to admit that it might have been because he was enjoying himself *too* much. He didn't need to find more things that drew him to Celeste, when he already couldn't seem to get the woman out of his head.

"So what do you do in California?" Chase asked.

The man treated all the Nichols sisters as if he were an older brother. He seemed especially protective of Faith, though she hardly seemed to notice.

"Construction. I've got a fairly good-size operation, with offices in San Diego, Los Angeles and Sacramento."

"Delaney Construction. Is that you?" Rafe piped up.

He nodded, intensely proud of what he had built out of nothing. The company had become a powerhouse over the past decade, even in the midst of a rough economy.

"You do good work," Rafe said. "A buddy of mine is

one of your carpentry subs. Kevin O'Brian. I flew out for a few weeks last spring to help him on a job, a new hospital in Fullerton."

"Right. He's a good man."

"That's what he said about you."

"Wow. Small world," Hope said.

He and the men spent a few moments talking about some of the unique challenges of working in the construction industry in Southern California.

"Have you ever thought about moving your operations out to this neck of the woods?" Chase asked. "We don't have a lot of hospitals and the like going up, but there are always construction projects around here, especially in the Jackson area."

The question took him by surprise. Three months ago he would have given an emphatic no to that question. He had a business in Southern California, contacts and subcontractors and jobs he had fought hard to win.

He glanced at Olivia. He had other things to concern himself with now, like what might be best for his daughter.

Small-town life seemed to agree with her, he had to admit. Maybe she would be able to heal better if she were away for longer than just a few weeks from the life they had both known in California.

A change of scenery appeared to have helped the Nichols sisters move beyond the trauma in their past.

"I haven't," he answered truthfully. "It's definitely something to think about."

He glanced across the table to see Celeste listening in, though she was pretending not to.

What would she think if he stuck around town a little longer than a few weeks?

Probably nothing, he told himself. They meant nothing to each other.

"What are you doing with that property of your grandmother's?" Mary asked.

"I'm hoping to put it up for sale in the next few weeks."

"You're not planning to subdivide it, are you?" she asked, her gaze narrowed.

He could probably make more money if he did that, but somehow he didn't think his grandparents would approve.

"That's a nice piece of land there by the Cold Creek," Brannon said. "Somebody could build a beautiful house on it if they were so inclined."

If he were going to stay here—which he most definitely *wasn't*, based on a simple dinner conversation—he probably would take the bones of the house and add on to it, opening up a wall here or there and rebuilding the kitchen and bathrooms.

It was a nice, comfortable house, perfectly situated with a gorgeous view of the mountains, but it was too small and cramped for comfort, with tiny rooms and an odd flow.

All this was theoretical. He planned to sell the property as-is, not take on another project. He had enough to do right now while he was helping his daughter recover the shattered bits of her life and learn to go on without the mother she had adored.

The conversation drifted during the dinner from topic to topic. The Nicholses seemed an eclectic group, with wide-ranging interests and opinions. Even the children joined in the discussion, discussing their projects at school, the upcoming show, the movie deal they were celebrating.

He was astonished to discover he enjoyed every moment of it. This was exactly what a family should be, he thought, noisy and chaotic and wonderful.

He had never known this growing up as an only child whose parents had stayed together much longer than they should have. He had learned to live without a family over the years, but it made his chest ache that his daughter would never have it, either.

Her sisters were matchmaking.

Celeste could tell by the surreptitious glances Faith and Hope sent between her and Flynn, the leading little questions they asked him, the way they not-so-subtly discussed the upcoming movie deal, careful to focus on Celeste's literary success, as if they were trying to sell a prize pig at the market.

It was humiliating, and she could only hope he hadn't noticed.

How could they possibly think Flynn might be interested in her in the first place? If they had bothered to ask her, she would have explained how ludicrous she found the very idea.

They didn't ask her, of course. They'd simply gone ahead and invited the poor man to dinner. Why he agreed to come, she had no idea. By the time dessert rolled around, she still hadn't figured it out—nor did she understand how he and Olivia seemed to fit in so effortlessly with her family.

Hope and Faith and Aunt Mary all liked him, she could tell, and Chase and Rafe treated him with courtesy and respect.

As for her, she liked having the two of them here entirely too much.

She tried to reel herself back, to force herself to remember this was only temporary. They were only at the ranch for the evening. Her sisters' matchmaking intentions were destined to failure. Not only *wasn't* he interested in her, but he had made it abundantly clear he was going back to California as soon as he could.

"Practice went well, don't you think?" Hope asked, distracting her from that depressing thought. "The kids seemed to be into it, and what I heard was wonderful."

"It won't win any Tony Awards, but it should be fun," she answered.

"With all you have going on around here, I still can't figure out why you decided to throw a show for local senior citizens," Flynn said.

Hope took the chance to answer him. "We've always had so much community support over the years here at The Christmas Ranch, from the very moment Uncle Claude opened the doors. The people of Pine Gulch have been great to us, and we wanted to give back a little. I guess we picked senior citizens because so many of them feel alone during the holiday season."

"Many of these people have been friends with me and my late husband for years," Mary added. "This seemed a good chance to offer them a little holiday spirit."

"I think it's nice," Louisa declared. "So do my friends. That's why they agreed to do it."

Celeste smiled at her niece, who had a very tender heart despite the tragedy of losing her father.

"I do, too," she answered.

"Is Sparkle going to show up at the party?" Barrett asked.

"I think we're going to have to see about that next week," Faith answered her son. "He's been acting a little down the past few days."

Celeste frowned at her sister. "What's wrong with him?" she asked, alarmed.

"Oh, I'm sure it's nothing," she answered. "He's just off his feed a bit. I ended up bringing him up here to his stall at the main barn to see if being back with the horses for a day or two would cheer him up."

Sparkle had a particularly soft spot for Mistletoe, an old mare who used to be Uncle Claude's. "I'm sure that's it," Celeste said.

"Maybe he just misses *you*, CeCe," Hope suggested. "You haven't been down to see him in a while."

Celeste rolled her eyes. "Right. I'm sure he's pining away."

It was true that she and Sparkle were old friends. The reindeer was warm and affectionate, far more than most of their small herd.

"You ought to go down to the barn to say hello while you're here," Faith suggested.

"Can I go meet Sparkle?" Olivia asked, her eyes huge as she followed the conversation. "I would *love* to."

She *had* told the girl she would take her to meet the inspiration for the books she loved so much. "He enjoys company. I'm sure he would love to meet you."

"Can we go now?" the girl pressed.

She looked at the table laden with delicious dishes she had done nothing to help prepare. Yes, she could claim a good excuse—being busy directing the show and all—but Uncle Claude and Aunt Mary had always been clear. If you didn't help cook a meal, you were obligated to help clean it up.

"I need to help clear these dishes first," she said.

"Oh, don't worry about this," Faith said.

"Right. We can take care of things," Hope insisted.

"Yes, dear," Aunt Mary added. "We've got this completely covered. It won't take a moment to clean this up. Meantime, why don't you take our guests down to the barn to meet Sparkle?"

Who were these women and what had they done with her family members? She frowned, fighting the urge to roll her eyes at all of them for their transparent attempts to push her together with Flynn. For heaven's sake, what did they think would possibly happen between the two of them with his daughter along?

"I don't know," Flynn said, checking his watch. "It's getting late."

"It's not even eight o'clock yet!" Olivia protested. "Since I don't have to get up for school, I haven't been going to bed until nine thirty."

"I suppose that's true."

"So we can go?"

He hesitated, then shrugged. "If Celeste doesn't mind taking us. But we can't stay long. She's already had a long day."

"Oh, yay!" Olivia jumped up instantly from the table and headed for her coat.

"Does anyone else want to go down to the barn with us?" Celeste asked.

She didn't miss the way Barrett practically jumped out of his chair with eagerness but subsided again with a dejected look when his mother shook her head firmly.

Oh, she hoped Flynn hadn't noticed her crazy, delusional, interfering sisters.

He rose. "We'll probably need to head out after we stop at the barn. It's late and I have to get this young lady home to bed, whatever she says."

"Understandable," Aunt Mary said with a warm, affectionate smile for both of them.

With a sweet, surprising charm, he leaned in and kissed her aunt's plump cheek. "Thank you for the delicious meal. We both truly enjoyed it."

She heard a definite ring of truth to his words, even as he looked a little surprised by them. She had the feeling he hadn't expected to enjoy the meal—which again made her wonder why he had agreed to come.

"You are most welcome," Aunt Mary said. "I hope both of you will come again before you return to California. Your grandmother was a dear, dear friend, and I miss her terribly. Having you and your daughter here helps ease that ache a little."

He looked touched. "I miss her, too. I only wish I could have visited her more the past few years."

Mary patted his hand. "She told me you called her every Sunday night without fail, and sometimes during the week, too. She was very proud of that fact, especially as so many young people these days get so busy with their lives that they forget that their parents and grandparents might be a touch lonely without them."

"A phone call was nothing. I can't tell you how much I appreciate all of her friends here in Pine Gulch who helped keep her busy and involved."

Celeste liked to consider herself one of that number. Charlotte had volunteered at the library almost up to the end of her life, never letting her physical ailments or the frailties of age prevent her from smiling and try-ing to lift someone else.

"She was always so proud of you," Mary went on. "Especially because of what you came from."

He gave a snort at that. "What I came from? Beverly Hills? Yeah. I overcame so much in life. I don't know why nobody has come out with a made-for-television movie about my sad life."

Mary made a face. "Charlotte was proud of many things about you, but perhaps most of all that despite every advantage you had, you always stayed grounded and didn't let your head get turned by your mother's fame or fortune. Now that I've met you, I understand what she meant. You're a good boy, Flynn Delaney."

She smiled and patted his hand again. Flynn looked a bit taken aback at anyone calling him a boy, but he only had time to give Aunt Mary a bemused sort of look before Olivia cut off anything he might have said in response.

"Are you ready, Daddy? I can't wait to see Sparkle. I can't *wait*."

"Yes. I'm ready. We can grab our coats on the way out. Thank you all again."

"You're so welcome," Faith and Hope said at the same time, almost as if they had rehearsed it. Chase and Rafe both nodded in the odd way men had of speaking volumes with just a simple head movement.

"Bye, Olivia. We'll see you at the next practice," Louisa said cheerfully.

They put on their coats quickly and headed out into the December evening.

The snow had increased in intensity, still light but

more steady now. The air was still, though, with no wind to hurl flakes against them.

The night seemed magical somehow, hushed and beautiful with the full moon trying to push through the cloud cover.

Celeste was fiercely aware of him as they made their way to the barn. He was so very…male, from the jut of his jaw to his wide shoulders to the large footsteps his boots made in the snow beside her much smaller ones. He made her feel small and feminine in comparison.

To her relief, she didn't have to make conversation. Olivia kept up a steady stream of conversation about the ranch. She couldn't help noticing the girl had talked more that day than she had in all their previous encounters combined. Either she was more comfortable with Celeste now, or she was beginning to return to the girl she had been before the shooting.

If she wasn't mistaken, the girl had hardly limped that afternoon or evening. That had to be a good sign, she supposed.

"Here we are," she said when they reached the barn. The smell of hay and animals and old wood greeted them, not at all unappealing in its way.

She flipped on the lights and heard Mistletoe's distinctive whinny of greeting. She took time as they passed the old horse to give Misty a few strokes and an apple she pulled from her pocket before she led them to Sparkle's stall next door.

"Olivia, this is Sparkle. Sparkle, meet my good friend Olivia."

After a moment of coyness, the reindeer headed to the railing of the stall.

"I've never seen a real reindeer before. He's small!"

"Reindeer are generally much smaller than people think they should be." She petted him, much the way she had Mistletoe. He lipped at her, trying to find a treat.

"Would you like to feed him an apple?"

"Can I?"

She glanced down at the girl and decided not to miss this opportunity. "I don't know. You'll have to use your left arm. He prefers it when people feed him from that side."

That was an out-and-out lie. Sparkle would eat with great delight any apple that came his way, but she decided Olivia didn't need to know that.

Flynn made a low sound of amusement beside her that seemed to ripple down her spine. She barely managed to hold back her instinctive shiver as she handed the apple to Olivia.

The girl narrowed her gaze at Celeste, obviously trying to figure out if this was some kind of a trick. In the end, the appeal and novelty of feeding a reindeer outweighed her suspicions.

She took the apple with her injured left hand and, with effort, held it out to the reindeer, who nibbled it out of her hand. Olivia giggled. "Can I pet him?"

"Sure. He won't hurt you."

She rubbed his head for a moment. "What about his antlers?"

"Go ahead. Just be gentle."

She reached out and tentatively touched an antler. "It's hard and soft at the same time. Weird!"

Sparkle visited with her for a moment, and it was plain he was happy to find a new friend. Any malaise the reindeer might have been feeling was nowhere in evidence. Maybe he really *had* been pining for her, but she doubted it. Maybe, like the rest of them, he just needed a little break from the hectic pace of the holiday season.

"What's special about this particular reindeer?" Flynn asked.

She considered how to answer. "Well, he was the first reindeer Uncle Claude ever obtained, so he's been here the longest. And he's always been so much more affectionate than the others—not that they're mean or anything, just…standoffish. Not Sparkle. He's always been as friendly as can be. It rubs off on everyone."

They watched the reindeer a few moments longer. When she heard a little sound from the stall at the end of the barn, she suddenly remembered what other treasure the barn contained. Clearly, she didn't spend enough time here.

"I nearly forgot," she said. "There's something else here you might like to see."

"What?" Olivia asked eagerly. The girl loved animals; that much was obvious. Perhaps she and Flynn ought to look into getting a dog when they returned to California.

She didn't want to think about that now, not when the night seemed hushed and sweet here in the quiet barn.

"Come and see," she answered. She led the way and pulled open the stall gate. Olivia peered in a little warily but her nervousness gave way to excitement.

"Puppies! Dad, look!"

"I see them, honey."

The half dozen black-and-white pudgy things belonged to Georgie, one of the ranch border collies.

"Can I pet them?"

"Sure. I'll warn you, they're probably not super

clean. You're going to want to wash your hands when you're done."

"I will. I promise."

She knelt down and was immediately bombarded with wriggling puppies.

Celeste felt her throat tighten as she watched this girl who had been through so much find simple joy in the moment. Flynn had almost lost her. It seemed a miracle that they were here in this barn on a snowy night watching her giggle as a puppy licked her hand.

"She did all right today at the rehearsal," she said in a low voice to Flynn as they watched together. "I know you were concerned about the noise and confusion, but she handled it well. Wouldn't you agree?"

They were standing close enough together that she could feel his sigh. "I suppose."

"Does that mean you'll bring her to the next rehearsal, then?"

He gave a small sound that was almost a laugh. "Anybody ever tell you that you're relentless?"

"A few times, maybe," she said ruefully. *More than a few* was closer to the truth.

Needing a little distance, she eased down onto the bench next to the stall. To her surprise, he followed and sat beside her.

"Fine," he answered. "You win. I'll bring her to the next one. That doesn't mean I have to like it."

She glanced at his daughter playing with the puppies a dozen feet away, then turned back to Flynn. "Why do you have a problem with her performing?" she asked, her voice low. "Especially when it seems to be something she enjoys?"

"I don't *want* her to enjoy it," he answered in an

equally low tone. "If I had my way, I would have her stay far away from any kind of stage or screen."

She frowned at the intensity of his words. "Because of your mother or because of Elise?"

"Either. Both. Take your pick." He watched as a puppy started nibbling on Olivia's ponytail, which only made her giggle again as she tried to extricate it from the little mouth.

After a moment he spoke with fierce resolve. "I want my daughter to find happiness in life based on her own decisions and accomplishments, not because of how many pictures of her holding a latte from Starbucks showed up in the tabloids this week. There's an artificiality to that world that crumbles to nothing in a heartbeat. Take it from someone who grew up on the edge of that spotlight."

She thought of what Aunt Mary had said about his grandmother's pride in him for staying grounded. Unlike his mother or his wife, he hadn't sought that spotlight. He had gone into a career outside Hollywood and had built a successful business on his own merits. She had to admire that.

"That must have been tough for you," she said.

He shrugged. "How can I complain, really? It sounds stupid, even to me. I grew up with the sort of privileges most people only dream about. A-list celebrities hanging out in my swimming pool, a BMW in the driveway on my sixteenth birthday, vacations in Cannes and Park City and Venice."

By worldly standards, her family had been very poor. Her parents had given everything they had to helping others, to the point that she remembered a period in their lives when she and her sisters each had had only two or three outfits that they swapped back and forth.

She hadn't necessarily enjoyed moving from country to country, never feeling as if she had a stable home. In truth, she still carried lingering resentment about it, but she had always known she was deeply loved.

She had a feeling that for all his outward privilege, Flynn had missed out on that assurance, at least from his parents. She was grateful he had known the unwavering love and devotion of his grandmother.

"We don't get to choose the circumstances of our birth families, do we?" she said softly. "The only thing we have control of is the life we make for ourselves out of those circumstances."

His gaze met hers and the intensity of his expression left her suddenly breathless. Something shimmered between them, something bright and fierce. She couldn't seem to look away, and she again had the oddest feeling he wanted to kiss her.

Now? Here? With his daughter just a few feet away? She must have been imagining things. Still, the idea of him leaning forward slightly, of his mouth sliding across hers, made nerves jump in her stomach and her knees feel suddenly weak.

She felt as if she stood on the brink of something, arms stretched wide, trying to find the courage to jump into the empty space beyond.

She could lose her heart so easily to this man.

The thought whispered into her mind and she swallowed hard. With the slightest of nudges, she would leap into that empty space and doubtless crash hard back to earth.

Careful, she warned herself, and looked away from

him, pretending to focus on his daughter and the cute, wriggling puppies.

After a long pause, he finally spoke. "Despite everything you and your sisters have been through, you've made a good life for yourself here in Pine Gulch."

"I'd like to think so." Okay, maybe she was a little lonely. Maybe there were nights she lay in bed and stared at the ceiling, wondering if she was destined to spend the rest of her nights alone.

"I guess you know a little about being in the spotlight now, don't you?" Flynn said.

She forced a little laugh. "Not really. My particular spotlight is more like a flashlight beam. A very tiny, focused flashlight. That's the nice thing about being only a name on a book cover."

"That will change when the Sparkle movie hits the big screen," he predicted.

Oh, she didn't want to think about that. Just the idea made her feel clammy and slightly queasy. "I hope not," she said fervently. "I like being under the radar."

He frowned. "Why agree to let someone make the movie, then? You had to know that's only going to increase your celebrity status. You won't be able to stay under the radar for long."

In her heart, she knew he was right. What had she gotten herself into?

She hadn't had a choice, she reminded herself. Not really.

"I love my family," she said. "They're everything to me."

"It only took me a few minutes at dinner tonight to figure that out. You have a great family. But what does that have to do with signing a movie deal you don't appear to want?"

For someone who loved the magic and power in words, sometimes in conversation she felt as if she never could manage to find the right ones.

"Things haven't been…easy around here the past few years, even before my brother-in-law's accident. My uncle was a wonderful man but not the best businessman around, and the ranch hasn't exactly been thriving financially."

"I'm sorry to hear that."

"The, um, increased interest in The Christmas Ranch after the first Sparkle book came out last season helped a great deal but didn't completely solve the cash flow woes." She felt her face heat a little, as it always did when she talked about the astonishing success of the book. "With the deal Hope and I will be signing for the movie rights, we can pay off the rest of the ranch's debts and push the operation firmly into the black, which will lift considerable pressure from Faith. How could I turn down something that will benefit my family so much?"

He studied her for a moment, that funny intensity in his expression again. "So it's not necessarily what you really want, but you're willing to go through with it anyway for your family."

"Something like that," she muttered.

"If having a movie made out of your book doesn't sit well with you, couldn't you have found an alternative revenue stream?"

She shrugged. "Hope and I talked at length about this. Our agent and publisher were clear. *Someone* was going to make a Sparkle movie—which, believe me, is an amazing position to find ourselves in. The terms of this particular deal were very favorable for Hope and for me, and we were both impressed by the other projects this particular production company has engineered. The moment seemed right."

"I'm *glad* they're making a Sparkle movie," Olivia said suddenly. Celeste had been so busy explaining herself, she hadn't realized the girl had left the puppies on the floor of the stall and rejoined them. "I can't wait to see it."

Flynn smiled at his daughter with that sweet tenderness that tugged at her heart. "We'll probably be back in California, and you can tell everyone else at the movie theater that you actually had the chance to meet the real Sparkle and the women who created the fictional version."

"I guess." Olivia didn't look as excited about that prospect as Celeste might have expected. In fact, she appeared downright glum.

Why? she wondered. Was the girl enjoying her time in Pine Gulch so much that she didn't like thinking about their eventual return to California?

"Maybe we could come back and see the movie here," Olivia suggested.

"Maybe."

Celeste felt a sharp little kick to her heart at the noncommittal word. They wouldn't be back. She was suddenly certain of it. After Flynn sold his grandmother's house, he would have no more ties here in Pine Gulch. She likely would never see him or his daughter again.

This was why she needed to be careful to guard her heart better. She already hurt just thinking about them leaving. How much worse would it be if she let herself take that leap and fell in love with him?

He stood up and wiped the straw from the back of Olivia's coat where she had been sitting on the floor of the stall.

"We should probably take off," he said. "You need to tell Celeste thank-you for bringing you out here to meet Sparkle and to play with the puppies."

"Do we have to go?" she complained.

"Yes. It's late and Celeste probably has to work at the library tomorrow."

She nodded and was suddenly overwhelmed by a wave of fatigue. The day had been long and exhausting, and right now she wanted nothing more than to be in her comfy clothes, cuddled up with her animals and watching something brainless on TV.

"Okay," Olivia said in a dejected voice. "Thank you for bringing me down here to meet Sparkle and play with the puppies."

"You are very welcome," Celeste said. "Anytime you want to come back, we would love to have you. Sparkle would, too."

Olivia seemed heartened by that as she headed for the reindeer's stall one last time.

"Bye, Sparkle. Bye!"

The reindeer nodded his head two or three times as if he was bowing, which made the girl giggle.

Celeste led the way out of the barn. Another inch of snow had fallen during the short time they had been inside, and they walked in silence to where his SUV was parked in front of the house.

She wrapped her coat around her while Flynn helped his daughter into the backseat. Once she was settled, he closed the door and turned to her.

"Please tell your family thank you for inviting me to dinner. I enjoyed it very much."

"I will. Good night."

With a wave, he hopped into his SUV and backed out of the driveway.

She watched them for just a moment, snow settling on her hair and her cheeks while she tried to ignore that little ache in her heart.

She could do this. She was tougher than she sometimes gave herself credit for being. Yes, she might already care about Olivia and be right on the brink of falling hard for her father. That didn't mean she had to lean forward and leave solid ground.

She would simply have to keep herself centered, focused on her family and her friends, her work and her writing and the holidays. She would do her best to keep him at arm's length. It was the only smart choice if she wanted to emerge unscathed after this holiday season.

Soon they would be gone and her life would return to the comfortable routine she had created for herself.

As she walked into the house, she tried not to think about how unappealing she suddenly found that idea.

Chapter 9

She didn't have a chance to test her resolve, simply because she didn't see Flynn again for longer than a moment or two over the next few days.

At the Thursday rehearsal, he merely dropped Olivia off and left after making sure to give Hope—not Celeste—a card with his cell phone number on it.

She supposed she should take that as some sort of progress. From what she gathered, he hadn't let Olivia out of his sight since the accident. She had to feel good that he felt comfortable enough with her and her family to leave the girl at The Christmas Ranch without him.

On the other hand, she had to wonder if maybe he was just trying to avoid her.

That really made no logical sense. Why would he feel any sort of need to avoid her? *He* wasn't the one who was developing feelings that could never go anywhere.

Still, she had to wonder, especially when he did the same thing Saturday morning for their final practice before the performance, just dropping Olivia off as most of the other parents had done.

She should be grateful he'd brought the girl at all, especially when he obviously wasn't thrilled about the whole thing.

It was too bad, really, because Olivia was a natural in front of an audience. She seemed far more comfortable onstage than the other children.

The performance was nothing elaborate, a rather hodgepodge collection of short Christmas skits mixed with songs and poems, but considering the few practices they'd had, the show came together marvelously.

When they finished the second run-through Saturday morning, Celeste clapped her hands.

"That was amazing!" she exclaimed. "I'm so proud of each one of you for all your hard work. You are going to make some people very, very happy next week."

Jolie Wheeler raised her hand. "Can we take the costumes home to show our moms and dads?"

None of the costumes was anything fancy, just bits and pieces she and Hope had thrown together with a little help from Faith and a few of the parents. "We need to keep them here so we can make sure everyone has all the pieces—the belts and halos and crowns—they need for the performance. When you take them off, put your costume on the hanger and everything else in the bag with your name on it in the dressing room. Remember, you will all have to be here at five thirty sharp so we can get into costume and be ready for the show. We'll have the performance first, and then you are all welcome with your families to stay for dinner with our guests, if you'd like. There should be plenty of food for everyone."

"Then can we take the costumes home?" Jolie asked.

She smiled at the adorable girl. "We need to keep them here just in case we decide to do another show at The Christmas Ranch next year."

"Rats," Jolie complained and a few others joined her in grumbling. What they wanted to do with a few hokey costumes, Celeste had no idea, but she had to smile at their disappointment.

"You'll all just have to be in the show next year so you can wear them again," she said.

Not that she intended to be part of it, even if Hope begged her. Writing the little show had taken her almost as long as a full-fledged children's book.

"Thank you all again for your hard work, and I'll see you Tuesday evening at five thirty if you need help with your hair and makeup."

The children dispersed to the boys' and girls' dressing rooms—really just separate storage spaces that had been temporarily converted for the show. She cleaned up the rehearsal space and supervised the pickup of the children.

Finally, only Louisa, Barrett, Joey and Olivia were left. They didn't seem to mind. Indeed, they had gone to the game drawer Hope kept in her office to keep the children occupied when they were hanging out at the lodge and were playing a spirited game of Go Fish with a Christmas-themed deck of cards.

Though she had a hundred things to—including finishing the paint job on the backdrop for the little stage they had rigged up—she sat down at the table near the refreshment booth where they were playing.

"You did so well today. All of you."

"Thanks," Louisa said. "It's really fun. I hope we do it again next year."

Not unless Hope found some other sucker to be in charge, she thought again.

"I've had lots of fun, too," Olivia said. "Thanks for inviting me to do it."

"You're very welcome. How are things going at your great-grandmother's house?"

As soon as she asked the question, she wished she hadn't. It sounded entirely too much as if she was snooping. She might as well have come out and asked when they were leaving.

"Good, I guess. We have two more rooms to do. My dad said we'll probably go back to California between Christmas and New Year's."

She tried to ignore the sharp pang in her chest. "I'm sure you'll be glad to be back in your own house."

"You're lucky! You can go swimming in the ocean," Louisa said.

"Sometimes. Mostly, it's too cold, except in summer."

"And you can go to Disneyland whenever you want," Joey added.

"No, I can't," she protested. "I have to go to school and stuff."

They talked more about the differences between their respective homes. Olivia was quite envious that they could ride horses and go sledding all winter long while the other children thought California was only palm trees and beaches.

While the seasonal staff of The Christmas Ranch started arriving and getting ready for the busiest day

of their season, the children continued their game, and
Celeste sat at the table next to them working on a draw-
ing for a complicated part of the stage she was hoping
Rafe could help her finish later that day.

Finally, about forty-five minutes after practice ended,
Flynn burst through the front doors looking harried.
"Sorry I'm late. I was taking a load of things to the
county landfill and it took longer than I expected."

"Don't even worry about it. The kids have been enjoying themselves. Haven't you?"

"Yep," Barrett said. "'Cause I won Go Fish three
times and Joey and Olivia both won once. Louisa didn't
win any."

"Next time, watch out," his sister declared.

Flynn smiled at the girl, that full-fledged charming smile Celeste remembered from when he was a
teenager. She had to swallow hard and force herself to
look away, wondering why it suddenly felt so warm in
the lodge.

"How was practice?" he asked.

"Good," she answered. "Great, actually. Everyone
worked so hard."

"I can't wait for you to see the show, Dad," Olivia
declared. "It's going to be *so* good. Celeste says all the
ladies will cry."

He looked vaguely alarmed. "Is that right? Will I cry,
too? I'd better bring a big hankie, just in case."

She giggled hard, then in the funny way kids have,
she looked at Barrett and Louisa and something in their
expressions made her laugh even harder, until all three
were busting up. Their laughter was infectious and Celeste couldn't help smiling.

* * *

Flynn gazed at the three children, certain he was witnessing a miracle.

This was really his daughter, looking bright and animated and…happy.

This was the daughter he remembered, this girl who found humor in the silliest things, who was curious about the world around her and loved talking with people. He'd feared she was gone forever, stolen by a troubled man who had taken so much else from her.

Seeing her sitting at a table in the St. Nicholas Lodge, laughing with Celeste and her niece and nephew, he wanted to hug all three of the children. Even more, he wanted to kiss Celeste right on that delicious-looking mouth of hers that had haunted his dreams for days.

Her smiling gaze met his and a wave of tenderness washed over him. She had done this. He didn't know how. She had seen a sad, wounded girl and had worked some kind of Sparkle magic on her to coax out the sweet and loving girl Olivia used to be.

Her smile slid away and he realized he was staring. He drew in a deep breath and forced himself to look away.

His gaze landed on a piece of paper with what looked like a complicated drawing. "I didn't know you were an artist."

She looked embarrassed. "I'm *so* not an artist, Hope is. I'm just trying to work up a sketch I can show Rafe. I'm trying to figure out how to build wings on the side of the stage so the children have somewhere to wait offstage. There's no time to sew curtains. I just need some sort of screen to hide them from view.

He studied her sketch, then took the paper from

her and made a few quick changes. "That shouldn't be hard," he said. "You just have to build a frame out of two-by-fours and then use something lightweight like particle board for your screen. If it's hinged and connected there, it should be solid and also portable enough that you can store it somewhere when you're not using it."

She studied the drawing. "Wow. That's genius! You know, I think that just might work. Can you just write down what supplies you think it might need? Rafe will be back from Jackson Hole shortly, and I can put him to work on it if he has time."

He glanced at the stage, then at his daughter, still smiling as she played cards with the other two children. Though he knew he would probably regret it—and he certainly had plenty of things still to take care of at Charlotte's house—he spoke quickly before he could change his mind.

"If you've got some tools I can use and the two-by-fours, I can probably get the frame for it done in no time."

She stared at him, green eyes wide behind those sexy glasses she wore. "Seriously?"

He shrugged. "I started out in carpentry. It's kind of what I do. This shouldn't be hard at all—as long as Olivia doesn't mind hanging around a little longer."

"Yay!" Louisa exclaimed. "She can come to the house and decorate the sugar cookies we made last night with Aunt Celeste while our mom was Christmas shopping."

Olivia looked suitably intrigued. "I've never decorated sugar cookies."

"Never?" Celeste exclaimed. She looked surprised

enough that Flynn felt a pinch of guilt. Apparently this was another area where he had failed his daughter.

Olivia shook her head. "Is it hard?"

"No way," Louisa answered. "It's easy and super, super fun. You can decorate the cookies any way you want. There's no right or wrong. You can use sparkly sugar or M&M's or frosting or whatever you want."

"The best part is, when you mess it up, you get to eat your mistakes," Barrett added. "Nobody even cares. I mess up a *lot*."

Olivia snickered and Flynn had a feeling *she* would be messing up plenty, too. What was it with all these Christmas traditions that filled kids with more sugar when they least needed another reason to be excited?

He had struck out miserably when it came to Christmas traditions this year. At least they had the little Christmas tree at his grandmother's house for decoration, but that was about it.

Olivia had insisted she hoped Santa Claus wouldn't come that year, but he had disregarded her wishes and bought several things online for her. A few other presents would be waiting back in California, sort of a delayed holiday, simply because the new bike her physical therapist suggested was too big for the journey here in his SUV.

Next year would be different, he told himself. By this time next year they would be established in a routine back in California. They could hang stockings and put up a tree of their own and decorate all the sugar cookies she wanted, even if he had to order ready-made plain cookies from his favorite bakery.

The idea of returning to a routine after the stress of

the past few months should have been appealing. Instead, it left him remarkably unenthused.

"May I go, Dad? I really, really, *really* want to decorate cookies."

He was torn between his desire to keep her close and his deep relief that she was so obviously enjoying the company of other children. She would enjoy the cookie decorating far more than she would enjoy sitting around and watching him work a band saw.

"Are you sure your aunt won't mind one more?" he asked Celeste.

"Are you kidding? Mary loves a crowd. The more the merrier, as far as she's concerned." She smiled a little. "And look at it this way. You'll probably come out of the whole thing with cookies to take home."

"Well, in that case, how can I say no? A guy always needs a few more cookies."

"Yay! I can go," Olivia told the other children as if they hadn't been right there to hear her father's decision.

"Put the cards away first and then get your coats on. Then you can walk up to the house."

"You're not coming?" Olivia asked.

"I'll be up later," she answered with a smile. "But first I have to finish painting some of the scenery."

The children cleaned up the cards and returned them to a little tin box, then put on their coats, hats and mittens. As soon as they were on their way, Celeste turned to him with a grateful smile. She looked so fresh and lovely that for a crazy moment, he wished they were alone in the lodge with that big crackling fire.

Instead, an older woman was setting out prepackaged snacks in what looked like a concessions area and another one was arranging things on a shelf in a gift store. Outside the windows, he could see families beginning to queue up to buy tickets.

"Is there somewhere I can get going on this? A workshop or something?"

"Oh." She looked flustered suddenly and he wondered if something in his expression revealed the fierce attraction simmering through him. "Yes. There's a building behind back where Rafe keeps his tools. That's where I've been painting the scenery, too. I'll show you."

She led the way through the lodge to a back door. They walked through the pale winter sunshine to a modern-looking barn a short distance away.

In a pasture adjacent to the barn, he saw several more reindeer as well as some draft horses.

"This is where we keep the reindeer at night during the holiday season," she explained. "There's Sparkle. Do you see him?"

As far as he could tell all the reindeer looked the same, but he would take her word for it. "Is he feeling better?"

"Much. Apparently he only wanted a few days off."

"Olivia will be happy to hear that."

"He'll need his strength. This afternoon and evening will be crazy busy."

"For the reindeer, too?" he asked, fascinated by the whole idea of an entire operation devoted only to celebrating the holidays.

"Yes. Hope will probably hook them up to the sleigh for photo ops and short rides. The draft horses, of course, will be taking people on sleigh rides around the ranch, which is a highlight of the season. You should take Olivia. She would love it. It's really fun riding through the cold, starry night all bundled up in blankets."

It did sound appealing—especially if he and Celeste were alone under those blankets…

He jerked his brain back to the business at hand. He really needed to stop this.

"We're only open a few more nights," she said. "But if you want to take her, let me know and I'll arrange it."

As much as he thought Olivia would enjoy the sleigh ride, he wasn't at all certain that spending more time at The Christmas Ranch with Celeste and her appealing family would be good for either of them.

"We'll see," he said, unwilling to commit to anything. "Shall we get to it?"

"Right. Of course."

She led him into a well-lit, modern building with stalls along one wall. The rest seemed to be taken up with storage and work space.

She led him to an open area set up with a band saw, a reciprocating saw, a router and various other power tools, as well as a stack of two-by-fours and sheets of plywood.

"You might not need to have Rafe run to the lumber yard. You might have everything here."

"Great."

She pointed to another area of the barn where other large pieces of plywood had been painted with snowflakes. "I need to finish just a few things on the scenery, so I'll be on hand if you need help with anything."

The best help she could offer would be to stay out of his way. She was entirely too tempting to his peace of mind, but he couldn't figure out a way to say that without sounding like an idiot, so he just decided to focus on the job at hand.

"Do you mind if I turn on some music?" she asked.

"That's fine," he answered. Her place, her music.

It wasn't Christmas music, he was happy to hear. Instead, she found some classic-rock station and soon The Eagles were harmonizing through the barn from a speaker system in the work area.

She returned to her side of the area and started opening paint cans and gathering brushes, humming along to the music. Though he knew he needed to get started, he couldn't seem to look away.

He liked watching her. She seemed to throw herself into everything she did, whether that was directing a ragtag group of children in a Christmas show, telling stories to a bunch of energetic school kids or writing a charming story about a brave reindeer.

He was fascinated with everything about her.

He had to get over it, he told himself sternly. He needed to help build her set, finish clearing out his grandmother's house and then go back to his normal life in California.

He turned his attention to the pile of lumber and found the boards he would need. Then he spent a moment familiarizing himself with another man's work space and the tools available to him. Rafe Santiago kept a clean, well-organized shop. He would give him that.

The moment he cut the first board, he felt more centered than he had in a long time. He was very good at building things. It gave him great satisfaction to take raw materials and turn them into something useful, whether that was a piece of furniture or a children's hospital.

For nearly an hour, they worked together in a comfortable silence broken only by the sounds of tools and the music. He made good progress by doing his best to pretend she wasn't there, that this growing attraction simmering through him would burn itself out when it no longer had the fuel of her presence to sustain it.

The barn was warmer than he would have expected, especially with the air compressor going to power the tools, and soon he was down to his T-shirt. Before she started painting, she had taken off the sweater she wore, but it wasn't until he took a break and looked up from connecting two boards that he saw the message on it: Wake up Smarter. Sleep With a Librarian.

For an instant his mind went completely blank as all the blood left his head at the image. Unfortunately, his finger twitched on the trigger of the unfamiliar nail gun, which was far more reactive than any of the guns he was used to.

He felt a sharp biting pain as the nail impaled the webbing between the forefinger and thumb of his left hand to the board. He swore and ripped out the nail, mortified at his stupidity.

It wasn't the first time he'd had an accident with a nail gun or a power tool—in his line of work, nobody made it through without nicks and bruises and a few stitches here or there, especially starting out—but it was completely embarrassing. He hadn't made that kind of rookie mistake in years. Apparently, she wasn't very good for his concentration.

"What happened?" she asked.

"Nothing. It's fine." It was, really. The nail hadn't gone through anything but skin.

"You're bleeding. Let me see."

"It's just a poke. Hazard of the job."

"I think Rafe keeps a first-aid kit somewhere in here." She started rifling through cabinets until she found one.

"I don't need anything. It's almost stopped bleeding."

It still burned like hell, but he wasn't about to tell her that.

"I'll feel better if you let me at least clean it up."

"Really, not necessary."

She ignored him and stepped closer, bringing that delicious springtime scent with her that made him think of sunlit mornings and new life.

"Hold out your hand."

Since he was pretty certain she wouldn't let up until he cooperated, he knew he had no choice but to comply. Feeling stupid, he thrust out his arm. She took his injured hand in both of hers and dabbed at it with a wipe she'd found inside the kit.

"It's not bad," she murmured. "I don't think you're going to need stitches."

He did his best to keep his gaze fiercely away from that soft T-shirt that had caused the trouble in the first place—and the curves beneath it.

The gentle touch of her fingers on his skin made him want to close his eyes and lean into her. It had been so long since he'd known that kind of aching sweetness.

She smiled a little. "Do you remember that time I fell on my bike in front of your grandmother's house?"

"Yes." His voice sounded a little ragged around the edges, but he had to hope she didn't notice.

"You were so sweet to me," she said with soft expression as she applied antiseptic cream to the tiny puncture wound. "I couldn't even manage to string two words together around you, but you just kept up a steady stream of conversation to make me feel more comfortable until my aunt Mary could come pick me up. I was so mortified, but you made it feel less horrible."

He swallowed. He'd done that? He didn't have much memory of it, only of a quiet girl with big eyes and long dark hair.

"Why would you be mortified? It was an accident."

She snorted a little. "Right. I ran into your grandmother's mailbox because I wasn't paying attention to where I was going. It was all your fault for mowing the lawn without your shirt on."

He stared down at her. "*That's* why you crashed?"

She looked up and he saw shadows of remembered embarrassment there. "In my defense, I was thirteen years old, you were a much older boy and I already had a huge crush on you. It's a wonder I could say a word."

"Is that right?" he asked softly. Her fingers felt so good on his skin, her luscious mouth was *right there* and he wanted nothing but to find a soft spot of hay somewhere for the two of them to collapse into.

"Yes," she murmured, and he saw answering awareness in her eyes. "And then you made it so much worse by being so kind, cleaning me up, calling my aunt, then fixing my bike for me. What shy, awkward bookworm alive could have resisted that, when the cutest boy she'd ever met in real life was so sweet to her?"

He didn't want to be sweet right now. At her words, hunger growled to life inside him, and he knew he would have to appease it somehow.

Just a kiss, he told himself. A simple taste and then they both could move on.

He lowered his mouth and felt her hands tremble when his lips brushed hers.

She tasted just as delicious as he would have imagined, sweet and warm and luscious, like nibbling at a perfectly ripe strawberry.

She froze for just a moment, long enough for him to wonder if he'd made a terrible error in judgment, and then her mouth softened and she kissed him back with a breathy sigh, as if she had been waiting for this since that day half a lifetime ago.

Her hands fluttered against his chest for just a moment, then wrapped around his neck, and he pulled her closer, delighting in her soft curves and the aching tenderness of the kiss.

Chapter 10

Life could take the strangest turns sometimes.

If someone had told her a week ago that she would be standing in The Christmas Ranch barn on a Saturday afternoon kissing Flynn Delaney, she would have advised them to see somebody about their delusions.

Here they were, though, with her hands tangled in his hair and his arms wrapped around her and his mouth doing intoxicating things to her.

She wanted the moment to go on forever, this sultry, honeyed magic.

Nothing in her limited experience compared to this. She'd had a couple of boyfriends in college, nothing serious and nothing that had lasted more than a month or two—and absolutely nothing that prepared her for the sheer sensual assault of kissing Flynn.

She made a little sound in her throat and he deepened

the kiss, his tongue sliding along hers as his arms tightened around her. Sensation rippled through her, and she could only be grateful when he pushed her against the nearest cabinet, his mouth hot and demanding.

She couldn't seem to think about anything other than kissing him, touching him, finding some way to be closer to him. She wrapped her arms more tightly around his neck, wanting this moment to go on forever.

They kissed for a long time there with the scents of sawdust and hay swirling around them. Even as she lost herself in the kiss, some tiny corner of her brain was trying to catalog every emotion and sensation, storing it up so she could relive it after he was gone. The taste of him, of coffee and mint and sexy male, the silky softness of his hair, the delicious rasp of his whiskers against her skin, his big, warm hands slipping beneath the back of her T-shirt to slide against her bare skin…

"Celeste? Are you in here?"

She heard her brother-in-law's voice and felt as if he had just thrown her into the snow. Rafe and Hope must have returned earlier than they'd planned.

She froze and scrambled away from Flynn, yanking her T-shirt back down and trying frantically to catch her breath.

He was having the same trouble, she realized, as he quickly stepped behind one of the power tools to hide the evidence of his arousal.

Had *she* done that to him? She couldn't quite believe it.

"Celeste?" she heard again.

"In…" The words caught in her throat and she had to clear them away before she spoke again. "In here."

An instant later Rafe walked into the work space. He

stopped and gazed between the two of them and she saw his mouth tighten, a sudden watchful glint in his eyes.

Rafe was a tough man, extremely protective of each Nichols sister—probably because he had once saved all their lives. His sharp gaze took in the scene and she doubted he could miss her heightened color, her swollen lips, their heavy breathing.

She was sure of it when he aimed a hard, narrow-eyed look at Flynn.

She could feel herself flush more and then told herself she was being ridiculous, feeling like a teenager caught necking on the front porch by her older brother. She was a grown woman, twenty-eight years old, and she could kiss half the men in town if she wanted.

She'd just never wanted to before.

"Hope said you might need some help building a few things for the set."

"Flynn has been helping me."

"So I see," Rafe drawled.

"Thanks for letting me use your shop," Flynn said. "I tried to be careful with the tools, but your nail gun got away from me." He held up the hand she had bandaged.

"It's got a fast trigger. Sorry about that. Anything I can do to help you wrap things up so you can get out of here?"

"Another pair of hands never hurts," Flynn answered.

Celeste finally felt as if her brain cells were beginning to function again.

"I'm about done painting. I…think I'll just clean my brushes and leave you to it. I should probably head up to the house to help Aunt Mary with the cookie decorating."

She couldn't meet either of their gazes as she walked past the men, feeling like an idiot.

"Nice shirt," Rafe murmured in a low voice as she passed him.

Baffled, she glanced down and then could have died from mortification. It was the Sleep with a Librarian shirt that Hope and Faith had given her one Christmas as a joke. She never wore it, of course—it wasn't her style *at all*—but she'd thrown it on that morning under her sweater, knowing she was going to be painting the scenery later and it would be perfect for the job.

She gathered her brushes quickly and headed for the sink in the small bathroom of the barn.

While she cleaned the brushes, she glanced into the mirror and saw it was worse than she had thought. Her hair had come half out of the messy bun, her lips were definitely swollen and her cheeks were rosier than St. Nicholas's in "'Twas the Night Before Christmas."

Oh, she wanted to *die*. Rafe knew she had just been making out with Flynn, which meant he would definitely tell Hope. Her sisters would never let her hear the end of it.

That was the least of her problems, she realized.

Now that she had kissed the man and knew how amazing it was, how would she ever be able to endure not being able to do it again?

What just happened here?

Even after Celeste left to clean her brushes, Flynn could feel his heart hammering, his pulse racing.

Get a grip, he told himself. It was just a kiss. But for reasons he didn't completely understand, it somehow struck him as being so much more.

He couldn't seem to shake the feeling that something momentous had occurred in that kiss, something terrifying and mysterious and tender.

Why had he kissed her?

The whole time they'd shared the work space, he had been telling himself all the reasons why he needed to stay away from her. At the first opportunity and excuse, he had ignored all his common sense and swooped right in.

What shy, awkward bookworm alive could have resisted that, when the cutest boy she'd ever met in real life was so sweet to her?

She'd once had a crush on him. He didn't know why that made him feel so tender toward the quiet girl she had been.

That kiss had rocked him to the core and left him feeling off balance, as if he'd just slipped on the sawdust and landed hard on his ass. For a moment, he closed his eyes, remembering those lush curves against him, her enthusiastic response, the soft, sexy little sounds she made.

"What are you doing here?" For one horrible moment he thought Rafe was calling him out for kissing Celeste, until he realized the other man was gazing down at the set piece he was building.

Focus, he told himself. Get the job done, as he'd promised.

"She wants some kind of wings on the side of the stage for the children to wait behind until it's their turn to go on," he explained. He went into detail about his plan and listened while Rafe made a few excellent suggestions to improve the design.

"This shouldn't take us long to finish up," the other

man said. "In fact, I probably could handle it on my own, if you want to get out of here."

That sounded a little more strongly worded than just a suggestion. "I'm good," he answered, a little defiantly. "I like to finish what I start."

He was aware as they went to work of her cleaning up her brushes, closing up the paint cans, putting her sweater back on to hide that unexpectedly enticing T-shirt.

He was also aware that she hadn't looked at him once since she'd jerked out of his arms when her brother-in-law had come in.

Was she regretting that they had kissed? He couldn't tell. She *should* regret it, since they both had to know it was a mistake, but somehow it still bothered him that she might.

Did he owe her some kind of apology for kissing her out of the blue like that? Something else he didn't know.

He had been faithful to his vows, as misguided as they had been, and his relationships since then had been with women who wanted the same thing he did: uncomplicated, no-strings affairs.

Celeste was very different from those women— sweet and kind and warm—which might explain why that kiss and her enthusiastic response had left him so discombobulated.

A few minutes later she finished at the sink and set the brushes to dry.

"I guess that's it," she said, still not looking at Flynn. "The brushes are all clean and ready for Hope when she has time to come down and finish. I'm just going to head up to the house to check on the cookie decorating. Thanks again for doing this, you guys."

She gave a vague, general sort of smile, then hurried out of the barn.

He and Rafe worked in silence for a few more moments, a heavy, thick tension in the air.

The other man was the first to speak.

"Do you know what happened to Celeste and her sisters when they were kids?"

Rafe's tone was casual, but the hard edge hadn't left his expression since he had walked into the work space earlier.

"In Colombia? Yeah. She told me. I can't imagine what they must have gone through."

Rafe's hard expression didn't lighten. "None of them talks about it very much. Frankly, I'm surprised she told you at all."

He didn't know why she had, but he was touched that she would confide that very significant part of her life to him.

He also didn't know why Rafe would bring it up now. It didn't seem the sort of topic to casually mention in general conversation. Something told him Rafe wasn't a man who did things without purpose.

"She was the youngest," the man went on. "Barely older than Louisa, only about twelve. Just a little kid, really."

His chest ached, trying to imagine that sweet vulnerability forced into such a traumatic situation. It was the same ache he had whenever he thought about Olivia watching her mother's murder.

"They went through hell while they were prisoners," Rafe went on. "The leader of the rebels was a psycho idiot bastard. He didn't give them enough to eat that entire month they were there, they were squished into squalid quarters, they were provided no medical care or decent protections from the elements, they underwent psychological torture. It's a wonder they made it through."

His hand tightened on the board he held, and he wanted to swing it at something, hard. He didn't need to hear about this. It only seemed to heighten these strange, tender feelings in his chest.

"It affected all of them in various ways," Rafe went on. "But I think it was hardest on Celeste. She was so young and so very softhearted, from what Hope tells me. She's always been a dreamer, her head filled with stories and music. The conditions they were forced into must have been particularly harsh on an innocent young girl who couldn't really comprehend what was happening to her family."

The ache in his chest expanded. He hated that she had gone it and wished, more than anything, that he could make it right for her.

"Why are you telling me this?"

Rafe gave him a steady look, as if weighing how to respond. He could see in his eyes that her brother-in-law knew exactly what they had been doing just before he walked in. Flynn fought the urge to tell the man to back off, that it was none of Rafe's damn business.

"I was there," Rafe finally said. "Did she tell you that?"

Flynn stared. "Where?"

"In Colombia. I was part of the SEAL team that rescued the Nichols family. It was my very first mission. A guy doesn't forget something like that."

Rafe was big and tough enough that somehow Flynn wasn't surprised he'd been a SEAL. He supposed the only remarkable thing about the situation was that the man seemed content now to live in a small town in Idaho, running a holiday attraction.

"So you saw their father get shot."

Rafe's jaw tightened. "Yeah. I saw it. And I saw Celeste weep and weep during the entire helicopter flight when she realized what had happened. I thought she would jump right out after her father."

Flynn swallowed at the image. After the past three months he hadn't thought he had much of his heart left to break, but he was most definitely wrong.

"I also shot two revolutionaries who were trying to keep us from leaving with them," Rafe went on. "You might, in fact, say I've had CeCe's back since she was eleven years old."

Yeah. The man definitely knew he had walked in on them kissing.

"She's very important to me," the other man said. "The whole Nichols family is mine now."

He met Flynn's gaze and held it as if he wanted to be perfectly clear. "And make no mistake. I protect what's mine."

He could choose to be offended, he supposed. He hadn't been called out for kissing a woman in...*ever*. Somehow he couldn't drum up anything but respect for Rafe. He was actually touched in an odd way, grateful that she had someone looking out for her.

"Warning duly noted." He made his own voice firm. "But anything between Celeste and me is just that. Between the two of us."

Rafe seemed to accept that. "I just don't want to see her hurt. Despite everything she's been through, CeCe somehow has still managed to retain a sweetness and a generosity you won't find in many people on this planet. If you mess with that, I won't be the only member of this family who won't be happy about it. Trust me. You do *not* want to tangle with the Nichols women."

This, more than anything else the man had said, resonated with truth. She had become a friend, someone he liked and respected. He didn't want to hurt her, either, but he couldn't see any other outcome. He had a business, a life in LA. Beyond that he wasn't in any position right now to start a new relationship with anyone, not when Olivia was still so needy.

He had made a mistake, kissing her. A mistake that couldn't happen again.

He gave the other man a steady look. "I got it. Thanks. Now can we just finish this job so I can grab my daughter and go home?"

After a moment, Rafe nodded and turned back to work, much to Flynn's relief.

The walk from the lodge to the main house helped a great deal to cool her flaming cheeks, but it didn't do much for the tumult inside her.

Oh, that kiss. How was she supposed to act around him now when she was afraid that every second she was near him she would be reliving those wild, hot moments in his arms? His hands on her skin, his mouth on hers, all those muscles pressing her against the cabinet.

She shivered in remembered reaction. How was she supposed to pretend her world just hadn't been rocked?

It had happened. She couldn't scrub those moments from her memory bank—indeed, she had a feeling they would haunt her for a long time—but surely she was mature enough to be able to interact with him in a polite, casual way. What other choice did she have?

When she reached the house, she drew in a deep breath, hoping all trace of those heated moments was gone from her features in case either of her eagle-eyed sisters was inside, then she pushed open the door.

The scents of cinnamon and pine and sugar cookies greeted her and the warmth of the house wrapped around her like one of Aunt Mary's hand-knitted scarves. As she stood in the entry, she had a sudden, familiar moment of deep gratitude for her aunt and uncle who had taken in three lost and grieving girls and given them safe shelter from the hard realities of life.

This was home. Her center.

Some of the storm inside her seemed to calm a bit. This was how she made it through, by focusing on what was important to her. Her family, her stories, the ranch. That was what mattered, not these fragile feelings growing inside her for Flynn and Olivia.

Before she could even hang up her coat, she heard the click of little paws on the floor. A moment later Linus burst into the room and greeted her merrily. She had nearly forgotten she'd brought him up to the house during the rehearsal to hang out with Mary, since Lucy had been in one of her snooty moods where she just wanted to be left alone.

"Hi, there. There's my darling boy." She scooped him up in her arms, and he licked her face and wriggled in her arms as if they had been away from each other for years instead of only a few hours.

"Have you been good?" she asked. He licked her cheek in answer, then wiggled to be let down again. She followed him and the sound of laughter to the kitchen, where she found her niece and nephews decorating cookies with Aunt Mary and Olivia.

"Look at all our cookies!" Barrett said. "The old people are going to *love* them."

He was such an adorable child, with a huge reservoir of compassion and love inside him for others.

This was a prime example—though she decided at some point she probably would have to gently inform him that the senior citizens coming to the show next week might not appreciate being called "old people."

"What a great job."

"Look at this one, Aunt CeCe. See how I made the stars sparkle with the yellow sugar things?" Joey, joined at the hip with Barrett, thrust his cookies at her.

"Fabulous."

"And look at my Christmas trees," Barrett said.

"I see. Good work, kid. And, Lou, I love how you swirled the icing on the candy canes. Very creative."

She turned to Olivia. "What about you? Have you decorated any?"

"A few." She pointed to a tray where a dozen angel cookies lay wing to wing. They all had hair of yellow frosting, just like the blonde and lovely Elise Chandler. Celeste had a feeling that wasn't a coincidence.

"I love them. They're beautiful, every one."

"Decorating cookies is *hard*," Joey declared. "You have to be careful you don't break them while you're putting on the frosting."

"But then you get to eat them when they break," Barrett pointed out.

"They've all been very good not to eat too many broken cookies," Aunt Mary said from the stove, where she was stirring something that smelled like her delicious ham-and-potato soup.

"Can you help us?" Louisa asked.

She had a million things to do before the show—not to mention a pile of unwrapped gifts in the corner of her office at home—but this suddenly seemed to take precedence over everything else.

"Of course," she answered her niece with a smile. "I can't imagine anything I would enjoy more."

Mary replaced the lid on the stockpot on the stove and turned down the burner. "Since you're here to supervise now, I think I'll go lie down and put my feet up. If you don't mind anyway. These swollen ankles are killing me today."

"Go ahead, my dear. You've done more than enough."

"I've got soup on the stove. The children had some earlier, but there's more than enough for anyone who pops in or out."

Celeste left the children busy at the table and headed over to hug her aunt before she reached in the cupboard for a bowl. "I know Hope and Rafe are back. I bumped into Rafe." She felt herself blush when she said it and hoped Aunt Mary wouldn't notice. "What about Faith? Is she around?"

"No. She ran into Idaho Falls for some last-minute g-i-f-t-s," Aunt Mary spelled, as if the children were tiny instead of excellent readers. Fortunately none of the children seemed to be paying attention to them.

"Poor girl," her aunt went on. "She's been too busy around the ranch to give Christmas much thought, and now here it is just a few days away."

The reminder instantly made Celeste feel small. She was fretting about a kiss while her sister had lost a husband and was raising two children by herself—albeit with plenty of help from Aunt Mary, Rafe, Hope and Celeste.

She was so grateful for her loving, supportive family—though she experienced a pang of regret for Flynn, who had no one.

She sat down at the table with her soup and listened to the children's chatter while she ate each delicious spoonful. When she finished, she set her bowl aside and turned to the serious business of cookie decorating.

"All right. Help me out, kids. What kind of cookie should I decorate first?"

"The angels are really hard," Olivia said.

Well, she'd already faced down a bunch of holiday-excited children and been kissed until she couldn't think straight. What was one more challenge today? "Bring on an angel, then."

Aunt Mary always had Christmas music playing in the house and the children seemed to enjoy singing along. Olivia didn't join them, she noticed. The girl seemed a little withdrawn, and Celeste worried maybe the day had been too much for her.

After she had decorated her third cookie, the song "Angels We Have Heard on High" came over the stereo.

"Ooh, I love this one," Louisa said. Her niece started singing along to the Glorias with a gusto that made Celeste smile.

"My mom is an angel now," Olivia said in a matter-of-fact sort of tone that made emotions clog Celeste's throat.

"I know, sweetheart," she said softly. "I'm so sorry."

"Our dad is an angel, too," Barrett informed her.

"Mom says he's probably riding the prettiest horses in heaven right now," Louisa said.

"My mom is in jail," Joey offered. That made her just as sad for him.

"Aren't you lucky to have Uncle Rafe and Aunt Hope, though?"

"Yep," he answered.

Barrett nodded. "And we still have our mom. And you have your dad," he reminded Olivia.

"Your mom *and* your dad are angels, aren't they?" Louisa said to Celeste. "I asked my mom once why Barrett and me don't have a grandma and a grandpa, and she told me."

The pain of losing them still hurt, but more like an old ache than the constant, raw pain she remembered.

"They both died," she agreed. "It's been a long time, but I still feel them near me."

At some moments she felt them closer than others. She was quite certain she had heard her father's voice loud and clear one wintry, stormy night when she was driving home from college for the holidays. As clear as if he had been sitting beside her, she'd heard him tell her to slow down. She had complied instantly and a moment later rounded a corner to find a car had spun out from the opposite lane into hers. She was able to stop in time to keep from hitting it, but if she hadn't reduced her speed earlier, the head-on collision probably would have killed her and the other driver.

"Do you ever *see* your mom and dad angels?" Olivia asked, studying Celeste intently.

Oh, the poor, poor dear. She shook her head. "I don't see them as they were, but whenever I see the angel decorations at Christmastime, it helps me think about them and remember they're always alive in my heart."

"I really need to ask my mom something," Olivia said, her little features distressed. "Only I don't know how."

Celeste reached for the girl's hand and squeezed it. Oh, how she recalled all those unspoken words she had wanted to tell her parents, especially her father, who had died so abruptly. With her mother, she'd had a little more time, though that didn't ease the difficulty of losing her.

She chose her answer carefully, trying to find the right words of comfort.

"When you see an angel decoration you really like, perhaps you could whisper to the angel what you need to say to your mom. I believe she'll hear you," she said softly, hoping she was saying the right things to ease the girl's grief and not just offering a useless panacea.

Olivia considered that for a long moment, her brow furrowed. Finally she nodded solemnly. "That's a good idea. I think I'll do that."

She smiled and gave the girl a little hug, hoping she had averted that particular crisis. "Excellent. Now, why don't we see how many more cookies we can decorate before your father comes in?"

"Okay."

They went to work, singing along to the Christmas music for another half hour before the doorbell rang.

"I'll get it!" Joey announced eagerly. He raced for the door and a moment later returned with Flynn.

She had known it would be him at the door, but somehow she still wasn't prepared for the sheer masculine force of him. Suddenly she couldn't seem to catch her breath and felt as if the vast kitchen had shrunk to the size of one of Louisa's dollhouse rooms.

The memory of that kiss shivered between them, and she could feel heat soak her cheeks and nerves flutter in her stomach.

She shoved aside the reaction and forced a smile instead. "That was faster than I expected. Are you finished?" she asked.

He shrugged. "Your brother-in-law is a handy dude. With both of us working together, it didn't take us long."

"Wonderful. I can't tell you how much I appreciate it, especially with everything else you have going on. Thank you."

He met her gaze finally, and she thought she saw an instant of heat and hunger before he blinked it away. "You're very welcome."

His gaze took in the table scattered with frosting bowls, sugar sprinkles and candy nonpareils. "This looks fun," he said, though his tone implied exactly the opposite.

"Oh, it is, Daddy," Olivia declared. "Look at all the cookies I decorated! About a hundred angels!"

More like fifteen or sixteen, but Celeste supposed it had felt like much more than that to a seven-year-old girl.

She handed over one of the paper plates they had been using to set the decorated cookies on when they were finished. "Here, fill this with several cookies so you and your dad can take some home to enjoy."

"They're for the old people, though, aren't they?"

"I think it would be just fine for you to take five or six. We'll have plenty. Don't worry," she answered, declining again to give a lecture on politically correct terminology.

"Are you sure?"

"Yes. Go ahead. Pick some of your favorites."

Olivia pondered her options and finally selected five cookies—all blonde angels, Celeste noted—and laid them on the paper plate while Celeste found some aluminum foil to cover them.

"Here you go," she said, holding them out to Flynn.

"Thanks," he murmured and took the plate from her. Their hands brushed and she gave an involuntary shiver that she seriously hoped he hadn't noticed.

His gaze met hers for just an instant, then slid away again, but not before she saw a glittery, hungry look there that made her feel breathless all over again.

"Find your coat," he told his daughter.

"Can we stay a little bit longer?" Olivia begged. "Louisa and Barrett and Joey said they're going to have sleigh rides later. I've never been on a sleigh ride."

"We have a lot to do today, bug. We've already hung around here longer than we probably should have."

If he and his daughter had left earlier, the kiss never would have happened. Judging by the edgy tension that seethed between them now—and despite the flash of hunger she thought she had glimpsed—Celeste had a feeling that was what he would have preferred.

"Please, Daddy. I would *love* it."

As he gazed at his daughter a helpless look came into his eyes. She remembered him saying he hated refusing Olivia anything after what she had been through.

"How long do these sleigh rides take?" he asked Celeste.

"Less than an hour, probably."

"They're super fun at night," her niece suggested helpfully. "You could go home and do your work and then come back later. Then you can see all the lights and stuff. There's even caroling."

"Ooh. Caroling!" Olivia looked delighted at the idea, while her father looked vaguely horrified.

"I must agree. It is really fun," Celeste said.

He sighed. "Would that work for you, Liv? We can go home and try to finish another room at the house, and then come back later."

"Will you all be there?" she asked her new friends.

"Sure! We love to take the sleigh rides."

Olivia looked enchanted by the idea.

"Our last sleigh ride for regular visitors of The Christmas Ranch is back at the St. Nicholas Lodge about 8:00 p.m. Why don't you meet us at the lodge a little before that, and we can take one that's not as crowded?"

"Oh, yay! I can't wait!" Olivia exclaimed. She spontaneously hugged Celeste, and she looked so adorably sweet with her eyes bright and pink frosting on her cheek that Celeste couldn't help it, she kissed the top of the girl's head.

When she lifted her head, she found Flynn gazing at her with a strange look on his features that he quickly wiped away.

"I guess we'll see you all later tonight, then," he said.

He didn't sound nearly as thrilled as his daughter about the idea.

Chapter 11

All afternoon Celeste did her best not to dwell on that stunning kiss.

Knowing she would see him again that evening didn't help. The whole busy December day seemed filled with sparkly anticipation, even though she tried over and over again to tell herself she was being ridiculous.

It didn't help matters that her sisters both attempted to back out of the sleigh ride and send her alone with the children. She couldn't blame them, since it had been completely her idea, but she still wanted them there. Though she knew the children would provide enough of a buffer, she didn't want to be alone with Flynn.

Finally she had threatened Hope that if she didn't go on the sleigh ride with them, Hope would have to direct the show Tuesday night by herself.

As she expected, Rafe had obviously told Hope what he had almost walked in on earlier in the barn. Her sisters hadn't come out and said anything specific about it, but after the third or fourth speculative look from Hope—and the same from Faith—she knew the word was out in the Nichols family.

If not for her beloved niece and nephews, she sincerely would have given some thought to wishing she had been an only child.

"You owe me this after dragging me into the whole Christmas show thing," Celeste said fiercely to Hope at dinner, when her sister once more tried to wriggle out of the sleigh ride.

Hope didn't necessarily look convinced, but she obviously could see that Celeste meant what she said. "Oh, all right," she muttered. "If I'm going out in the cold that means you have to come, too, Fae."

Faith groaned. "After an afternoon of tackling the stores on the busiest shopping day of the year, I just want to put my feet up and watch something brainless on TV."

Barrett added his voice. "You *have* to come, Mom. It won't be as fun without you. You've got the *best* caroling voice."

"Yeah, and you're the only one who knows all the words," Louisa added.

Faith gave her children an exasperated look but finally capitulated. "Fine. I guess somebody has to help you all carry a tune."

After dinner they all bundled up in their warmest clothing and traipsed down to the St. Nicholas Lodge. Even Rafe came along, which she supposed she was grateful for, though he kept shooting her curious little looks all evening.

They arrived at the lodge just as Flynn and Olivia walked in from the parking lot. Olivia wore her pink-and-purple coat with a white beanie and scarf. She looked adorable, especially when she lit up at the sight of them.

"Hi, everybody! Hi!" she said. "We're here. Dad didn't want to come, but I told him we promised, so here we are."

Celeste had to laugh at that, especially when Flynn's color rose. "It's good to see you both," she said.

It wasn't a lie. The December night suddenly seemed magical and bright, filled with stars and snow and the wonder of the season.

Olivia skipped over to her, hardly even limping in her excitement for the evening. "Guess what, Celeste?"

"What, sweetheart?"

"Today when we were cleaning we found boxes and boxes and *boxes* of yarn and scrapbook paper and craft supplies. Would you like to have them for your story times at the library? Dad said he thought you might."

"Seriously?" She stared, overwhelmed and touched that he would think of it.

"You don't have to take them," he said quickly. "I just didn't want to send everything to Goodwill if you could find a use for it."

"Are you kidding?" she exclaimed. "Absolutely! I can definitely use craft supplies. Thank you so much!"

"Good, because they're all in the back of the SUV. I took a chance that you would want them and figured if you didn't, I could drop them in the box at the thrift store in town after we were done here."

"Smart." She considered their options. "My car is still here in the parking lot from this morning. I can just pull next to you, and we can transfer them from your SUV to mine."

"Do you want to do it now or after the sleigh ride?"

"Go ahead and do it now while you're thinking about it," Hope suggested. Celeste narrowed her gaze at her sister, wondering if this was some sneaky way to get the two of them alone together, but Hope merely gave her a bland look in response.

"Sure," she said finally. "That way we won't forget later."

They walked out into the cold air, and she tried not to think about the last time they had been together— the strength of his muscles beneath her hands, the delicious taste of him, all those shivery feelings he evoked.

"I'm parked over there," he said, pointing to his vehicle.

"I parked at the back of the lot this morning to leave room for paying guests. Just give me a minute to move my car next to yours."

"I could just carry the boxes over to where you are."

"It will only take me a minute to move." She took off before he could argue further and hurried to her very cold vehicle, which had a thin layer of soft snow that needed to be brushed away before she could see out the windshield. Once that was done, she started it and drove the few rows to an open spot next to his vehicle, then popped open the hatch of her small SUV.

By the time she opened her door and walked around to the back, he was already transferring boxes and she could see at least half dozen more in the back of his vehicle.

She stared at the unexpected bounty. "This is amazing! Are you sure Olivia wouldn't like to keep some of this stuff?"

He shook his head. "She went through and picked out a few pairs of decorative scissors and some paper she really liked, but the rest of it was destined for either Goodwill or the landfill."

"Thank you. It was really kind of you to think of the library."

"Consider it a legacy from Charlotte to the library."

"I'll do that. Thank you."

He carried the last of the boxes and shoved it into her cargo area, then closed the hatch.

"There you go."

"Thanks again."

She expected him to head directly back to the lodge. Instead, he leaned against her vehicle and gave her a solemn look. The parking lot was mostly empty except for a family a few rows away loading into a minivan, probably after seeing Santa Claus inside.

"Do I owe you an apology?" he asked.

She fidgeted, shoving her mittened hands into her pockets. "An apology for what?"

He sighed. "We both know I shouldn't have kissed you, Celeste. It was a mistake. I didn't want to leave you with the…wrong impression."

Oh, this was humiliating. Was she so pathetic that he thought because she had told him she'd once had a crush on him, she now thought they were *dating* or something, because of one stupid kiss?

Okay, one *amazing*, heart-pounding, knee-tingling kiss. But that was beside the point.

"You don't owe me anything," she said.

He gazed up at the stars while the jingle of the sleigh returning to the lodge and the sound of shrieking children over on the sledding hill rang out in the distance.

"Here's the thing. Right now, my whole attention has to be focused on helping my daughter. I'm not…looking for anything else. I can't."

She leaned against the cold vehicle next to him and tried to pretend she was sophisticated and experienced, that this sort of moment happened to her all the time—a casual conversation with a man who had kissed her deeply just a few hours ago and was now explaining why he couldn't do it again.

"It was a kiss, Flynn. I get it. I've barely given it a thought since it happened."

He wasn't stupid. She didn't doubt he could tell that was a blatant lie, but he said nothing. He simply gave her a careful look, which she returned with what she hoped was a bland one of her own.

"Good. That's good," he said. "I just wanted to clear the air between us. The last thing I want to do is hurt you or, I don't know, give you the wrong idea. You've been nothing but kind to Olivia and to me."

"Do you really think I'm so fragile that I could be hurt by a single kiss?"

The question seemed to hang between them, bald and unadorned, like a bare Christmas tree after the holidays.

He had a fierce wish that he'd never started this conversation, but the implications of that kiss had bothered him all afternoon as he'd carried box after box out of Charlotte's house.

He meant what he said. She had been very sweet to him and Olivia. His daughter was finally beginning to heal from the trauma she had endured, and he knew a big part of the progress she'd made the past week was because of all the many kindnesses Celeste and her family had shown them.

It seemed a poor repayment for him to take advantage of that because he couldn't control his base impulses around her.

He also couldn't seem to shake the guilt that had dogged him since that conversation with Rafe. The other man hadn't come out and blatantly told him to leave her alone, but Flynn hadn't missed the subtle undercurrents.

"Your brother-in-law and I had quite a talk this afternoon while we were finishing the screens for you."

"Is that right?"

Her cheeks looked pink in the moonlight, but he supposed that could have been from the cold night air.

"He's very protective of you and wanted to be clear I knew you had people watching out for you."

She made a low noise in the back of her throat. "My family sometimes drives me absolutely crazy."

Despite the awkwardness of the conversation, he had to smile. "They're wonderful, all of them. It's obvious they love you very much."

"A little too much, sometimes," she muttered. "They apparently don't think I can be trusted to take care of myself. Sometimes it really sucks to be the youngest sibling."

He couldn't imagine having any siblings. While he was lucky to have very tight friends, he knew it wasn't the same.

"I think it's nice," he answered. "Having your sisters close must have been a great comfort after you lost your parents."

Her lovely features softened in the moonlight. "It was," she murmured. "They may drive me crazy, but I would be lost without them. Don't tell them I said that, though."

He smiled a little. "I wish I had that same kind of support network for Olivia, but I'm all she has right now. I can't forget that."

"I understand. You're doing a great job with her. Don't worry. Children are resilient. She's working her way over to the other side in her own time."

His sigh puffed out condensation between them. "Thanks."

"And you can put your mind at ease," she said briskly. "You're not going to break my heart. Trust me, I don't have some crazy idea that you're going to propose to me simply because we shared one little kiss."

"It wasn't a little kiss. That's the problem," he muttered.

As soon as he said the words, he knew he shouldn't have, but it was the truth. That kiss had been earthshaking. Cataclysmic. He would venture to call it epic, which was the entire problem here. He knew he wouldn't forget those moments for a long, long time.

He wasn't sure how he expected her to respond but, as usual, she managed to surprise him. She flashed him a sideways look.

"What can I say? I'm a good kisser."

The unexpectedness of her response surprised a laugh out of him that echoed through the night. She seemed like such a sweet, quiet woman, but then she had these moments of sly humor that he couldn't seem to get enough of.

It made him wonder if she had this whole secret internal side of herself—contained and bundled away for protection—that she rarely showed the rest of the world.

She intrigued him on so many levels, probably because she was a study in contradictions. She could be tart and sweet at the same time, firm yet gentle, deeply vulnerable yet tough as nails.

Most of all, she seemed *real*. For a guy who had grown up surrounded by the artificial illusion of Hollywood, that was intensely appealing.

"It looks as if the other sleigh ride is done," she finally said. "The kids are probably anxious to get going."

"Right. Guess I'd better get my carol on."

She laughed, as he had hoped. At least the tension between them since the afternoon had been somewhat diffused.

As they walked, he was aware of a jumble of feelings in his chest. Regret, longing and a strange, aching tenderness.

For just a moment, he had a crazy wish that things could be different, that he had the right to wrap his hand around hers and walk up to the sleigh ride with her, then sit beneath a blanket cuddled up with her while they rode in a horse-drawn sleigh and enjoyed the moonlit wonder of the night together.

He could handle the regret and the longing. He was a big boy and had known plenty of disappointments in his life.

But he didn't have any idea what to do with the tenderness.

Celeste decided a sleigh ride through the mountains on a December evening was a good metaphor for being in love.

She was bumped and jostled, her face cold but the rest of her warm from the blankets. It was exhilarating and exhausting, noisy and fun and a little bit terrifying when they went along a narrow pass above the ranch that was only two feet wider on each side than the sleigh.

She'd been on the sleigh ride dozens of times before. This was the first time she'd taken one while also being in love, with these tangled, chaotic feelings growing inside her.

She was quickly reaching the point where she couldn't deny that she was falling hard for Flynn. What else could explain this jumbled, chaotic mess of emotions inside her?

"Oh. Look at all those stars," a voice breathed beside her, and she looked down to where Olivia had her face lifted to the sky.

She wasn't only falling for Flynn. This courageous, wounded girl had sneaked her way into Celeste's heart.

She would be devastated when they left.

When they'd climbed into the sleigh, Olivia had asked if she could sit beside Celeste. The two of them were sharing a warm blanket. Every once in a while the girl rested her cheek against her shoulder, and Celeste felt as if her heart would burst with tenderness.

"I never knew there were so many stars," Olivia said, her voice awestruck.

"It's magical, isn't it?" she answered. "Do you know what I find amazing? That all those stars are there every single night, wherever you are in the world. They're just hidden by all the other lights around that distract us away from them."

The whole evening truly *was* magical—the whispering jingle of the bells on the draft horses' harnesses, the creak of the old sleigh, the sweet scent of the snow-covered pines they rode through.

Except for Mary—who had stayed behind in the warm house—Celeste was surrounded by everyone she loved.

"I wish we could just go and go and never stop," Olivia said.

Unfortunately, the magic of sleigh rides never lasted forever. She had a feeling that, at least in her case, the magic of being in love wouldn't last, either. The *in love* part would, but eventually the heartache would steal away any joy.

"We'll have to stop at some point," the ever-practical Faith said. "The horses are tired. They've been working all night and are probably ready to have a rest."

"Besides that," Joey added, "what would we eat if we were stuck on a sleigh our whole lives?"

"Good point, kid," Rafe said. "We can't live on hot chocolate forever."

Olivia giggled at them and seemed to concede their point.

"I thought we were supposed to be caroling. We haven't sung *anything*," Louisa complained.

"You start us off," her mother suggested.

Celeste was aware that while both her sisters seemed to be dividing careful looks between her and Flynn, they did it at subtle moments. If she were very lucky, he wouldn't notice.

Louisa started, predictably enough, with "Jingle Bells." The children joined in with enthusiasm and soon even the adults joined them. Flynn, on the other side of Olivia, had a strong baritone. Under other circumstances, she might have been entranced by it, but Celeste's attention was fixed on his daughter as she sang.

Why hadn't she noticed during their rehearsals and the songs they had prepared that Olivia had such a stunning voice, pure and clear, like a mountain stream? It was perfectly on pitch, too, astonishing in a child.

She wasn't the only one who noticed it, she saw. Hope and Faith both seemed startled and even Rafe gave her a second look.

Flynn didn't seem to notice anything, and she thought of those stars again, vivid and bright but obscured by everything else in the way.

"What next?" Joey asked. "Can we sing the one about Jolly Old St. Nick?"

"Sure," Faith said. Of the three sisters, she had the most musical ability, so she led the children as the sleigh bells jingled through the night. With each song, Olivia's natural musical talent became increasingly apparent to everyone on the sleigh, but both she and Flynn seemed oblivious.

"What's that place with all the lights?" Olivia asked after they finished "Silent Night."

"That's the Christmas village," Barrett answered her. "It's awesome. Can we stop and walk through it?"

"You've seen it, like, a million times," his sister chided.

"Yeah, but Olivia hasn't. It's way more fun to see it with somebody else who has never been there. It's like seeing it for the first time all over again."

"You are so right, kiddo," Hope said, beaming at the boy. "Bob, do you mind dropping us off here so we can take a little detour through the village?"

"Not at all. Not at all."

The driver pulled the team to a stop, and everybody clambered out of the sleigh and headed toward the collection of eight small structures a short distance from the main lodge.

This was one of her favorite parts of the entire Christmas Ranch. With the lights strung overhead, it really did feel magical.

Each structure contained a Christmas scene peopled with animatronic figures—elves hammering toys, Mrs. Claus baking cookies, children decorating a Christmas tree, a family opening presents.

"This is quite a place," Flynn murmured beside her.

"The Christmas village is really what started the whole Christmas Ranch. You probably don't know this, but my family's name of origin was Nicholas. As in St. Nicholas."

"The big man himself."

"Right. Because of that, my aunt and uncle have always been a little crazy about Christmas. Before we came to live with them, my uncle Claude built the little chapel Nativity over there with the cow who nods his head at the baby Jesus and the two little church mice running back and forth. It became a hobby with him, and after that he came up with a new one every year."

With a pang, she dearly missed her uncle, a big, gruff man of such kindness and love. He had taught her and her sisters that the best way to heal a broken heart was to forget your troubles and go to work helping other people.

"He decided he wanted to share the village with the whole community, so he opened the ranch up for people to come and visit. The reindeer herd came after, and then he built the whole St. Nicholas Lodge for Santa Claus, and the gift shop and everything."

"This is really great. I have no idea how he did it. It's a fascinating exercise in engineering and physics."

She frowned up at the star above the chapel, just a dark outline against the mountains. "Usually the star up there lights up. I'm not sure what's wrong with it. I'll have to mention it to Rafe. He has learned the ins and outs of all the structures in the village. I don't know how everything works. I just love the magic of it."

Olivia appeared to agree. The girl seemed enthralled with the entire village, particularly the little white chapel with its Nativity scene—the calm Madonna cradling her infant son, and Joseph watching over them both with such care while a beautiful angel with sparkly white wings watched overhead.

"You guys are welcome to hang out, but we're going to head back to the house," Faith said after about fifteen minutes. "It's cold and I know my two are about ready for bed."

"We need to go, too," Hope said, pointing to a sleepy-looking Joey.

"Thank you all for taking us on one more ride," Flynn said. "I appreciate it very much. Olivia loved it."

"You're very welcome," Hope said. "It was our pleasure."

The rest of her family headed back up to the ranch house while Celeste and Flynn walked with Olivia to the lodge's parking lot.

"I'm glad you both came," Celeste said when they reached their vehicles.

"This is definitely a memory we'll have forever, isn't it, Liv?" Flynn said as he opened the backseat door for his daughter. "When we're back in California enjoying Christmas by the ocean, we'll always remember the year we went caroling through the mountains on a two-horse open sleigh."

She had to smile, even though his words seemed to cut through her like an icy wind whipping down the mountain.

"We'll see you Tuesday for the performance."

He nodded, though he didn't look thrilled.

"We'll be there. Thanks again."

She nodded and climbed into her own vehicle, trying not to notice how empty and cold it felt after the magic of being with them on the sleigh ride.

Chapter 12

"Are you sure we're not too early?" Flynn asked his daughter as they pulled up in front of the St. Nicholas Lodge on the night of the show. "It doesn't start for quite a while."

She huffed out her frustrated-at-Dad sigh. "I'm sure. She told me five thirty. This is when I'm supposed to be here, Celeste said, so they can help me get ready with my hair and makeup and stuff. I get to wear makeup onstage so my face isn't blurry."

Yeah, he was terrible with hair and didn't have the first idea what to do about makeup. Here was a whole new stress about having a daughter. Soon enough she was going to want to know about that stuff. Good thing he had friends in LA with wives who could help a poor single dad out in that department.

She opened the passenger door the moment he pulled

into a parking space. "Okay. Thanks, Dad. I'll see you at the show."

When he turned off the engine and opened his own door, she gave him a look of surprise. "You don't have to come in yet."

He shrugged. "I'm here. I might as well see if they need help with something—setting up chairs or whatever."

"Okay," she said, then raced for the door without waiting to see if he followed. Clearly, he was far more nervous about this whole performance thing than she was.

She had made amazing progress in a short time. In a matter of days she already seemed much more at ease with herself and the world around her than she had been when he brought her to Pine Gulch. She used her arm almost without thinking about it now, and she hardly limped anymore.

He wasn't foolish to think all the pain and grief were behind them. She would be dealing with the trauma for a long time to come, but he was beginning to hope that they had turned a corner.

Children are resilient. She's working her way over to the other side in her own time.

He gave no small amount of credit to the Nichols family, for their warmth and acceptance of her. She had made friends with the children and she also completely adored Celeste.

Would he be able to keep that forward momentum when they returned to California? He had no idea, but he would sure as hell try—even if that meant figuring out the whole hair-and-makeup thing on his own sometime down the line.

He pushed open the front doors after her and walked into the lodge, only to discover the place had been transformed into an upscale-looking dining room.

What had been an open space was now filled with round eight-top tables wearing silky red tablecloths and evergreen and candle centerpieces. The huge Christmas tree in the corner blazed with color and light, joined by merry fires flickering in the river-rock fireplaces at both ends of the vast room. Glittery white lights stretched across the room and gleamed a welcome.

The air smelled delicious—ham and yeasty rolls and, if he wasn't mistaken, apple pie.

Like iron shavings to a magnet, his gaze instantly found Celeste. She was right in the middle of everything, directing a crew of caterers while they laid out table settings.

His stomach muscles tightened. She looked beautiful, with her hair up in a dark, elegant sweep and wearing a simple tailored white blouse and green skirt. Again, the alluring contradictions. She looked prim and sexy at the same time.

"Hi, Celeste," Olivia chirped, heading straight to her for a hug, which was readily accepted and returned.

He didn't understand the bond between the two of them, but he couldn't deny the strength of it.

"Looks as if you've been busy," he said, gesturing to the tables.

"Hope and Rafe did all this while I was working at the library today. It looks great, doesn't it?"

"Wonderful," he agreed. "I was going to see if there was anything I could do to help, but you seem to have everything under control."

"I don't know if I'd go that far," she answered with

a rather frazzled-sounding laugh. "I don't know what I was thinking to agree to this. If Hope ever tries to rope me into one of her harebrained ideas again, please remind me of this moment and my solemn vow that I will never be so gullible again."

He smiled even as he was aware of a sharp ache in his chest. He wouldn't be around to remind her of anything. Some other guy would be the one to do that—a realization that he suddenly hated.

"Thanks for bringing Olivia early. She wanted her hair fixed the same as Louisa's."

"She said it was going to be a big bun on her head," Olivia said. "That's what I want."

Celeste smiled at her. "Find your costume first, and then Louisa's mom is on hair-and-makeup duty in the office, and she'll help you out."

"Okay," she said eagerly, then trotted away.

Without the buffer of his daughter, he suddenly couldn't escape the memory of that earthshaking kiss a few days earlier. When she smiled like that, her eyes huge behind her glasses, he wanted to reach out, tug her against him and taste her one more time.

"How are you?" she asked.

He didn't know how to answer. That strange, irresistible tenderness seemed to twist and curl through him like an unruly vine. As he had no idea what to do with it, he said the first thing he could think of in a futile effort to put distance between them.

"Good. It's been a busy few days. We've made a lot of progress with Charlotte's house. We're now down to one room and a few cupboards here and there."

She didn't answer for about three beats, and he

thought he saw her hand tighten. Would she miss them when they left? Olivia, no doubt. What about him?

"That's a huge job," she finally said. "I imagine you must be relieved to be nearing the finish line."

Relieved? No. Not really. It had been a strange, disquieting experience sorting through the pieces of his grandparents' lives, all the treasures and papers and worthless junk they had left behind. It made a man wonder what would remain of his own life once he was gone. Right now he didn't feel as though he had all that much to show for his years on the planet.

"I thought it would take me until at least New Year's, but we're ahead of schedule."

"That's great," she said. Was that cheerful note in her voice genuine or forced?

"At this point, I'm thinking we'll probably take off the day after Christmas. Maybe we'll drive to San Diego for a few days before we head back up the coast to LA."

"Oh. So soon? I... That will be nice for you, to be back in the warmth and sunshine after all this snow we've had."

Logically, he knew it *should* be what he wanted, to go home and begin cobbling together the rest of their lives, but he still couldn't manage to drum up much enthusiasm for it.

"If I don't get the chance to talk to you again, I wanted to be sure to give you my thanks for all you've done to help Olivia."

Surprise flickered in those lovely eyes. "I didn't do anything," she protested.

"You know that's not true," he said. "You have been nothing but kind to her from the first moment we met you at the library that day. You gave her an unforgettable birthday celebration and have helped her feel the Christmas spirit when I would have thought that impossible this year. She's beginning to return to her old self, and I give a great deal of the credit for that to you and your family."

Her smile was soft and sweet and lit up her face like a thousand twinkly lights. He was struck again by how truly lovely she was, one of those rare women who became more beautiful the more times a man saw her.

"She's a remarkable girl, Flynn. I feel honored to have had the chance to know her. I'll miss her. I'll miss both of you."

Before he could come up with a reply to that—before he could do something stupid like tell her how very much he would miss her, too—one of the catering crew came up to her to ask a question about the dessert trays. After an awkward little pause, she excused herself to help solve the problem.

I'll miss her. I'll miss both of you.

The words seemed to echo through the vast lodge. While his daughter's life had been changed for the better because of their stay here in Pine Gulch, he wasn't sure he could say the same thing for his own.

He would miss Celeste, too. Rather desperately, he realized suddenly. As he stood in her family's holiday lodge surrounded by the trappings of the season, he realized how very much she had impacted his world, too.

"Got a minute?"

He had been so lost in thought he hadn't notice Rafe come in. Though there was still a certain wariness between the two of them, Rafe seemed to have become much more accepting of him after their time together working in the barn the other day.

He liked and respected the other man. In fact, Flynn suspected that if he and Olivia *were* to stick around Pine Gulch, he and Rafe would become friends.

"I have more than a minute," he answered. "I'm just the chauffeur right now, apparently, delivering Olivia to get her hair fixed."

"Perfect. While you've got your chauffeur hat on, I've got about twenty older ladies in need of rides. None of them likes to drive after dark, apparently, and especially not when it's snowing. Naturally, Hope promised them all she would find a way to get them here without thinking of the impossible logistics of the thing. Chase was supposed to help me shuttle them all, but he got tied up with something at his ranch and won't be free until right before the show starts. Everybody else is busy right now with the kids, so I'm in a pinch."

He was honored to be asked, even though he wasn't part of the community. "Sure. I'm happy to help, but I don't know where anybody lives. You'll have to tell me where to go."

"I've got a list right here with addresses and names. I figure if we split it up, we'll have time to get everybody here before the show, but it's going to be tight. You sure you don't mind?"

He didn't. It felt good to be part of something, to feel as though he was giving back a little for all that had been done for him and Olivia.

"Not at all. Let's do it."

"Where's my dad?" Olivia asked. "I thought he was going to be here to watch."

She looked absolutely beautiful in the little angel costume she wore for the show—and for the special part they had just practiced at the last minute.

The costume set off her delicate features and lovely blond hair to perfection.

Celeste's gaze drifted from her to the other children in their costumes. They all looked completely adorable. Somehow, by a Christmas miracle, they were really going to pull this off.

"Do you see my dad?" Olivia asked.

She frowned and looked around the beautiful screens Rafe and Flynn had built to serve as the wings to their small stage. She saw many familiar, beloved neighbors and friends, but no sign of a certain gorgeous man.

"I can't see him, but I'm sure he'll be here."

"Who are you looking for?" Hope asked, looking up from adjusting Joey's crooked crown.

"Flynn."

"I don't think he's back yet from picking up the last group of ladies."

Celeste stared at her sister. "What ladies?"

"Oh, didn't you know? Rafe asked him to help shuttle some of the ladies who wanted to come to the dinner and show, but didn't want to be stuck driving after dark."

She gaped at her sister. "Seriously? Flynn?"

"Yeah. He's already dropped off one carload earlier, and then I think Rafe sent him out again."

She pictured him driving through the snow to pick up a bunch of older ladies he didn't even know, and her throat seemed suddenly tight and achy. What a darling he was, to step up where he was needed.

How was she supposed to be able to resist a man like that?

She was in love with him.

She drew in a shaky breath as the reality of it crashed over her as if the entire plywood set had just tumbled onto her head. It was quite possible that she had been in love with him since that summer afternoon so many years ago when he had picked her up from her bike, dried her tears and cleaned up her scratches and scrapes.

Was that the reason she had never really become serious about any of the other men she dated in college? She'd always told herself she wasn't ready, that she didn't feel comfortable with any of them, that she was too socially awkward. That all might have been true, but perhaps the underlying reason was because she had already given her heart to the larger-than-life boy he had been.

In the past few weeks she truly had come to know him as more than just a kind teenager, her secret fantasy of what a hero should be. She had come to admire so many other things about him. His strength, his goodness, the love he poured out to his daughter.

How could she *not* love such a wonderful man? She loved him and she loved Olivia, too. Her heart was going to shatter into a million tiny pieces when they left.

"What if he doesn't make it back?" Olivia fretted now. "He'll miss my big surprise."

Celeste drew in a breath and forced herself to focus on the show. There would be time for heartbreak later.

"He'll make it back. Don't worry. He wouldn't miss seeing you."

Actually, Flynn missing Olivia's big surprise might not be such a bad thing. She wasn't quite sure he would like it, but it was too late for regrets now.

Olivia still seemed edgy as the music started. Her

uneven gait was more pronounced than usual as she followed the other children onstage for their opening number.

Just as the last child filed on, she saw him leading three older women: Agnes Sheffield, her sister and their friend Dolores Martinez.

She watched around the wings as he took their coats, then helped them find empty seats. Agnes touched his arm in a rather coquettish way. As he gave the octogenarian an amused smile, Celeste fell a little in love with him all over again.

Darn man. Why did he have to be so wonderful?

At last, when everyone was settled and the children were standing on the risers, Destry Bowman, one of the older girls, took the microphone.

"We welcome you all to the first ever holiday extravaganza at The Christmas Ranch. Consider this our Christmas gift to each of you."

The children immediately launched into the show, which was mostly a collection of familiar songs with a few vignette skits performed by the older children. After only a few moments, she could tell it was going to be considered an unqualified success.

She saw people laughing in all the right parts, catching their breath in expectation, even growing teary eyed at times, just as she'd predicted to the children. Most of all, she hoped they had a little taste of the joy and magic of the season, which seemed so much more real when experienced through the eyes of a child.

This was different from writing a book. Here she could see the immediate impact of what she had created and helped produce.

Seeing that reaction in real time made her rethink

her objections to the upcoming Sparkle movie. Maybe it wouldn't be such a bad thing. The story was about finding the joy and wonder of Christmas through helping others, as Uncle Claude and Aunt Mary had taught them. If Sparkle could help spread that message, she didn't see how she could stand in the way.

Finally, it was time for the last number, which they had changed slightly at the last minute.

"Are you ready, sweetheart?" she whispered to Olivia.

The girl nodded, the tinsel halo of her angel costume waving eagerly.

As all the children were onstage, she stepped out to the audience so she could watch. From this vantage point, she had a clear view of Flynn. His brow furrowed in confusion at first to see Olivia at the microphone, then when the piano player gave her a note for pitch and she started singing the first verse to "Silent Night" by herself a cappella, his features went tight and cold.

Her voice was pure and beautiful, as it had been the other night while they were caroling, and she sang the familiar song with clarity and sweetness. She saw a few people whispering and pointing and thought she saw Agnes Sheffield mouth the words *Elise Chandler* to Dolores.

When Olivia finished, the piano started and all the children sang the second verse with her, then Destry Bowman signaled the audience to join in on the third.

What they might have lacked in musical training or even natural ability, the children made up for in enthusiasm and bright smiles.

Beside her, Hope sniffled. "They're wonderful, CeCe. The whole show is so good."

She smiled, even though emotions clogged her own throat.

They finished to thunderous applause, which thrilled the children. She saw delight on each face, especially the proud parents.

A moment later, Hope took the stage to wrap up things. "Let's give these amazing kids another round of applause," she said.

The audience readily complied, which made the children beam even more. The show had been a smashing success—which probably meant Hope would want to make it a tradition.

"I have to give props to one more person," she went on. To Celeste's shock, Hope looked straight at her. "My amazing sister Celeste. Once again, she has taken one of my harebrained ideas and turned it into a beautiful reality. Celeste."

Her sister held out her hand for her to come onstage. She had never wanted to do some serious hair pulling more than she did at right that moment.

She thought about being obstinate and remaining right where she was, but that would only be even *more* awkward. With no choice in the matter, she walked onstage to combined applause from the performers and the audience.

Face blazing, she hurried back down the stairs and off stage as quickly as possible, in time to hear Hope's last words to the audience.

"Now, Jenna McRaven and her crew have come up with an amazing meal for you all, so sit back and enjoy. Parents, your kids are going to change out of their costumes and they'll be right out to join you for dinner. As a special treat for you, the wonderful Natalie Dalton and Lucy Boyer are going to entertain you during dinner with a duet for piano and violin."

The two cousins by marriage came out and started the low-key dinner music Hope had arranged while the caterers began serving the meal.

"You all did wonderfully," Celeste told the cast when they gathered offstage. "Thank you so much for your hard work. I'm so proud of you! Now hurry and change then come out and find your family so you can enjoy all this yummy food."

With much laughing and talking, the children rushed to the two dressing rooms they had set aside. She was picking up someone's discarded shepherd's crook when her sister Faith came around the screen.

"Great work, CeCe. It was truly wonderful." She gave one of her rare smiles, and in that moment, all the frenetic work seemed worth it.

"I'm glad it's over. Next year it's your turn."

"Great idea." Hope joined them and turned a speculative look in Faith's direction.

"Ha. That will be the day," Faith said. "Unlike Celeste, I know how to say no to you. I've been doing it longer."

Celeste laughed and hugged her sisters, loving them both dearly, then she hurried back into the hallway to help return costumes to hangers and hurry the children along.

Just before she reached the dressing room, Flynn caught up with her, his face tight with an emotion she couldn't quite identify.

Still caught up in the exhilaration of a job well done, she impulsively hugged him. "Oh, Flynn. Wasn't Olivia wonderful? She didn't have an ounce of stage fright. She's amazing."

He didn't hug her back and it took a moment for her to realize that emotion on his face wasn't enthusiasm. He was furious.

"Why didn't you tell me she was going to sing a solo?"

She didn't know how to answer. The truth was, she *had* worried about his reaction but had ignored the little niggling unease. For his own reasons, Flynn objected to his daughter performing at all, let alone by herself. But the girl's voice was so lovely, Celeste had wanted her to share it.

Her heart sank, and she realized she had no good defense. "I should have told you," she admitted. "It was a last-minute thing. After we went caroling and I heard what a lovely voice she had, I decided to change the program slightly. I didn't have a lot of time to fill you in on the details since we decided to make the change just tonight, but I should have tried harder."

"You couldn't leave well enough alone. I told you I didn't want her doing the show in the first place, but my feelings didn't seem to matter. You pushed and pushed until I agreed, and then you threw her onto center stage, even though I made my feelings on it clear."

"She loved it!" she protested. "She wasn't nervous at all. A week ago, she was freaking out in a restaurant over a bin of dropped dishes, and today she was standing in front of a hundred people singing her heart out without flinching. I think that's amazing progress!"

"Her progress or lack of progress is none of your business. You understand? She's my daughter. I get to make those choices for her, not some small-town librarian who barely knows either of us."

She inhaled sharply as his words sliced and gouged at her like carving knives.

Her face suddenly felt numb, as frozen as her brain. That was all she was to him. A small-town librarian who didn't even know him or his daughter. It was as if all the closeness they had shared these past few days, the tender moments, didn't matter.

As if her *love* didn't matter.

She drew in another breath. She would get through this. She had endured much worse in her life than a little heartbreak.

Okay, right now it didn't exactly seem *little*. Still, she would survive.

"Of course," she said stiffly. "I'm sorry. I should have talked to you first. Believe it or not, I had her best interests at heart. Not only do I think she has an amazing voice, but I wanted her to know that even though something terrible has happened to her, her life doesn't have to stop. She doesn't have to cower in a room somewhere, afraid to live, to take any chances. I wanted to show her that she can still use her gift to bring light and music to the world. To bring joy to other people."

The moment she said the words, realization pounded over her like an avalanche rushing down the mountain.

This was what the Sparkle books did for people. It was what *she* did for people. All this time she had felt so uncomfortable with her unexpected success, afraid to relish it, unable to shake the feeling that she didn't deserve it.

She had a gift for storytelling. Her mother and father had nurtured that gift her entire life, but especially when their family had been held captive in Colombia.

Tell us a story, CeCe, her father would say in that endlessly calm voice that seemed to hold back all the chaos. He would start her off and the two of them would spin a new tale of triumph and hope to distract the others from their hunger and fear. She told stories about dragons, about a brave little mouse, about a girl and a boy on an adventure in the mountains.

Tears welled up as she remembered how proud and delighted her parents had been with each story. Maybe that was another reason she'd struggled to accept her Sparkle success, because they weren't here to relish it with her.

Yes, it would have been wonderful. She would have loved to see in the pride in their eyes, but in the end, it didn't matter. Not really. Her sisters were here. They were infinitely thrilled for her, and that was enough.

More important, *she* was here. She had a gift and it was long past time she embraced it instead of feeling embarrassed and unworthy anytime someone stopped her to tell her how much her words meant to them.

"Excuse me," she mumbled to him, needing to get away. Just as she turned to escape, her niece, Louisa, came out of the dressing room holding a book.

"Aunt CeCe, do you know where Olivia went? We were talking about *The Best Christmas Pageant Ever*. She'd never read it, and I told her I got an extra copy at school and she could have it. I want to make sure I don't forget to give it to her."

She turned away from Flynn, hoping none of the glittery tears she could feel threatening showed in her eyes.

"She's probably in the dressing room."

"I don't think so. I just came from there and I didn't see her."

"Are you looking for Olivia?" Barrett asked, joining them from the boy's dressing room. "She left."

She frowned at her nephew even as she felt Flynn tense beside her. "Left? What do you mean, she left?"

He shrugged. "She said she wanted to go see something. I saw her go out the back door. I thought it was kind of weird because she didn't even have a coat on, just her angel costume."

Celeste stared down at the boy, her heart suddenly racing with alarm. The angel costume was thin and not at all suitable for the wintry conditions in the Idaho mountains. Even a few minutes of weather exposure could be dangerous.

"How long ago was this?" Flynn demanded.

"I don't know. Right after we were done singing. Maybe ten minutes."

"She can't have gone far," Celeste said.

"You don't know that," Flynn bit out.

He was right. Even in ten minutes, the girl *might* have wandered into the forest of pine and fir around the ranch and become lost, or she could have fallen in the creek or wandered into the road. In that white costume, she would blend with the snow, and vehicles likely wouldn't be able to see her until it was too late.

Her leg still wasn't completely stable. She could have slipped somewhere and be lying in the snow, cold and hurt and scared…

Icy fingers of fear clutched at her, wrapping around her heart, her lungs, her brain.

"We can't panic," she said, more to herself than to

him. "I'll look through the lodge to find her first, and then I'll get Rafe and everyone out there searching the entire ranch. We'll find her, Flynn. I promise."

Chapter 13

He heard her words as if from a long distance away, as if she were trying to catch his attention with a whisper across a crowded room.

This couldn't be real. Any moment Olivia would come around the corner wearing that big smile he was beginning to see more frequently. He held his breath, but she didn't magically appear simply because he wished it.

Cold fear settled in his gut, achingly familiar. He couldn't lose her. Not after working so hard to get her back these past few months.

"We'll find her, Flynn," Celeste said again, the panic in her voice a clear match to his own emotions.

She cared about his daughter, and he had been so very mean to her about it. He knew he had hurt her. He had seen a little light blink out in her eyes at his cruel words.

Her progress or lack of progress is none of your business. She's my daughter. I get to make those choices for her, not some small-town librarian who barely knows either of us.

He would have given anything at that moment to take them back.

He didn't even know why he had gotten so upset seeing Olivia up onstage—probably because he still wanted to do anything he could to protect her, to keep her close and the rest of the world away.

He didn't want her to become like her mother or his, obsessed with recognition and adulation. At the same time, he had been so very proud of her courage for standing in front of strangers and singing her little heart out.

None of that mattered right now. She was missing and he had to find her.

He hurried to find his coat, aware of a bustle of activity behind him as Rafe jumped up, followed by Hope and Faith.

The instant support comforted him like a tiny flickering candle glowing against the dark night in a window somewhere. Yeah, they might be temporary visitors in Pine Gulch, but he and Olivia had become part of a community, like it or not.

Celeste's brother-in-law stopped for an instant to rest a hand on Flynn's shoulder on his way to grabbing his own coat off the rack. "Don't worry, man. We'll find her. She'll be okay."

He wanted desperately to believe Rafe.

He couldn't lose her again.

They would find her.

A frantic five-minute search of the lodge revealed

no sign of one little girl. She wasn't in any of the bathrooms, the kitchen area, the closed gift shop or sitting beside any of the senior citizens as they enjoyed their meal, oblivious to the drama playing out nearby.

Rafe texted Celeste that he had searched through the barn with no sign of her. Faith and Hope had gone up to the house to see if they could find her there. Rafe told her he wanted to take a look around the reindeer enclosure for a little blonde angel next and then head for some of the other outbuildings scattered about the ranch.

As soon as she read the word *angel*, something seemed to click in her brain. Angel. She suddenly remembered Olivia's fascination the other night with the angel above the little chapel in the Christmas village.

Excitement bubbled through her, and she suddenly knew with unshakable certainty that was where she would find the girl.

She grabbed her coat off the rack—not for her, but for Olivia when she found her—and raced outside without bothering to take time throwing it on.

Though Hope and Rafe had elected to close the rest of the ranch activities early that night—the sleigh rides, the sledding hill, the reindeer photography opportunities—because all hands were needed for the dinner and show, they had chosen to keep on the lights at the Christmas village for anyone who might want to stop and walk through it.

She nodded to a few families she knew who were enjoying the village, the children wide-eyed with excitement, but didn't take time to talk. She would have to explain away her rudeness to them later, but right now her priority was finding Olivia.

When she reached the chapel, she nearly collapsed

with relief. A little angel in a white robe and silver tinsel halo stood in front of it, hands clasped together as she gazed up at the Madonna, the baby and especially the angel presiding over the scene.

Before she greeted the girl, Celeste took a precious twenty seconds to send a group text to Flynn, her sisters and Rafe to call off the search, explaining briefly that she had found Olivia safe and sound at the Christmas village.

With that done, she stepped forward just in time to hear what the girl was saying.

"Please tell my mom I don't want to be sad or scared all the time anymore. Do you think that's okay? I don't want her to think I don't love her or miss her. I do. I really do. I just want to be happy again. I think my daddy needs me to be."

Oh, Celeste so remembered being in that place after her parents had died—feeling so guilty when she found things to smile about again, wondering if it was some sort of betrayal to enjoy things like birthday cakes and trick-or-treating and the smell of fresh-cut Christmas trees.

She swallowed down her emotions and stepped forward to wrap her coat around Olivia. As she did, she noticed something that made her break out in goose bumps.

"If it means anything," she murmured, "I think your mom heard you."

The girl looked up. Surprise flickered in her eyes at seeing Celeste, but she gave her a tremulous smile and took the hand Celeste held out. "Why do you think so?"

"Look at the star."

Sure enough, the star above the chapel that had

been out the other night flickered a few times and then stayed on.

Celeste knew the real explanation probably had to do with old wiring or a loose bulb being jostled in and out of the socket by the wind. Or maybe it was a tiny miracle, a sort of tender mercy for a grieving child who needed comfort in that moment.

"It *is* working," Olivia breathed. "Do you think my mom turned it on?"

"Maybe."

The star's light reflected on her features. "Do you... do you think she'll be mad at me for being happy it's Christmas?"

"Oh, honey, no." Heedless of the snow, Celeste knelt beside the girl so she could embrace her. "Christmas is all about finding the joy. It's about helping others and being kind to those in need and holding on to the people we love, like your dad. I heard what you said to the angel, and you're right. It hurts his heart to see you sad. Dads like to fix things—especially *your* dad—and he doesn't know how to fix this."

"When I cry, he sometimes looks as if he wants to cry, too," she said.

Celeste screwed her eyes shut, her heart aching with love for both of them. She didn't know the right words to say. They were all a jumble inside her, and she couldn't seem to sort through to find the right combination.

When she looked up, the peaceful scene in the little church seemed to calm her and she hugged the girl close to her. "It's natural to miss your mom and to wish she was still with you. But she wouldn't want you to give up things like sleigh rides and Christmas carols and playing with your friends. If that angel could talk,

I think that's exactly what she would tell you your mom wanted you to hear."

Olivia seemed to absorb that. After a moment she exhaled heavily as if she had just set down a huge load and could finally breathe freely. She turned to Celeste, still kneeling beside her, and threw her arms around her neck.

That ache in her chest tightened as she returned the embrace, wondering if this would be her last one from this courageous girl she had come to love as much as she loved her father.

"Thanks for letting me be in the show," Olivia said. "It made me really happy. That's why I wanted to come out here, to see if the angel could ask my mom if it was okay with her."

Celeste hadn't known Elise Chandler, but from what little she did know, she had a feeling the woman would love knowing her daughter enjoyed entertaining people.

"I'm glad you had fun," she answered. "Really glad. But you scared everybody by coming out here without telling anyone. In fact, we should probably find your dad, just to make absolutely sure he got the message that you're safe."

"I'm here."

At the deep voice from behind them, she turned around and found Flynn watching them with an intense, unreadable look in his eyes.

Her heartbeat kicked up a notch. How much had he heard? And why was he looking at her like that?

Olivia extricated herself from Celeste, who rose as the girl ran to her father.

Flynn scooped her into his arms and held her tight, his features raw with relief.

"I'm sorry I didn't tell you where I was, Daddy."

"You know that's the rule, kiddo. Next time, you need to make sure you tell me where you're going so I know where to find you."

"I will," she promised.

As he set her back to the ground, her halo slipped a little and he fixed it for her before adjusting Celeste's baggy coat around the girl's shoulders. "I've been worried about you, Livie."

He didn't mean just the past fifteen minutes of not knowing where she was, Celeste realized. He was talking about all the fear and uncertainty of the past three months.

Her love for him seemed to beam in her chest brighter than a hundred stars. How was she going to get through all the days and months and years ahead of her without him?

"I don't want to be sad anymore," Olivia said. "I still might be sometimes, but Celeste said the angel would tell me Mom wouldn't want me to be sad *all* the time."

His gaze met hers and she suddenly couldn't catch her breath at the intense, glittering expression there. "Celeste and the angel are both very wise," he answered. He hugged her again. "You'll always miss your mom. That's normal when you lose someone you love. But it doesn't mean you can't still find things that make you happy."

"Like singing. I love to sing."

He nodded, even though he did it with a pained look. "Like singing, if that's what you enjoy."

The two of them were a unit, and she didn't really have a place in it.

She thought of his words to her. *She's my daughter. I*

get to make those choices for her, not some small-town librarian who barely knows either of us.

They stung all over again, but he was right. For a brief time she had been part of their lives, but the time had come to say goodbye.

"Since you're safe and sound now, I really should go," she said with bright, completely fake cheer. "Why don't you hurry back to the lodge and change out of your angel costume, then you can grab some dinner?"

"I *am* hungry," Olivia said.

She smiled at the girl, though it took all her concentration not to burst into tears. A vast, hollow ache seemed to have opened up inside her.

"I'm sure Jenna McRaven can find both of you a plate. It all looked delicious."

"Good idea."

"I'll see you both later, then," she answered.

Even though they would be heading in the same direction, she didn't think she could walk sedately beside him and make polite conversation when this ache threatened to knock her to her knees.

Without waiting for them, she hurried back toward the lodge. As she reached it, the lights gleamed through the December night. Through the windows, she saw the dinner still in full swing. Suddenly, she couldn't face all that laughter and happiness and holiday spirit.

She figured she had done her part for the people of Pine Gulch. Let her sisters handle the rest. She needed to go home, change into her most comfortable pajamas, open a pint of Ben & Jerry's and try to figure out how she could possibly face a bleak, endless future that didn't contain a certain darling girl and her wonderful father.

* * *

By another Christmas miracle, she somehow managed to hold herself together while she hurried through the cold night to her SUV, started the engine and drove back to the foreman's cottage.

The moment she walked into the warmth of her house, the tears she had been shoving back burst through like a dam break and she rushed into her bedroom, sank onto her bed and indulged herself longer than she should have in a good bout of weeping.

She was vaguely aware that Linus and Lucy had followed her inside and were watching her with concern and curiosity, but even that didn't ease the pain.

While some part of her wanted to wish Flynn had never returned to Pine Gulch so that she might have avoided this raw despair, she couldn't be so very selfish. Olivia had begun her journey toward healing here. She had made great progress in a very short amount of time and had begun regaining all she had lost in an act of senseless violence.

If the price of her healing was Celeste's own heartache, she would willingly pay it, even though it hurt more than she could ever have imagined.

After several long moments, her sobs subsided and she grew aware that Lucy was rubbing against her arm in concern while Linus whined from the floor in sympathy. She picked up both animals and held them close, deeply grateful for these two little creatures who gave her unconditional love.

"I'm okay," she told them. "Just feeling sorry for myself right now."

Linus wriggled up to lick at her salty tears, and she

managed a watery smile at him. "Thanks, bud, but I think a tissue would be a better choice."

She set the animals back down while she reached for the box on the table beside her bed.

She would get through this, she thought as she wiped away her tears. The pain would be intense for a while, she didn't doubt, but once Flynn and his daughter returned to California and she didn't have to see either of them all the time, she would figure out a way to go forward without them.

She would focus instead on the many things she had to look forward to—Christmas, the new book release, the movie production, a trip to New York with Hope to meet with their publisher at some point in the spring.

With a deep breath, she forced herself to stop. Life was as beautiful as a silky, fresh, sweet-smelling rose, even when that beauty was sometimes complicated by a few thorns.

She rose and headed to the bathroom, where she scrubbed her face in cold water before changing into her most comfortable sweats and fuzzy socks.

The mantra of her parents seemed to echo in her head, almost as if they were both talking to her like the angels Olivia had imagined. If they were here, they would have told her the only way to survive heartache and pain this intense was to throw herself into doing something nice for someone else.

With that in mind, she decided to tackle one more item on her holiday to-do list—wrapping the final gifts she planned to give her family members. It was a distraction anyway, and one she badly needed. She grabbed the gifts from her office and carried them to the living room, then hunted up the paper, tape and scissors.

With everything gathered in one place, she turned on the gas fireplace and the television set and plopped onto the floor.

Lucy instantly nabbed a red bow from the bag and started batting it around the floor while Linus cuddled next to her. She had just started to wrap the first present when the little dog's head lifted just seconds before the doorbell rang.

It was probably one of her sisters checking on her after her abrupt exit from the dinner. She started to tell them to come in, then remembered she had locked the door behind her out of habit she developed while away at school.

"Coming," she called. "Just a moment."

She unlocked the door, swung it open and then stared in shock at the man standing on the porch. Instantly, she wanted to shove the door shut again—and not only because she must look horrible in her loose, baggy sweats, with her hair a frizzy mess and her makeup sluiced away by the tears and the subsequent cold water bath.

"Flynn! What are you doing here?"

He frowned, concern on his gorgeous features. "You didn't stick around the lodge for dinner. I tried to find you to give your coat back but you had disappeared."

"Oh. Thanks."

She took the wool coat from him, then lowered her head, hoping he couldn't see her red nose, which probably wasn't nearly as cute as Rudolph's.

Though she didn't invite him in, he walked into the living room anyway and closed the door behind him to keep out the icy air. She should have told him not to bother, since he wouldn't be staying, but she couldn't find the words.

"Are you feeling okay?" he asked.

Sure. If a woman who was trying to function with a broken heart could possibly qualify as *okay*. She shrugged, still not meeting his gaze. "It's been a crazy-busy few days. I needed a little time to myself to get ready for Christmas. I've still got presents to wrap and all."

She gestured vaguely toward the coffee table and the wrapping paper and ribbon.

He was silent for a moment and then, to her horror, she felt his hand tilt her chin up so she had no choice but to look at him.

"Have you been crying?" he asked softly.

This had to be the single most embarrassing moment of her life—worse, even, than crashing her bicycle in front of his grandmother's house simply because she had been love struck and he hadn't been wearing a shirt.

"I was, um, watching a bit of a Hallmark movie a little earlier and, okay, I might have cried a little."

It wasn't a very good lie and he didn't look at all convinced.

"Are you sure that's all?" he asked, searching her expression with an intensity she didn't quite understand.

She swallowed. "I'm a sucker for happy endings. What can I say?"

He dropped his hand. "I hope that's the reason. I hope it's not because you were upset at me for acting like an ass earlier."

She tucked a strand of hair behind her ear. "You didn't at all. You were worried for your daughter. I understand. I was frantic, too."

"Before that," he murmured. "When we were talking about Olivia's solo in the show. I was cruel to you, and I'm so, so sorry."

She didn't know how to respond to that, not when he was gazing at her with that odd, intense look on his features again.

"You were a concerned father with your daughter's best interests at heart," she finally said. "And you didn't say anything that isn't true. I *am* a small-town librarian, and I'm very happy in that role. More important, I don't have the right to make decisions for Olivia without asking you. I should have told you about her solo. I'm sorry I didn't."

He made a dismissive gesture. "That doesn't matter. While she was missing, I prayed that if we found her, I would drive her myself to acting lessons, singing lessons, tap-dancing lessons. Whatever she wants. As long as she's finding joy in the world again and I can help her stay centered, I don't care what she wants to do. She's not my mother or Elise. She's a smart, courageous girl, and I know she can handle whatever comes her way. These past few months proved that."

In that moment she knew Olivia would be fine. Her father would make sure of it. It was a great comfort amid the pain of trying to figure out how to go on without them.

"I realized something else while we were looking for Olivia," Flynn said. He stepped a little closer.

"What's that?" she whispered, feeling breathless and shaky suddenly. Why was he looking at her like that, with that fierce light in his eyes and that soft, tender smile?

Her heart began to pound, especially when he didn't

answer for a long moment, just continued to gaze at her. Finally, he took one more step and reached for her hand.

"Only that I just happen to be in love with a certain small-town librarian who is the most caring, wonderful woman I've ever met."

Nerves danced through her at the words, spiraling in circles like a gleeful child on a summer afternoon.

"I... You're what?"

His hand was warm on hers, his fingers strong and firm and wonderful. "I've never said that to anyone else and meant it. Truly meant it."

She took a shaky breath while those nerves cartwheeled in every direction. "I... Exactly how many other small-town librarians have you known?"

He smiled a little when she deliberately focused on the most unimportant part of what he had said. "Only you. Oh, and old Miss Ludwig, who had the job here in Pine Gulch before you. I think my grandmother took me into the library a few times when I was a kid, and I *definitely* never said anything like that to her. She scared me a little, if you want the truth."

"She scared me, too," she said. *You scare me more*, she wanted to say.

He leaned down close enough that only a few inches separated them. "You know what I meant," he murmured, almost against her mouth. "I've never told a woman I loved her before. Not when the words resounded like this in my heart."

"Oh, Flynn." She gave him a tremulous smile, humbled and awed and deeply in love with him.

He was close enough that she only had to step on tiptoes a little to press her mouth to his, pouring all the emotion etched on her own heart into the kiss.

He froze for just a moment and then he made a low, infinitely sexy sound in his throat and kissed her back with heat and hunger and tenderness, wrapping his arms tightly around her as if he couldn't bear to let her go.

A long while later he lifted his head, his breathing as ragged as hers and his eyes dazed. She was deliriously, wondrously happy. Her despair of a short time earlier seemed like a distant, long-ago memory that had happened to someone else.

"Does that kiss mean what I hope?" he murmured.

She could feel heat soak her cheeks and all the words seemed to tangle in her throat. She felt suddenly shy, awkward, but as soon as she felt the urge to retreat into herself where she was safe, she pushed it back down.

For once, she had to be brave, to take chances and seize the moment instead of standing by as a passive observer, content to read books about other people experiencing the sort of life she wanted.

"It means I love you," she answered. "I love you so very much, Flynn. And Olivia, too. I lied when I told you I was crying over a television show. I was crying because I knew the two of you would be leaving soon, and I…I didn't think my heart could bear it."

"I don't want to go anywhere," he said. "Pine Gulch has been wonderful for Olivia *and* for me. She might have been physically wounded, but I realized while I was here that some part of me has been emotionally damaged for much longer. This place has begun to heal both of us."

He kissed her again with an aching tenderness that made her want to cry all over again, this time because of the joy bubbling through her that seemed too big to stay contained.

She didn't know what the future held for them. He had a company in California, a life, a home. Perhaps he could commute from Pine Gulch to Southern California, or maybe he might want to take Rafe's advice and open a branch of his construction company here.

None of that mattered now, not when his arms and his kiss seemed to fill all the empty corners of her heart.

A long time later, he lifted his head with reluctance in his eyes. "I should probably go find Olivia. I left her with Hope and Rafe at the lodge. I'm sure she's having a great time with the other kids, but I hate to let her out of my sight for long."

"I don't blame you," she assured him.

He stepped away, though he didn't seem to want to release her hands. "I doubt Rafe was buying the excuse when I told him that I needed to return your coat. Something tells me he knows the signs of a man in love."

She could feel her face heat again. What would her family say about this? She didn't really need to ask. They already seemed to adore Olivia, and once they saw how happy she was with Flynn, they would come to love him, too.

"Do you want to come with me to pick her up?" he asked.

She wanted to go wherever he asked, but right now she still probably looked a mess. "Yes, if you can give me ten minutes to change."

"You look fine to me," he assured her. "Beautiful, actually."

When he looked at her like that, she felt beautiful, for the first time in her life.

"But if you *have* to change—and if I had a vote— I'm particularly fond of a particular T-shirt you own."

"I'll see what I can do," she answered with a laugh. She kissed him again while the Christmas lights from her little tree gleamed and the wind whispered against the window and joy swirled around them like snowflakes.

Epilogue

"Are you ready for this?"

Celeste took her gaze from the snowflakes outside to glance across the width of the SUV to her husband.

"No," she admitted. "I doubt I will *ever* be ready."

Flynn lifted one hand from the steering wheel to grab hers, offering instant comfort, his calm blowing away the chaotic thoughts fluttering through her like that swirl of snow.

"*I'm* ready," Olivia piped up from the backseat. "I can't *wait*."

"You? You're excited?" Flynn glanced briefly in the rearview mirror at his daughter. "You hide it so very well."

Olivia didn't bother to pay any attention to his desert-dry tone. "This is the coolest thing that's ever happened in my whole life," she said.

Since Olivia wasn't yet a decade old, her pool of experiences was a little shallow, but Flynn and Celeste both declined to point that out.

The girl was practically bouncing in the backseat, the energy vibrating off her in waves. Celeste had to smile. She adored Olivia for the lovely young lady she was growing into.

The trauma of her mother's tragic death had inevitably left scars that would always be part of her, but they had faded over the past two years. Olivia was a kind, funny, creative girl with a huge heart.

She had opened that big heart to welcome Celeste into their little family when she and Flynn married eighteen months earlier, and Celeste had loved every single moment of being her stepmother.

Now Olivia breathed out a happy sigh. "I think I'm more excited about the Pine Gulch premiere of *Sparkle and the Magic Snowball* than the real one in Hollywood tomorrow."

"Really?" Celeste said in surprise. "I thought you'd be thrilled about the whole thing."

Olivia loved everything to do with the film industry, much to Flynn's dismay. Celeste supposed it was in her blood, given her mother's and her grandmother's legacies. Someday those Hollywood lights would probably draw her there, too—something Flynn was doing his best to accept.

"It will be fun to miss school and fly out and stay at our old house. I mean, a movie premiere in Hollywood with celebrities will be glamorous and all. Who *wouldn't* be excited about that?"

In the transitory glow from the streetlights, her features looked pensive. "But I guess I'm more excited about this one because this is our home now," she said after a moment. "This is where our family is and all our friends. Everyone in Pine Gulch is just as excited about the new Sparkle movie as I am, and I can't wait to share it with them."

Oh. What a dear she was. If the girl hadn't been safely buckled in the backseat, Celeste would have hugged her. It warmed her more than her favorite wool coat that her stepdaughter felt so at home in Pine Gulch and that she wanted all her friends and neighbors to have the chance to enjoy the moment, too.

"Good point," Flynn said, smiling warmly at his daughter. "The whole town has been part of the story from the beginning. It's only right that they be the first to see the movie."

"Yep. That's the way I feel," Olivia said.

Her father gave Celeste a sidelong glance before addressing Olivia again. "Good thing your stepmother is so fierce and fought all the way up to the head of the studio to make sure it happened this way. What else could they do but agree? They're all shaking in their boots around her. She can be pretty scary, you know."

Olivia giggled and Celeste gave them both a mock glare, though she knew exactly what he was doing. Her wonderful husband was trying to calm her down the best way he knew how, by teasing away her nerves.

She *had* fought for a few things when it came to her beloved Sparkle character, but wanted to think she had been easygoing. That was what the studio executives had told her anyway. She considered herself extremely fortunate that her vision for the characters and the story matched the studio's almost exactly.

A moment later, Flynn pulled up to the St. Nicholas Lodge, which had been transformed for the night into a theater.

Somebody—Rafe, maybe—had rented a couple of huge searchlights, and they beamed like beacons through the snowy night. The parking lot was completely full and she recognized many familiar vehicles. Unfortunately, they couldn't fit everyone in town into the lodge so the event had become invitation only very quickly. For weeks, that invitation had become the most sought-after ticket in town.

Though the official premiere the next night in California would be much more of a full-fledged industry event, a red carpet had been stretched out the door of the lodge, extending down the snowy walkway to the edge of the parking lot.

Had that been Faith's doing? Probably. Where on earth had she managed to find a length of red carpet in eastern Idaho? Their older sister was proud of and excited for both Celeste and Hope.

The past two years since they'd signed the contract licensing the Sparkle stories to the animation studio they had chosen to work with seemed surreal. Besides two more bestsellers, they now had a *second* Sparkle animated movie in the works.

Now that she was here, about to walk into the makeshift theater to see people enjoying *her* story come to life on the screen—and it would be enjoyable, she knew, given what she had seen so far of the production— Celeste felt humbled and touched. It didn't seem real that life and fate, her own hard work and her sister's beautiful artwork had thrust her into this position.

"A red carpet," Olivia squealed as she finally noticed—and caught sight of the people lined up in the cold on either side of it, as if this was the real premiere filled with celebrities to gawk over. "How cool is that? That looks like my friend Louise from school. Oh, there's Jose. And Mrs. Jacobs. My whole class is here!"

"I guess you can't escape Hollywood, even here in Pine Gulch," Celeste said quietly to Flynn as he parked in the VIP slot designated for them. "I'm sorry."

He made a rueful face, but she knew him well enough after these deliriously happy months together to know he didn't really mind. He had been her biggest supporter and her second most enthusiastic fan—after Olivia, of course.

"For you, darling, it's worth it," he replied. He tugged her across the seat and pulled her into his arms for a quick kiss. "I'm so proud of you. I hope you know that. I can't wait for the whole world to discover how amazing you are."

Her heart softened, as it always did when he said such tender things to her.

Two years ago, she'd had a pretty good life here in Pine Gulch—writing her stories, working at the library in a job she loved, spending time with her sisters and her niece and nephew and Aunt Mary.

But some small part of her had still been that little girl who had lost both of her parents and was too afraid to truly embrace life and everything it had to offer.

Flynn and Olivia had changed her. At last, she fully understood the meaning of joy. Sparkle might have his magic snowball that could save Christmas, but the true magic—the only one that really mattered—was love.

These past two years had been a glorious adventure— and in seven months, give or take a few weeks, they would all be in for a new turn in their shared journey.

She pressed a hand to her stomach, to the new life growing there. Flynn caught the gesture and grinned—a secret smile between the two of them. He pressed a hand there as well, then reached for his car door.

"Let's go meet your adoring public," he told her.

She didn't need an adoring public. She had everything she needed, right here, in the family they had created together.

* * * * *

To Sarah Stone, our angel, for a year full of adventure. We can't thank you enough!

Dear Reader,

I don't know about you, but Christmas at my house is all about easy. With a packed calendar of parties, shopping, wrapping and generalized chaos, I try to find the simplest ways to do things while still enjoying some favorite traditions. This recipe is perfect for those of you who (like me!) love homemade candy but not all the fuss. All my best to you and yours this joyous season.

EASY VANILLA MICROWAVE CARAMELS

4 tbsp butter
1 cup brown sugar
½ cup corn syrup
⅔ cup sweetened condensed milk
1 tsp vanilla
butter (for greasing pan)
nonstick aluminum foil or parchment paper
waxed paper, cut into 4"–5" squares

Butter an 8" x 8" pan. Line the pan with nonstick foil or parchment paper, folding any excess over the outside edges; set aside. Mix the butter, brown sugar and corn syrup in a microwave-safe glass bowl or measuring cup. Microwave on High for two minutes. Stir mixture and return to microwave for two minutes. Add sweetened condensed milk and stir well. Microwave for 3½ minutes. Remove from microwave and stir in vanilla. Pour into prepared pan, scraping any residue from the sides of the bowl. Set aside and let cool to room temperature. When the caramel has cooled, remove liner from the pan. Cut into approximately 1" squares with a well-buttered knife. Butter your hands well, then place one caramel in the middle of a waxed-paper square. Roll the paper into a cylinder and twist the ends. Store the wrapped candies in a cool, dry place.

RaeAnne

CHRISTMAS IN COLD CREEK

Chapter 1

Much as he loved Pine Gulch, Trace Bowman had to admit his town didn't offer its best impression in the middle of a cold, gray rain that leached the color and personality from it.

Even the Christmas decorations—which still somehow could seem magical and bright to his cynical eye when viewed on a snowy December evening—somehow came off looking only old and tired in the bleak late-November morning light as he parked his patrol SUV in front of The Gulch, the diner that served as the town's central gathering place.

That sleety rain dripping from the eaves and awnings of the storefronts would be snow by late afternoon, he guessed. Maybe earlier. This time of year—the week after Thanksgiving—in Pine Gulch, Idaho, in the western shadow of the Tetons, snow was more the norm than the exception.

He yawned and rotated his neck to ease some of the tightness and fatigue. After three days of double shifts, he was ready to head for his place a few blocks away, throw a big, thick log on the fire and climb into bed for the next week or so.

Food first. He'd eaten a quick sandwich for dinner around 6:00 p.m. More than twelve hours—and the misery of dealing with a couple of weather-related accidents—later and he was craving one of Lou Archuleta's sumptuous cinnamon rolls. Sleep could wait a half hour for him to fill up his tank.

He walked in and was hit by a welcome warmth and the smell of frying bacon and old coffee. From the tin-stamped ceiling to the row of round swivel seats at the old-fashioned counter, The Gulch fit every stereotype of the perfect small-town diner. The place oozed tradition and constancy. He figured if he moved away for twenty years, The Gulch would seem the same the moment he walked back through the doors.

"Morning, Chief!" Jesse Redbear called out from the booth reserved for the diner's regulars.

"Hey, Jesse."

"Chief."

"Chief."

Greetings assailed him from the rest of the booth, from Mick Malone and Sal Martinez and Patsy Halliday. He could probably have squeezed into their corner booth but he still headed for an empty stool at the counter.

He waved at them all and continued his quick scan of the place, an old habit from his days as a military MP that still served him well. He recognized everyone in the room except for a couple he thought might be staying at the hotel and a girl reading a book in the corner. She looked to be his niece, Destry's, age and he had to wonder what a nine-year-old girl was doing by herself at The Gulch at 7:30 a.m. on a school day.

Then he noticed a slender woman standing at one of the back booths with an order pad in her hand. Since when did The Gulch have a new waitress? He'd been busy working double shifts after the wife of one of his men had a baby and he hadn't been in for a week or two, but last he knew Donna Archuleta, the wife of the owner, seemed to handle the breakfast crowd fine on her own. Maybe she was finally slowing down now that she'd hit seventy.

"Hey, Chief," Lou Archuleta, Donna's husband and the cook, called out from behind the grill before Trace could ask Donna about the solitary girl or the new waitress. "Long night?"

How did Lou know he'd been working all night? Was he wearing a sign or something? Maybe the man had just figured it out from his muddy boots and the exhaustion he was pretty sure was probably stamped on his features.

"It was a rough one. That freezing rain always keeps us hopping. I've been helping the state police out on the highway with a couple of weather-related accidents."

"You ought to be home in bed catching up." Donna, skinny and feisty, flipped a cup over and poured coffee into it for him. The last thing he needed was caffeine when he wanted to be asleep in about five minutes from now, but he decided not to make an issue of it.

"That's my plan, but I figured I'd sleep better on a full stomach."

"You want your regular?" she asked in her raspy ex-smoker's voice. "Western omelet and a stack?"

He shook his head. "No stack. I'm in the mood for one of Lou's sweet rolls this morning. Any left?"

"I think I can find one or two for our favorite man in blue."

"Thanks."

He eased his tired bones onto a stool and caught a better look at the new waitress. She was pretty and slender with dark hair pulled back in a haphazard sort of ponytail. More curious than he probably should be, he noted her white blouse seemed to be tailored and expensive. The hand holding a coffeepot was soft-looking with manicured nails.

What was someone in designer jeans doing serving coffee at The Gulch?

And not well, he noted as she splattered Maxwell House over the lip of Ronny Haskell's coffee cup. Ronny didn't seem to mind. He just smiled, somewhere in the vicinity of her chest region.

"Do you want something else to drink?" Donna asked him, apparently noticing he hadn't lifted his cup.

He gave her a rueful smile. "To be honest, I need sleep more than caffeine today. A small orange juice will do me."

"I should have thought about that. One OJ coming up."

She headed toward the small grill window to give his order to her husband and returned a minute later with his juice. Her hand shook a little as she set it down and he noted more signs of how Donna and Lou were both growing older. Maybe that's why they'd added a server to help with the breakfast crowd.

"Busy morning," he commented to Donna when she came back with the sweet roll, huge and gooey and warm.

"Let me tell you something. I've survived my share of Pine Gulch winters," she said. "In my experience, gloomy days like this make people either want to hunker down at home by themselves in front of the fire or seek out other people. Guess we've got more of the latter today."

The new waitress eased up to the window and tentatively handed an order to Lou before heading back to take the order of a couple of new arrivals.

"Who's the new blood?" he asked with a little head jerk in her direction.

Donna stopped just short of rolling her eyes. "Name's Parsons. Rebecca Parsons. But heaven forbid you make the mistake of calling her Becky. It's *Becca.* Apparently she inherited old Wally Taylor's place. His granddaughter, I guess."

That was news to Trace. He narrowed his gaze at the woman, suddenly put off. Wally had never spoken of a granddaughter. She sure hadn't been overflowing with concern for the old man. In his last few years, Trace had just about been his neighbor's only visitor. If he hadn't made a practice of checking on him a couple of times a week, Wally might have gone weeks without seeing another living soul.

Trace had been the first to find out that he'd passed away. When Trace hadn't seen him puttering around his yard for a couple of days or out with his grumpy mutt, Grunt, he'd stopped by to check and found him dead in his easy chair with the Game Show Network still on, Grunt whining at his feet.

Apparently his granddaughter had been too busy to come visit him but she hadn't blinked at moving in and taking over his house. It would serve her right if he dropped Grunt off for her. Lord knew he didn't need a grouchy, grieving, hideously ugly dog underfoot.

"That her kid?" he asked Donna.

She cast a quick look toward the booth where the girl was still engrossed in whatever she was reading. "Yeah. Fancy French name. *Gabrielle.* I told Becca the girl could spend an hour or so here before school starts, long as she behaves. This is her second morning here and she hasn't looked up from her book, not even to say thank-you when I fixed her a hot chocolate with extra whipped cream, on the house."

She seemed to take that as a personal affront and he had to smile. "Kids these days."

Donna narrowed her gaze at his cheek. "I'm just saying. Something's not right there."

"Order up," Lou called. "Chief's omelet's ready."

Donna headed back to the window and grabbed his breakfast and slid it expertly onto the counter. "You know where to find the salt and pepper and the salsa. But of course you won't need anything extra."

She headed off to take care of another customer and he dug into his breakfast. In the mirror above the counter, he had a perfect view of the new waitress as she scrambled around the diner. In the time it took him to finish his breakfast, he saw her mess up two orders and pour regular instead of decaf in old Bob Whitley's cup despite his doctor's orders that he had to ease up on the real stuff.

Oddly, she seemed to be going out of her way to avoid even making eye contact with him, though he thought he did intercept a few furtive glances in his direction. He ought to introduce himself. It was the polite thing to do, not to mention that he liked to make sure new arrivals to his town knew the police chief was keeping an eye out. But he wasn't necessarily inclined to be friendly to someone who could let a relative die a lonely death with only his farty, bad-tempered dog for company.

Fate took the decision out of his hands a moment later when the waitress fumbled the tray she was using to bus the table just adjacent to him. A couple of juice glasses slid off the edge and shattered on the floor.

"Oh, drat," the waitress exclaimed under her breath. The wimpy swear word almost made him smile. Only because he was so damn tired, he told himself.

On impulse, he unfolded himself from the bar stool. "Need a hand?" he asked.

"Thank you! I…" She lifted her gaze from the floor to his jeans and then raised her eyes. When she identified him her hazel eyes turned from grateful to unfriendly and cold, as if he'd somehow thrown the glasses at her head.

He also thought he saw a glimmer of panic in those interesting depths, which instantly stirred his curiosity like cream swirling through coffee.

"I've got it, Officer. Thank you." Her voice was several degrees colder than the whirl of sleet outside the windows.

Despite her protests, he knelt down beside her and began to pick up shards of broken glass. "No problem. Those trays can be slippery."

This close, he picked up the scent of her, something fresh and flowery that made him think of a mountain meadow on a July afternoon. She had a soft, lush mouth and for one brief, insane moment, he wanted to push aside that stray lock of hair slipping from her ponytail and taste her. Apparently he needed to spend a lot less time working and a great deal more time recreating with the opposite sex if he could have sudden random fantasies about a woman he wasn't even inclined to like, pretty or not.

"I'm Trace Bowman. You must be new in town."

She didn't answer immediately and he could almost see the wheels turning in her head. Why the hesitancy? And why that little hint of unease he could see clouding the edges of her gaze? His presence was obviously making her uncomfortable and Trace couldn't help wondering why.

"Yes. We've been here a few weeks," she finally answered.

"I understand your grandfather was Wally Taylor."

"Apparently." She spoke in a voice as terse and cool as the freezing rain.

"Old Wally was an interesting guy. Kept to himself, mostly, but I liked him. You could always count on Wally not to pull any punches. If he had an opinion about something, you found out about it."

"I wouldn't know." She avoided his gaze, her voice low. He angled his head, wondering if he imagined sudden sadness in her eyes. What was the story here? He thought he remembered hearing years ago that Wally had been estranged from his only son. If that was the case, Trace supposed it wasn't really fair to blame the son's daughter for not maintaining a relationship with the old codger.

Maybe he shouldn't be so quick to judge the woman until he knew her side of things. Until he had reason to think otherwise, he should be as friendly to her as he would be to anyone else new in his town.

"Well, I'm just up the road about four lots, in the white house with the cedar shake roof, if you or your daughter need help with anything."

She flashed a quick look toward the girl, still engrossed in her book. "Thank you. Very neighborly of you, Chief. I'll keep that in mind. And thank you for your help with my mess. Eventually I hope to stop feeling like an idiot here."

"You're welcome." He smiled as he picked up the last shard of glass and set it on her tray.

She didn't return his smile but he wanted to think she had lost a little of her wariness as she hurried away to take care of her tray and pick up another order from Lou at the grill window.

Definitely a story there. He just might need to dig a little into her background to find out why someone with fine clothes and nice jewelry who so obviously didn't have experience as a waitress would be here slinging hash at The Gulch. Was she running away from someone? A bad marriage? An abusive husband?

Now that the holidays were in full swing, the uptick in domestic-disturbance calls made that sort of thing a logical possibility. He didn't like to think about it. That young girl looked too bright and innocent to have to face such ugliness in her life. So did the mother, for that matter.

Rebecca Parsons. Becca. Not Becky. An intriguing woman. It had been a long time since one of those had crossed his path here in Pine Gulch.

He sipped at his juice and watched her deliver a plate of eggs and bacon to Jolene Marlow. A moment later she was back at the window, telling Lou apologetically that the customer had asked for sausage and she hadn't written it down.

"She ever done this before?" Trace asked Donna with a jerk of his head toward Becca, as the other woman passed by on her way to refill another customer's cup.

Donna sighed. "I don't think so. I'm sure she'll pick up on it a little better any minute now." She frowned at him. "Don't you be giving her a hard time, pullin' your 'I'm just looking out for my town' routine. I get the feeling she's had a rough go of things lately."

"What makes you think?"

Donna cast a look to make sure Becca and the girl were both out of earshot before she lowered her voice. "She came in here three days ago practically begging for a job. Said she just needed something to tide her over for a few weeks and asked if she could work over the holidays for us. Smart girl knew to hit Lou up for the job instead of me. She must have seen he was the softy around here."

Trace decided he would be wise to keep his mouth shut about his opinions on that particular topic. Donna probably didn't need reminding about all the free meals she gave out to anyone who looked down on his luck or the vast quantities of food she regularly donated to the senior-citizens center for their weekly luncheons.

"Just be nice to her, okay? You were friendly with Wally, about the only one in town who could say that."

"He died alone with only that butt-ugly dog for company. Where was this granddaughter?"

Donna patted his shoulder in a comforting sort of way, giving her raspy smoker's cough. "I know Wally and his boy had a terrible falling-out years ago. You can't blame the granddaughter for that. If Wally blamed the girl for not visiting him, he never would have left his house to her, don't you think?"

Donna was right, damn it, as she so often was. He supposed he really would have to be a good neighbor to her and not just give lip service to the phrase.

That particular term made him think about her lips once more, lush and full and very kissable. He gave an inward groan. He really needed to go home and get some sleep if he was going to sit here and fantasize about a woman who might very well be married, for all he knew.

The chief of police. Just what she needed.

Becca hurried from table to table, refilling coffee and water, taking away plates, doing every busywork she could think of so she wouldn't have to interact with the gorgeous man who passed for the Pine Gulch long arm of the law.

It didn't seem right somehow. Why couldn't Trace Bowman be some kind of stereotype of a fat old guy with a paunch and a leering eye and a toothpick sticking out of the corner of his mouth? Instead, he was much younger than she might have expected the chief of police to be, perhaps only midthirties. With brown hair and those piercing green eyes and a slow heartbreaker of a smile, he was masculine and tough and very, very dangerous, at least to her.

She should *not* have this little sizzle of awareness pulsing through her every time she risked another look at him. Police. Chief. Did she need any other reason to stay far, far away from Trace Bowman?

With habits ingrained from childhood, she catalogued all she had picked up about him from their brief encounter. He either worked or played hard, judging by the slight red streaks in his eyes, the circles under them and the general air of fatigue that seemed to weigh down his shoulders. Since he was still in uniform and his boots were mud-splattered, she was willing to bet it was the former.

He probably wasn't married—or at least he didn't wear a wedding ring. She was voting on single status for Pine Gulch's finest. If he had a wife, wouldn't it be logical he'd be going home for a home-cooked breakfast and maybe a quickie after a long night instead of coming into the diner? It was always possible he had a wife who was a professional and too busy to arrange her schedule around her husband's, but he gave off a definite unmarried vibe.

He didn't seem particularly inclined to like her. She might have wondered why not if he hadn't made that comment about being her grandfather's neighbor. He apparently thought she should have visited more. She wanted to tell him how impossible that would have been since she'd never even *heard* of Wally Taylor until she received the notification of his death and his shocking bequest, right when her own life in Arizona had been imploding around her.

A customer asked her a question about the breakfast special, distracting her from thoughts of the police chief, and she forced herself to smile politely and answer as best she could. As she did she was aware of Trace Bowman standing up from the counter and tossing a few bills next to his plate, then shoving his hat on and heading out into the cold drizzle.

The minute he left, she took her first deep breath

since she'd looked up and seen the uniform walking into The Gulch.

The man didn't particularly like her and she had the vague sense that he was suspicious of her. Again, *not* what she needed right now.

She hadn't done anything wrong, she reminded herself. Not really. Oh, maybe she hadn't been completely honest with the school district about Gabi's identity but she hadn't had any other choice, had she?

Even knowing she had no reason to be nervous, law enforcement personnel still freaked her out. Old, old habit. Savvy civil servants ranked just about last on her mother's list of desirable associates. Becca would be wise to follow her mother's example and stay as far away from Trace Bowman as possible.

Too bad for her, he lived not far from her grandfather's house.

She glanced at her watch—one of the few pieces of jewelry she hadn't pawned—and winced. Once again, time was slipping away. She felt as if she'd been on her feet for days when it had been only an hour and a half.

She rushed over to Gabrielle, engrossed in reading *To Kill a Mockingbird*, a book Becca would have thought was entirely too mature for her except she'd read it herself at around that age.

"It's almost eight. You probably need to head over to the school."

Her half sister looked up, her eyes slightly unfocused, then released a heavy sigh and closed her book. "For the record, I still don't think it's fair."

"Yeah, yeah. I know. You hate it here and think the school is lame and well below your capabilities."

"It's a complete waste of my time. I can learn better on my own, just like I've always done."

Gabi was eerily smart for her age. Becca had no idea how she'd managed so well all these years when her education seemed to have been haphazard at best. "You've done a great job in school so far, honey. You're ahead of grade level in every subject. But for now school is our best option. This way you can make friends and participate in things like music and art. Plus, you don't have to be by yourself—and I don't have to pay a sitter—while I'm working."

They had been through this discussion before. Her arguments still didn't seem to convince Gabi.

"I can find her, you know."

She gave a careful look around to make sure they weren't being overheard. "And then what? If she'd wanted you with her, she wouldn't have left you with me."

"She was going to come back. How is she supposed to find us now, when you moved us clear across the country?"

Moving from Arizona to eastern Idaho wasn't exactly across the country, but she imagined it seemed far enough to a nine-year-old. She also wasn't sure what other choice she'd been given because of the hand Monica had dealt her.

"Look, Gab, we don't have time to talk about this right now. You have to head to school and I have to return to my customers. I told you that if we haven't heard from her by the time the holidays are over, we'll try to track her down, right?"

"That's what you *said*."

The girl didn't need to finish the sentence for Becca

to clearly understand. Gabrielle had spent nine years full of disappointments and empty promises. How could Becca blame her for being slow to trust that her sister, at least, meant what she said?

"We're doing okay, aren't we? School's not so bad, right?"

Gabi slid out of the booth. "Sure. It's perfect if you want me to be bored to death."

"Just hide your book inside your textbook," Becca advised. It had always worked for her, anyway, during her own slapdash education.

With a put-upon sigh, Gabi stashed her book into her backpack, slipped into her coat and then trudged out into the rain, lifting the flowered umbrella Becca had given her.

She would have liked to drive her sister the two blocks to school but she didn't feel she could ask for fifteen minutes off during the busiest time of the morning, especially when the Archuletas had basically done her a huge favor by hiring her in the first place.

As she bused a table by the front window, she kept an eye on her sister. Between the umbrella and the red boots, the girl made a bright and incongruously cheerful sight in the gray muck.

She had no idea what she was doing with Gabi. Two months after she'd first learned she had a sister after a dozen years of estrangement from her mother, she wasn't any closer to figuring out the girl. She was brash and bossy sometimes, introspective and moody at others. Instead of feeling hurt and betrayed after Monica had dumped her on Becca, the girl refused to give up hope that her mother would come back.

Becca was angry enough at Monica for both of them.

Two months ago she'd thought she had her life completely figured out. She owned her own town house in Scottsdale. She had a job she loved as a real-estate attorney, she had a wide circle of friends, she'd been dating another attorney for several months and thought they were heading toward a commitment. Through hard work and sacrifice, she had carved her own niche in life, with all the safety and security she had craved so desperately when she was Gabi's age, being yanked hither and yon with a capricious, irresponsible con artist for a mother.

Then came that fateful September day when Monica had tumbled back into her life after a decade, like a noxious weed blown across the desert.

"Order up," Lou called from the kitchen. She jerked away from the window to the reality of her life now. No money, her career in tatters, just an inch or two away from being disbarred. The man she'd been dating had decided her personal troubles were too much of a liability to his own career and had dumped her without a backward glance, she had been forced to sell her town house to clean up Monica's mess, and now she was stuck in a sleepy little town in southeastern Idaho, saddled with responsibilities she didn't want and a nine-year-old girl who wanted to be anywhere else but here.

Any minute now, somebody was probably going to write a crappy country music song about her life.

To make matters even more enjoyable, now she'd raised the hackles of the local law enforcement. She sighed as she picked up the specials from Lou. Her life couldn't get much worse, right?

Even if Trace Bowman was the most gorgeous man she'd seen in a long, long time, she was going to have to do her best to keep a polite distance from the man. For now, she and Gabi had a place to live and the tips and small paycheck she was earning from this job would be enough to cover the groceries and keep the electricity turned on.

They were hanging by a thread and Chief Bowman seemed just the sort to come along with a big old pair of scissors and snip that right in half.

Chapter 2

Trace leaned back in his chair and set his napkin beside his now-empty plate. "Delicious dinner, Caidy, as always. The roast was particularly fine."

His younger sister smiled, her eyes a translucent blue in the late-afternoon November light streaming through the dining room windows. "Thanks. I tried a new recipe for the spice rub. It uses sage and rosemary and a touch of paprika."

"You know sage in recipes doesn't really come from the sagebrushes out back, right?"

She made a face at the teasing comment from Trace's twin brother, Taft. "Of course I know it's not the same. Just for that, you get to wash *and* dry the dishes."

"Come on. Have a little pity. I've been working all night."

"You were on duty," Trace corrected. "But did you

go out on any actual calls or did you spend the night bunking at the firehouse?"

"That's not the point," Taft said, a self-righteous note in his voice. "Whether I was sleeping or not, I was *ready* if my community needed me."

The overnight demands of their respective jobs had long been a source of good-natured ribbing between the two of them. When Trace worked the night shift, he was out on patrol, responding to calls, taking care of paperwork at the police station. As chief of the Pine Gulch fire department and one of the few actual full-time employees in the mostly volunteer department, Taft's job could sometimes be quiet.

They might bicker about it, but Trace knew no other person would have his back like his twin—though Caidy and their older brother, Ridge, would be close behind.

"Cut it out, you two." Ridge, the de facto patriarch of the family, gave them both a stern look that reminded Trace remarkably of their father. "You're going to ruin this delicious dessert Destry made."

"It's only boysenberry cobbler," his daughter piped in. "It wasn't hard at all."

"Well, it tastes like it was hard," Taft said with a grin. "That's the important thing."

Dinner at the family ranch, the River Bow, was a heralded tradition. No matter how busy they might be during the week with their respective lives and careers, the Bowman siblings tried to at least gather on Sundays when they could.

If not for Caidy, these Sunday dinners would probably have died long ago, another victim of their parents' brutal murders. For a few years after that fateful time a decade ago, the tradition had faded as Trace and his siblings struggled in their own ways to cope with their overwhelming grief.

Right around the time Ridge's wife left him and Caidy graduated from high school and started taking over caring for the ranch house and for Destry, his sister had revived the traditional Sunday dinners. Over the years it had become a way for them all to stay connected despite the hectic pace of their lives. He cherished these dinners, squabbles and all.

"I worked all night, too, but I'm not such a wimp that I can't take care of my fair share," he said with a sanctimonious look at his brother. "You sit here and rest, Taft. I wouldn't want you to overdo. I'll take care of the dishes."

Of course his brother couldn't let that insult stand, just as Trace expected. As a result, Taft became the designated dishwasher and Trace dried and put away the dishes while Destry and Ridge cleared the table.

Taft was just running water in the sink when Destry came in on her father's heels, her eyes as huge and plaintive as one of Caidy's rescued mutts begging for a treat. "Please, Dad. If we wait much longer, it will be too late."

"Too late for what?" Taft asked innocently.

"Christmas!" Destry exclaimed. "It's already the last Sunday in November. If we don't cut down our tree soon, the mountains will be too snowy. Please, Dad? Please, please, please?"

Ridge heaved a sigh. He didn't need to express his reluctance for Trace to understand it. None of his siblings had been very crazy about Christmas for nearly a decade, since their parents were killed just before Christmas Eve ten years ago.

"We'll get one," his brother assured Destry.

"What's the point of even putting up a tree if we wait much longer? Christmas will be over."

"It's not even December yet!"

"It's *almost* December. It will be here before we know it."

"She sounds like Mom," Taft said. "Remember how she used to start hounding Dad to cut the tree a few weeks before Thanksgiving?"

"And she always had it picked out by the middle of the summer," Caidy answered with a sad little smile.

"Please, Daddy. Can we go?"

Trace had to smile at his niece's persistence. Destry was a sharp little thing. She was generally a happy kid, which he found quite amazing considering her mother was a major bitch who had left Ridge and Destry when the little girl was still just a toddler.

"I guess you're right." Ridge eyed his brothers. "Either of you boys up for a ride to help me bring back the tree? We can get one for your places, too."

Taft shrugged. "I've got a date. Sorry."

"You have a date on a Sunday afternoon?" Caidy asked with raised eyebrows.

His brother seemed to find every available female between the ages of twenty-two and forty. "Not really a date. I'm going over to a friend's house to watch a movie and order pizza."

"You just had dinner," Caidy pointed out.

Taft grinned. "That's the thing about food…and other things. No matter how good the feast, you're always ready for more in a few hours."

"How old are you? Sixteen?" Ridge asked with a roll of his eyes.

"Old enough to thoroughly enjoy my pizza and everything that goes along with it," Taft said with another grin. "But you boys have fun cutting down your Christmas trees."

"You in?" Ridge asked Trace.

Since he didn't have a pizza buddy right now—or any other kind of euphemistically termed acquaintance—Trace figured he might as well. "Sure. I'm up for a ride. Let's go find a tree."

He could use a ride into the mountains. It might help clear the cobwebs out of his head from a week of double shifts.

The decision had been a good one, he decided a half hour later as he rode his favorite buckskin mare, Genie, up the trail leading to the evergreen forest above the ranch. He had needed to get out into the mountains on horseback again. The demands of his job as head honcho in an overworked and underfunded police department often left him with too little leisure time. He ought to make more time for himself, though. Right now, with feathery snowflakes drifting down and the air smelling crisp and clean, he wouldn't want to be anywhere else.

He loved River Bow Ranch. This was home, despite the bad memories and their grim past. Counting Destry now, five generations of Bowmans had made their home here, starting just after World War I with his great-grandfather. It was a lovely spot, named not only for the family name but also for the oxbow in Cold Creek that was a beautiful nesting spot in the summer for geese and swans.

Below the ranch, he could see the lights of Pine Gulch gleaming in the dusk. His town. Yeah, it might sound like something out of an old Western, but he loved this little slice of western heaven. He'd had offers from bigger departments around Idaho and even a couple out of state. A few of them were tempting, he couldn't deny that. But every time he thought about leaving Pine Gulch, he thought about all the things he would have to give up. His family, his heritage, the comfort of small traditions like breakfast at The Gulch after an overnight shift. The sacrifices seemed too great.

"Thanks for coming with us," Destry said, reining her tough little paint pony next to his mare.

"My pleasure. Thanks for asking me, kid." His niece was turning into a good rider. Ridge had set her on the back of a horse from just about the moment she could walk and it showed. She had a confident seat, an easy grace, that had already won her some junior rodeo competitions.

"Are you finally going to put up a tree this year, Uncle Trace?"

"I don't know. Seems like a lot of trouble when it's only me."

He hated admitting that but it was true. He was tired of being alone. A year ago, he thought he was ready to settle down. He'd even started dating Easton Springhill. From here, he could see across the canyon and up to where she ran her family's place, Winder Ranch.

Easton wasn't for him. Some part of him had known it even as he'd tried to convince himself otherwise. Just *how* wrong she'd been for him had become abundantly clear when Cisco Del Norte came back to town and he saw for himself just how much Easton loved the man.

The two of them were deliriously happy now. They had adopted a little girl, who was just about the cutest thing he'd ever seen, all big eyes and curly black hair and dimples, and Easton was expecting a baby in the spring. While Trace still wasn't crazy about Cisco, he had to admit the guy made Easton happy.

He had tried to convince himself he was in love with Easton but he recognized now that effort had been mostly based on hope. Oh, he probably could have fallen in love with her if he'd given a little more effort to it. Easton was great—warm and compassionate and certainly beautiful enough. They could have made a good life together here, but theirs would never have been the fierce passion she shared with Cisco.

A passion he couldn't help envying.

Maybe he would always be the bachelor uncle. It wasn't necessarily a bad role in life, he thought as Destry urged her pony faster on the trail.

"Almost there!" she exclaimed, her face beaming.

A few moments later they reached the thickly forested border of the ranch. Destry was quick to lead the way to the tree she had picked out months ago and marked with an orange plastic ribbon, just as their mother used to do.

Ridge cut the tree quickly with his chain saw while Destry looked on with glee. Caidy and a couple of her dogs had come up, as well—Trace had left Grunt, the ugly little French bulldog he'd inherited from Wally Taylor, back at the ranch house since the dog couldn't have kept up with the horses on his stubby little legs.

His sister didn't help cut down the tree, only stood on the outskirts of the forest, gazing down at town.

"How about you?" his brother asked. "You want us to cut one for you while we're up here?"

His brother asked every year and every year Trace

gave the same answer. "Not much sense when it's just me. Especially since I'll be working through Christmas, anyway."

Since he didn't have a family, he always tried to work overtime so his officers who did could have a little extra time off to spend with their children.

Caidy glanced over at them and he saw his own melancholy reflected in her eyes. Christmas was a hell of a time for the Bowman family. It probably always would be. He hated that she felt she had to hide away from life here with the horses and the dogs she trained.

"Hey, do you think we could cut an extra tree down for my friend?" Destry asked him.

"I don't mind. You'll have to ask your dad, though."

"Ask me what?" Ridge asked, busy tying the sled to his saddle for his horse to pull down the mountain.

"I wanted to give a tree to one of my friends."

"That shouldn't be a problem. We've got plenty of trees. But are you sure her family doesn't already have one?"

Destry shook her head. "She said they might not even put up a tree this year. They don't have very much money. They just moved to Pine Gulch and I don't think she likes it here very much."

Trace felt the same sort of tingle in his fingertips he always got when something was about to break on a case. "What's this friend's name?"

"Gabi. Well, Gabrielle. Gabrielle Parsons."

Of course. Somehow he'd known, even before Destry told him the name. He thought of the pretty, inept waitress with the secrets in her eyes and of the girl who had sat reading her book with such solemn concentration in the midst of the morning chaos at The Gulch.

"I met her the other day. She and her mother moved in near my house."

Both Ridge and Caidy gave him matching looks of curiosity and he shrugged. "She's apparently old Wally Taylor's granddaughter. He left the house to her, though I gather they didn't have much of a relationship."

"You really do know everything about what goes on in Pine Gulch," Caidy said with an admiring tone.

Trace tried his best to look humble. "I try. Actually, the mother is waitressing at The Gulch. I stopped there the other day for breakfast and ended up with the whole story from Donna."

"What you're saying, then," Ridge said, his voice dry, "is that *Donna* is the one in town who knows when every dog lifts his leg on a fire hydrant."

Trace grinned. "Yeah. So? A good police officer knows how to cultivate sources wherever he can find them."

"So can we cut a tree for Gabrielle and her mom?" Destry asked impatiently.

He remembered the secrets in the woman's eyes and her unease around him. He had thought about her several times in the few days since he'd seen her at the diner and his curiosity about why she had ended up in Pine Gulch hadn't abated whatsoever. He had promised himself he would try to be a good neighbor. What was more neighborly than delivering a Christmas tree?

"I don't see the problem with that. I can drop it off on my way home. Help me pick a good one for them."

Destry gave a jubilant cheer and grabbed his hand. "I saw the perfect one before. Come on, over here."

She dragged him about twenty feet away, stopping in front of a bushy blue spruce. "How about this one?"

The tree easily topped nine feet and was probably that big in circumference. Trace smiled at his niece's eagerness. "I'm sorry, hon, but if I remember correctly, I think that one is a little too big for the living room of their house. What about this nice one over here?" He led her to a seven-foot Scotch pine with a nice, natural Christmas-tree shape.

She gave the tree a considering sort of look. "I guess that would work."

"Here, you can help me cut it down, then." He fired up Ridge's chain saw and guided his niece's hands. Together they cut the tree down and Trace tied it to his own horse's saddle.

"I hope Gabrielle will love it. You're going to take it to her tonight, right?" she demanded, proving once more that she was nothing like her selfish mother except in appearance. Destry was always thinking about other people and how she could help them, much like Trace's mother, the grandmother she had never met.

"I promise. But let's get it down the hill first, okay?"

"Okay." Destry smiled happily.

As they headed back toward River Bow Ranch while the sun finally slipped behind the western mountains, a completely ridiculous little bubble of excitement churned through him, like he was a kid waiting in line to see Santa Claus. He tried to tell himself he was only picking up on Destry's anticipation at doing a kind deed for her friend, but in his heart Trace knew there was more to it.

He wanted to see Becca Parsons again. Simple as that. The memory of her, slim and pretty and obviously uncomfortable around him, played in his head over and over. She was a mystery to him, that was all. He wanted only to get to know a few of her secrets and make sure she didn't intend to cause trouble in his town.

If anybody asked, that was his story and he was sticking to it.

Chapter 3

How did parents survive this homework battle day in and day out for *years*?

Becca drew in a deep, cleansing breath in a fierce effort to keep from growling in frustration at her sister and smoothed the worksheet out in front of them. They had only four more math problems and one would think she was asking Gabi to rip out her eyelashes one by one instead of just finish a little long division.

"We're almost done, Gab. Come on. You can do it."

"Of course I *can* do it." Though she was a foot and a half shorter than Becca, Gabi still somehow managed to look down her nose at her. "I just don't see why I have to."

"Because it's your homework, honey, that's why." Becca tried valiantly for patience. "If you don't finish it, you'll receive a failing grade in math."

"And?"

Becca curled her fingers into fists. Her sister was ferociously bright but had zero motivation, something Becca found frustrating beyond belief considering how very hard she had worked at school, the brief times she had been enrolled. In those days, she would rather have been the one ripping out her eyelashes herself rather than miss an assignment.

Not that her overachieving ways and conscientious study habits had gotten her very far.

She gazed around at the small, dingy house with its old-fashioned wallpaper and the water stains on the ceiling. She had a sudden memory of her elegant town house in an exclusive gated Scottsdale community, trim and neat with its chili-pepper-red door and the matching potted yucca plants fronting the entry. She suddenly missed her house with a longing that bordered on desperation. She would never have that place back. Her mother had effectively taken it from her, just like she'd taken so many other things.

She pushed away her bitterness. She had made her own choices. No one had forced her to sell her town house and use the equity to pay back her mother's fraud victims. She could have taken her chances that she might have been able to slither out of the mess Monica had left her with her career—if not her reputation—intact.

Again, not the issue here. She was as bad as Gabi, letting her mind wander over paths she could no longer change.

"If you flunk out of fourth grade, my darling sister, I'll have to homeschool you and we both know I'll be much tougher on you than any public school teacher. Come on. Four more questions."

Gabi gave a heavy sigh and picked up her pencil again, apparently tired of pitting her formidable will against Becca's. She finished the problems without any noticeable effort and then set down her pencil.

"There. Are you happy now?"

As Becca expected, her sister finished the problems perfectly. "See, that wasn't so tough, now, was it?"

Gabi opened her mouth to answer but before she could get the words out, the doorbell rang, making them both jump. The sudden hope that leaped into Gabi's eyes broke Becca's heart. She wanted to hug her, tell her all over again that Monica wasn't likely to come back.

"I'll get it," the girl said quickly, and disregarding all Becca's strictures about basic safety precautions, she flung open the door.

If ever a girl needed to heed stranger danger, it was now, Becca thought with a spurt of panic at the sight of the Pine Gulch chief of police standing on her doorstep. Trace Bowman looked dark and dangerous in the twilight and all her self-protective instincts ramped up into high gear.

Gabi looked disappointed for only a moment before she hid her emotions behind impassivity and eased away from the door to let Becca take the lead.

"Chief Bowman," she finally murmured. "This is… unexpected."

Not to mention unfortunate, unwelcome, unwanted.

"I know. Sorry to barge in like this but I've been charged with an important mission."

She glanced at Gabi and saw a flicker of curiosity in her sister's eyes.

The police chief seemed to be concealing something out of sight of the doorway but she couldn't tell what it was from this angle.

"What sort of mission?" Becca was unsuccessful in keeping her wariness from her voice.

"Well, funny story. My niece, Destry, apparently is in the same school class as your daughter."

She couldn't correct his misstatement since she was the one who had perpetrated the lie. She shot a quick look at Gabi, willing her to keep her mouth shut. At the same time, she realized how rude she must appear to the police chief, keeping him standing on the sagging porch. She ought to invite him inside but she really didn't want him in her space. On the porch was still too close.

"Yes, Gabi's mentioned Destry."

"She's a great kid. Always concerned about those she counts as friends."

And he was telling her this why, exactly? She smiled politely, hoping he would get to the point and then ride off into the sunset on his trusty steed. Or maybe that pickup truck she could see parked in the driveway.

To her surprise, he appeared slightly uncomfortable. She thought she detected a hint of color on his cheekbones and he cleared his throat before he spoke again. "Anyway, Destry said Gabrielle told her you didn't have a Christmas tree yet and your daughter didn't know if you'd be putting one up this year."

She narrowed her gaze at Gabi, who returned the look with an innocent look. They had talked about putting a tree up. She'd promised her sister they would find something after payday the next week. She had to wonder if the concern from Chief Bowman's niece was spontaneous or if Gabi had somehow planted the seed somewhere.

"I'm sure we'll get something. We just… Between moving in and settling into school and work, we haven't had much free time for, um, holiday decorating. It's not even December yet."

"I tried to tell Destry that but when we went up into the mountains this afternoon to find a tree for the ranch house, she had her heart set on cutting one for you, too. Look at it this way. One less thing you have to worry about, right?"

Finally he moved the arm concealed around the door-jamb so she could see that he was indeed holding a Christmas tree, dark green and fragrant.

"You don't get any fresher than this one. We just cut it about an hour ago."

A tree? From the chief of police? What kind of town was this?

She hadn't put up a Christmas tree in, well, ever. It had seemed far too much trouble when she was living alone. Besides, she had never had all that much to celebrate, busy with clients and contracts and court filings.

For an instant, she was transported to her very best memory of Christmas, when she was seven or eight and Monica had been working to empty the bank account of a lonely widower who had either been genuinely fond of Becca or had been very good at pretending. He had filled his house with Christmas decorations and presents. A wreath on the door, stockings hanging on the mantel, the whole bit.

She had really liked the old guy—until he'd called the police on Monica when he began to suspect she was stealing from them, and Becca and her mother had had to flee just a few steps from the law.

Now here was the chief of police standing on her doorstep with this lovely, sweet-smelling Christmas tree. "I…oh."

She didn't know what to say and her obvious discomfort must have begun to communicate itself to Trace Bowman.

"I can find another home for it if you don't want it," he finally said as the pause lengthened.

"Oh, please." Gabrielle clasped her hands together at her heart as if she were starring in some cheesy melodrama and trying desperately to avoid being tied to the railroad tracks by some dastardly villain. It was completely an act. *The part of Pleading Young Girl will be played tonight by the incomparable Gabrielle Parsons.*

Becca had no choice but to give in with as much grace as she could muster. And then figure out how she was going to afford lights and ornaments for the dratted thing.

"A tree would be lovely, I'm sure. Thank you very much." She *was* grateful. Her half sister might have the soul of a thirty-year-old con artist in a nine-year-old's body, but she was still a child. She deserved whatever poor similitude of Christmas Becca could manage.

"I didn't know if you would have a tree stand so I snagged a spare from the ranch house. If you'll just let me know where you want it, I can set this baby up for you."

"That's not necessary. I'm sure I can figure it out."

"Have you ever set a real tree up before?"

Real or fake, she didn't know the first thing about a Christmas tree. Honesty compelled her to shake her head.

"It's harder than it looks. Consider the setup all part of the service."

He didn't wait for her to give him permission; he just carried the tree through the door and into her living room, bringing that sweet, wintry-tart smell and memories of happier times she had nearly forgotten.

"It's beautiful," Gabi exclaimed. "I think that might be the most beautiful tree I've ever seen."

Becca studied her sister. She couldn't say she'd figured out all her moods yet, but Gabi certainly looked sincere in her delight. Her eyes shone with excitement, her face bright and as happy as she'd seen it yet over the past two months. Maybe Becca was entirely too cynical. It was Christmas. Gabi had a right to her excitement.

"It really is a pretty tree," she agreed. "Where would you like Chief Bowman to put it, kiddo?"

"Right there facing the front window, then everyone will see it."

Gabi was full of surprises tonight. She usually preferred to stay inconspicuous to avoid drawing attention to herself. Becca had been the same way, trained well by a mother who was always just a pace or two ahead of the law.

Trace carried the tree over to the window and positioned it. The tree fit perfectly in the space, exactly the right height, as if he'd measured it.

"Right here?" he asked, his attention focused on Gabi.

"Maybe a little more to the left."

With a slightly amused expression, he moved the tree in that direction. When Gabi nodded he slanted a look at Becca. She shrugged. Christmas tree positioning wasn't exactly in her skill set. Right along with waiting tables and trying to raise a precocious nine-year-old girl.

"Gabrielle, would you mind going back out onto porch for the tree stand I left there?" he asked. "I don't want to move from the perfect spot."

She hurried out eagerly and returned shortly with the green metal tree stand.

"Okay, I'm going to lift the tree and you set the stand with the hole right underneath the trunk. Got it?"

She nodded solemnly. When Trace effortlessly lifted the tree, she slid the stand where he indicated. Becca couldn't help but compare her eagerness to help Trace with the tree to her grave reluctance a few moments earlier to finish four measly math problems.

For the next few moments, Trace held the tree and instructed Gabi to tighten the bolts of the stand around the trunk in a particular order for the best stability.

Becca watched their efforts with a growing amusement that surprised her. She shouldn't be enjoying this. This was the police chief, she reminded herself, but it was hard to remember that when he was laughing with Gabi about the tree that seemed determined to list drunkenly to the side.

"I'm beginning to see why people prefer artificial trees."

"Oh, blasphemy!" He aimed a mock frown in her direction. "What about that heavenly smell?"

"A ninety-nine-cent car air freshener can give you the same thing without the sap and the needles all over the carpet."

He shook his head with a rueful smile but didn't argue and she was painfully aware of the highly inconvenient little simmer of attraction. He was an extraordinarily good-looking man, with those startling green eyes and a hint of afternoon shadow along his jawline. Avoiding him would be far easier if the dratted man didn't stir up all kinds of ridiculous feelings.

"I'll clean up the needles, I promise."

To Becca's surprise, Gabrielle seemed to glow with excitement. She was such a funny kid. Becca was no closer to figuring out this curious little stranger than she was two months ago when Monica had dumped her in her lap.

"Okay, moment of truth." Trace stepped back to look at his handiwork. "Does that look straight to you two?"

Gabrielle moved toward Becca for a better perspective and cocked her head to the side. "It looks great to me. What about you, Be—um, *Mom*?"

Gabi stumbled only slightly over the word but it was still a surprising mistake. Her sister was remarkably adept at deception. No surprise there since she'd been bottle-fed it since birth. Becca glanced at the police chief but he didn't seem to have noticed anything amiss and she spoke quickly to distract him.

"Looks straight to me, too."

"I think you're both right. It *is* straight. Amazing! That didn't take long at all. You've got some serious tree setup skills, young lady."

Much to Becca's astonishment, her sister giggled. Actually giggled. Gabrielle blinked a little, clearly surprised at the sound herself.

"Now what are we going to decorate it with?" the girl asked.

"I've got a couple strings of lights out in the truck. We can start with that."

"I can probably find something around here," Becca said quickly. "If not, I can pick some up tomorrow."

She didn't want him here. It was too dangerous. The more time they spent with the police chief, the greater the chance that either she or Gabi would slip again and he would figure out things weren't quite as they seemed. She had the distinct impression he was suspicious enough of them and she didn't want to raise any more red flags.

Her unwilling attraction to him only further complicated the situation. She just wanted him to leave so she could go back to duct-taping her life back together.

"I've already got the lights out in my truck. Why go to so much trouble of tracking down more?"

"You've already done more than enough."

"Here's something good to know about me." Trace grinned. "I'm the kind of guy who likes to see things through."

For an insane instant, she imagined just how he would kiss a woman—with thorough, meticulous intensity. Those green eyes would turn to smoke as he took great care to explore and taste every inch of her mouth with his until she was soft and pliant and ready to throw every caution out the window....

She blinked away the entirely too appealing image to find Trace watching her. His eyes weren't smoky now, only curious, as if wondering what she was thinking. Heat rushed to her cheeks with her blush, something she hadn't done in a long time. He wouldn't be talked out of helping them decorate the tree. Somehow she knew she was stuck in this untenable situation and continuing to protest would only make him wonder why she was so ardently determined to avoid his company.

Gabi was obviously pleased to have him here and it seemed churlish of Becca to make a deal about it. How long would it take to decorate a tree, anyway?

"Thank you, then. I think I saw a box of old ornaments up in the attic in my...my grandfather's things."

"Great. I guess we're in business." He headed for the door and returned a moment later with a box that had Extra Christmas Lights written on it with black permanent marker in what looked like a woman's handwriting. He didn't have a wife, she knew, so who had written those words? Maybe he had an ex or a steady girlfriend. Not that it was any of her business who might be writing on his boxes, she reminded herself.

He immediately started untangling the light strings and she watched long, well-formed fingers move nimbly for a moment then jerked her attention away when she realized she was staring.

"Gabi, come help me look for the ornaments."

Reluctance flitted across the girl's features as if she didn't want to leave Trace Bowman's presence, either, but she followed Becca up the narrow stairs to the cramped storage space under the eaves adjacent to the room Gabi had claimed as her own bedroom.

The space smelled musty and dusty and was piled with boxes and trunks Becca had barely had time to even look at in the few weeks they'd been in Pine Gulch. She pulled the string on the bare-bulb light and could swear she heard something scurry. They needed a cat, she thought. She didn't want to add one more responsibility to her plate but a good mouser would be just the thing.

"I think I saw the ornaments somewhere over by the window. Help me look, would you?"

She and Gabi began sorting through boxes filled with the detritus of a lonely old man's life. It made her inexpressibly sad to think about the grandfather she hadn't even known existed. Monica had told her very little about the paternal side of her heritage. She had known her father had died when she was just a baby and Monica had told her she didn't have any other living relatives on either side.

Big surprise. She'd lied. This was just one more thing her mother had stolen from her.

"He's nice, isn't he?"

She glanced at Gabi, who was looking toward the doorway and the stairs with a pensive sort of look.

"He's the police chief, Gab. You know what that means."

"We haven't done anything wrong here."

"Except tell the world I'm your mother."

She never should have done it, but it was one of those tiny lies that had quickly grown out of control. When she'd tried to enroll Gabi in school after they arrived in Pine Gulch, Becca had suddenly realized she didn't have any sort of guardianship papers or even a birth certificate. Worried that Gabi would be taken from her and placed into foster care, she had fudged the paperwork at the school. Thinking the school authorities would be more likely to take her word for things if she was Gabi's mother rather than merely an older sister, she had called upon the grifting skills she hadn't used in years to convince the secretary she didn't know where Gabi's birth certificate was after a succession of moves—not technically a lie.

The secretary had been gratifyingly understanding and told Becca merely to bring them when she could find them. From that moment, they were stuck in the lie. She didn't want to think about Trace Bowman's reaction if he found out she was perpetrating a fraud on the school and the community. She wasn't a poor single mother trying to eke out a living with her daughter. She was stuck in a situation that seemed to grow more complicated by the minute.

"I still think he's nice," Gabi said. "He brought us a Christmas tree."

She wanted to warn her sister to run far, far away from sexy men bearing warm smiles and unexpected charm. "You're right. That was a very kind thing to do. Actually, it was his niece's idea, right? You must have made a good friend in Destry Bowman."

"She's nice," Gabi said, avoiding her gaze. "Where do you think you saw the ornaments?"

An interesting reaction. She frowned at Gabi but didn't comment, especially when her sister found the box of ornaments just a moment later, next to a box of 1950s-era women's clothing.

Her grandmother's, perhaps? From the attorney who notified her of the bequest, she had learned the woman had died years ago, before she was born, but other than that she didn't know anything about her. Since coming to Pine Gulch, she had been thinking how surreal it was to live in her grandfather's house when she didn't know anything about him, surrounded by the personal belongings of a stranger.

She had picked up bits and pieces since she'd arrived in town that indicated that her father and grandfather had fought bitterly before she was born. She didn't know the full story and wasn't sure she ever would, but Donna told her that her father had apparently vowed never to speak to his own father again. She could guess the reason. Probably her mother had something to do with it. Monica was very good at finding ways to destroy relationships around her.

Kenneth Taylor had been killed in a motorcycle crash when Becca was a toddler and her parents had never been married. Her only memories of him were a bushy mustache and sideburns and a deep, warm voice telling her stories at night.

She'd been curious about her father's family over the years, but Monica had refused to talk about him. She hadn't even known her grandfather was still alive until she'd heard from that Idaho Falls attorney a few months earlier, right in the middle of her own legal trouble. When he had told her she had inherited a small house in Idaho, the news had seemed an answer to prayer. She had been thinking she and Gabi would wind up homeless if she couldn't figure something out and suddenly she had learned she owned a house in a town she'd never visited.

This sturdy little Craftsman cottage was dark and neglected, but she knew she could make a happy home here for her and Gabi, their lies notwithstanding.

As long as the police chief left her alone.

Females with secrets. He'd certainly seen his share of those.

Trace carefully wound the colored lights on the branches of their Christmas tree, listening to Becca and Gabi talk quietly as they pulled glass ornaments from a cardboard box. Something was not exactly as it appeared in this household. He couldn't put his finger on what precisely it might be but he'd caught more than one unreadable exchange of glances between Becca and her daughter, as if they were each warning the other to be careful with her words.

What secrets could they have? He had to wonder if they were on the run from something. A jealous ex? A custody dispute? That was the logical conclusion but not one that sat comfortably with him. He didn't like the idea that Becca might be breaking the law, or worse, in danger somehow. That would certainly make his attraction for her even more inconvenient.

He couldn't have said why he was still here. His plan when Destry had begged him to do this had been to merely do a quick drop-off of the tree, the stand and the lights. He'd intended to let Becca and Gabi deal with the tree while he headed down the street for a comfortable night of basketball in front of the big screen with his squash-faced little dog at his feet.

Instead, when he had shown up on the doorstep, she had looked so obviously taken aback—and touched, despite herself—that he had decided spending a little time with the two of them was more fascinating than even the most fierce battle on the hardwood.

He wasn't sorry. Gabi was a great kid. Smart and funny, with clever little observations about life. She, at least, had been thrilled by the donated Christmas tree, almost as if she'd never had a tree before. At some point, Gabi had tuned in on a Christmas station on a small boom box–type radio she brought from her bedroom. Though he still wasn't a big fan of the holiday, he couldn't deny there was something very appealing about working together on a quiet evening while snowflakes fluttered down outside and Nat King Cole's velvet voice filled the room.

It reminded him of happier memories when he was a kid, before the Christmas that had changed everything.

"That's the last of the lights. You ready to flip the switch?"

"Can I?" Gabi asked, her eyes bright.

"Sure thing."

She plugged in the lights and they reflected green and red and gold in her eyes. "It looks wonderful!"

"It really does," Becca agreed. "Thank you for your help."

Her words were another clear dismissal and he decided to ignore it. He wasn't quite ready to leave this warm room yet. "Now we can start putting up those ornaments."

She chewed her lip, clearly annoyed with him, but he only smiled and reached into the box for a couple of colored globes.

"So where were you before you moved to Pine Gulch?" he asked after a few moments of hanging ornaments. Though he pitted his question as casual curiosity, she didn't seem fooled.

Becca and her daughter exchanged another look and she waited a moment before answering. "Arizona," she finally said, her voice terse.

"Were you waitressing there?"

"No. I did a lot of different things," she said evasively. "What about you? How long have you been chief of police for the good people of Pine Gulch?"

He saw through her attempt to deflect his questions. He was fond of the same technique when he wanted to guide a particular discussion in an interview. He thought about calling her on it but decided to let her set the tone. This wasn't an interrogation, after all. Only a conversation.

"I've been on the force for about ten years, chief for the last three."

"You seem young for the job."

"I'm thirty-two. Not that young. You must have been a baby yourself when you had Gabi, right?"

He thought he saw a tiny flicker of something indefinable in the depths of her hazel eyes but she quickly concealed it. "Something like that. I was eighteen when she was born. What about you? Any wife and kiddos in the picture?"

Again the diversionary tactics. Interesting. "Nope. Never married. Just my brothers and a sister."

"And you all live close?"

"Right. My older brother runs the family ranch, the River Bow, just outside town. We run about six hundred head. My younger sister helps him around the ranch and with Destry. Then my twin brother, Taft, is the fire chief. You might have seen him around town. He's a little hard to miss since we're identical."

"Wow. There are two of you?"

"Nope. Only one. Taft is definitely his own man."

She smiled a little as she reached to hang an ornament on a higher branch. Her soft curves brushed his shoulder—completely accidental, he knew—and his stomach muscles contracted. He hadn't felt this little zing of attraction in a long, long time and he wanted to savor every moment of it, despite his better instincts reminding him he knew very little about the woman and what he did know didn't seem completely truthful.

She moved away to the other side of the tree and picked up a pearly white globe ornament from the box.

He thought her color was a little higher than it had been before but that could have been only the reflection from the Christmas lights.

"You haven't had the urge to explore distant pastures? See what's out there beyond Pine Gulch?"

"Been there, done that. I spent four years as a Marine MP, with tours in the Middle East, Germany, Japan. I was ready to be back home."

He didn't like to think about what had happened after he came home, restless and looking for trouble. He'd found it, far more than he ever imagined, in the form of a devious little liar named Lilah Bodine.

"And the small-town life appeals to you?"

"Pine Gulch is a nice place to live. You won't find a prettier place on earth in the summertime and people here watch out for each other."

"I'm not sure that's always a good thing, is it? Isn't that small-town code for snooping in other people's business?"

What in her past had made her so cynical? And what business did she have that made her eager to keep others out of it?

"That's one way of looking at it, I suppose. Some people find it a comfort to know they've always got someone to turn to when times are tough."

"I'm used to counting on myself."

Before he could respond to that, Gabi popped her head around the side of the Christmas tree, a small porcelain angel with filigree wings in her hand. "This was the last ornament in the box," she said. "Where should I put it?"

Becca looked at the tree. "Well, we don't have anything at the top. Why don't we put her there?"

"That seems about right," Trace said. "A tree as pretty as this one deserves to have an angel watching over it."

"Okay. I'll have to get a chair."

"Why?" He grinned at the girl and picked her up. She seemed skinny for her age and she giggled a little as he hefted her higher to reach the top of the tree. She tucked the little angel against the top branch and secured her with the clip attached to her back.

"Perfect," Gabi exclaimed when she was done.

He lowered her to the ground and the girl hurried to turn off the light switch to the overhead fixture and the two lamps until the room was dark except for the gleaming, colorful tree.

They all stepped back a little for a better look. Much to his surprise, as he stood in this dark, dingy little house with that soft music in the background and the snow drifting past the window and the tree lights flickering, he felt the first nudge of Christmas spirit he'd experienced in a long, long time.

"It's magical," Gabi breathed.

Becca leaned down and hugged her. "You know what, kiddo? *Magical* is exactly the right word."

They all stood still for a moment. Becca was the first to break the spell.

"I'm sorry we kept you so long." She smiled at him and he had the feeling it was the most genuine smile she'd ever given him. "You didn't need to stay to help us decorate the whole thing."

"You didn't see me rushing for the door, did you?" he answered. "I could have left anytime. If I hadn't been enjoying myself, I would have been gone. I don't usually get into Christmas, but this was fun."

She gave him a curious look, as if surprised that he

could possibly enjoy something so tame as decorating a tree. He wasn't sure he could explain it to her when he didn't quite understand it himself.

"Would you like some cocoa?" she asked, and he had the vague impression the invitation hadn't been planned.

He was tempted by the offer, more tempted than he should have been, but he was beginning to think regaining a little distance between them would be smart.

"Another time, maybe. I've got an early day tomorrow. I dropped my dog off at home after we cut the tree down and I probably need to head back and put him out."

She nodded and walked him to the door, where he retrieved his parka from the hook by the door. "Well, thank you again," she said. "It really was a kind thing to do. Please tell your niece we appreciate it."

"I'll do that." He shrugged into his coat. He reached for the door handle, then completely on impulse, leaned in and kissed her cheek. She smelled delicious, sweetly female, and her skin was warm against his mouth.

It was a crazy gesture and totally unlike him and he had no idea what had compelled him. Must be some weird holiday insanity. When he drew away, she was staring at him, her eyes as huge as Gabi's had been when she first saw the tree.

"Good night," he said quickly and opened the door before she could respond.

What just happened there? he wondered as he climbed into his pickup for the half-block drive to his house. He really had planned to just drop off the tree and go. Instead, he had spent more than an hour helping her set up the tree and then decorate it. And then he had complicated matters by that ridiculous brush of his mouth on her cheek.

He felt sorry for the woman and her kid. That was all. She was obviously in a tight spot financially. She was alone in a new town without friends or family. He was only helping her out, doing just what any good neighbor would do.

He refused to think he allowed himself any other motive. He wasn't at all eager to throw his heart out there again—and if he did, he certainly wouldn't hand it over to a woman like Becca who was obviously hiding something from him. He'd learned his lesson about lying women.

Chapter 4

"Would any of you like a refill?" With the pot of decaf in one hand and the good stuff in the other, Becca smiled at The Gulch regulars, a group that had met there every single morning since she'd started working at the diner.

She had come to find great comfort in their consistency, listening to them bicker and joke around with each other and other restaurant patrons. Though they all apparently came from very different demographic and socioeconomic backgrounds, they seemed like a family, dysfunctions and all.

"Top me off, would you?" Mick Malone gestured to his cup and she was rather proud of herself for remembering he drank only decaf. She managed to pour his refill without spilling a drop, another mark of just how far she'd apparently come in the nearly two weeks since she'd started working at the diner.

"Another stack, Sal? I can have Lou throw a few more cakes on the griddle."

"This ought to hold me until lunch, darlin'."

She smiled at the older cowboy. He had to be in his seventies and so skinny he probably had trouble keeping his jeans up, but the guy had the metabolism of a hummingbird, apparently, and could eat every other one of the regulars under the table.

"Anyone else need anything?"

"I'll take one of those pretty smiles if you've got another one to spare." Jesse Redbear, missing his left front tooth, gave her a flirtatious grin that lifted all his wrinkles. She shook her head but couldn't resist a smile.

"That's the one." He winked at her. "I think I'm good now."

She shook her head again. "I'll check on you all again in a minute," she said, then moved to the other side of her section to check on a couple of customers who had just sat down.

She couldn't say she would be sorry to leave waitressing behind when she finished the requirements to transfer to the Idaho state bar, but she had certainly learned a lot the past few weeks working at The Gulch. She had learned that sometimes the stingiest-looking customers could be the biggest tippers, that keeping beverages topped off could go a long way and that sometimes a friendly, apologetic smile could make all but the most dour customers forgive her frequent mistakes.

"Order up," Lou called from the grill, and she finished taking the newcomers' orders then headed back to pick up the breakfast specials for a young family she'd seen around town before. When the bell chimed on the door, heralding a new arrival, she looked up just as everyone else did.

The chief of police walked in looking dark and gorgeous, and her stomach fluttered wildly, until she noticed the pretty ski-bunny type who came in with him, hanging on his arm as if she were a bounty hunter and he was prey about to escape.

They didn't take a table, just stood for a moment near the entrance. To Becca's dismay, he gave the woman a playful kiss and it was obvious they'd just spent the night together. Her stomach dived down to her feet and she thought of how stupid she'd been to have cherished that sweet little kiss on the cheek he'd given her nearly a week earlier when he'd come to help them with their Christmas tree.

"Come have a cup of coffee at least," he said in a low bedroom voice.

"I can't stay," the woman protested. "I'm already late for work. I'll see you later, though, right?"

"Plan on it." He kissed her again, and the ditzy-looking woman left the diner with a longing sort of backward glance.

Becca somehow wasn't surprised when he sat down in her section. Annoyed with herself for the completely unreasonable jealousy seething through her, she set the menu down in front of him with a little more brusqueness than normal. "Good morning, Chief. Do you want coffee this morning?"

She heard the coolness in her voice and he must have picked up on it, too, because he finally met her gaze with a surprised sort of look. Becca faltered. This wasn't Trace Bowman. It must be his twin, she realized with growing mortification.

"I'm so sorry. You're not Chief Bowman."

"Actually, I am. Just not the *only* Chief Bowman."

Trace's twin was the fire chief, she remembered belatedly. Now that she had a better look at him, she realized that while they were identical twins, there were definite differences. This Bowman was a little broader in the shoulders, his hair was a little shaggier and he didn't come across quite as dangerously masculine.

And apparently he was the ladies' man of the family. He gave her a charmer of a grin. "I'm the better-looking chief."

"I'm sorry. I forgot you were twins."

"I'm Taft Bowman, with the Pine Gulch Fire Department." He held out a hand to shake hers and she had no real choice but to reach out to return the gesture.

"I'm Rebecca Parsons."

"Right. You're new in town, Wally Taylor's granddaughter. You must be the one with the kid our Destry's age."

Our Destry. She had to admit, she was touched by his words, as if the entire Bowman clan seemed to take responsibility for the little girl. That sort of family unity was completely beyond anything in her experience.

"That's right." She gave him a smile she hoped was slightly warmer. "Do you need time to look at the menu or do you know what you want?"

This was another thing she'd learned in her few weeks working at The Gulch. Townsfolk generally already had their orders picked out before they ever walked through the doors.

"I'm in the mood for a ham-and-cheese omelet this morning. Think you can talk Lou into making one for me?"

Apparently Taft Bowman had enough experience with Lou that he knew he could sometimes be in a mood. "I'll certainly ask him. He's done a few other omelets this morning, so keep your fingers crossed. I think you should be safe."

His green eyes that seemed just like Trace's gleamed appreciatively as he smiled at her. He was every bit as good-looking as his brother and she wondered why his smile didn't stir her hormones in the slightest. She was as unmoved by his flirting as she had been by Jesse Redbear's.

Maybe it was because the fire chief was an obvious player, judging by the woman who had just left. But she had a feeling if Trace had looked at her that way, she would have dissolved into a puddle all over the peeled plank floor of The Gulch.

"The fire chief would like a ham-and-cheese omelet."

Lou frowned as he turned some sizzling bacon on the grill. "That can probably be arranged."

She realized after she gave the order that she'd forgotten to ask Trace's brother if he wanted coffee. By the time she turned back to remedy her mistake, he had swiveled around in his booth and was talking to a couple of middle-aged women at the next table, who simpered and blushed at his teasing.

She fought an amused smile as she headed back toward his booth. "Coffee, Chief?"

He aimed that flirtatious grin at her. "Thanks. Give me the high-octane stuff."

She had only started to pour when the door opened again and the *other* Chief Bowman walked inside. How could she ever have mistaken Taft for his brother? They weren't anything alike, she saw now. Her stomach gave a silly little swoop and she remembered again the soft brush of his mouth on her skin.

"Um. Ow."

She jerked her gaze away at the calm words and was horror-stricken to realize she had splashed hot coffee on the fire chief's leg.

"Oh. Oh! I'm so sorry. Let me just…" She pulled off the towel tucked into her apron and began dabbing at the spot. He eased back in the booth and gave her an amused look, and she was painfully aware of Trace walking toward their table. When he reached it, he stood there for a moment watching her dab at his brother's thigh before he cleared his throat.

"What have we here?"

"Just a little coffee mishap," his twin said. "No worries. It's probably not even a third-degree burn."

"I've been doing so well all morning," she wailed, then glared at Trace. "Why did you have to come in and ruin everything?"

Oh, she hadn't meant to say that. She was suddenly aware that both men were watching her with interest. Heat rushed to her face and she wanted to sink through the floor with mortification. Trace Bowman made her nervous and off balance and now everyone in the diner within earshot knew it.

She took a deep breath and pulled the towel away from the fire chief, praying for composure.

"I really am sorry," she said to him.

"I'm fine," he said again. "My Levi's took the brunt of it."

To her vast relief, Lou rang the bell in the window. "Order up," he called.

"That would be your omelet, Chief."

Trace, just sliding into the booth across from his brother, gave her a teasing smile. "How'd you know I was in the mood for an omelet?"

"Get your own. That one's mine." Taft gave him a mock scowl.

Trace raised an eyebrow with a meaningful look she didn't understand. "Funny. I was just going to say the same thing to you."

She didn't have time to figure out the subtext between them as she headed back toward the grill to pick up the order. Nor did she understand why, when faced with two equally gorgeous men, did only one of them seemed to possess the power to turn her into a babbling idiot?

"Here's the chief's omelet," Lou said. "Comes with a short stack."

"Thanks."

"What about the other chief?"

She let out a breath. She did *not* want to have to deal with the man this morning. "He said something about an omelet as well but I'll have to go check to make sure."

Lou refrained from rolling his eyes but he still looked faintly exasperated, probably wondering why she hadn't asked when she was just at the booth, but he didn't push her. Becca grabbed the eggs and pancakes and returned to the Bowman brothers' booth.

She slid the plates down in front of the fire chief, along with a small syrup container. At least she didn't spill that all over him, too.

"Anything else I can do for you?"

The fire chief opened his mouth, a teasing gleam in his green eyes, but then she heard a dull thud from under the table and his flirtatious expression shifted to one of almost pain. "I'm good. Really, really great. Thanks."

She looked suspiciously at Trace but he only smiled blandly.

"Are you ready to order?" she asked.

"I think I know what I want."

She reached into her apron pocket for her order pad and was happy her fingers trembled only a little when she gripped her pencil. "I'm ready. Go ahead."

"I changed my mind about the omelet. Think I'm in the mood for something sweet. I'll have the French toast. Oh, and a side of scrambled eggs. Thank you."

"Coffee?"

"Decaf."

She poured for him, focusing all her concentration on not spilling a single drop. After she finished giving his order to Lou, the large group at the corner booth next to the Bowman brothers left and she hurried over to bus their table. Though she didn't intend to eavesdrop on the conversation of Trace and his brother, she couldn't help overhearing a little of it as she cleared away plates.

"Any guesses what might be going on with her?" Taft asked the police chief.

"No. Something's up, though. I stopped by the ranch last night to drop off a book I'd borrowed from Caidy, and Destry stayed in her room the whole time."

"That's not like her." The easy charm of the fire chief faded into concern. "Wonder if she's sick."

Becca frowned as she wiped down the table with a clean cloth. She hoped not. Gabrielle seemed to be spending a lot of time with Trace's niece. If Destry got sick, chances were Gabi would get it, too. Becca couldn't afford to miss work to stay home with her sister if Gabi caught some nasty bug.

"Caidy said she seemed to be feeling fine. No fever or complaining about any symptoms of sore throat or stomachache or anything. She's just been really quiet and sad for a few days. Caidy said she's not eating much and she didn't want to go on a ride with her yesterday after school."

"That's *really* not like her."

"I talked to Caidy this morning and she said Destry refused to stay home, said she was fine. Caidy's worried about her, too."

She didn't hear the rest as she had finished clearing off the corner booth and had no excuse to linger here, especially when she had other customers with needs. For the next ten minutes, she did her best to ignore the Bowman brothers, though she was aware of them—okay, aware of *Trace*—as she took orders, seated new customers, poured coffee refills.

When Lou announced his order was ready, Becca ordered herself to be calm and collected. He was just another customer, she told herself as she set the fluffy eggs and cinnamon French toast on a tray.

She might have even believed it if her nerves didn't jump like crazy, simply from being this close to him.

"Thank you." His warm smile of appreciation didn't help matters whatsoever. She wanted to bask in that smile like a kitten in a sunbeam.

Becca quickly did her best to clamp down on the inappropriate response. She didn't need a man to further snarl up her life, especially when she seemed to be doing a fine job of that all on her own.

"More coffee?" she asked them.

Trace nodded and she refilled his cup first then used the other pot of regular to top off his brother's.

"Anyway, you know how Ridge can be," Taft said, obviously continuing the conversation between them. "If something doesn't moo or neigh, he doesn't pay it much attention."

"Hey, Becca. You live with a nine-year-old girl," Trace said suddenly.

"Yes," she said carefully.

"We're both a little concerned for our niece, Destry. She's been acting weird this week. Secretive, you know."

"It *is* almost Christmas. Maybe she's working on a special present."

"That's a possibility, but it's not reading that way to me," Trace said.

"She's usually the only one in the family who's excited about Christmas," Taft said. "Not this year, though. I offered to take her Christmas shopping over the weekend so we could get something for her dad and Caidy, and she shut me down right away."

"Why?"

"No idea," Trace answered. "That's what we were hoping you could shed some insight about. You being a girl and also being the mother to a girl the same age."

Her stomach twisted a little at the reminder of her lie and she could feel herself flush. "I meant, why doesn't more of your family enjoy Christmas?"

The two men exchanged a look, both suddenly solemn. "Memories," Trace finally said. "Our parents died around Christmastime. This year is the ten-year anniversary of their deaths."

She had known, somehow, that he carried a deep pain

around the holiday. When he had been at their house the other night helping with the tree, he had laughed and joked with them, but she had seen a shadow in his eyes a few times.

"I'm sorry," she said. "I shouldn't have pried. No wonder you want to avoid the holiday altogether."

"We might want to, but we understand that Destry's just a kid. Since she was little, we've all tried to put on a good show for her."

Again she was struck at the Bowman siblings' love and concern for the little girl. For a crazy moment, she was consumed with envy. She would have loved this sort of extended family when she was a child. Instead, all she'd had was Monica.

Gabrielle had more than that, she suddenly realized. Gabi had *her.* She could guess that her younger sister probably didn't have that many warm, cherished Christmas memories. Not with Monica raising her in the same haphazard way she had raised Becca. But Gabi had an older sister who could give her everything she had missed for the past nine years. Christmas carols and sleigh rides, home-baked cookies and stockings on the mantel.

She had been trying to merely survive the holidays until she found a little better footing, but Gabi deserved more than that. Like it or not, she needed to step up for her little sister's sake, just as the Bowmans tried to do for their niece.

"Any ideas what we can do for Des?" Taft asked.

They were asking the wrong person. She was just about the last one on earth with many insights into the mind of a nine-year-old girl. "You're going to have to figure out what's wrong first. What does she say when you ask?"

"Nothing," Trace said. "She says she's fine."

"I can ask my… Gabi if you'd like. They seem to be friends. If anyone can wiggle out the truth about what might be bothering Destry, it's Gabrielle."

"That would be great." Taft smiled at her and she wondered again at the capriciousness of fate. She had absolutely no reaction to his smile other than a pleasant warmth.

When she met Trace's glittery green gaze, that warmth exploded into a churning, seething firestorm, and she wanted to stand there and bask in the heat of it.

"Excuse me, miss? Can I get more water?"

At the voice from a neighboring table, Becca jerked her attention back to her job and the ten other tables full of customers who needed her. "Excuse me. I'm sorry."

She grabbed up the water pitcher and refilled the water glasses at the neighboring table, reminding herself as she attended to her other customers of all the reasons why fraternizing with local law enforcement was a bad idea.

She might not be running a con but she was definitely living a lie. If he found out the truth—that Gabi was her younger sister, not her daughter, and that Becca didn't have any kind of official custody arrangement with their mother—authorities could conceivably take the girl from her and put her into foster care. She couldn't let that happen to her sister.

The Bowman brothers seemed to be taking their time over their food and she tried not to pay any more attention to them than strictly necessary to make sure they had adequate service. The other customers kept her busy, especially the large group of college-age snow-mobilers, in town for the weekend, that ended up taking the corner booth near Trace and his brother.

They were demanding and petulant and becoming louder by the minute, to the point where she almost expected Lou to come out from behind the grill and start swinging his frying pan around.

They were also not nearly as respectful as the local customers. Their flirting with her had a hard edge to it and when she reached to refill one coffee cup, the young man on the end of the booth tried to cop a quick feel.

She instinctively squeaked and backed away. Before she'd even caught her breath, Trace was looming behind her. For a large man, he moved with deadly stealth, turning from amiable to dangerous in the space of a heartbeat.

He'd been a military policeman, she remembered him saying. She could quite clearly picture him knocking a couple of shaved marine heads together for disturbing the peace. He had the harsh, indestructible look of a leatherneck. Definitely not someone to mess around with.

"Thank you for breakfast, Becca." He barely looked at her when he spoke, his attention on the rough group of snowmobilers.

"You're welcome," she said. She could probably handle a group of kids on her own but she couldn't deny she was grateful to Trace for stepping in.

"You think you could top off my coffee one more time before I go?"

"Sure. Right away, Chief Bowman."

She quickly escaped the tension and returned to the neighboring booth, where she quickly refilled his coffee. Taft said something to her about the weather and she answered distractedly, her attention still focused on Trace, who had now bent down and murmured something to the college kids. She couldn't hear what he said but she saw the boy who had tried to grope her blanch as if he'd just driven his snowmobile into an icy lake.

He nodded vigorously and then all of the kids dug into their food while Trace moved leisurely back to his own booth.

She felt compelled to say something. "Thank you. I could have handled the situation, but…thank you."

"No problem. They shouldn't bother you again."

"Just out of curiosity, what did you use on the little punks?" the fire chief asked. "The line about how you keep the band castrator we use on the cattle in the back of your squad car and aren't afraid to use it?"

He gave a slow smile that ramped her heartbeat up a notch. "No, but that's always a good one. I just told them we have old-fashioned ideas around here about the way men ought to treat women. And that I have a special jail cell at the station house for little punks who come to town looking for trouble. They shouldn't bother you again. You let me know if they do."

"I will," she mumbled and moved quickly away before she did something completely ridiculous like burst into tears.

She was more shaken by the incident than she wanted to admit—more by her reaction to what Trace had done than by a stupid little punk trying for a cheap thrill.

Becca had been taking care of herself virtually since birth, since Monica had all the maternal instincts of a blowfly. Despite that, she had worked hard to become a competent, self-assured adult. She had been on her own since she became an emancipated minor at sixteen and had convinced herself she didn't need anyone.

So why did she literally go weak in the knees when a sexy police chief stepped up to watch over her?

She had no answer for that. She only knew she couldn't make up for the inadequacies of her childhood by seeking someone to watch over her as an adult. Right now her focus needed to be Gabi and nurturing her baby sister the way their mother never had.

Chapter 5

"I'm not going to stand for it, you hear me?" Ralph Ashton's face was florid, his eyes an angry, snapping brown. "I pay taxes in this town, have done for sixty-five years now. When I'm being robbed blind, I've got a right to expect the police to do more than stand around scratching their behinds."

Trace fought for patience as he stood in the narrow aisle of the store the man had owned for years. Like an old-fashioned general store, Ashton's sold everything from muck boots to margarine, pitchforks to potato chips. In his early eighties now, Ralph Ashton had been running the place since he was a teenager. He should have stepped down years ago but he still insisted he was perfectly competent to manage the day-to-day operations of the store, much to the frustration of his children—and the frustration of law enforcement officials who had to deal with his frequent complaints about shoplifters.

"You're absolutely right, Mr. Ashton. I'm sorry we haven't been able to figure out who's stealing candy bars out of your inventory. I still think it's probably kids pulling a prank, but maybe there's more to it."

"It's high time you did something about this. Set up a sting or something."

"If you would stop erasing your security film every twelve hours, I might have a better chance of figuring things out."

"You know how expensive that film is?"

They had had this argument often and Trace knew a losing cause when he stared it in the eye. He was about to respond when a new customer came into the store. His pulse jumped when he saw Becca Parsons pull a shopping cart out of the row and head off in the other direction.

Though it was a wintry December day with snow falling steadily, she was like a breath of springtime, like standing in a field of daffodils while birds flitted around him building nests....

The whimsy of that sudden image popping into his head left him unnerved and he quickly turned back to Mr. Ashton.

"If you want to catch the shoplifters, you might have to spend a little money to do it."

"I've spent money! I pay my taxes. I have rights, don't I? It's a disgrace. That's what it is. These rotten kids are bleeding me dry and you won't even dust for fingerprints. I'm calling the mayor. Right now. See if I don't."

The old man was growing increasingly agitated, Trace saw with concern. He nodded in a placating sort of way. "I understand your frustration, Mr. Ashton.

Honestly, I do. I'm sorry we haven't had more luck. Let's talk about our options. Why don't you sit down and take a rest? Where's Rosalie?" Ashton's grand-daughter usually did her best to take over as many store responsibilities as Ralph would let her.

"Useless thing. She took her mother to a doctor's appointment in Idaho Falls. Seemed to think the assistant manager could run the place on his own." He spoke as if that was the most ridiculous idea he had ever heard, as if he were the only one fit to make decisions.

Trace didn't like Ralph Ashton—the guy had been a grumpy old cuss ever since he could remember—but he still had to respect the man's dedication to his business and he couldn't help the stirring of pity when he saw the tremble of Ralph's hands as he straightened a row of canned peaches on the shelf above them.

"Look, I'll fingerprint the rack if you'll agree to go sit down in Rosalie's office and work on some paperwork or something. The assistant manager can still find you if he needs help with anything."

"You're just trying to get rid of me and then you're going to duck out and leave me to deal with these lousy shoplifters on my own."

Trace gave him a stern look. "I said I'll check for fingerprints and I will. You can watch me the whole time through the security cameras. You know we Bowmans keep our word, Mr. Ashton."

Ralph gave him a considering look. "True enough. Your parents were good folks. I always used to say your dad was about the only honest man in town. If he said he would pay you in a few weeks, you'd get your money right on the dot."

The reminder of Trace's father seemed to convince

the man. "I do have plenty of paperwork. Just let me know when you're done."

He stumped off, his cane making a staccato beat through the store. Trace gave a heavy sigh and turned back to the candy rack. This was a completely futile exercise when half the people in town bought gum and candy bars from Ashton's Mercantile, but he would keep his word and humor the guy. And then maybe he would have a good, long talk with Rosalie about increasing their security budget a little and maybe stationing a stocker nearby after school to keep a better eye out.

He was just lifting his eighth set of prints—for all he knew, it could have been his own since he'd bought a tin of wintergreen Altoids a few days earlier—when Becca turned onto his aisle, her shopping cart full of budget items like macaroni-and-cheese boxes and store-brand cereal. She did have some baking supplies—butter, sugar, flour, as well as some cake decorating sprinkles and colored icing—and he guessed Christmas cookies were in her immediate future.

When she spotted him, her eyes lit up with warmth but she quickly concealed her expression. He'd never known a woman so guarded with her emotions. What made her so careful? Was it something about him or did she have that reaction to everyone? He very much wanted to find out. He remembered his ridiculous imagery of earlier, how she seemed to bring springtime into the store with her despite the snow he could see through the front doors, which was now blowing harder than ever.

He found it more than a little unsettling how happy he was to see her or how many times in the past week since he last saw her that he had driven past her house at the end of a long shift and been tempted to turn into the driveway toward those glowing lights. He hadn't been this interested in a woman in a long time.

"How have you been? I haven't seen you in a while."

"You haven't been into The Gulch lately. At least not during my shift."

"I've stopped in a few times for dinner." *But you weren't there.* He decided it would be better to leave that particular disappointment unspoken.

"Lou and Donna have been really great to let me work mostly the breakfast and lunch crowds so I can be with Gabi after school and in the evenings."

"They're good that way."

She smiled. "That's exactly the word. They're *good.* Really nice people."

He raised an eyebrow. "You sound surprised."

"Not surprised, exactly. I'm just not…used to it, I guess. They've been extraordinarily kind to me."

"That's the way they are."

"I keep thinking how lucky I am that The Gulch was the first place I applied for a job when I came to town. I'm amazed they've let me stay, if you want the truth." She gave him a rueful smile. "I'm really not waitress material. You may have noticed."

"You're doing fine."

"I'm not, but I'm trying. I'm amazed at how patient and kind they've been with me. I keep looking for an ulterior motive but so far I can't find anything."

He wondered again at her life before she moved into her grandfather's house. What experience with the world led a woman to become so cynical that she constantly seemed braced for hurt and didn't know how to accept genuine kindness when it came her way?

"They don't have an ulterior motive, I can promise you. That's just who they are. Lou and Donna care about Pine Gulch and the people in it. You'll find when you've been around a little longer that this town is lucky enough to have more than a few people like the Archuletas. Good, honest, hardworking people who watch out for each other."

"I'm beginning to see that," she murmured. She made a vague gesture at the candy rack and his evidence bag open in front of him. "What are you doing?"

In light of the claim he'd just made about Pine Gulch and the town's inhabitants, he felt a little sheepish replying, "Okay, not everyone is honest. Ralph Ashton, who owns the store, seems to think he's been the victim of a dastardly crime spree. He's losing more inventory than usual from his candy stock."

"So you're fingerprinting the display rack? Forgive me, Chief Bowman, but that seems a little extreme, doesn't it?"

"I'm humoring Mr. Ashton," he admitted. "He's an elderly man and rather set in his ways. I tried to explain this was an exercise in futility since every single person in town has bought candy off this rack at some point. But he's got a bad heart and I didn't want to stress him more by arguing with him. Seemed easier to just lift a few prints."

She gazed at him for a long moment, as if he were a completely alien species she had just wandered across in the mountains.

Right now, he felt like one. "I know. It's stupid."

She shook her head, something warm and soft in her eyes. "I don't think it's stupid. I think it's…sweet."

He wasn't sure he really wanted her thinking he was sweet. He had been a police officer for the past decade and a military policeman for four years before that. He'd passed sweet a long, long time ago—if he'd ever been there at all. Before he could correct her misconception, he heard a high, childish voice shriek out his name.

"Trace! Trace! Trace!"

Both of them looked at the approaching cart, pushed by a woman with a swinging blond ponytail and a delighted smile that was only matched by the cherubic two-year-old with the inky black curls and the huge dark eyes who was waving madly at him from the front seat of the cart. "Hi, Trace. Hi, Trace!"

He smiled at Easton Springhill Del Norte and her adopted daughter, Isabella. "Hey, you. Two of my favorite people!"

Belle held her arms out for him to hug her in that generous, loving way she'd been blessed with despite her haphazard early years. "How's my girl?" he asked and was rewarded with an adorable giggle.

"I'm good. Mommy said I could have a juice box in the car if I'm good while we're shopping."

"That's a brave mommy. You'll have to be careful not to spill it."

"I won't. I'm a big girl."

"I know you are." He eased her back into the seat and kissed Easton on the cheek, strangely aware of Becca watching them. "Becca, this is my favorite two-and-a-half-year-old, Miss Isabella Del Norte, and her mother, Easton."

Becca gave a stiff sort of smile. "Hi. I think you've come into the diner a few times."

"Oh, right." Easton beamed. "You're the new waitress, Wally Taylor's granddaughter. It's great to formally meet you."

"How are you, East?"

"I'm great." She gestured to her baby bump, about the size of a bocce ball. He knew she was expecting in March. "Beginning to waddle. Another few weeks and I won't be able to get up on a horse, I'm afraid. Cisco's already making noises about me taking a break from calving this year."

"You look beautiful," he told her, completely the truth. She had always been lovely to him, but he couldn't deny that since Cisco Del Norte had stopped his wandering and settled down in Pine Gulch and they had married, Easton had bloomed.

Trace could admit now that he'd been worried the man would break her heart all over again and leave like he'd been doing since they were just kids, but by all appearances, Cisco seemed like a man who wasn't going anywhere, who loved his family and raising horses and living in a small Idaho town. He'd even helped Trace out a few months ago on a drug case with South American ties, Cisco's specialty after years as an undercover drug agent.

A few years ago, Trace had wanted much more than friendship with Easton. They had dated several times and he had been pretty sure they were moving toward something serious when Cisco had returned home. When he saw how much Easton loved the other man, Trace had stepped aside. What else could he have done? He couldn't regret it, not when their joy together was obvious to everyone around them, but once in a while when he saw her, he couldn't help the little pang in his heart for what might have been.

"I need to finish shopping and check out," Becca said. "I'll see you later."

"I'm sorry we interrupted your conversation," Easton said. "It's wonderful to meet you."

Becca gave a polite smile and headed around the next aisle. He watched her go for a moment. When he turned back, he found Easton studying him carefully.

"She seems very nice."

"How do you know? You barely exchanged two words with her."

She gave a shrug and tucked a stray blond lock behind her ear "I've got a vibe about these things. She's very pretty. I heard she has a daughter. Any husband in the picture?"

"East." He glared at her, which she parried with an innocent look.

"What? I was just asking."

"As far as I can tell, no. No husband in the picture."

"Good. That's very good. I'll have to make sure Jenna sends her an invite to the Cold Creek Christmas party at the McRavens' so I can get a chance to sit down with her for a real visit."

"You don't need to vet women for me, East," he growled. "I do fine on my own."

"Do you?" Though her voice was teasing, he didn't miss the concern in her eyes. "You know I love you and only want the best for you. You deserve to be happy, Trace."

He wasn't sure a woman like Becca Parsons, who obviously didn't trust him, was the route to happiness.

"I am happy. I've got a great life, full of interesting people and darling little shoplifters." He grabbed the pack of gum out of Belle's chubby little fingers that she must have lifted when neither he nor Easton were looking.

"Belle. No, no," Easton exclaimed.

"I like gum."

Trace laughed. "I'm sure you do, honey. But you'd better be careful or Ralph Ashton will throw you in the slammer."

This was about the only time she *really* missed Arizona.

Since she left for work, the snow had been falling steadily. At least four inches now covered the sidewalk and driveway that she had just shoveled first thing in the morning before she headed for the breakfast shift.

What she wouldn't do for a few saguaro cactuses in her line of vision right about now, the beige and browns and grays of living in the desert. Instead, she was surrounded by snow and icicles and that very cold wind that seemed to sneak through her parka to pinch at her with icy fingers.

For three days, Mother Nature had been relentlessly sending flurries their way.

It was the worst kind of snow, too—not a big whopping storm that could be taken care of in one fell swoop, but little dribs and drabs spread over several days that had to be shoveled a few inches at a time.

She was already tired of it and had been reminded several times by customers at The Gulch that winter was really only beginning. She did have to admit she was looking forward to what everyone told her were spectacular summer days—and wondrously cool nights. During the summer in Phoenix, it was often still ninety degrees at midnight.

"We tell people hereabouts, if they complain about

the winter, they don't deserve the summer," Donna had told her a few days earlier.

She scooped another shovelful of snow, wishing her budget would stretch for a snowblower. As it was, she would be lucky to be able to give Gabi a few toys and books for Christmas. She was picking up a few things here and there for the girl. Money was tight but she was managing—and she was more excited about the holidays than she might have believed possible even a few weeks earlier.

Much to Becca's befuddlement, Gabi loved to shovel the snow. She ought to leave the driveway for another few hours until her sister came home from school, but Becca was afraid if she waited much longer, it would be so deep it would take hours to clear. As it was, by the time she finished the curve of sidewalk leading to the house, her biceps burned and her lower back was already beginning to ache.

She started on the driveway when she heard an approaching vehicle heading down the street. To her surprise, the vehicle slowed and then stopped in front of her house. Through the whirl of snow she recognized the white Pine Gulch Police Department SUV and she suddenly felt as warm as a Phoenix afternoon in July.

Trace climbed out of the SUV and headed toward her. He wore a brown shearling-lined police-issue parka and a Stetson and he looked rough and gorgeous. She, by contrast, felt frumpy and bedraggled in her knit hat and gloves and the old peacoat that wasn't quite as effective as it should be against the weather.

He smiled warmly and she suddenly felt breathless from more than just the exertion of shoveling.

She hadn't seen him since that day in the store, nearly

a week earlier, though she had seen his vehicle pass by a few times when she'd been up late at night.

He looked tired, she thought, with a pang of sympathy for his hard work on behalf of the good people of Pine Gulch.

"Need a hand?" he asked.

She ought to tell him no. Every moment she spent with him only seemed to make her hungry for more. But the driveway was long, the snow heavy, and she was basically a weak woman.

"As long as it has a shovel attached to it, sure."

He opened the back of his SUV and pulled out a snow shovel, then dug in without a word.

They worked mostly in silence on different ends of the driveway, but she didn't find it uncomfortable. She wanted to ask him about the woman in the grocery store and what his feelings for her were. They were plainly friends but she gained the distinct impression in the store that the two of them had shared more than that. Did it bother him to see her with one child and another on the way? Was he still in love with her?

None of those questions were any of her business, she reminded herself, shoveling a little more briskly.

Trace was obviously much more proficient at this particular skill than she was—and much stronger—and what would have taken her at least an hour was done in less than half that.

"Thank you," she said when the last pile had been pushed to the side of her driveway. "That was a huge help."

"I told you, people in Pine Gulch take care of each other."

She was beginning to believe it. Much to her surprise, Becca was beginning to enjoy living in Pine Gulch. What had started out as only a temporary resting place while she tried to figure out what to do next had become familiar. She liked the fact that when she went to that quaint little grocery store in town, Trace hadn't been the only person who had stopped to talk to her. She had been greeted by two different people she'd waited on at the diner, each of whom had stopped her to make a little friendly conversation and wish her Merry Christmas.

"Just out of curiosity, why do you have a shovel in your vehicle?"

He smiled at the question. "For digging out stranded cars or helping the citizens of Pine Gulch with their snow removal needs. Even the reluctant ones."

She flushed. "I let you help, didn't I? I'm grateful. Believe me, you saved me all kinds of work. For the most part, I guess I'm used to taking care of myself."

"Nothing wrong with that. You should fit right in here in eastern Idaho. We're known for our self-sufficient resilience."

"You were probably on your way somewhere, weren't you?"

"Just home for a few hours of downtime and to put the dog out before I head back at six for another shift. I'm shorthanded right now, if you haven't figured that out."

"Well, I appreciate you spending a little of your downtime helping me shovel when you've got your own to do. Would you like me to go help you with your driveway?"

"No need. I pay a neighbor kid to come over with his dad's snowblower. It puts a little change in his pocket and keeps him out of trouble. Plus, it makes things a little more convenient for me. With my shifts being all over the place, I never know when I'll be available to shovel the snow. This way I don't have to worry about it. I can give you his name if you'd like."

She considered her meager budget and how much paying someone to clear her driveway would probably cost through a long eastern-Idaho winter. Cheaper than buying a snowblower herself, she supposed, but until she was able to finish the waiver requirements for transferring her bar membership—which included a hefty fee, unfortunately—she would have to make do.

"I'm okay. I like the exercise," she lied. He didn't appear to buy the excuse. To divert his attention, she said the first thing she could think of. "Would you like to come in for some cocoa? It's the least I can do to repay you for helping me."

She didn't really expect him to say yes. Why would he want to spend any more of his brief leisure time with her? To her surprise he kicked the rest of the snow off his shovel and propped it against his truck. "I'd like that. Thanks."

Now she'd done it. She couldn't rescind the invitation without sounding like an idiot. At the same time, she wasn't sure being alone with Trace on a snowy December afternoon was the greatest of ideas, not with this awareness that seemed to pop and hiss between them.

She would be polite, would make him some cocoa and then send him on his way. She had absolutely no reason to be nervous.

Reasonable or not, nerves jumped inside her as she opened the door to her grandfather's house and led him inside.

* * *

He should be stretched out on his recliner taking a nap right about now. For the past three weeks, he'd been running on about five hours of sleep a night or less and he was beginning to feel the effects. He should have just helped her shovel and then headed home. Her invitation to come inside had taken him completely by surprise and he'd agreed before he'd really thought through the wisdom of it.

"The tree looks great," he said. She and Gabi had added a popcorn-and-cranberry garland and homemade ornaments. Paper-cut snowflakes hung in the windows and across the door frame and it appeared as if she had cut some of the greenery from the evergreens out in the yard and tucked them on the fireplace mantel and on the banister up the stairs, threaded with lights and a few glossy ornaments. More greenery and ribbons wound through the old chandelier above the dining room table.

In the few weeks since he had been here helping them put up the Christmas tree, Becca had created a warm, welcoming haven out of Wally Taylor's dark and gloomy house. The house no longer looked like a sad old bachelor's house, years past its prime. Somehow on a budget of obviously shoestring proportions, Becca had created a cozy space full of color and light—plump, bright pillows on the old sofa, new curtains, a colorful quilt over the recliner.

He hoped the efforts she had expended into creating a comfortable nest for her and for and her daughter indicated Becca intended to stay in Pine Gulch, at least for a little while.

"You've been hard at work. The place looks great," he said, ignoring the little spurt of happiness lodged in his chest when he thought about her giving his town a chance.

She looked embarrassed at the compliment. "It's still a dark, crumbling old house with outdated linoleum and ugly carpet. I can't do anything about that right now until I save a little more. But I own it outright and nobody can take it away from me."

An interesting comment that made him even more curious about her background. He wondered again what had led her here and what sort of insecurity and instability she might have faced that made her cling so tightly to the house.

"Let me take your coat," she said. "Sit down here by the fire and warm up a little while I fix the cocoa."

"I'll let you take my coat but this isn't The Gulch. You don't have to serve me here. I can help with the cocoa."

"It's not The Gulch but it is my home and you're a guest here."

As she reached for his coat, her fingers brushed his and that subtle awareness simmered to life between them again. Had he ever noticed the curve of her cheekbone before, that particularly unique shade of her eyes?

She was so lovely, soft and restful, and he just wanted to stand here for a moment with the little fireplace crackling merrily and the snow still falling steadily outside and simply enjoy looking at her.

He grabbed her fingers in both of his hands around his coat. "Your hands are cold," he murmured.

She stared at him, her eyes suddenly wide. He could hear the ticking of a clock somewhere in the house and the shifting of the house and the sudden whoosh as the furnace clicked on. A low hunger thrummed between them, glittery and bright. He could step forward right now and pull her into his arms, capture that lusciously soft mouth with his. He might not learn all her secrets that way but it would be a start.

The fire suddenly crackled and Becca blinked and the moment was gone.

She cleared her throat and tugged her still-cold fingers away. "I'll, uh, hang up your coat and see about the cocoa."

She headed back through the house. He followed her into the kitchen, with its dark-wood paneling and old-fashioned appliances. She had tried to brighten this room up, too, with new white curtains, a set of brightly colored dish towels hanging on the stove and a watercolor print on the wall above the small crescent table, an Impressionist painting of a small cottage with an English garden blooming around it.

She stood at the stove, pouring milk into a saucepan.

"I thought when you said cocoa you were going to make it from the mix," he said.

"I like the old-fashioned way, with powdered cocoa and milk. It only takes a minute, though. Would you like a cookie? Gabi and I made them last night."

"I would, thank you. I'm afraid I'm weak when it comes to holiday goodies."

He picked one up and tasted shortbread and raspberries from the jam center. "These are delicious!"

"Thanks."

"Is it a family recipe?" he probed, hoping to get some insights into her background.

She shrugged. "Probably. Someone else's family, anyway. I found it online."

Okay, so much for that subtle line of questioning, he

thought ruefully. But after a moment she added, somewhat reluctantly, "I don't remember my own mother ever making cookies."

"She wasn't the domestic sort, then?" he asked.

Her laugh was small with a hint of bitter undertone that made him sad. "That, Chief Bowman, is an understatement."

He would have liked to pursue it but she once again deflected his inquiries by turning the conversation back to him. "What about your family?" she asked as she measured vanilla. "Was your mother the cookie-baking type?"

"Sometimes, when the mood struck her. When she wasn't busy with her work."

"What did she do?"

"She was an artist. Oil on canvas."

"Really?" She narrowed her gaze. "Margaret Bowman. Was that your mother?"

He blinked, surprised. His mother had only just started becoming commercially successful when she was killed. "Yes. How did you know?"

"I saw one of her paintings of Cold Creek Canyon in springtime hanging in the library the other day. It was absolutely stunning. It gave me a little hope that maybe there's more to Pine Gulch than snow."

He had forgotten that he and his siblings had donated one of her paintings to the library in memory of their mother. "Mostly she did it for fun and passion. I think she loved collecting art as much as she enjoyed creating it."

Her polite smile encouraged him to add more. "When she was a young girl growing up in southern Utah outside Zion National Park, she and her mother became friends with Maynard Dixon, who had a home there," he said of the great Western artist. "Dixon was fond of my mother and encouraged her talent. He even gave her a small oil painting depicting the area. Later she and my father acquired three more Dixon paintings, as well as a couple of Georgia O'Keeffes and a small Bierstadt. They were the cornerstone of their collection."

"You must feel so fortunate to have such beautiful pieces to enjoy in your family."

The familiar anger and helplessness burned through him. "We don't. Not anymore. The Dixons and O'Keeffes and the Bierstadt were stolen ten years ago, along with the rest of their collection, the night my parents were murdered."

She paused from stirring the milk on the stove, her eyes shocked and sympathetic.

"I'm so sorry, Trace. You said they died. I thought... perhaps an accident."

"No accident. They were victims of a robbery and had the misfortunate to have seen the bastards who broke in."

"How terrible."

Usually he hated talking about this, hated the pity and that hint of avid curiosity he would see in people's eyes when the topic came up. With Becca, her concern felt genuine and he found an odd sort of solace in it.

"I don't care about the artwork, you know? I never did. The paintings were beautiful, but I would have ripped them off the wall myself and given them to any passing beggar on the street if it could have saved my parents."

"I'm sorry."

"It breaks my heart they never had the chance to even

know Destry, to see where Ridge has taken the ranch, to watch Caidy grow into a beautiful young woman."

His voice trailed off and he flushed, embarrassed that he had revealed so much of himself to her, but she only continued watching him with that quiet compassion. "You said they died right before Christmas."

"Right. December twenty-third, ten years ago."

"How difficult for you and your family. That must have made it even harder, coming so close to Christmas."

He never talked about this part, but for reasons he couldn't explain he felt compelled to add the rest. "I was home on leave from the marines. I'd just finished my second deployment to the Middle East and had only three months left in my commitment to the military. I was trying to figure out what to do with my life, you know? Trying to figure out if I should re-up or get out. I spent most of my leave partying. Drinking. Staying out late. Living it up. Don't get me wrong, I loved my parents, my family, but I was a stupid kid. I met a girl and we were…"

His voice trailed off and he was angry all over again at his stupidity. He should have known something was wrong. He'd been a military policeman, for God's sake. But a devious little witch had thrown his natural instincts all to hell.

"I think I can figure out what you were doing," Becca said, a hint of dryness in her tone.

His jaw worked. "She was in on it. Her job was to keep me busy and away from the ranch while the rest of the crew went in and did the job. My parents weren't supposed to be home. My sister had a school choir concert. But at the last minute, she got sick and so they all stayed home. My dad surprised the thieves and he was shot first. My mom tried to run and they got her next. Caidy was hiding in the house the whole time. She still won't talk about it."

Her eyes drenched with sympathy, she poured cocoa into a mug with a snowman on it and then set it in front of him before taking the seat across the table from him.

"That's why you became a police officer? Your parents' murders?"

He looked into the murky depths of his drink where he could still see the swirl of cocoa from her spoon. "Yeah. Something like that. The age-old quest for truth, justice and all that idealistic garbage."

"I don't think it's garbage. Not at all! What's idealistic about wanting to protect the town and the way of life you love? It's honorable. You've tried to build on your parents' legacy, to keep Pine Gulch a safe place. At heart, you just want to make sure others don't have to cope with the same pain you and your brothers and sister have to live with. I get it."

He gazed at her for a long moment, then shook his head. "How do you do that?"

"What?"

"You're as good as any detective." He sipped at his cocoa, decadently rich. "You've definitely got a gift for getting people to reveal things they wouldn't normally talk about. I never intended to dredge up old history."

"I'm sorry if I was probing," she said, her movements and her tone suddenly stiff.

He had the oddest feeling he'd offended her somehow. What had he said? He combed through their conversation but didn't have the first idea what he'd done. "You weren't probing at all, Becca. That's not what I meant. I'm the one who mentioned my parents in the first place. I opened the door."

On impulse, he reached across the table for her fingers. Where they had been cold from shoveling snow before, her time in the kitchen and holding the mug of cocoa had left them warm, and he slid his thumb across the soft knuckle of her forefinger. "To be honest, if anything, I'm surprised at myself for telling you all the grisly details. It's a...touchy subject and I usually don't like to talk about it."

"Thank you for sharing it with me," she said solemnly.

Her fingers trembled a little in his. This close to her, he could see she had a little scar at the corner of her mouth and he wondered where it came from. He very much wanted to kiss her, even though he knew it probably wasn't very smart. He sensed once his mouth touched hers, he wouldn't want to stop. He would be perfectly happy to go on kissing her all afternoon while the snow fluttered down outside.

Any trace of fatigue seemed to have completely left his system. Instead, a fierce hunger settled low in his gut. With a long sigh, he finally surrendered to it, leaning across the table and brushing his mouth against hers.

She inhaled a sexy little breath at the first touch of his mouth on her warm, soft lips and then she kissed him back. She tasted sweet and rich, intoxicating, with that earthy undertone of cocoa, and he wanted to sink into her and never bother climbing back out.

Chapter 6

This couldn't be happening.

She couldn't really be kissing the chief of police in the kitchen of her grandfather's house while the old refrigerator hummed and the wind blew snow under the eaves.

No, it was real enough. She seemed hyperaware of each of her senses. The noises of the house seemed magnified, each taste and smell more intense.

He tasted of cocoa and hot male and he smelled like laundry soap and starch and a very sexy aftershave with wood and musk notes.

As she had expected, Trace Bowman kissed like a man who knew exactly how to cherish a woman, who would make sure she always felt safe and cared for in his arms. He explored her mouth as if he wanted to taste every millimeter of it and wouldn't rest until he knew every single one of her secrets.

What started as just a casual sort of brush of his mouth against hers quickly seemed to ignite until she couldn't manage to string together any sort of coherent thought except *more*.

With their mouths still connected, he pulled her to her feet so that he could tug her closer and he leaned back against her counter, taking her with him. His heat and the strength of him seemed to enfold her and she wanted to stay right here with her arms wrapped around his waist and his mouth licking and tasting her until she could barely stand up.

She could feel his heartbeat—though perhaps that was hers, racing a mile a minute.

In her entire life, she had never gone from zero to *take-me-now* so quickly. She had known, somehow. From that first day, she had guessed that if she ever kissed Trace Bowman it would be an unforgettable experience, a kiss with the power to make her forget everything else except this.

She had no idea how long they kissed. It might have been days, for all she would have cared. They might have continued indefinitely, except the mantel clock suddenly chimed through the house, yanking her back to her senses.

She slid her mouth away, nearly shivering at the sudden chill. Calling on every skill at deception she had tried to suppress her entire adult life, she eased back and tried not to reveal that she wanted nothing more than to climb right back into his arms.

He stared at her, his breathing ragged and his eyes a hazy, hungry green. After a moment, he let out a breath. "Again. Not what I intended."

She had kissed men before. Heavens, she'd been

nearly engaged three months ago. But she had never been so completely rocked off her foundation by the touch of a man's mouth on hers.

Becca swallowed, reminding herself she was a mature woman who had graduated from law school, passed the Arizona state bar, been an associate at an extremely successful real-estate law firm in Phoenix. This was only a kiss. Nothing to leave her reeling and stunned.

The smart thing to do would be to get out in front of this before she blew the whole thing out of proportion.

"Was that a just-between-neighbors kiss or a let's-jump-into-bed-right-this-minute kiss?"

For an instant, he looked taken aback by her frankness and then he gave a rough-sounding laugh. "If we have to categorize it, why don't we say it was more a we've-got-something-between-us-so-why-don't-we-just-see-where-this-goes? sort of thing."

She was tempted. So tempted. Trace Bowman was the kind of man she had dreamed about since she was old enough to know the difference between real men and her mother's usual boy toys. Decent and kind, he loved his family, he seemed grounded, he worked hard. Not to mention the minor little fact that he was the most gorgeous man she'd ever met and made her forget her own name.

But she had a million reasons why let's-see-where-this-goes wasn't a possibility for her right now. In some ways, she almost would have preferred the let's-jump-into-bed scenario. Her mind was already there, imagining tangled limbs and hard muscles and toe-curling passion.

"Look, I appreciate your help with shoveling the snow and the Christmas tree and everything. You've been very kind to Gabi and me and I'm grateful. It's just…to be perfectly honest, I'm just trying to keep my head above water here. Our situation is…complicated. I'm not in a really good place right now for, um, seeing where things go with you right now."

She couldn't gauge his reaction to what she said. Something flashed in his expression but he concealed it quickly and she couldn't tell if it was hurt or disappointment or neither. Finally he nodded. "Fair enough. Maybe once you've had time to settle in a little more, you'll be more of a mind to stop and look around and enjoy the view."

"Maybe," she said in what she hoped was a noncommittal tone. For just a moment she allowed her mind to imagine how things could be with Trace. More incredible kisses like that. Someone to lean on. Warm feet cuddling with hers on cold December nights.

Heavenly. If circumstances were different, she would love nothing more. He seemed like the genuine thing, a decent and caring man who wouldn't walk away at the first sign of trouble. But how could she ever allow herself to be involved with a police officer now when she and Gabi were basically living a lie? Before she could ever be in a relationship with Trace, she would have to tell him the truth about her, about Gabi, about Monica— and if she did that, admitted her deception, she knew Trace would be furious and hurt and wouldn't *want* any more delicious let's-see-where-this-goes kisses.

The sound of the front door opening and then closing again distracted her from the ache of regret settling somewhere near her heart.

"Why is there a cop car outside?" Gabi called out from the entry. "Is everything okay? Becca?"

With an inward cringe, she shot a quick glance at Trace to see if he noticed her "daughter" calling her by her first name. His expression was shuttered and expressionless and, again, she couldn't gauge his reaction.

Becca quickly straightened her sweater and smoothed a hand over her hair to make sure it wasn't flying in every direction. "In here, honey," she called, forcing a smile.

A moment later, Gabi walked into the kitchen, still wearing her snow-dotted parka and backpack. "Oh," she exclaimed when she saw Trace, and to Becca's consternation something that looked suspiciously like guilt flashed in her little sister's eyes before she blinked it away.

Oh, Gabi. What are you up to?

Gabi took in the plate of cookies on the table, the two coffee mugs half-full of cocoa and both of them standing only a foot or so apart, and her eyes narrowed with wary confusion.

"Hi, Gabrielle." Trace's smile could have melted every icicle dripping from the roof. "You're home from school early, aren't you? School doesn't get out for another hour."

Gabi took off her beanie with a too-casual shrug that did nothing to alleviate Becca's worry. "I had a stomachache. I think I just need to lie down."

For about a second and a half, Becca was tempted to let her. The whole stomachache thing was an obvious lie but until she could get Trace out of the house, she couldn't call her sister on it. Whatever trouble she suddenly suspected Gabi might be tangled up in, this was something better handled outside the presence of an entirely too sexy police chief.

Aware of him watching their byplay with interest, she forced an expression of maternal concern. "Honey, you can't just leave school like that, especially with all the snow out there. You should have called me so I could come pick you up."

"I figured you'd be busy." Gabi's gaze shifted from Becca to Trace and back again. "Looks like I was right."

She flushed, grateful Gabi hadn't barged in five minutes earlier. "Did you tell your teacher or anyone else in the office you were leaving?"

Gabi didn't say anything and Becca's stomach twisted. The last thing they needed was trouble at school, any unusual behavior that might raise eyebrows and cause unwanted speculation. Gabi darn well knew they were trying to fly straight in Pine Gulch. Well, mostly straight.

"I didn't think about it," she said defensively. "We had a late-afternoon recess. I went in to go to the bathroom and decided to just grab my backpack and come home. I thought it would be okay. I mean, school was almost over, right? We're only a few blocks from the school anyway and I just thought it would be faster for me to walk home instead of calling you."

She needed to get Trace out of here so she could have a straight conversation with Gabi without the darn chief of police looking on. She let out a breath, hating this tension churning through her. Lies and deception. Her entire life from her earliest memories was a writhing, tangled mess of them and she hated it.

"I'll call the school and let them know you've come home so they don't worry about you. We wouldn't want them reporting you missing to the police or something."

She tried to make a joke of it but neither Trace nor Gabi even cracked a smile.

"Next time, you need to go through the proper channels, okay? I can come to the school to pick you up, no matter what I might be in the middle of doing." Like kissing the Pine Gulch police chief until she couldn't think straight.

"Okay. May I please go to my room to lie down?"

Definitely un-Gabi-like behavior. She frowned at her sister but didn't know how to probe while Trace was still there.

"Yes. It should be warm and toasty up there. I'll come check on you in a few minutes." She rubbed a hand over Gabi's hair, a little damp from the snowflakes that had seeped through her beanie.

"I'm sorry," Gabi muttered.

"No worries. I'll call the school. Go get some rest."

The girl escaped quickly and Becca pulled her cell phone from her pocket. She had added Pine Gulch Elementary to her address book when they first moved to town and she found it quickly and dialed.

"Hello," she said when the secretary answered. "This is Rebecca Parsons. I'm sorry for the mix-up, but my sis—" She caught herself just in time and didn't trust herself to look at Trace to see if he'd caught her mistake. "My *daughter*, Gabrielle, just came home with a stomachache. I'm afraid she walked here on her own without letting her teacher or anyone at the office know."

She listened to the secretary's stern admonitions about following procedures. "Yes, I've told her she shouldn't have left like that. We had a long talk about it and I don't believe she'll do it again. I just wanted you to know she is home and safe and will be out for the remainder of the day."

"Tell her to drink fluids and get plenty of rest," the secretary said. "There are some nasty bugs going around right now. We've had five children go home sick today."

"I'll do that. Thank you, Mrs. Gallegos."

She ended the call and turned back to Trace. "Apparently there's a mini-epidemic at Pine Gulch Elementary School."

"Should I be calling in the Center for Disease Control?" He asked the question with a smile that made her heartbeat skip, made her wish she could forget everything and just sink into his kiss once more.

"I don't believe so. Good to know it's an option, though."

"Since it looks as if you've got your hands full, I'll take off. Thank you for the cookies and cocoa and... everything."

Her mind replayed the heat of his mouth on hers, his body hard and solid, his arms wrapping her close...

"Thank you for helping me clear the driveway."

"You're welcome. I'm afraid you're only going to have to head out again in a few hours and do it all over again."

Through the kitchen window, she could see big, fluffy flakes slanting past and she sighed. "You know, if I were in Phoenix right now, I wouldn't have to worry about the snow."

Or the ache in her feet from standing all morning in the diner or keeping the power bill paid or how she was going to put food on the table for a growing nine-year-old girl after her mother cleared out her savings and her equity.

Or sexy, perceptive police chiefs that made her want to throw all her troubles to the wind and jump into his arms.

"I'm glad you're not in Phoenix," he said with a half smile, and despite all the stress and worry and snow, for this moment, she was, too.

After Trace donned his police-department coat and Stetson again and headed out the door, Becca returned to the kitchen and fixed a tray of saltines and some of the orange-pineapple juice Gabi liked, then headed up the stairs.

Though there were two other bedrooms besides her own on the main floor, Gabi had chosen a room up here, a small, cramped little space under the eaves with a sharply angled ceiling and dormers at both ends.

She knocked outside the door and after a long pause, Gabi finally said, "Come in."

With her first weekly paycheck from The Gulch, she and Gabi had driven to Idaho Falls where the shopping selection was a little better and purchased a can of pale lavender paint and a cheerful comforter set to make the space more homey.

Despite those feeble decorating efforts, Gabi hadn't done anything to put the stamp of her considerable personality in the room. Other than the warm, fluffy comforter and the fresh coat of paint over the tired old beige, the room seemed barren and lifeless.

Becca understood her sister's psyche entirely too well. Given her track record with Monica, Gabi didn't expect to be here long, so why bother trying to make the room feel more like home? Her heart ached for her sister, for all the rooms she had probably settled into, only to be yanked out again when Monica moved on to the inevitable greener pasture.

"How are you feeling?" she asked, setting the small tray on the narrow table beside the bed.

"Okay."

She reached out to feel Gabi's forehead and wasn't really surprised when the girl flinched away from the contact. Gabi didn't want to let Becca past her defenses any more than she wanted to settle into the house.

"You don't have a fever. Not that I'm an expert, you understand, but as far as I can tell you don't feel warm. Do you think you're going to be sick?"

"No. I'm okay now. It was probably just something I ate."

Her gaze shifted to the drawer of the bedside table then quickly away again, making Becca wonder if Gabi had perhaps stashed junk food in there and was eating it until she was sick. That was another hallmark of someone with an uncertain childhood—stockpiling food for those times when Monica was too busy with her latest scheme to remember minor little details like feeding her child.

One part of her wanted to let Gabi keep whatever security measures she needed to feel safe, but this was one of those situations where Becca knew she needed to be the adult, not hearken back to that scared child, tucking a jar of peanut butter and a spoon under her bed, just in case. She resolved to find a moment over the weekend to look through Gabi's room when she had a chance.

Not now, though, when Gabi said she had a stomachache.

"Can I get you anything?" Becca asked.

"No. I think I'll just try to finish the book I'm supposed to for my oral report next week and then maybe take a nap."

Though she detested her homework, there were moments when Gabi sometimes acted more like a particularly responsible college student than a nine-year-old. Becca still found them unnerving.

She couldn't shake the feeling that something else was going on with Gabi, that the girl was perhaps in some kind of trouble. She wasn't great at reading her sister but there was an air of suppressed excitement about Gabi underneath her mien of solemn illness. Becca's early years with Monica had left her rather good at sensing subtexts and layers. It had also taught her the futility of fighting a losing battle. Right now, Gabi seemed completely closed off to her.

"Does anything sound good to you for dinner?"

Gabi's shove rippled the comforter tucked under her chin. "I'm not hungry. Just fix whatever sounds good to you. If I'm feeling okay, I'll try to eat something later."

"Okay. Get some rest." She smoothed her sister's hair away from her face, wondering how it was possible for this curious little creature to become so dear to her in a few short, extremely stressful months. Oh, she might occasionally long for the life she'd had before Monica and Gabi had burst back into it, probably in the way any new parent might pine for their single, carefree life at random moments.

Protecting and caring for Gabi had become the most important thing in her world. She loved Gabi and would do anything necessary, even wait tables for ten hours a day, to make sure her sister never had to squirrel food away again.

She tucked the comforter a little more snugly around her sister, then turned toward the door. Gabi's voice stopped her before she reached it and she turned.

"I really am sorry I left school like that. I just…didn't want to be at school anymore. I mean, not if I was going to be sick or something. I didn't want to puke in front of the other kids. Will we be in trouble now?"

"I called and spoke with the school secretary. I promised her it wouldn't happen again. It won't, right?"

"No. It was a stupid mistake. I should have followed the rules better."

Gabi sounded so disgusted with herself, Becca was compelled to return to the bed and pull her sister into a hug.

Though Gabi tended to shy away from physical encounters like a kitten who'd had one to many encounters with a stern broom, this time she yielded in Becca's arms and she could swear she even felt her sister return the hug for a moment before she dropped her arms and eased away.

Progress. One little step was still forward momentum.

"Get some rest now. I'm sure Donna won't mind if I take tomorrow off and I'm not working Sunday so that will give you the weekend to recover."

"You don't have to take time off. I'm fine staying here by myself."

She wasn't going to let that happen anytime soon. "We'll see. Maybe I can see if Morgan Boyer can babysit you again."

"I don't know why you won't let me stay alone. Mom did it all the time."

She was *not* their mother. She had spent her entire adult life making sure of that. "We'll figure something out." She headed for the hallway. "I'll leave your door open. Call down the stairs if you need anything."

"I won't."

Of course not. Gabi thought she was this self-contained little adult who didn't need help from anyone. She left the door ajar but by the time she made it to the bottom of the stairs, she heard the click of Gabi closing it firmly behind her.

Becca sighed, fighting the urge to march back up the stairs and open the door again. Gabi was doing her best to keep her out. The only thing she could do was keep pouring love on her sister and she had to hope she would eventually reach through that prickly skin to the sweet girl she knew lived inside Gabi.

Chapter 7

Sunday evening, Trace sat in the two-storied great room at River Bow enjoying the warmth of the fireplace and the flickering Christmas tree lights and the sight through the huge picture window of the last rays of the dying sun reflecting a pale orange on the snow.

He'd had a hell of a few days and was in dire need of a little quiet. The storm Friday and Saturday had snarled up the roads, resulting in numerous traffic accidents. And then that stupid jackass Carl Crenshaw had spent all day Saturday watching college football games and steadily drinking, trying to drown his sorrows at being laid off from the county road crew. When his wife tried to get him to turn the television off for dinner, he'd ripped down the mounted trophy six-point deer rack he'd shot the previous fall and gone after his wife with it, while their three kids watched.

Now Connie was in the hospital in Idaho Falls with a broken arm and multiple stab wounds and Carl was in the county jail and their three little kids had probably been traumatized for life.

Trace needed a little peace and lighthearted chatter. Unfortunately, he wasn't finding much of it here. His twin brother could usually be counted on for a laugh but he was on duty. Ridge was busy with ranch paperwork, Caidy had kicked him out of the kitchen and Destry seemed subdued and distracted.

She sat silently beside him reading a book while he flipped through channels, not in the mood to watch football after the Crenshaw domestic dispute. Wally Taylor's ugly little dog sat at her feet, chewing on a rawhide bone Caidy had produced for him when they arrived.

Finally her silence became too much and he turned off the television. "Okay, spill. What's going on? Doesn't Christmas vacation start later this week? You should be hyped up on sugar and bouncing off the walls right about now."

She gave him an exasperated look. "I'm nine years old, Uncle Trace. I don't bounce off walls."

A few months ago on her birthday, she'd basically done exactly that, but he decided not to embarrass her by reminding her of it. "Okay, maybe you're too old for bouncing off walls but you should at least be in a good mood," he said. "It's Christmas! What are you asking Santa to bring you?"

"Nine years old, remember?" she pointed out. "I don't believe in fairy tales like Santa Claus and the Easter Bunny anymore."

"Now, that's just sad," he said. She was growing up, no longer the cute little bug who used to jump into his arms when he walked through the door. In a few short years she would be a teenager—ack!—and not have time for him anymore. Before that happened, he would have to make sure all the young men in town remembered her uncle was the chief of police.

"Okay, scratch Santa, then. What are you asking your dad to get you for Christmas?"

Caidy walked in at that moment carrying a bowl of her creamy, delicious mashed potatoes, which she set on the dining table. "Wrong question."

"Why's that?" he asked.

"We're having issues in that arena," Ridge answered, coming down the hall from the ranch office with a stack of paperwork in his hand.

"What's the matter?" Trace winked at Destry. "Are you asking for a new Ferrari again?"

She frowned. "No. It's not a big deal. I don't know why everybody's so mad."

"Nobody's mad, honey," Caidy said. "Just concerned about what's going on. You have to admit, it's unusual."

He thought things had been better with his niece. After he and Taft had talked about the problem a few weeks ago, she had seemed to cheer up and had become excited about Christmas again. Apparently he was out of the loop around the ranch. He'd missed dinner the week before thanks to his crazy December schedule and hadn't given Destry much thought.

"What's so unusual? What's going on?" he asked as they all converged on the table and took their usual places.

"It's not a big deal," Destry repeated. "I only asked for money this year instead of presents. You'd think I robbed a bank or something."

"Money for what?"

"There's the rub," Ridge muttered. "She doesn't want to tell us. She insists it's her business. I don't know how any kid can expect her parents to just hand over cash for Christmas or anything else without having the first idea what it's going to be used for."

"It's not like I'm going to buy drugs or something! I wouldn't do anything bad with it, I swear, Dad."

"Then you shouldn't have a problem telling me what you want to do with the money," Ridge countered as he grabbed a fresh roll out of the basket and set it on the edge of his plate. "How do I know you're not going to run off and buy a train ticket to Hollywood?"

"You know I wouldn't do that. Jeez, Dad."

"Then what?"

"I don't know. Stuff. Books and clothes. Songs on iTunes. I'm nine years old. Maybe I would just like some money to spend the way I want it."

She looked down at her plate when she spoke but Trace didn't miss the slight flush on her high cheekbones. She was a lousy liar and they all knew it. She could never look any of them in the eye when she told a whopper. Ridge glanced at Trace, a help-me-out-here sort of look in his eyes, as if his position as chief of police gave him automatic lie-detector status.

"You get an allowance, right?" he asked. "Maybe you can talk to your dad about a raise. Why do you need more than that?"

"I just do." She spoke with the stubbornness she had inherited from her father. And her uncles and aunt, for that matter. None of the Bowmans had a reputation for backing down from an argument.

"Well, if money is what you want, I think that's what you should get."

His pronouncement was met with a grateful look from Destry, but Caidy and Ridge just glared at him.

"No, it's not," Ridge said.

"Why not? Makes it easier on the rest of us. Then we don't have to waste our time shopping for things she doesn't want. Like, I don't know, those new pink-and-black Tony Lamas with the flowers on them that somebody mentioned a few months ago."

He thought he had her there. For a few seconds, her eyes softened with wistful yearning but then she blinked and her expression grew resolute once more.

"Thanks, Uncle Trace." She rose from the table and came around to his side and wrapped her arms around his neck for a quick hug before returning to her seat. "Will you tell Uncle Taft?"

He nodded. "I'll tell him. But you know Taft and how much he likes to shop for pink flowered boots."

She giggled. "Dad, do you want me to say grace?"

Though Ridge was still glowering at Trace, he nodded to his daughter. "Make sure you ask a special blessing for your uncles to be safe while they work."

"I always do," Destry said, which sent a lump rising in Trace's throat.

After the dinner of pot roast and potatoes and Caidy's moist, delicious rolls, he and Ridge were relegated to kitchen duty while Caidy and Destry worked on home-work on the recently cleared dining room table.

"So what's really going on with the whole Christmas-present thing?" he asked his older brother as he washed dishes.

"Damned if I know. She came home from school

with this harebrained request earlier this week and refuses to talk about it. She just says she wants money instead of presents." He shrugged. "Doesn't matter. I bought her a new saddle clear back last summer and I've been hiding it in the barn. Caidy's done most of the rest of her Christmas shopping already on the internet. We're not sending everything back."

Ridge dried and put the gravy bowl that had been their mother's on the top shelf of the cupboard. "Maybe you can talk to her. See if she'll tell you what's going on and why she needs money more than pink cowboy boots."

Trace frowned. "Why me?"

"You're the trained investigator. If you can't get anything out of her, I don't know who can."

"This is a little different than weaseling a confession out of a hardened criminal."

"With all your experience, getting a nine-year-old girl to tell you her secrets should be a breeze, right?"

He wasn't having much luck convincing Becca Parsons to confide her worries in him. But unlike the beautiful but secretive waitress, Destry already loved and trusted him. She might be a little more willing to confide in him.

After they finished washing the dishes and returning them to the cupboards, Ridge returned to the ranch computer in his office and Trace sauntered out to the dining table, where Destry and Caidy were working on a math assignment while Grunt plopped at their feet.

"How's the homework coming?"

She scribbled one more equation, then set down her pencil and closed her math book with satisfaction. "Done. Finally."

"Good. I was thinking, I bet my favorite girl has been lonely. You want to come out with me to give Genie an apple?"

He counted on Destry's love for all the horses on the ranch to help persuade her to walk with him out to the barn for a little heart-to-heart.

"Sure," she exclaimed, looking much happier than she'd been all evening. "Just let me grab my coat."

A few moments later, they walked outside and headed for the barn. Grunt waddled along behind them, accompanied by a couple of the border collies Caidy rescued and trained. The December night was still, the kind of winter night when the world seemed to be holding its breath, waiting for something magical.

He walked the familiar path between the house and the barn, remembering all those years of having to wake before the sunrise to take care of chores before school. Though he had decided when he was a kid that ranching wasn't for him, he was still grateful for the lessons he'd learned here and the memories.

This had been the perfect place to grow up. Hidden trails to explore, a creek to play in on hot summer afternoons, a barn made for jumping into the hay from the loft. Wintertime had been sledding down the hill behind the barn, racing Taft on snowmobiles across the pasture, midnight rides into the mountains under a cold, starry night.

They had all been extraordinarily happy here, until that fateful night a decade ago. He pushed away the grim note, instead forcing himself to breathe in the scent of pine and cattle and that distinctive scent of impending snow.

At the barn, he headed immediately for his favorite

horse, the buckskin mare he had trained seven or eight years earlier. She whinnied with delight when she saw him, more so when he produced her favorite treat, an apple, from his pocket.

While she lipped the treat, he rubbed her neck and withers while Destry refilled water troughs from the hose in the barn then came to stand beside him.

"I need to get out here one evening and take her for a ride," he said.

"Can I come with you?"

He had the strangest idea of taking Becca and her daughter along with them. They would enjoy it, he thought. Would she agree to come? Maybe he would broach the idea after the holidays, when things settled down a little for him. She wanted only friendship between them but maybe if she spent a little more time with him, she might be persuaded to consider something more.

"Sure thing, munchkin. It's a date."

They moved next to *her* horse, the sturdy little paint pony she had named the rather unoriginal Patches when she was about five years old. She chattered to Trace about school, about her friends, about her homework, about a slumber party she would be attending over Christmas vacation. Finally he swung the conversation toward his reason for inviting her out to the barn.

"So just between the two of us, what's the real story about your Christmas presents? Why do you want money instead of girl stuff this year?"

She was quiet for a moment but he could see in her eyes that she was bursting to talk about it. "You promise you won't tell my dad or Aunt Caidy?"

"Why would I want to tell them?" he said, careful not

to make any vows he wasn't prepared to keep. People seemed to think they could lie to children with impunity but he'd never subscribed to that belief.

She seemed to take his evasion as proof he would stay mum. She looked around the barn one more time, as if fearing invisible eavesdroppers. Or maybe she was worried Grunt would tell tales. Then she turned back to him.

"I want to give it to my friend."

"Your friend?"

Destry nodded. "She's really sick. Maybe dying. Her mom… They can't afford the surgery she needs to get better. I don't want her to die. She's only nine. My age. Me and my friends decided to help her. Maybe we can even raise enough money so she can have the surgery."

Okay, he hadn't been expecting that. He tried to keep his finger pretty firmly on the pulse of Pine Gulch and he hadn't heard anything about a sick child who needed surgery. "What's wrong with her?"

"I don't know for sure what it's called but she has some kind of problem with her heart. It makes her tired and sometimes she can't even play at recess. She just has to sit on the swings. Don't you think that's sad?"

"Very sad," he agreed. "What friend is this?"

She looked away from him, her eyes on her horse. "I promised I wouldn't tell. She doesn't like people to know she's sick, so she only told about five of us in the class. Nobody else knows."

He frowned. "Really? Not even Ms. Hartford?"

"I don't think so. She said people treat her differently when they find out and she just wants to be normal."

That sounded feasible, if a little odd. "You can tell me, Des. I can keep a secret. It's part of my job sometimes. Maybe I can help you persuade your dad to forget about the Christmas presents this year if you let me in on it."

She chewed her lip, mulling it over. Patches nickered and Destry finally shook her head. "I can't, Uncle Trace. I promised."

"Does she act sick?"

"Just tired a lot. Friday she was so tired she couldn't stay awake in class. She ended up going home at afternoon recess."

He stared at her, picturing Gabi Parsons coming into the kitchen of Becca's house with her parka covered in snow. Had she looked like someone with a heart condition? She had seemed subdued and a little pale except for the spots of cold-weather color on her cheeks.

Gabi had a heart condition? She was sick, possibly dying? Oh, *damn*.

He thought of how solemn she seemed all the time and the significant looks that sometimes passed between Becca and her daughter. It was definitely possible. That could explain everything—the worry in Becca's eyes when she looked at the girl, her desperate efforts to provide for her child, that sense of fear, almost despair, he picked up sometimes.

He had picked up plenty of clues over the weeks that she had tumbled into tough times. Medical costs could certainly explain that. Maybe she had come to Pine Gulch to live in her grandfather's house so she could save money on rent in order to afford an expensive operation her child needed.

A tiny jagged pain lodged in his chest at the thought of Becca coping with this kind of fear on her own, of poor Gabi facing tests and hospitalizations and the thought that she might not survive.

No wonder she had pushed him away after that stunning kiss. The last thing she probably had any energy for or interest in was a new relationship, despite the attraction that simmered between them. He wished, more than anything, that she had trusted him enough to confide a few of her troubles to him. He couldn't have eased her burden, but sometimes the sharing of it offered its own comfort.

"You're not going to tell, right?" Destry asked anxiously. "You promised. Not my dad, not Aunt Caidy, not anybody."

He forced a smile for his niece through the ache in his heart. "What would I tell? I don't know a single thing except that Genie still likes apples."

She smiled back, nudging his shoulder with her head much the way his horse did when she was happy with him. What a great kid, he thought. At an age when most kids were completely egocentric, thinking the entire world should bow to their demands, Des was willing to give up all her Christmas presents to help her friend.

Becca should know how much Gabi's friends cared about her. Perhaps that would help lift her spirits.

Chapter 8

She was *not* a crafty person. So what was she doing the week before Christmas with knitting needles and a skein of yarn, trying to fumble her way through making a scarf and hat set for Gabi?

This was completely stupid, an exercise in frustration. She was trying only because Donna Archuleta loved to knit and always brought a bag with needles and yarn and her latest project to work on during her rare downtime at the diner. Becca had made the mistake of asking her about it one morning and the next thing she knew, Donna had brought her a spare pair of needles and yarn and had taught her a few basic stitches.

With the zeal of a true devotee, Donna had insisted this would help Becca deal with the stress of moving and the holidays and starting a new job. Those were the stresses Donna knew about. For obvious reasons,

Becca hadn't told Donna about the strain of working to fill the requirements for reciprocal bar admission to practice law in Idaho or the inherent difficulties of trying to be a parental figure to a girl she hadn't known a few months ago.

She dropped a stitch, her fourth in about an hour. Donna made it seem so effortless but Becca mostly found it a pain in the neck. She was determined to finish it, though, mostly to prove she could.

After fifteen more minutes, she dropped another stitch. Rats. She dug out the crochet hook and tried fixing it with the technique Donna had explained, but it was frustrating business.

Though it was just past nine, she knew she ought to be in bed. She had enjoyed the day off but had to be at The Gulch at six-thirty for the breakfast shift, another day of standing on her achy feet and pouring coffee. A few more moments, she told herself.

Christmas was only a week away and she regretted she didn't have more presents for Gabi, or the endless budget to buy them. A homemade matching scarf and beanie set was pretty tame as far as gifts went, but maybe it would help cheer Gabi out of her moodiness. The yarn had been free from Donna, so all she needed to spend on this was her time and aggravation.

She frowned up the stairs. Her sister had gone to bed an hour earlier, claiming exhaustion. Becca wasn't buying it. Something was definitely going on with the girl. She hadn't exhibited any signs of sickness or laid claim to any further stomachaches, but all weekend she had been acting strangely. Giddy one moment— as if she knew a secret no one else did—then morose and defeated the next. She seemed to have lost her appetite, too, and hadn't even seemed to enjoy making more cookies.

Becca had done her best to finesse the truth out of her sister but apparently her persuasive skills were on the rusty side. Gabi insisted everything was fine, that school was going well, that she was coming to enjoy her new friends. Her efforts to dig deeper than that with her sister earned her nothing. Apparently she was as lousy at parenting as she was at knitting. She sighed again. Okay, she wasn't *that* bad at knitting. She held up the scarf under the light. The crochet-hook trick had helped, though the yarn pulled a little more tightly in that area. Just like taking care of Gabi, she was doing her best. The job might not be perfect but she was trying, right?

She picked up the needles again and had finished another row when she heard a quiet rapping on the door. The hands on the carved mantel clock showed 9:20 p.m. Who on earth would be dropping in this late? Though this was Pine Gulch and not one of the bad neighborhoods in Phoenix, she was still wary. She was a single woman, alone here with her "daughter," and everyone who came into The Gulch probably knew it.

She set the knitting on the table beside her chair and moved to the door cautiously, wishing she had an extra set of needles so she could wield one as a weapon. Since she had only the one—the crochet hook had that unfortunate, well, hook that didn't seem particularly deadly—she picked up an umbrella from the stand behind the door. She wasn't going to let anybody hurt Gabi on her watch.

After a careful peek through the curtain on the old-fashioned door, she dropped the umbrella back in the stand, though her nerves weren't eased in the slightest to find the police chief standing on her doorstep.

As she reached for the doorknob, she had one of those random flashbacks of sneaking out the back door of a rented dive somewhere in Arkansas and slipping away through an alley while the police hammered on the front.

She wasn't doing anything wrong here, she reminded herself. Trace was a friend, of sorts—the closest thing, anyway, she had to a friend here in Pine Gulch besides Donna Archuleta.

She opened the door and shivered at the blast of cold air. It was snowing again, drat it. That was the first thing she noticed. Then she picked up the tension in his shoulders, the tight set to his mouth. He was obviously upset about something.

"May I come in?" he asked after she greeted him.

All her self-protective instincts urged her to make some polite excuse and slam the door. *It's not a good time. I just started a bath. I have to stir a pot of gravy on the stove. I'm in the middle of brain surgery.* Anything to keep at bay these dangerous feelings she was beginning to have for this dangerous man.

She remembered their kiss of a few days earlier, the heat of his mouth, the wild jumble of sensations twisting her insides. All weekend, she had tried to put those moments out of her mind but the memory of being in his arms would flash into her head at the oddest moments, like song lyrics she couldn't shake.

She was many things but she wasn't a coward. "Of course." She opened the door wide enough for him to step into the warmth of her living room. Little snow crystals had settled in his dark hair and they gleamed under her entry light.

"Sorry to barge in like this. You were probably in the middle of something."

"Not really. Nothing productive, anyway. I was trying to knit a scarf for Gabi."

"That sounds productive."

"Not when you're as lousy at it as I am. I'm glad for the break." That much was true, anyway.

"Please, come in. Can I get you something?"

"No. I'm fine. Thank you." He gazed at her for a moment, then shook his head. "Scratch that. I'm not fine. I'm in a dilemma and I'm not sure how to deal with it."

And he was coming to *her* for advice? She wasn't quite sure how to respond.

"I need to talk to you about something, but I gave my word to a C.I.—confidential informant—that I wouldn't reveal this information," he went on. "I keep my word, Becca."

"I'm sure you do," she answered. Everything she had come to know about Trace indicated he was a man of honor who would protect anyone who placed her trust in him.

Much to her surprise and further confusion, he reached out and gripped her fingers in his, cool from the night air. "On the other hand, I wouldn't be betraying any confidences or revealing any new information to *you*, obviously. How could I be, when you know all this already, right?"

Did she? Because right now all she knew was confusion and concern and the insane urge to stand here all night simply holding his hand.

"I'm just going to come right out and say it. I'm so sorry for everything. Why didn't you tell me?"

A tiny flicker of unease stirred in her stomach. "I'm afraid you're going to have to be more specific. Why didn't I tell you *what?*"

"Everything. About Gabi."

That unease grew to genuine foreboding. Somehow he must have discovered Gabi wasn't her daughter but her sister and that she had no formal guardianship of her. How? Had Gabi told someone at school, perhaps his niece? Did everyone in town know? Was he there to take Gabi away?

Wait. Don't panic. Not yet. To her surprise, he didn't seem condemning about her lies, merely sympathetic. She never would have expected such sanguinity from him.

She drew in a breath and slid her hand away from his and tucked it in the front pocket of her hoodie. "How did you…um…find out about Gabi?"

He smiled but it seemed oddly sad around the edges. "I can't tell you that. My C.I., remember? Look, you don't have to talk about it if you don't want to. Obviously you're a very private person and I understand and can respect that. But if you need anything, even just a shoulder, I'm here. How long have you been dealing with this on your own?"

It felt like forever. She thought of those terrible early weeks after Monica ran off when Gabi had been lost and frightened, grimly determined her mother was going to show up again any minute now. Becca had been furious with her mother, of course, for abandoning her child that way without a word…and then she realized

Monica had forged her name on several checks and withdrew nearly all her savings.

This was all before the forged mortgage paperwork had begun to show up and she realized how deeply her mother had entrenched Becca in her latest deception. It was the latest betrayal in a lifetime of them. Becca was a real-estate attorney. Monica had to know that even the slightest whiff of mortgage fraud could lead to disbarment.

Fortunately, the senior partners at her firm had trusted her when she explained the situation. They had helped her clean up the mess, though it had taken the rest of her savings and all her equity in her town house, all while she was also dealing with a damaged nine-year-old girl who didn't want to be with her.

Tears burned behind her eyelids. She was so very tired of carrying the weight of this by herself. She longed to share even a tiny portion of the burden with someone else for a few moments.

"About four months," she finally admitted.

"But this can be fixed, right?" His eyes were dark with sympathy and something else, almost like sorrow. She frowned. Something was wrong here. His reaction seemed far disproportionate to the situation.

"I don't see how," she said warily. "If you have any ideas, I'd love to hear them."

"Well, won't the surgery help?"

She stared at him, confused all over again. That unease bloomed again in her stomach. "I'm sorry. Back up the truck here. What surgery are you talking about?"

"Gabrielle's surgery. For her heart condition."

She blinked, feeling as if she'd stepped off a ledge

somewhere into an alternate universe. "Gabi has a heart condition?"

The sorrow in his eyes seemed to cloud over, like fog tendrils snaking through trees, giving way to a confusion that matched her own. Silence stretched between them and he finally sat down heavily on her grandfather's sagging old sofa. "Doesn't she?"

"No. Why on earth would you think so?"

His features seemed to harden. "Oh, I don't know. Maybe because my niece is asking for money in lieu of presents for Christmas this year so she can give the money to Gabi so you can afford her heart surgery."

That unease now exploded into full-blown panic and her stomach roiled. *Gabi, what have you done?*

"I'm sure there's some misunderstanding." *Please, God, let there be some misunderstanding.* "Gabi doesn't have a heart condition, I promise. She's perfectly healthy."

If anything, he looked even harder, like chiseled stone. "Explain to me, then, why my niece is asking for money this year instead of Christmas presents to pay for an unnecessary surgery for your daughter?"

Because Gabi had been fed a steady diet of schemes and cons by their mother and the sweet taste of the grift flowed through her veins. She didn't know whether to be more sad for her sister or for her victims.

"I can't answer that," she said grimly. "But I promise you, I'll find out."

"According to Destry, there are five other girls at Pine Gulch Elementary who also want to give up their Christmas this year to help your daughter."

Nausea churned through her. They were going to be in so much trouble. *Oh, Gabi. How could you do this?*

She closed her eyes for a moment, trying to figure out how to wade through these treacherous waters. Her face flamed and she was very much afraid she was going to be sick. She was exhausted suddenly. How many times had she been in this position, forced to make excuses— mostly to herself—for the people in her life? She had thought she was being so healthy and strong after cutting ties with her mother when she was barely sixteen. Those years had been terribly difficult, but the peace and serenity, the hard-fought security, had been worth the sacrifices.

Now here she was again in the same situation, and this time couldn't just walk away from her sister. Gabi didn't have anyone else.

"Gabi can be…overdramatic. She is also prone to, um, exaggeration. She might have started a story and gotten carried away."

His gaze narrowed. "Destry said she's dying."

Darn you, Gabi. They had to live in Pine Gulch. Her sister had to go to school now with these little girls she'd tried to con. Becca had to work at the café, where she was bound to encounter the little marks' angry parents.

Monica should have taught her one of the most basic rules of grifting: only an ill bird fouls its own nest.

"She's not dying, I promise," she assured Trace. Though by the time Becca was through with her, she might wish otherwise.

"I guess I'm going to have to take your word for it. I have to tell you, this whole thing seems really strange to me. I just can't see your average nine-year-old girl making up a story like this on her own."

And just like that, suspicion now swung back to her. *She* must have put Gabi up to it. What other explanation could there be? They were both in on it, planning to collect their ill-gotten gains by playing on the sympathetic instincts of gullible locals and then ditch Pine Gulch. It was a likely scenario, one she might have come up with herself.

She should have expected it, since the same thing had been happening her entire life.

Despite her frustration with her sister for shoving Becca into the firing line, thrusting her into this miserable position once more, she was aware of a vague feeling of hurt. Trace had kissed her. He had seemed determined to forge a friendship with her despite all her back-off signals and had urged her to give this attraction between them a chance. Yet he was very quick to jump to conclusions at the first sign of trouble.

It was irrational, she knew. The man *shouldn't* trust her. She had been lying about Gabi and her relationship to the girl since the moment she and Trace met. She had absolutely no right to feel hurt.

"Gabi is not your average nine-year-old," she said as calmly as she could muster.

"Has she made up a story like this before?"

Hundreds of times. She sighed. Gabi probably had been telling lies since she could talk. The girl deserved a normal life, but Becca didn't have the first idea how to convince her she wouldn't find one unless she shed all the bad habits of her first nine years.

"She has a vivid imagination." She picked her words carefully. "Sometimes it can get her into trouble. I'm sorry, Trace. I'll talk to her. I'll make sure she clears this whole thing up tomorrow at school, I promise."

"Destry has been really upset about this. I think this is the reason she has been acting so strangely the last few weeks, not eating and not showing much interest in her usual activities. She's a compassionate little girl and thinking Gabi was dying has shaken her up. I wouldn't be surprised if it's the same with the other girls.

"It was cruel of Gabi to play on their sympathies. Cruel and wrong. I absolutely agree. I will make sure she comes clean, I promise."

"Is she sleeping now?"

"Yes. And to be honest with you, I should be, too. I have to work an early shift in the morning." She rose, hoping he would take the hint. Coping with all the complicated layers of her attraction to him was beyond her capabilities right now when she needed to deal with this latest stress that no amount of knitting in the world could ever ease.

To her relief he stood, as well.

"She's really not dying." He said the words as both a statement and a question and Becca shook her head.

"She's fine, Trace."

"I'm glad for that, at least. It ripped my guts out to think of you having to cope with that kind of pain and worry by yourself."

She had plenty of pain and worry, just not that particular pain and worry. This was a very good reminder that life could always seem worse. At least she and Gabi were both healthy.

"Thank you for coming to tell me, Trace." She opened the door for him. "I'll deal with Gabi, you can be sure."

He looked as if he wanted to say something more but he finally nodded. "Good night, then," he said and walked out into the cold night air.

After she closed the door behind him, Becca leaned

against it, her emotions in turmoil. This was *her* fault. She had sensed something was up with Gabi even before her sister came home from school pretending to be sick the previous Friday. Instead of confronting it head-on and worming the truth from her sister, she had opted to ignore her instincts, ignore the whole situation. Because she had chosen the path of least resistance, Gabi's lies had now tangled them both up into a mess she didn't know how to escape.

Beneath her guilt with herself and her frustration with her sister and renewed worry about how they would be able to make a life here in Pine Gulch once Gabi's latest deception became common knowledge, Becca was aware of an aching sadness for what she had lost.

She might have told herself she couldn't allow a relationship with Trace, but some part of her still yearned. This was a firm reminder that they could never be more than casual friends. He was a sworn officer of the law and she came from a long line of felons and thieves. The smartest thing to do now would be to cling tightly to whatever hard-fought distance she could find, no matter how much it hurt.

Chapter 9

Though she had been tempted to wake Gabi as soon as Trace drove away through the December night, Becca forced herself to wait until the morning. Their confrontation would come soon enough. Better to wait until she had a cooler head and a calmer heart.

Instead, she endured a mostly sleepless night, worrying about her sister and about how she was going to teach right and wrong—moral choice and accountability—to a girl who had spent nine years watching her mother take what she wanted regardless of the consequences to anyone around her.

She grabbed only a few hours of sleep and woke gritty-eyed, with an aching sadness trickling through her.

Used to fending for herself from all those years with Monica, Gabi always woke to her own alarm clock. She was dressed and sitting at the small table in the dingy kitchen with her cereal bowl when Becca finished show-ering and pulling her hair into her customary ponytail.

"Morning." Gabi smiled at her, much more at ease than she'd seemed all weekend. The irony didn't escape Becca. She reminded herself that somewhere inside Gabi was as sweetly innocent as any other nine-year-old girl, she just needed more help and guidance now than most, as difficult as it might seem.

She drew in a deep breath. Now that the moment had come, she didn't know where to start. Better to just plunge right in, she decided, like that first moment of walking outside into the frigid air.

"I had a late-night visit from the police chief last night. Gabi, we need to talk."

Gabi froze, the spoon still in her mouth. Alarm flick-ered in her eyes but it was quickly concealed. She pulled the spoon out and returned it to the bowl before she spoke.

"Those girls gave me that stuff. I didn't do anything. I was going to give it back today, I swear."

She closed her eyes, her worst fears confirmed. The girls in her class thought she was dying of a heart con-dition and Gabi was certainly smart enough to work the situation to her advantage.

"What stuff?"

Gabi pressed her lips together as if she wanted to call her words back. After a long pause, she reached into her backpack and withdrew a handful of items, then spread them on the breakfast table. An iPod Touch, a handheld game system, a slim silver cell phone. What fourth-grader had a cell phone? Becca wondered. Prob-ably most of them.

"You told them you're sick, didn't you? That you have

a bad heart. That's why the girls in your class gave you those things."

To her credit, Gabi looked genuinely upset. Her face crumpled and a tear leaked from one eye. Either she truly regretted her actions or Monica had a serious contender for the most deceptive Parsons female. "I didn't mean for…for all this to happen, Becca. I swear, I didn't mean it."

"Why would you lie about something so terrible?"

"At first it was just a joke, you know?"

"No. I don't understand this at all. Explain how you could joke about having a serious heart condition."

"I didn't want to go to PE one day. We were doing that stupid crab soccer that I hate and I can't do. So I told one of the girls I had a heart problem and she helped me get out of class."

"Why didn't you just say you hated crab soccer?"

"I don't know. It was stupid. I felt bad about it right after and was going to tell her the truth, but…" Her voice trailed off and she looked truly miserable.

"What?"

"They were all so nice to me afterward, you know? Writing me notes, bringing me lunch, watching out for me on the playground." She looked down at the table. "I didn't want to be here and thought school was stupid. But after I lied about being sick, I felt, I don't know, *important*, I guess. They were even talking about having a benefit for me. I thought it was cool."

"And then the girls started giving you iPods and cell phones and talking about going without Christmas presents so they could give you the money instead?" She used her hard, sharp attorney's voice and Gabi looked up, startled and guilty.

"I didn't ask for any of that stuff, I swear! They all just gave it to me. I think they thought it would make me feel better or something. I was going to give it back and tell them you wouldn't let me keep it."

"But you weren't going to tell them you were lying."

Her sister's silence was answer enough and her frustration overwhelmed her. "For heaven's sake, Gabi. Pine Gulch is our *home* now. We're not going anywhere. Haven't you figured that out? These are neighbors and friends, not marks who are so stupid they deserve to be conned. People you can grift and then never see again. I can't believe Monica never explained the difference of that to you. What are those girls going to think now when they find out it's not true, that you don't have a heart condition and you're not dying?"

She could see by the shock on Gabi's features that the thought had never occurred to her. And why would it? She and Monica had never lived more than a few months at a time anywhere, always moving on to the next city, the next job. Her poor sister had never had a normal life. As far as Becca knew, she'd probably never had a real friend who lasted more than a few weeks. Of course she wouldn't have her focus on the long-term implications.

Her sister's words confirmed the assumption. "They won't want to be my friends now, will they?"

Oh, darn. She wanted to step in and fix this for her sister but she knew this was one of those problems Gabi simply had to deal with on her own. How could Becca undo a lifetime of her mother's example and help Gabi see she could find a better way of life than using other people for her own advantage?

The only thing that gave her hope was the knowledge

that she had grown up under the exact same circumstances and somehow came out the other side with this sometimes inconvenient moral compass she couldn't shake.

"It's going to take some work. Put yourself in their position. You lied to them. They won't like thinking you made a fool of them. Now you're going to have to be honest—tell them what you told me, about wanting them to like you. Believe it or not, honesty can take you a lot further than lies and deception."

Judging by her skeptical expression, Gabi didn't look as if she were buying that particular concept. Becca couldn't really blame her.

Gabrielle was quiet all the way to the diner. She tried rather halfheartedly to convince Becca she didn't feel well, still feeling sick from Friday, and thought she should stay home one more day.

Becca only raised her eyebrow and stared down her sister, and after a moment Gabi mumbled something about how she would probably feel better once she was at school. When they arrived, she slid into her favorite booth looking out over Main Street and propped her book open in front of her.

As Becca waited on customers, she tried to keep a careful eye on her sister. She was fairly positive she didn't see Gabi turn the page one single time. Still, Gabi barely looked up even when Becca set a hot chocolate topped with fluffy whipped cream in front of her.

A little remorse could go a long way, she reminded herself as she waited on The Gulch regulars. Gabi needed to suffer a little for what she'd done to deceive her friends. Pain was a harsh but effective teacher.

The regulars had been joined by one of their occasional members, the mayor of Pine Gulch, Quinn Montgomery, a distinguished-looking man in his sixties with a teasing glint in his eyes.

She passed out their orders, ending with the mayor. "Here you go, sir. Egg-white omelet with extra green peppers, just the way you like."

"Thank you, my dear." He gave her a warm smile. "I don't know how you keep straight what everyone prefers."

She returned his smile as she refilled coffee at the table. "My steel-trap mind, Mayor. It serves me well."

He laughed out loud at that. "Where can I get one of those? My Marjorie is always telling me I'd forget my head if it wasn't screwed on."

Becca smiled and moved on to the next table, feeling slightly better than she had since she woke up.

She might trip over her feet and struggle to pour a simple cup of coffee without spilling it all over the customer and herself, but Becca had been given the gift of a keen memory. She never would have survived law school that first terrible year without it.

She sometimes suspected her excellent memory for customer names and preferences might be the only reason Lou and Donna hadn't fired her after the first week for gross incompetence. She was not cut out to be a waitress, though she wanted to believe she was no longer a complete disaster.

A couple of construction workers next to the regulars' booth were just giving her their orders when the door to the diner opened and the chief of police walked in wearing khakis and his Pine Gulch PD parka, looking dark and masculine. Her heartbeat skittered and she shifted her body so she was turned away from the door, reluctant to face him after the awkwardness of the night before.

"Did you catch that?"

She looked down at the construction worker with a bushy beard that had taken over his face. So much for her memory. With Trace Bowman around, she forgot completely where she was and what she was doing. "I'm sorry. Can you repeat that?"

With a frustrated sigh, he gave her his order again, making sure she wrote it down dutifully this time. When she finished, she turned to head toward the kitchen to place the order with Lou and discovered Trace had stopped to talk to the mayor and the other regulars, which meant she had no choice but to walk right past him.

She might have expected him to gaze at her with wariness or even disdain after basically finding out her sister was running a con on the whole elementary school. Instead, he greeted her with a smile that felt very much like a warm kiss on the cheek.

"Thanks for meeting me here," she heard the mayor say as she moved past. "We've got to figure out what we can do about that pesky intersection once and for all. Three fender-benders there in two weeks are three too many. Becca, you mind if we take an empty booth?"

She turned back. "Um, no. Of course not. Take whichever table you'd like."

"Can you give me a minute first, Mayor?" Trace asked. "I see someone I need to have a word with."

"No problem. Do what you need to do."

Becca expected Trace to go talk to one of the other patrons. Instead, he headed toward the booth in the corner where Gabi sat pretending to read, the whipped cream now dissolved into her untouched hot chocolate.

Oh, she wished she had a customer nearby who needed something. She was consumed with curiosity and no small amount of dread. Would he lecture Gabi, chide her for lying? She wouldn't be able to hear them over the noise of clinking glasses and the hum of conversation in the diner.

She could *see* Gabi's reaction, however. Her sister's expression as she saw the chief of police headed toward her was painful to see, a mix of fear and embarrassment. Trace said something to her, and to her shock Becca watched a small smile blossom on her sister's features, the first one she'd seen all morning.

They talked for a moment longer and then Gabi actually laughed. Becca couldn't hear the sound of it from her position but she could see her sister's genuine smile, the way her eyes lit up as some of the fine-wrought tension seeped out of her.

In that instant as she gazed at the two of them, something hard and tight seemed to dislodge around her heart and crumble to pieces. The noises of the diner seemed to fade and she couldn't breathe suddenly as the shocking realization thundered through her.

She was falling for Trace Bowman, this man who took time out of his hectic schedule and left the mayor himself waiting so that he could cajole a smile and a laugh from a frightened young girl.

Oh, she was an idiot. He was a police officer. The *chief* of police, for heaven's sake. If he knew who she was, what she came from, he would want nothing to do with her. How could she have been so very foolish? She should have taken better care to keep him at a distance.

From the moment she had met him here at The Gulch, she should have done everything she could to discourage his attempts at friendship.

She knew what was at stake here. As she had told her sister just that morning, Pine Gulch was their home now. They had nowhere else to go. She was trying to be admitted into the bar, to open her own law practice.

Only an ill bird fouls its own nest. Her nest was well and truly fouled. Disastrously messed up. How would she be able to live here, make a life with Gabi, when she was foolishly falling in love with the chief of police?

"Hey, Becca, you mind topping me off?" Jesse Redbear gave her his toothless smile. The sounds of the diner filtered back through her head and she realized she was standing stupidly in the middle of the floor gazing into space with the pot of regular in her hand.

She forced herself to move forward. Out of somewhere deep inside, she manufactured a smile. "Here you go. Sorry about that."

"Everything okay, hon? You look kind of pale." Sal Martinez gave her a worried look.

"I'm fine. Just fine." She shoved this latest disaster into the compartment in her head labeled "later" and pasted on what she hoped was a charming smile. "I can't believe it's snowing again. Doesn't it ever stop around here?"

"Sure," Jess said with his wheezy two-pack-a-day laugh. "We hardly ever have snow in July and August."

"Something to look forward to, then," she answered, then moved away. She would worry about Trace Bowman and her very inconvenient feelings for him later. For now, she had a shift to finish, responsibilities to meet.

A nest to protect.

* * *

As he sat down with the mayor and listened while Quinn outlined the complaints he'd received about the intersection of Aspen Grove and Skyline Road, Trace couldn't seem to keep himself from watching Becca out of the corner of his gaze.

He found everything about her fascinating, from how she tucked her hair behind her ear, to the way she nibbled on the end of her pencil as she took orders, to the little wrist flip she did as she delivered a customer's order.

He wasn't the only one drawn to her. Because of her quiet dignity and warmth, people just seemed to want to be around her. The old coots who were The Gulch regulars were completely enamored. They flirted and joked and teased. She didn't appear to mind. She flirted right back with them. He imagined just the tips from the breakfast regulars would go far to help her with her budgetary needs.

Soon she made her way through the dining room toward the open table Quinn had found near the hall leading to the bathroom, though she still seemed to be avoiding his gaze.

"Mayor, would you like more coffee?"

"I'm good, thanks."

Finally she met his gaze and he saw wariness there and something else, something that looked like barely veiled panic.

"Chief Bowman, are you ready to order?" she asked, pulling out her notebook and pencil.

The idea of her in a position of servitude bothered him for reasons he couldn't have explained, but he didn't have a choice in this situation. "I'm going to have to go with what works. I'll have my usual. Western omelet and a stack."

"A man who knows what he wants."

"I'm beginning to," he murmured.

Her eyes widened and she stared at him for a long moment. Currents zinged between them and he couldn't believe everybody else in the diner didn't notice. Finally she wrenched her gaze away and nearly stumbled in her haste to escape their table and head toward Lou and the grill to give his order.

"In the short-term, we need a four-way stop there at the minimum, wouldn't you agree?" the mayor said.

Trace turned his attention back to the conversation and responded appropriately, though half his mind was still occupied with Becca and Gabi. A few moments later, he saw her glance at her watch and then head to the girl's table, probably to remind her it was time for school.

Gabi's face was all puckered and tight like she wanted to cry. Poor kid. He didn't blame her for not wanting to go to school. When he had spoken with her earlier, he had mainly intended only to tell her he was relieved she wasn't dying, but the moment she saw him, Gabi had looked even more miserable, if possible. Her features had dissolved into distress and she had stammered out an explanation about wanting to get out of PE and the story exploding beyond her control. She was visibly upset and had even apologized to *him* for her deception, when he had merely been a bystander in the whole situation.

He hadn't lectured her. Instead, he had told her about the time he and his twin brother had tried to deceive their teachers by trading places in school and he'd learned later his brother had only come up with the idea so he could get out of three tests he had that day. What had started as a funny joke had turned into the worst day of his young life.

The poor girl had laughed at the story but she was still quite obviously very sorry for what she had done. He'd also given her the benefit of his life experience by telling her things that seem impossible to face are never as hard as they appear. Like yanking a bandage, it was usually better to do it fast and get it over with.

She wouldn't have an easy time of it in school that day but she would get through it.

On some level, he could relate. He knew what it was to regret something with every breath, to wonder how he could ever face the people he had wronged. After his parents' murders, he had expected Caidy and his brothers to hate him for his unwitting part. If he hadn't been so self-absorbed with Lilah Bodine, he would have been at the ranch with his parents. He didn't know if he could have stopped the home invasion robbery but he might have been able to use the negotiation skills he'd gained as an MP to keep the situation from exploding as it had done.

Instead, he'd been drinking and partying, making out with a lying little bitch while his parents died violent and tragic deaths, his younger sister emotionally scarred for life.

His siblings hadn't blamed him. He still didn't understand why but he was deeply grateful for their forbearance. He pushed the thought away as he watched Becca help Gabi into her coat and backpack. He couldn't hear their conversation but he saw Becca pull her daughter into a hug. "I'm sorry, honey, but you have to face this," he heard her say.

Gabi released a heavy sigh and started trudging toward the door as if she were heading toward a month of math exams. She had to pass his table as she went and he impulsively reached out a hand and grabbed her arm. "Everything will be okay, Gabi. Any girl tough enough to set up a Christmas tree on the first try can handle this."

She didn't look convinced but she still gave him a hesitant smile that seemed to reach right in and nestle next to his heart. "Thanks," she said.

"You're welcome."

When he looked up, he found Becca watching him with an unreadable look in her eyes. Just before Gabi reached the door, Becca called out to her to wait for a moment, then she turned to Donna, working behind the counter. "Donna, do you mind if I take my break a little early so I can run Gabi to school? It's snowing pretty hard out there."

"No problem," the older woman answered. "I can cover your section."

Becca hurried to the back room and returned a moment later minus her apron and carrying her coat and purse.

While she was gone, Trace and the mayor finished their plan of attack on the hazardous intersection—a new four-way-stop and better signage—and the mayor excused himself to meet with the head of the public works department that took care of the roads.

Trace was just about done with his omelet when Becca returned, her features tight with stress.

He had a ridiculous urge to pull her down beside

him, tuck her under his arm and let her lean on him for a moment. She gave him a distracted smile but moved into the back room again to change out of her coat and back into her apron.

He needed to head into the station but found himself reluctant to leave without talking to her again. When she bustled out and started making the rounds of the diner with coffee, he fought the urge to grab her hand and make her stop and rest for a moment. Finally she made it to his table.

"Looks like the mayor paid for your breakfast. Would you like more coffee before you leave, Chief Bowman?"

She had called him Trace when he kissed her. He found himself reliving that kiss in great detail and wanting nothing more than another taste. "I'm good. I've got to head into the station, anyway. Gabi made it to school, then?"

Her smile faltered a little and he saw worry in her eyes. "I stayed and watched her walk all the way through the front doors and even saw Jennie Dalton greet her at the entrance. I don't think she'll be able to duck outside again, not with the principal herself in view."

He had a feeling Gabi was clever enough to do just that but he decided not to worry Becca by sharing that particular opinion.

"She told me what you said, about being brave enough to face her lies and how much better she'll feel when she's made things right. Thank you."

"You're welcome. She's a good kid, Becca. I really do think she just told a little lie and then got carried away. It happens."

She opened her mouth to respond, then closed it again, obviously changing her mind. "I'm sure you're right, Chief," she said solemnly before heading to the kitchen.

The mayor had probably covered his tip as well, but Trace left a few bills on the table anyway, wanting to leave her a healthy but not exorbitant gratuity. She would hate feeling like an object of charity, he knew.

His day was hectic with snow-related trouble. Besides the usual car accidents, a section of roof collapsed on the auto parts store, injuring an employee and a customer. He only had time for the occasional worry for Becca and Gabi until he returned to his own house twelve hours later to find a basket on his doorstep, its contents hidden in red tissue paper.

It wasn't unusual this time of year for Pine Gulch citizens to drop off the occasional thank-you gift for the police department. People typically made these sorts of deliveries to the police station but since everyone in town knew where he lived, he had occasionally been the recipient of a box of fudge or some peanut brittle. He considered that one of the best things about living in Pine Gulch. The small police force had its detractors, certainly, but most of the residents seemed to appreciate the sacrifice and dedication of his officers.

He slid open the envelope and saw the note with its slanting, firm handwriting. "We made sugar cookies this afternoon and Gabi wanted to bring you some," Becca wrote. "Thank you for buoying up a frightened girl. She survived the day, with your help."

He unlocked the door to a barked greeting from his ugly, grumpy dog, who spent most of the day sleeping or sniffing around the perimeter of his yard as if guarding a demilitarized zone.

He patted the dog's head and scratched behind his

ears. Poor thing, spending so much time by himself. Trace tried to take him around town whenever he could, but Grunt seemed to prefer his own company, probably from all those years as a companion to a dour old man.

He ought to look around for a new home for Grunt. A family, maybe. Noisy and hectic. That would be good for him. Caidy had offered to take him to the ranch to add to her menagerie. Grunt wasn't crazy about horses and had a hard time keeping up with Caidy's more active ranch dogs, but he might still enjoy the company.

He nibbled on a cookie, then gave a tiny section to Grunt, who gobbled it up and came back looking for more. Trace knew he ought to just sit here and eat his cookies and stay away from his very lovely—and dangerous—neighbor. But he found himself consumed with curiosity to find out how things went for Gabi beyond this hastily penned note.

"Do you want to go for a walk?"

The dog yawned and planted his head down across his front paws. Trace shook his head in exasperation. "Too bad. We're going."

He grabbed the leash off the hook by the door and fastened it around the dog's collar, then surveyed his kitchen. He needed more of an excuse to drop by her house than merely taking his dog for a walk. When his gaze landed on the basket full of cookies, he smiled and reached into the cupboard for another container. After transferring the cookies from her basket to his container, he rummaged through the cupboard for one of his few precious remaining jars of pepper jelly that Caidy and Destry had made him in the summer. They knew it was his favorite, so every year Caidy put up a dozen jars just for him. He cherished each one but he was willing to part with one if it would get him through Becca's door.

By the time he hooked the leash on the dog's collar, Grunt had perked up a bit and shuffled around impatiently for Trace to unlock the door. The snow had stopped, he was glad to see. This had definitely been a record-breaker of a December so far. The snowmobilers were loving it.

Somebody with a snowblower had cleared all the sidewalks on the street, he was grateful to see. He followed the ridged tracks all the way to Wally Taylor's old house. Her curtains were open, and as he approached the house he saw her inside on the sofa, wrapped in a blanket with a book spread open on her lap, a lamp lit beside her and the Christmas tree lights sending shifting colors across her features.

Something hungry and insistent curled low in his gut. He wanted her, wanted this. The whole picture: a cozy fire on a bitter winter's night, a comfortable house made welcoming for the holidays and especially the warm and lovely woman waiting for him at the end of a hard day.

He didn't want these feelings, particularly not for a woman who didn't trust him and who pushed him away at every opportunity, but he was very much afraid it was too late.

She looked up from her book at that precise moment and her gaze met his through the frost-filigree glass of her window. Her eyes widened with surprise and something else. He wanted to think she was happy to see him but he couldn't be sure.

He gestured toward the front door, then walked up

onto the porch to wait for her to open it. When she did, her features were wary.

"Trace! Come in. It's freezing out there."

"I've got my dog. Do you mind if I bring him inside?"

"You have a dog?"

"Well, I've always assumed he's a dog, though he might be a mutant goblin of some sort."

She gazed down at his funny-looking dog with a look of fascination. "He's welcome to come inside."

Warmth enfolded him as he walked inside the house that smelled of Christmas, of pine trees and cookies and cinnamon.

"He's, um, an interesting-looking dog."

"He was your grandfather's, actually. Grunt, this is Becca."

The dog belched a greeting and Becca smiled a little before turning back to Trace. "What kind of dog is, um, Grunt?"

"The vet says French bulldog, mostly, with a few other breeds thrown in just to muddy the waters."

"Ah. Is everything okay? Please don't tell me you just found out Gabi's been spreading some other kind of lie. I don't think I can handle more."

He laughed, though he was thinking again how foolish he had been to come here. "No. Grunt needed to get out so I thought I would return your basket and tell you thanks for the cookies."

"That was all Gabi's idea. She insisted we take some to you."

"We shared one before we walked over and it was delicious. I'm not sure I can eat a dozen sugar Christmas trees on my own but I'll do my best."

She smiled. "I told Gabi it might be too many but she wanted you to have a basketful. You can always take them into the station for the other officers."

"I might do that." He paused and decided he might as well be honest. "Okay, returning your basket was only an excuse. Though I did include some of my prized pepper jelly."

"You make pepper jelly?"

"No. My sister and niece do. But I certainly prize it."

She genuinely laughed at that, something he considered a major accomplishment. "Okay. Why did you need an excuse?"

"I had to know how things went today for Gabi. Did the other girls shun her after she told the truth, that she wasn't sick?"

"No, actually." She returned to her seat on the sofa and he took that as invitation to sit down in the easy chair. Grunt sniffed around the house, probably looking for some lingering trace of his previous master, poor thing. "She said a few of the girls were angry but most of them seemed happy she wasn't really dying. Gabi said their reactions will help her know which girls are really her friends."

"How about Destry? Was she one of the angry ones?"

Becca's expression softened. "Gabi said she was one of the kindest of the girls. She even invited Gabi to a sleepover during the Christmas holidays."

He was grateful he wouldn't have to have a sit-down talk with his niece about compassion and forgiveness. "Des has faced her own rough road. Her mother walked out on her when she was just a toddler and I think that might have made her more compassionate than most kids her age."

"That can happen." She studied him for a long moment. "Are you just coming home from work, then? It's nine o'clock."

This was becoming a habit, seeing her at breakfast and then again at the end of the day. He probably shouldn't find such comfort in that.

"Yeah. It's been a crazy day. Slide-offs and fender-benders. For some reason, people completely lose all good sense when it snows."

"Did you eat dinner?"

"Not yet. I'll find something when I head home."

"I made soup tonight for dinner. Minestrone and breadsticks. We've got tons of leftovers. If you'd like, I could heat you up a bowl."

His stomach grumbled and he realized he hadn't eaten since breakfast, the last meal she'd served him.

"I didn't come here for you to fix me dinner, Becca."

Why did you come here? She didn't speak the words but he could see the question plainly in her eyes. He hoped she didn't ask, as he wasn't entirely sure he could answer.

"I'm happy to do it. Consider it my little way of helping the police department."

While she headed into the kitchen without waiting for him to answer, he shrugged out of his coat and draped it over a chair. Grunt jumped into Trace's recently vacated chair as if it had been his customary place.

"You miss him, don't you, bud?"

The grouchy dog gave a cross between a whine and a sigh and closed his eyes. Out of sheer curiosity, Trace picked up the thick book she had been reading and just about fell over at the title and the contents.

He carried the heavy legal journal into the kitchen and held it up. "Nice, relaxing reading for a winter's evening."

Her lips parted and her hands froze in the process of spooning soup into a bowl. He thought he saw embarrassment and perhaps a trace of guilt flit across her features. "I'm hoping to be accepted into the Idaho bar in the next few months," she said, almost defiantly. "As part of the process of reciprocal admission, I have to take some self-study classes on Idaho state law and procedures."

He stared at her, completely floored. Everything he thought he knew about her had just been shaken and tossed out the window.

"You're an attorney?"

"Yes. I have been for three years. But I can't technically practice in Idaho until I complete the process."

"What's an Arizona attorney doing slinging hash at a diner in tiny Pine Gulch, Idaho?"

She looked away, focusing her attention on the bowl in front of her. "That's a really long story. Do you want some grated romano cheese in your soup?"

Trace had plenty of experience with evasion in his profession and he knew sometimes the best strategy was to exercise a little patience. "Yes. Thank you."

For the next few moments, he was busy enjoying the very savory and delicious soup, rich in vegetables and broth. She heated up several breadsticks for him and slid them onto a plate, then sat down across the little table from him.

"So what's the story, Becca?" he finally asked.

She sighed. "After my, um, grandfather left me the

house, I decided Gabi and I could both use a change. This was a good opportunity for us. That's all."

"*That's* your long story?"

"The CliffsNotes version, anyway."

As he tried to reconcile this new picture of her, he realized the image of her as a lawyer gelled much more clearly in his mind than as a waitress. He knew many very clever and savvy waitresses but he had always sensed Becca didn't quite fit in that venue.

He also was smart enough to figure out there was more to her story than her very brief explanation.

"And Gabi's father? Where does he fit into the story?"

Her eyes flared with shock at the question but she hid it quickly behind a cool smile. "I believe he was just a minor footnote in the introduction. He's not in Gabi's life whatsoever and hasn't been for years."

He was happier about that than he ought to be. "Are you intending to open a practice here?" he asked.

"Eventually. That's the plan, anyway, when I save enough money. I still have some student loans I'm paying off and I'm trying not to go into more debt if I can help it."

He was *definitely* happier about that than he ought to be. Not the debt-paying part, though that was certainly honorable, but the part about her wanting to open a practice in Pine Gulch.

"What sort of law?"

"In Phoenix, I was involved in contract law. Real estate, specifically. I imagine if I want to practice in a small town like Pine Gulch, I'll have to branch out into whatever my clients might need."

He was still having trouble processing all this. "You

said you were a real-estate attorney in Phoenix. Were you working for a firm there or did you have your own practice?"

She looked toward the fire, not meeting his gaze. "I was an associate in a large firm."

"Was it tough to walk away from Phoenix? You probably had clients you'd worked with for a while there."

She jumped to her feet and headed to the fire to add a log from the small stack on the hearth. "We needed a new start," she repeated, her voice firm, and again he sensed there was more to the story. Her features were taut with fine-etched tension. She wasn't telling him something. He sensed it instinctively but he could think of no way to persuade her to trust him with her problems.

Grunt whined suddenly, probably wondering why Wally Taylor wasn't the one fueling the fire, why the old man didn't come shuffling out of the kitchen somewhere.

"I can't believe you kept my grandfather's dog," she said with a rueful shake of her head.

"I was afraid the local shelter wouldn't be able to find someone else to adopt him. He's not the most attractive dog."

"I hadn't noticed," she murmured dryly. Ugly dog or not, she walked toward the chair where the dog was now looking mournfully around the room. She scratched him on the scruff and Grunt sniffed her with considerable reserve on his smashed features. He apparently decided she would do because he darted his tongue out and licked her hand, a show of acceptance Trace wasn't sure he'd earned yet.

"He's really quite adorable, in a hideous sort of way."

He gave her a considering look. "Would you and Gabi like to adopt him?" he asked on impulse. "I was just thinking earlier that he needed a house with children in it. Besides that, I'm rarely home and he's alone all day. I think he's lonely and I'm sure he would be happier here in the only house he's ever known."

Shock flickered in her eyes and her gaze shifted from the dog to him and then back to Grunt again. "I... I don't..."

"You don't need to decide right this minute. Think about it. Anyway, it was only an idea. I can always take him out to the ranch. My little sister sort of has a thing for rescuing animals and he might enjoy living with the other dogs."

"I've never had a pet."

"Really? Never? Not even when you were a kid?"

"No. We...we were never in one place long enough to take care of an animal. My father died when I was small and my mom raised me alone. She...moved around a lot."

He found that inexpressibly sad. What sort of childhood must she have endured, always on the go? He felt blessed all over again that his parents had created such a warm and loving home for him in Pine Gulch, full of horses and art and music and unending acceptance.

Maybe that was the reason she had moved here, the chance to give her daughter the stable, comfortable home she'd never had.

"Well, give it some thought. If you think you and Gabi would like to make a home for Grunt here, let me know. He's house-trained and obedient, for the most part. A little on the lazy side but that's not a bad thing in a little dog. He doesn't bark much and despite his unfortunate looks, he's loyal to a fault."

He paused, debating his words before deciding to tell her. "When I found your grandfather, Grunt was stretched out at his feet. I don't think he had moved for that entire twenty-four hours from when Wally died and I found him. First thing he did was run to his water dish and lap up every drop."

She gazed at the dog again, her eyes soft. He saw clear longing there, despite the dog's scrunchy face and permanent scowl, but indecision flickered there, too. "Right now it's all I can do to take care of Gabi, you know? I've been thinking we need to get a cat to take care of the mice. A dog, though. I'm not sure I can add another creature into the mix."

"Maybe when things settle down. I'll keep the offer on the table."

"Thank you."

He rose and Grunt rose with him. "We should probably be going. You and I have both got early days tomorrow. Thank you for the soup and the cookies."

"It's small recompense for all you've done for us since we arrived in Pine Gulch." She was quiet for a moment, then she gave him that rare, full-fledged genuine smile that always seemed to take his breath away. "You've really made us feel welcome, Trace."

"I hope you give Pine Gulch a chance, Becca. It's a nice town. Even for lawyers."

She shook her head, giving Grunt one last pat as Trace shrugged back into his coat.

At the door, he paused and on impulse reached out and folded her fingers in his. "I'm just going to say this, okay? You can take it any way you want but just know that it's sincere. I hope you know that if you're ever in any kind of trouble, you can always come to me."

She blinked, clearly startled. "I...thank you."

"I mean it, Becca." Whatever was putting those shadows in her eyes, that strain in her features, he knew he probably couldn't fix it but he could at least let her know she had somebody else in her corner.

"Thank you," she murmured again.

He should just have grabbed his ugly little dog and headed out into the night. He might have, but then the light in her entry reflected in her eyes and he saw the glimmer of tears there and he was lost.

With that same unrelenting sense of inevitability, he sighed, released Grunt's leash and reached for her. She gasped a little and then settled against him, her body soft and yielding, and he lowered his mouth to hers.

Chapter 10

Foolish, foolish woman.

She knew better than this. She knew exactly the sort of trouble she was courting by allowing these seductive kisses. She was allowing him inside her life, inside her heart. When she wasn't with him, she was thinking about him. When she *was* with him, she could feel herself falling deeper and deeper.

A ribbon of need seemed to curl and twist around them, wrapping them tightly together. Lovely and sultry, but more dangerous than a pit viper.

She couldn't let her life become more tangled with his. Trace was exactly the wrong man for her. He couldn't have been *more* wrong if Monica had selected him herself.

She was coming to rely on him too much, on his kindness and his friendship, on the heat and wonder of these stolen kisses that seemed to make the world much less scary.

His mouth was warm and firm and he tasted buttery from the breadsticks. She leaned into him, soaking up his strength and his heat, wishing she could stay here all night with him in this delicious embrace and let all the troubles of the world stay outside the door.

He was still wearing his parka, though he hadn't zipped it, and she slid her hands inside, to the heat at his sides. He was like a solid column of muscle, with no ounce of anything but strength.

With his arms around her, she felt…safe, for the first time she could remember.

Was it any wonder she was falling for him? Trace was the kind of man who gave an ugly little dog a home because he worried no one else would. He loved his family, he was dedicated to his community, he was extraordinarily kind to her sister.

The word jarred her back to reality. Her sister. Not her daughter.

That was the critical point. How was she going to tell him that Gabi was her sister after she'd spent weeks lying to him?

She was no better than Gabi. She had perpetrated a fraud on the Archuletas, on Trace, on the whole town of Pine Gulch. When he found out she had lied to him, he would be furious with her. She pictured the warmth in those green eyes changing to cold anger and her stomach twisted.

Though it was the hardest thing she'd ever done, even harder than striking out on her own when she was sixteen and had no money and no place to live, Becca forced herself to slide her mouth from his, to step back a pace. Cool air rushed in to fill the place where his body had been pressed to hers and she shivered but forced herself to be resolute.

"This isn't a good idea, Trace."

He raked a hand through his hair, his breathing ragged and his eyes a warm, dazed green which she refused to find flattering.

"You're right. Not when Gabi is asleep upstairs."

"That's...not what I mean." She shoved her hands in her pockets to keep from reaching for him again, her nails digging into her palms as if that hard, sharp pain could help her stay focused. She hated this, abhorred the idea of hurting him when he had been nothing but kind to her, but she had to do whatever was necessary to discourage him. She had to make it absolutely clear that she didn't want any more of these wondrous kisses.

Somehow she had to pull off the biggest con of her life.

She drew in a sharp breath, ignoring the harsh pain that nestled somewhere under her heart. "Don't kiss me again, Trace," she said, her voice firm even while her insides were trembling. "I meant what I said. I don't want a relationship. Not now. Not with you."

His head jerked back an inch or two as if she'd just slapped him. His gaze met hers and she saw a confused hurt there that made her stomach feel hollow and achy, as if she'd just drop-kicked his ugly little dog in front of him.

"Wow. That's plain enough."

"You're a very nice man, Trace. I obviously find you attractive or I wouldn't have kissed you. But attraction isn't enough. Not for me, not at this stage in my life. You've been a good friend to...to both Gabi and me, but right now that's all I have room for in my life. I don't want to hurt you but it's not fair for me to let you think I might be open for more. I tried to tell you that before."

"Right. You did." He was angry now. She could see it in the flare of his eyes and the hard, implacable set of his jaw. "You told me and I stupidly ignored you."

"You're not stupid. This isn't your fault, Trace."

"It's about me, not you. Isn't that what people say when they're giving someone the brush-off."

Oh, she hated this. She wanted nothing but to have those strong arms around her, to press her cheek against that wonderfully solid chest and just hold on tight. But that was impossible, and the best thing for both of them was to make that perfectly clear to him so she wouldn't have to be tempted again and again to throw her good sense into the wind.

"In this case, it's true. It is about me. I'm sorry if you don't want to accept that but I can't change it."

"So that's it. 'Stay away, don't bother me again. Take your dog and get the hell out of here.'"

The pain in her heart spread through her entire chest cavity but she called on every deceptive skill her mother had ever taught her and gave him a hard little smile. "I wouldn't have phrased it exactly like that."

He stared at her for a long moment and she hated seeing that warm light that had been there when they kissed fade into anger and hurt. "I can't argue with that, can I? Come on, Grunt. Let's go home."

He picked up his dog's leash and opened the door. A cold wind blew inside, chilling every part of her that wasn't already icy. He gave her one last look, then walked out into the night, closing the door firmly behind him.

She watched him walk down her steps onto the sidewalk, then turn toward his house at the end of the street. Snow swirled around him. It might have been a trick of the low light from the street lamp and the pale moon filtering through clouds, but she could swear it increased in fury and intensity as he walked down the street.

Though she was freezing, she couldn't summon the energy to close the door. She stood there in the cold, looking out at the lights glimmering on all their neighbors' houses, her chest aching with a deep sense of loss.

Oh, how she wished things could be different. Why couldn't she have a normal life, with a cozy house—instead of this dark, depressing old place—with a boyfriend and a little dog and a regular job?

Instead, she had a sister who might be a pathological liar, a mother who wasn't happy if she wasn't defrauding someone out of considerable amounts of money, and she had just pushed away the most wonderful man she'd ever met because she was worried he would see through her lies.

Would see that she wasn't good enough for him.

There was the truth. Becca pressed a hand to the ache in her stomach. She was afraid in her heart that she was so scarred from her insecure childhood that she had nothing to give a man like Trace Bowman. Otherwise she would have just faced the truth head-on—told Trace about her mother, about the years of lies and pain, about trying to distance herself as much as she possibly could from Monica until that day her mother and sister had shown up in Phoenix. What had she done that was so wrong, really, other than lying to the school and perpetrating a fraud on the town she was trying to make her own?

She shivered, the cold seeping deep into her bones, and she finally forced herself to shut the door. She had made her choice to push him away and she would live with it. What else could she do?

Now she had to focus on Christmas a few days away, on making the holiday as perfect as she could for a girl who had never known the normal traditions of childhood.

A guy didn't die of a bruised ego. Or a broken heart, come to that.

He wasn't sure which one he was dealing with. Trace only knew that something burned in his chest and a dark mood had settled over him that no amount of holiday cheer could lift.

He sat in his patrol vehicle outside the diner wishing with everything inside him that he didn't have to go inside. He could see her through the half-curtain windows—making conversation, delivering plates, taking orders. She moved with that quiet grace with which she did everything and she looked so beautiful he couldn't seem to look away, like a kid staring into the sun even when he knew damn well it was bad for him.

He would have picked any other place in town to meet with the mayor again about the pesky intersection that apparently the mayor couldn't sleep until they fixed. He had even suggested The Renegade, the tavern on the outskirts of town. Hell, at this point he would have preferred meeting in his patrol car, but the mayor had insisted on The Gulch, much to his dismay. Said he hadn't eaten breakfast and was starving and needed to be seen patronizing local businesses.

Trace didn't want to go inside. He hadn't seen Becca

since Monday night, two nights ago, when she had basically sent him packing. He told himself he hadn't made a conscious effort to avoid her, but in his heart, he knew otherwise. He was avoiding her, pure and simple.

He didn't expect every woman he was interested in to fall madly in love with him. That was ego he simply didn't have. Taft was the womanizer between them, not Trace. But he had sensed something special with Becca. She certainly didn't kiss him like a woman who wanted nothing to do with him.

He obviously had no instincts about this sort of thing. The last woman he had wanted to pursue a serious relationship with had ended up dumping him, too. He'd thought he and Easton were on the brink of falling for each other when Cisco Del Norte came back to Pine Gulch and he realized East was crazy in love with the man.

Becca wasn't Easton Springhill. He wasn't wrong— she was developing feelings for him, just as he was for her. He had sensed it in the way she kissed him, had seen it in her lovely hazel-brown eyes, but for some reason she wouldn't let him inside.

He couldn't help wondering if she was still hung up on Gabi's father, but she had seemed quite clear the night before that the man wasn't in either of their lives and hadn't been for a long time.

He sighed. Didn't matter her reasons. The woman asked him to back off and he had no choice but to accept that. And while he might wish to avoid her for the next, oh, year or two, that was impossible in a small town like Pine Gulch. Like it or not, he was going to have to face her eventually. Might as well get it over with.

With another sigh, he climbed out of his vehicle.

When he pushed open the door to the diner, heads immediately turned to see if the newcomer was anybody interesting. A few people waved, a few deliberately turned away. Being the police chief of a small town didn't always help a guy win any popularity contests, not when he sometimes had to arrest someone's brother or kid or wife. It didn't bother him much anymore.

The mayor wasn't there yet. Damn. That would have eased this awkwardness a little. When Becca saw him, color rose in her cheeks and she faltered a little before she pulled back her shoulders and stepped toward him. She was wearing a little snowflake ribbon in her hair and more snowflakes dangled from her ears, and she gave him a nervous kind of smile.

"Hi. Um, would you like to sit at the counter or a table?"

He frowned. Neither. He'd like to be eating a brown-bag sandwich in his car right now. He forced a casual smile in response. "Table please. The mayor wanted to grab some lunch while we have a quick meeting. He should be here in a minute."

She directed him to an open seat. "Do you need a menu or would you like to wait until the mayor arrives before you order?"

He hated this distance between them and the tension that seemed to seethe and pop like those fizzy fireworks he used to buy on the Fourth of July.

"Coffee?"

"No. Just water, thanks." He really didn't want her waiting on him but didn't see any way around it unless he tried to have a conversation with the mayor at the crowded, noisy counter.

She brought him his water a moment later and he

sipped it, checking his watch about every thirty seconds. He had been there maybe three or four minutes when the front door opened. He looked up, hoping to see Mayor Montgomery. Instead, the stooped, white-haired figure of Agnes Sheffield walked in along with her quieter sister, Violet. The Sheffield sisters were fixtures of Pine Gulch and had lived there for their entire lives. They even married brothers, who were both long dead now.

To his dismay, Agnes spotted him and immediately abandoned her younger sister to stump over toward him, her cane beating a harsh tattoo on the diner's peeled wood floor.

"This is the last straw. I have had enough! You hear me, Chief Bowman?"

Yes, along with the entire diner and probably every storefront on Main Street. "Of course. What's the problem, Mrs. Sheffield?"

"I'll tell you what the problem is. I want an apology, at the very least. An official one, signed on Pine Gulch Police Department letterhead. You're lucky I'm not going to try to take that fool's badge."

"What fool would that be, ma'am?"

"Your officer. Rivera, something or other. Some kind of Mexican name. He gave me a ticket for reckless driving. Me. How absurd is that? I've never driven recklessly in my life, young man."

The woman had needed her keys taken away about three years and two cataract surgeries ago. Her son was a friend of his and Trace knew he should have talked to the man before now and not let the situation degenerate so far. She was becoming a danger to others on the road, and he was going to have to be firm, as difficult as it was.

"It's harassment. That's what it is. I didn't do anything wrong."

"I'll look into it," he promised. "Officer Rivera is a good man, though. None of my officers would give a ticket that wasn't warranted."

"There's always a first time. I say, I did nothing wrong. I might have driven over the yellow line a time or two but I was not weaving. It was snowy. Anybody might have made that mistake."

"But you know you don't see as well as you used to, right?" he asked gently.

Something like fear flickered in her pale blue eyes. He understood it—losing the freedom to remain behind the wheel could be a horrible blow to a woman as proud and independent as Agnes Sheffield.

"That may be, but I can still drive perfectly well."

On impulse, he reached out and took her weathered, wrinkled hand in his. It was cool and trembling. "Mrs. Sheffield. You would hate to cause an accident, wouldn't you? What if you didn't see the school crossing guard and drove through a crosswalk and hurt a child?"

"I wouldn't do that. I'm a fine driver."

"I'm sure you are." He paused. "How about this. After the holidays, you and I can go for a little drive. We can even take Officer Rivera along if you'd like. If you can show us both we're crazy, I'll rip up your citation and get you that apology. On official stationary, I promise."

"And if not?" she asked, her voice small and her tone no longer so truculent.

He squeezed her gnarled fingers. "Then we will just

have to figure out a way to get you around town to the grocery store and your doctor's appointments, okay? Maybe you can let Violet have a turn driving."

"Hmph. We'll see."

The mayor came into the diner before he could answer and greeted Agnes with his customary charm. Trace wasn't sure how he did it, but in about thirty seconds of conversation, Mayor Montgomery had Agnes blushing and tittering like a teenage girl.

He looked up and happened to catch Becca's gaze. She was staring at him with a strange expression in her eyes, something glittery and bright. When they made eye contact, she wrenched her gaze away and headed for their table.

"Mrs. Sheffield, I seated Violet at your favorite table. Mayor, what can I get you to drink?"

The next forty-five minutes were miserable. He forced himself not to stare at Becca every time she came to their table to take their orders or deliver their food. He tried to avoid making eye contact but despite his best efforts, he was aware of her every movement in his peripheral vision Finally they finished the meeting and wrapped up their lunch at about the same time.

"Thanks for meeting me over lunch," Mayor Montgomery said, wiping his mouth with his napkin. "It was the only time I had free today."

"My treat this time," Trace answered. "You paid last time."

"But I invited you."

They wrangled over the bill for a moment but Trace emerged victorious and the mayor excused himself for another meeting. Trace was waiting for the bill when the chimes on the door jangled. From his position facing the door, Trace saw the new customer was a smartly dressed woman in her mid- to late-forties but trying hard to look a couple decades younger. He didn't think he recognized her but there was something vaguely familiar about the shape of her jawline, the angle of her neck.

He was trying to place how he might know her when he suddenly heard a clatter. He turned at the sound and saw Becca staring at the door, broken plates and spilled food at her feet and shock in her eyes.

"Look what you did!" Agnes Sheffield exclaimed.

Becca looked as if somebody had just run her over with a delivery truck. Her features were pale, her eyes hollow and stunned. She stood frozen for a long moment, then seemed to collect herself enough to kneel down and begin cleaning up her mess.

"I'm sorry. I'm so sorry. I'll have Lou replace your food. Oh, did I spill on you?"

She started to wipe off a splatter of sauce from Agnes's sweater, all the while darting little panicky glances at the woman who had come in. Who was it? And why did her presence leave Becca so flustered?

Not his business, he reminded himself, unless the woman was here to stir up trouble in his town. He did feel compelled to help Becca clean up the mess, however.

"Need a hand?" He didn't wait for an answer, simply crouched beside her and started picking up shards of broken plate.

"I just… I need to tell Lou."

Donna approached them with a wet cloth and the mop. "I saw, darlin'. No worries. I've already had him throw another couple of chicken breasts on the grill. No charge for lunch today, you two," she said to the

Sheffield sisters. "And for your trouble, you can have a piece of pie on the house."

"What about one of your sweet rolls instead?" Agnes gave her a crafty look.

"Sure. I can probably find one of those for you," Donna answered.

"A fresh one. It has to be fresh."

"Of course. A fresh sweet roll coming up, Mrs. Sheffield."

"They ought to fire that girl if she can't handle a tray," he heard Agnes grumble to her sister, and he saw that Becca's leached-out color had been replaced by a pale pink as she cleaned up the mess.

"I can do this," she muttered to him.

"And I can help," he said simply. "Is everything all right?"

She met his gaze and he watched as she seemed to become calm and composed right in front of his eyes. He found her skill at locking away all her emotions quite remarkable, though he could still see a shadow in her eyes and he didn't miss the way she completely avoided looking at the newcomer, whom Donna was trying to seat at the counter.

"Everything's great," Becca muttered. "Couldn't be better. I don't know why I'm so clumsy this afternoon. I guess it's just already been a long day. I've been on my feet since six-thirty."

He might almost believe her if he hadn't seen that moment of panic in her eyes and her determined efforts not to pay any attention to the woman who had come in.

When they finished cleaning up the mess, she forced a smile. "Thank you. I forgot you were still waiting for your bill. Just give me a moment and we'll get you on your way."

She rose in one fluid motion and headed to the kitchen, taking the soiled tray with her. Donna had seated the other woman at a table across the diner from him. He was tempted to go over and introduce himself but thought that might not be wise, under the circumstances.

When Becca returned, she handed him his and the mayor's bill with another distracted smile that didn't come close to reaching her eyes, then she headed toward the woman.

He expected her to hand the woman a menu. Instead, Becca slid into the booth across from her. He had the right cash to cover the bill and could have just left it on the table, but he was too curious to see how this drama would play out. As he watched, Becca and the other woman spent a few moments of intense conversation, but with the general hubbub of the diner, he couldn't hear the conversation. Becca looked to him angry and frustrated but the other woman didn't appear to care much.

Who was she? Why did she seem so familiar to him, like a book he was almost certain he'd picked up once at the library? And why was Becca so upset to see her?

After perhaps a five minutes' conversation, he saw Becca's hands flutter to her jeans pocket. She seemed indecisive, her features tight with frustration, but finally she pulled out a keychain and extracted a single key, which she slid across the table to the other woman almost defiantly.

The woman gave a tiny, triumphant sort of self-satisfied smile that immediately set Trace's teeth on edge as she palmed the key. She slid out of the booth, kissed Becca's cheek and left the diner without ordering anything. Becca sat there for a moment, her features hollow and raw. He very much wanted to go to her, to ask her to tell him what was so terribly wrong, to promise her he would send the woman packing from his town if her presence bothered Becca so much.

Not that he could do such a thing, but he would have liked the chance to try.

As he watched, she smoothed her hands down her apron and stood almost defiantly, lifting her chin and returning to work.

She stopped at two other tables to check on customers before she worked her way to his. "Did you need dessert or anything?"

"I'm good. Thank you." Despite years of training and practical experience questioning suspects and witnesses, he couldn't come up with a clever way to ask her about what had just happened, so he ended up just blurting it out. "Who was your friend?"

"My...friend?"

"The woman you just gave your house key to."

She raised an eyebrow. "Am I under police surveillance now?"

He refused to let her bait him. "I tend to observe things around me. It's part of being a police officer. She obviously upset you."

"She didn't upset me. I was just...surprised to see her, that's all. That was my dear mother, here to spend the holidays with Gabi and me. Isn't that wonderful?"

Her cool tone of voice left him in no doubt the development was anything *but* wonderful to Becca. Her mother. That was why the woman seemed familiar, because he saw traces of her in the woman he was coming to lo— His mind jerked away from the word like a skittish horse at a rattlesnake pit. He saw pale traces of her in Becca.

"That will be nice for Gabi, to have her grandmother around."

"Won't it?" she said mechanically, then turned to leave. Though he knew it was crazy, he reached out and touched her arm. She trembled a little but at least she didn't jerk her hand away.

"I know I've said this before but I just want to repeat that you can come to me for any reason. No strings, Becca."

Their eyes met and he thought he saw a glimmer of yearning there before she became composed once more.

"Why would I need to do that?" she asked with that cool smile he was beginning to hate, then she headed away to attend to another customer.

Chapter 11

Monica. Here. In Pine Gulch.

Becca couldn't think straight, barely aware of what she was doing for the rest of her shift as she took orders, bused tables, poured drinks.

How had her mother found them? Becca hadn't discovered the inheritance from her grandfather until after Monica had left, and she had been very careful to cover their tracks. She had been vague and closemouthed with her former coworkers and neighbors about where they were going.

She had feared this very thing. Monica couldn't have anything good in mind to show up out of the blue like this. What could she possibly want? Would she dare try running one of her schemes here in Pine Gulch? Years of experience had taught her she couldn't put anything past her mother. If there was any sort of illicit money to be made in Pine Gulch, Monica would find a way to get in on the action.

She couldn't let her. Becca fought down her panic attack. If Monica started bilking the people of Pine Gulch out of their hard-earned savings, she and Gabi would have nowhere else to go.

She so wished she'd been able to send her mother packing when she showed up at the diner—which begged another question. Of all the places she might have shown up in town, how did she know Becca worked at the diner in town?

Monica *had* shown up, though, and told her she needed a place to stay. Becca had wanted nothing more than to tell her mother to go to hell. The words had hovered there on her tongue. She had almost said them but then Monica had given her an arch look.

"I saw a police car out there. Who does it belong to?" She had scanned the diner and her gaze had landed unerringly on Trace. Monica could spot a cop with a spooky kind of skill. "That handsome devil with the dark hair and those delicious green eyes, right? He's not in uniform. What is he? A detective?"

She hadn't wanted to answer but she knew Monica would probe until she did. "The police chief," she had muttered.

"Ahhh. Perfect. What would that gorgeous police chief do if I walked over and told him you kidnapped my daughter? I can make it a very convincing story. You know that."

Even as cold fear gripped her stomach, she had let her mother goad her into losing her temper. In retrospect, that had been ridiculous but she seemed to have very little control when it came to Monica.

"I didn't kidnap anyone!" she had snapped. "You left her with me and took off without a word. What was I supposed to do?"

"I never expected you to leave Arizona with her. I don't believe I gave any such permission."

Though the rational part of her knew perfectly well her mother wouldn't want to bring unnecessary attention to herself by reporting a completely nonexistent crime when she had plenty of real crimes that could be pinned on her, Becca had reacted.

"What do you want?" she had hissed.

Monica shrugged. "Nothing so terrible, darling, I promise. Just a place to stay for a few days. I want to spend Christmas with my daughters. Family, that's what the holidays are all about, right?"

The very idea nauseated her, but at the time she had been desperate to get Monica out of the diner. In the end, she had caved and given her mother the key to her grandfather's house.

She would be there now. Picking through her things, assessing their humble Christmas decorations. Probably looking for any weakness in Becca that she could use to her advantage somehow.

Now what was she supposed to do?

She had never been so relieved when her shift ended and Donna told her to go home. She hung up her apron and grabbed her coat off the hook, then drove home as quickly as she dared through the snowy streets of Pine Gulch. In her mind, she rehearsed a dozen ways she would send Monica packing.

She found her mother in the kitchen wearing the frilly pink apron Becca had won at a bridal shower for a coworker in Arizona, what seemed another lifetime ago. She was stirring something in a bowl while Christmas music played on the kitchen radio.

Becca narrowed her gaze. "What are you doing?"

"I thought I would make some peanut butter cookies. They were always your favorite and my Gabi loves them, too."

She had absolutely no recollection of her mother ever making cookies. "How did you find us?" she demanded.

As she might have expected, Monica ignored the question. "How can you stand all that snow? Oh, I'll admit it's lovely for a day or two but I can't imagine putting up with it for months at a time."

Fitting, she supposed. Her mother didn't like to be inconvenienced by anything. Weather, finances, pesky little things like, oh, morals, ethics and laws.

"Tell me the truth, Monica. What are you doing here? I'm not buying the whole 'holiday time with the family' line. What else is going on?"

"Why do I have to have an ulterior motive, darling? I missed my little Gabi. And you, of course." She smiled as she added vanilla to the dough.

"Gabi's fine. She's happy." *She doesn't need you coming in and screwing everything up.*

"Is she?"

Just those two words and suddenly everything became clear. She stared at her mother, those nerves clutching her stomach again. "She found a way to call you, didn't she?"

Monica opened her mouth as if to deny it and then must have decided she could work the truth to her advantage somehow. "Apparently, she borrowed the cell phone of a little friend from school."

Of course. The day Becca had found out about her

claiming she had a heart condition, she'd had an iPod and phone and other electronic gadgetry. Gabi must have known Becca would have figured it out if she'd somehow sneaked her cell phone to use it, so she'd figured out a work-around.

"Gabi knows that no matter where I am or what I might be doing, I've got one cell number she can always use to reach me in an emergency. She called me last week and told me where she was and of course I dropped everything to rush right here."

Her sister was nine years old, she reminded herself. She didn't know any other life than the twisted one Monica had provided for those years. Still, Becca was aware of a sharp ache in her chest. "You left her with me, Monica. You used me and embroiled me in mortgage fraud and cleared out my savings and then you took off. I had no choice but to clean things up the best way I could. I might have been disbarred."

"You weren't, were you?"

"By a *miracle*. Because I agreed to liquidate every asset I had to cover what you stole!"

Monica's smile was conciliatory. "I'll make it up to you. You know I'm good for it, right?"

Oh, of course she would make it up. Like all the other money she had taken from her over the years in one form or another. Becca wasn't going to hold her breath over that particular promise.

"I don't want you here. Neither does Gabi. She's finally got a comfortable, stable home. Someone willing to think about her first."

Monica sniffed. "You call this place comfortable? It's horrible!"

Though she had thought the very same thing herself

throughout the past month, decrying the layers of dark, unattractive wallpaper, the peeling linoleum, Becca suddenly wanted to defend her grandfather's house. This house had provided a haven for them when they hadn't had anywhere else to go and she didn't want to hear Monica malign it.

"There's nothing wrong with this house that a little tender loving can't take care of. We're working on it, little by little. Anyway, that's not the point. The point is, Gabi is fine here. You showing up like this out of the blue will only confuse her."

"She called me," Monica pointed out once more.

"That doesn't matter. Gabi—" *Is here*, she realized, her words cut off by the sound of the front door slamming. School was on an early schedule because Christmas vacation started the next day, she remembered.

"Whose car is out there?" Gabi called from the entry. Becca didn't have a chance to answer before her sister wandered into the kitchen. She stood in the doorway, her jaw sagging at the sight of their mother in an apron, spooning batter onto a cookie sheet.

"Mom?"

"Darling!" Monica took a moment to wipe her hands on a cloth, then rushed to Gabi and enfolded her in a huge hug. Gabi didn't return the hug. She merely stood still, arms at her side.

"What are you doing here?" she asked stiffly.

"You called me, honey. You told me where you were. I thought that meant you wanted me here."

Gabi shot a quick look at Becca, her eyes stricken. "I only wanted to make sure you were okay and let you know we were fine here. I didn't want you to worry. I never thought you would come out here."

"It's Christmas. Where else would I be than with my beautiful girls?"

Becca barely restrained herself from rolling her eyes. She hadn't spent Christmas with her mother in a dozen years. Even when she lived with Monica, her mother had never made any sort of fuss about Christmas.

"We're going to have a wonderful time, darling. We can sing carols and, look, I'm making cookies, and I can be here when you open your presents from Santa. Aren't you so happy that we can be together?"

"Um. Sure," Gabi said. She had that closed-up expression again that always worried Becca.

The rest of the afternoon and evening passed in a stilted awkwardness, with Monica showing over-the-top enthusiasm for everything except the house. She *loved* the snowflakes Gabi had made. She *adored* their humble paper-chain garland. She couldn't get enough of the stockings Becca and Gabi had made out of felt pieces clumsily stitched together.

She apparently didn't notice—or care—that neither of them shared her enthusiasm.

Becca didn't have a chance to talk with Gabi alone until after dinner, when Monica headed to the third bedroom—sniffing her nose at the twin bed and the boxes piled around her that Becca hadn't had a chance to organize yet—to make some phone calls. Gabi immediately headed into the shower as if she wanted to avoid questions. Becca waited several moments after she heard the water shut off for her sister to change into her pajamas before seeking her out.

To her surprise, she found Gabi on the floor of the darkened living room, lit only by the light from the Christmas tree Trace had brought and decorated with them.

Colored streaks dripped down Gabi's cheeks, the Christmas lights reflecting her tears.

"Oh, honey." Becca folded her sister in her arms, marveling anew how she could come to care so much for Gabi in a few months. Gabi was stiff and unyielding for a moment and then she sagged in her arms. A lump rose in Becca's throat when Gabi wrapped her arms around her, too.

"I've ruined everything," she said, sniffling. "I'm sorry, Beck. I never *ever* thought she would come out here."

She smoothed a hand over Gabi's damp hair. "It's not your fault. Monica likes the unexpected. She always has."

"I should never have called her."

She couldn't lie to the girl, after she had known a lifetime of dishonesty, by pretending everything was fine. "It certainly complicates things. But we'll be okay."

"She's going to ruin Christmas."

"Not if we don't let her."

"You promise?"

The trust in Gabi's voice staggered her, left her feeling completely unworthy. She hugged her tightly. "I promise," she answered, though she had absolutely no idea how she was going to keep her word.

Monica was definitely up to something.

Less than twenty-four hours after her mother had blown into town like a nasty, greasy rain cloud, Becca knew she was cooking up some new scheme. Monica was on her cell phone constantly and she insisted on taking every call in the guest bedroom amid the boxes and clutter where she couldn't be overheard.

She also had an unmistakable air of restless excitement around her. Most worrisome of all, she seemed especially watchful of Gabi. At odd moments, Becca would find her mother scrutinizing her sister with a considering expression that worried her to no end. If she caught Becca looking at her, Monica would revert to a bland smile that didn't fool either of them.

Becca had never felt so helpless, trapped by her quandary. She wanted to tell her mother to leave, that she wouldn't let her ruin Gabi's first real Christmas. But with no legal, official custody arrangement between them, she knew Monica could drive away with Gabi at any moment and Becca would have no power to stop her.

She had been so worried, she had almost called in sick that day at the diner, but she knew that wouldn't have been fair to Lou and Donna. The Gulch was bound to be busier than usual this close to Christmas, especially with school out for Christmas vacation. She just had to trust that Monica wouldn't do anything stupid—which seemed a little like hoping Mother Nature would decide to send a heat wave to Pine Gulch for Christmas.

Now, as she pulled into her driveway behind Monica's flashy red sports car, relief flooded her. Her mother and Gabi were still here.

If nothing else, her mother's reappearance in their lives had proved without question to Becca how very much she loved her sister. She didn't know exactly when her perception had changed, but she no longer considered her sister a burden. She loved Gabi and wanted, above all, to give her sister a safe, normal childhood. A nine-year-old girl ought to be busy going to birthday parties and dance class, not playing a part in her mother's latest con.

If Monica took Gabi away, Becca knew just what fate awaited her. More lies and manipulation. Gabi would have to become a player, willing or not, in whatever game Monica wanted to embroil her in next.

Becca refused to let that happen. She had given her word and she would do whatever it took to keep that promise.

The afternoon and evening were a repeat of the awkwardness of the day before. Though she did her best to keep her sister busy in the kitchen making homemade caramels she wanted to give to the Archuletas and The Gulch regulars the next day on Christmas Eve, Monica still managed to sneak Gabi away for a couple of private talks. Each time, Gabi would return subdued but she refused to talk about what was bothering her with Becca.

After they finished wrapping the caramels in little sections of waxed paper, Gabi finally said she was tired and wanted to go to bed. Though it was about an hour earlier than her usual bedtime, Becca didn't stop her as she headed upstairs to her bedroom.

"Well, I've got to make a few phone calls," Monica said, pushing away from the table, where she had sat and watched Gabi and Becca wrap the caramels.

"Before you do, I need to talk to you." Becca forced her voice to be forceful, declarative.

Monica gave a light laugh, though she seemed slightly disconcerted. "That sounds ominous. You mind if I eat a caramel while you lecture me?"

Without waiting for an answer, she unwrapped one of the sticky-sweet pieces of candy and began to chew it.

"I don't want to lecture you," Becca said. True enough.

She wanted to wring her mother's neck for coming here and stirring up such tension, taking so much of the joy out of the holidays. "I want the truth. What are you planning with Gabi?"

Monica opened her mouth with a look of feigned hurt. She could have made a good living in Hollywood if she'd turned her talents in that direction. She was a brilliant actress, which was why she was so good at convincing people to part with their money, whether they wanted to or not.

"I'm not sure what you mean."

"I'm not stupid, Monica. I know the signs. You're cooking up something and it involves Gabi."

"Why would you say that to me?"

Becca ground her back teeth, refusing to play the game. "Because I know you. You forget, I was exactly in Gabi's shoes until I cut off ties with you twelve years ago. Enough is enough, Monica. Gabi and I are making a good life here. She's got friends, she's starting to enjoy school. I'm thinking about getting a dog and a cat. She's safe and happy now, for once in her life, and I'm not letting you drag her off again."

Oh, she should have just shut up while she was ahead. As soon as she said the last part, she wanted to clamp her teeth together at her own stupid tactical error.

Big mistake, to throw everything out there like that and reveal how very protective she was of Gabi now. Monica would definitely capitalize on her mistake. She would have been much better off pretending she didn't want Gabi around. Monica would have been much quicker to leave the girl with Becca if she thought it was some kind of onerous burden on her.

"You're imagining things." Monica put on her

wounded look. "I don't know why you're always so quick to accuse me of things. I'm just here to spend the holidays with my girls."

Becca hated to ask but felt she had no choice. "You're not planning something *here*, are you?"

Monica's look of surprise seemed genuine enough. "In Pine Gulch? No. I learned my lesson here."

She stared. "What does that mean?"

"I haven't had good experiences in Pine Gulch. After your father died, I contacted your grandfather looking for help." Her mouth pursed and she looked every one of her nearly fifty years. "He threatened to take you away from me, the old bastard. I wasn't going to let that happen so I vowed not to come back. When I was pregnant with Gabi, some old acquaintances needed another player for a big job here. The payoff was going to be huge but the whole job turned into a complete disaster. Fortunately I only had a small part. Nobody could tie me to anything. All I did was a little recon work for a few days. It wasn't easy, I'll tell you that, and I was able to get out of town fast when things headed south. You know how I feel about violence. Just not my scene."

She wasn't interested in Monica's walks down Memory Lane. All she wanted was to protect her sister.

"Gabi is happy here," she repeated. "Don't you think she deserves a chance at a normal life?"

"Gabrielle is not you, Rebecca. All you ever wanted was that *normal* you're always going on about. Look at you now. Waiting tables in a two-bit diner in Nowhere, Idaho. I can't believe any daughter of mine would be happy, but I never did understand you. Now, Gabi. She loves adventure."

"She's happy here," she repeated to Monica.

Her mother smiled, tossing her waxed paper wrapper on the counter instead of the garbage can. "If that was true, she never would have called me. Good night, my dear. Sleep well."

She walked out of the kitchen, leaving Becca with more of her messes to clean up and an ache of fear in her stomach.

Chapter 12

The next morning, Christmas Eve, The Gulch was only open for breakfast and shortened lunch hours. Becca handed out her caramels and was delighted with the enthusiastic response. Much to her surprise, several of the regulars had little gifts for her, as well—a box of chocolate mints, a plate of cookies, a mug filled with hot cocoa packets. Donna and Lou left a wrapped gift for her on the shelf above where she hung her purse and coat.

Pine Gulch was a nice town, she thought. People here had gone far out of their way to make her feel welcome and she wouldn't soon forget it.

Her happy holiday glow lasted until a little after nine when the door opened and the police chief of this nice town walked in. He was wearing a uniform—something fairly unusual for him, and a PGPD parka and Stetson.

Her traitorous insides trembled, and for an instant,

she fiercely wished things could be different between them—especially that she had been honest from the day she showed up in town about Gabi and Monica. She had an equally fierce wish that Donna wasn't tied up in the office right now so Becca didn't have to deal with him this morning.

"Merry Christmas, Chief. Do you want a table or a booth?"

"Merry Christmas." He gave her a cool nod. "Neither, actually. I just need a sweet roll and a breakfast wrap to go. I've only got a minute before I have to head back on patrol."

"I guess police officers don't get Christmas off."

He shrugged. "I try to give my officers with kids as much time at home as I can during the holidays."

Donna chose that moment to emerge from the back room, more paper place mats in her hand from the storage closet there. "If I know you, Chief, you're going to be working double shifts from now until New Year's."

He shifted, looking embarrassed. "Don't make it a bigger deal than it is, Donna. My officers work hard all year. If I can give them a little more time with their families over the holidays, it's a small enough thing."

Becca gazed at this strong, honorable man, her heart suddenly pounding in her chest. He worked himself into the ground over the holidays, gave up time with his own family, so his officers could be with their children. How could a woman resist a man like that?

She wasn't in danger of falling in love with him, she realized, shock trembling through her. She was already there. She didn't know when it had happened—perhaps that day in the diner when he had protected her from the rowdy snowmobilers or perhaps earlier, when he had shown up at their house with a Christmas tree and that rueful smile.

Or maybe she fell in love when she met her grandfather's dog, Grunt, and discovered Trace was the sort of man who would take in an ugly little dog and give him a home simply because no one else stepped up to do it.

What if she dared tell him the truth? Surely he would understand and forgive her? She had to believe that. After all, she had only been trying to protect her sister.

While Lou fixed Trace's breakfast burrito, she grabbed one of the diner's famous cinnamon rolls from the double batch he had prepared that morning and slipped it into a sack. On impulse, she hurried to the back room for the last small gift bag full of caramels. She already knew Trace had a sweet tooth. Maybe a little candy would help make his long shift a little more bearable.

She was heading back to the dining room when her cell phone rang. Though she carried it with her, very few people had the new number she had obtained when she moved to Pine Gulch. A quick glance at her caller ID verified the call was from her mother's phone. For a moment, she was tempted to shut off the phone and not accept the call. But since Monica was with Gabi, there was always a chance it was some sort of emergency.

"Yes. Hello?" she finally answered, pitching her voice low.

"She's packing my stuff!"

Instead of her mother's voice, she heard Gabi's and the frantic words turned her insides to ice.

"What?" She could only pray she had misunderstood.

"She just went to the bathroom and I sneaked her

phone so I could call you. She's packing all my stuff. I think she's trying to leave before you get back."

Panic exploded through her. She had suspected this very thing, damn it. Why hadn't she brought Gabi to work with her? When would she ever learn that she couldn't trust Monica for a single second? "It's Christmas Eve!"

"I know." Gabi's voice wobbled. "I tried to tell her that we should wait until after the holidays, but she said we need to go, that she has people waiting in California, a man, and she's told him all about me. I've apparently been away at boarding school and now I get to spend Christmas with them."

No. No, no, *no*! She wouldn't let this happen. What could she do?

Feeling wild, trapped, she gazed out at the diner trying to formulate a plan and her gaze landed on Trace looking big and solid and reassuring as he stood at the counter talking to Donna.

Trace. *I hope you know that if you're ever in any kind of trouble, you can always come to me,* he had said to her.

She had to tell him. He was the only one who could help her. How he would do that, she had no idea, but she had to do whatever necessary to protect her sister.

"Stall her. However you can think of, just stall her, okay?"

Gabi was silent for about three seconds. "I'll try," she finally said, doubt threading through her voice. She was probably wondering whether she had put her trust in the right person. Becca didn't blame her for that.

"Hang in there. Whatever you do, don't let her know

you called me. You'll have to delete the record from her recently dialed calls. Do you know how to do that?"

"I can figure it out." Gabi sounded terribly young suddenly. Young and frightened. "I don't want to go, Becca. I like it here with...with you."

This was a vast outpouring of affection coming from her reserved little sister and Becca had to swallow down tears. "I know, sweetheart. I'm not going to let her do this. Your place is here with me now. Hang on, okay? Just stall her."

"Okay. I've got to go. I just heard the toilet flush."

Gabi ended the call and Becca drew a deep breath. After the next few moments, everything was going to be different. The time for lies and deception was over. Trace might hate her now but she couldn't worry about that.

She had to protect her sister, whatever the cost.

He had to stop coming in here.

He would just have to leave enough time in the mornings so that he could make his own breakfast at home before he left for the day or else somehow force himself to be content with a breakfast sandwich from the fast-food place at the other end of town.

It was too hard to come to The Gulch now with Becca here. Every time he saw her, he had to fight with everything inside him not to pull her into his arms and not let go.

"Here's your breakfast burrito. I don't know where Becca has run off to," Donna said, her dark eyes exasperated. "I swear she was putting a cinnamon roll into a bag for you. Let me just grab you another one."

"I saw her go to the back room a minute ago," he

said. Of course he hadn't missed that. He was aware of every move she made, pathetic lovestruck fool that he was.

"I'll just see what's going on," Donna started to say, but before she could move, Becca walked back into the room.

Something was terribly, terribly wrong.

He saw tension in every line of her body, from the tight set of her shoulders to her clenched fists, and her features were as colorless as they'd been that day her mother came into the diner.

She seemed to take a deep breath and then headed toward him. As she neared, he saw fear in her eyes, stark and cold. He instinctively reached his fingers toward his weapon, hovering there—braced for trouble, despite not knowing its source.

"What's wrong?"

She let out a shaky breath. "I need your help, Trace."

"You've got it," he said without hesitation.

She blinked, confusion in her eyes, as if she hadn't expected such ready willingness. Becca struck him as someone who had been carrying her troubles by herself for entirely too long. Maybe it was time she allowed someone else to lend a shoulder.

Her features softened, her mouth trembling, then she pressed her lips together. "I have to tell you something first. You won't like it."

"Sit down first. You look like you're going to fall over."

"I can't. There's no time. I need to..." She drew in a deep breath, her hands in tight fists at her side. "I just have to come right out and say this. Gabi isn't really my daughter."

He stared, the air leaving him a whoosh. He didn't know what to think, trying to process the shock of this revelation.

"It's a long story, one I don't have time to get into right now, but she's really my younger sister. Half sister, I guess. We share a mother. You met her the other day here at The Gulch."

Suddenly so much made sense—her protectiveness about Gabi, the vagueness about their past life together, those few times when Becca had seemed completely out of her element when it came to child-rearing.

"You were surprised to see your mother," he said. He had a thousand questions but that thought seemed to take precedence. "Surprised and not pleased."

"An understatement." Becca rubbed a hand over her face. "A few months ago, she dumped Gabi on me in Arizona and took off without a word. I had no idea where she was or how to reach her, which is usually the way I prefer the situation. But here she is again, out of the blue, and she wants to take Gabi away. We have to stop her."

He felt as if he had missed a step somewhere. There had to be more to this story than a difficult relationship with her mother. He was able to key in on the legalities, however. "You said she's the girl's mother. How can you stop her from taking her? Do you have official guardianship of Gabi?"

"No. I told you, she just dumped her on me. I have no formal custody whatsoever, which is why I thought it would be easier when we moved here to just say she was my daughter." She glanced at her watch. "Custody or not, I have to do something. Gabi doesn't want to go with Monica. She's finally got a home and security, friends at school. She's happy here. If Monica takes her, she'll…" Her voice trailed off and he sensed *this* was the crux of the whole situation, though he didn't know what led him to that conclusion.

"She'll what?"

She said nothing, looking at the floor, the other customers, the counter—anywhere but at him.

"Help me understand, Becca. What's so terrible about a mother wanting to be with her own daughter?"

"Monica doesn't want Gabi." Bitterness seeped from her words. "She only wants to use her in whatever scheme she's cooking up now."

"Scheme?"

She sighed and finally met his gaze, and he saw a lifetime of hurt there. "My mother is a con artist and a thief. She has spent her entire life using everyone around her. I became an emancipated minor when I was sixteen and severed all ties with her because I couldn't deal with the manipulation and lies anymore. I didn't even know about Gabi until a few months ago when my mother showed up in Phoenix with her. I hate myself when I think that. Because I refused to have anything to do with Monica, Gabi spent nine years with her. If I'd known, I might have been able to do something to help her get away years earlier."

She released a long breath. "I wasn't there for all that time, Trace. But I'm here now and I've promised Gabi I won't let Monica take her. Please, can you help me?"

He couldn't see a clear way to accomplish that particular job given the legal parameters of his position, but he wasn't prepared to admit that to her yet. "Can you prove your mother—Monica—is up to something in Pine Gulch?"

"No. Gabi said she's going to California." She frowned. "I think she was involved in a job here once. Years ago. She said something about everything going wrong. I don't see how that can help us, though."

She checked her watch again. "We have to hurry, Trace. She could be driving away right now. Please, will you help me stop her?"

He had rarely felt so helpless as he considered the best course of action. "Without evidence of wrongdoing, I can't just storm in and take your sister away from her mother. I wish it were that simple."

"So you're not going to help me. She's going to destroy Gabi's childhood just like she did…"

"Yours?"

In one short, tense conversation, so many things about Becca seemed vividly clear to him now. She was a series of layers, complex and mysterious. A challenge he found eminently intriguing.

At the core, though, was a woman trying to do the right thing for a young girl. If he could, he vowed he would figure out a way to help her.

"I can stall her," he finally said. "Maybe take her in for questioning on some open cases we have here while we bring in CPD. You said she was involved in something around here years ago?"

"She wouldn't talk much about it, only to say it turned violent unexpectedly and she left when she could. She said her part was small. I will say this for my mother, amoral she might be but she abhors violence. Says it's unnecessary and messy."

He frowned, a little niggle of unease lodging in his gut. "How long ago?"

"I'm not sure, exactly. I had nothing to do with her

for the last dozen years. She did say she was pregnant with Gabi, so that would have been about a decade ago. Somewhere in there. Her job was reconnaissance."

Was it possible that Becca's mother had been involved with the men who had killed his parents? He and the local authorities had been convinced more people had been involved than just the two men Caidy had seen shoot his parents and the woman who had been sent to distract him from coming home in the middle of the robbery.

He felt a little stir of anticipation at the possibility of a break in the case, a link to the people who had killed his parents. At the same time, he didn't miss the irony—he was in love with a woman who just might be the daughter of someone involved in that heinous crime.

He wouldn't worry about that right now, until he met the woman and had a chance to assess the situation.

"I need to go. I can't just stand here." Becca twisted her hands together. "Gabi said Monica is packing her things."

"Grab your coat. Let's go."

Her eyes widened with a dazed sort of shock as if she hadn't let herself believe he would truly help her. This only served to reinforce his belief that she had known very few people she could count on in her life. It made him sad, made him want to tuck her against his heart and promise her he would always be there when she needed him.

"I have to tell Donna."

"I heard, darlin'." The older woman stood a few feet away.

"All of it?" Becca looked worried, probably certain she would face censure for lying, but Donna stepped forward and squeezed her hands. "You go do what you have to in order to protect that little girl. We'll be fine. I can handle things here."

Eyes brimming with tears she didn't shed, Becca hugged her employer tightly for a moment, then left the room to grab her coat.

"I mean it," Donna said to him when Becca was out of earshot. "You do whatever you have to, Trace. She loves that girl, daughter or not. It sounds like this mother is a real piece of work. You teach her that in Pine Gulch, we take care of our own."

Oh, no pressure. Trace sighed. He would do what he could. But right now his options when it came to keeping a mother away from her child seemed pitifully inadequate.

He was helping her. Some part of her almost couldn't believe this wasn't some kind of trick, that he wasn't going to just take her to the police station and charge her with lying to a police officer or obstruction of justice.

Across the width of the vehicle, Trace watched the road and the tiny snowflakes fluttering down in front of the vehicle. He looked grim and dangerous, his jaw firm and his mouth hard—definitely not a man she would want to mess with under other circumstances. For an instant, she almost felt sorry for Monica for being oblivious as to what havoc was going to rain down on her in a very short time.

She was suddenly very grateful to have Trace Bowman on her side.

He *was* on her side. He had been from the beginning. She had been so stupid not to trust him from the moment she showed up in Pine Gulch. Most of the time she liked to tell herself her tumultuous childhood hadn't left any lasting damage. But once in a while she saw with stark clarity how stunted she was in certain areas. A willingness to allow herself to rely on others was right there at the top of the list. She had been on her own for so long—even before she officially severed ties with Monica—that she had a difficult time giving others any opportunity to see past her defenses in order to help her.

She hadn't expected this sweet, healing relief at knowing someone else was in her corner, helping her fight her own particular dragon.

On impulse, she reached out and touched his arm, feeling the heat and the strength through the thickness of his coat.

"Trace, I shouldn't have lied to you and everyone else about Gabi being my daughter. I'm sorry. When I tried to register her at school, I realized I didn't have a birth certificate or anything. It…seemed easier to say I was her mother than to try to explain the whole messy situation and have to admit I wasn't technically her legal guardian. I was worried the school would have to open an investigation with child protective services. I couldn't bear to think of her being taken away, going into foster care, not when I'm trying my best to give her a comfortable life. Foster care would have been horrible for her."

She'd had a few short bouts in foster care during those times Monica had been arrested and she wouldn't wish that on anyone, especially not the sister she loved.

"I wish you had trusted me."

Her life the past few months would have been so

much less stressful if only she hadn't been so stubbornly independent. "I should have."

He sent her a quick look across the vehicle, then turned his attention back to the road as they turned onto the street they shared. "Is that the reason you pushed me away? Because I'm a cop and you were afraid to spend more time with me for fear I would figure it out and take Gabi away?"

"I was raised from an infant not to attract the attention of the police. It's a little hard to break the habit. But yes, that's the main reason."

He said nothing but she thought she saw a glint of something unreadable in his green eyes and then they were at her grandfather's house.

In the driveway, Monica was placing a box in the trunk of her car, which was tricked out with every available luxury.

Trace pulled into the driveway behind her, effectively blocking her escape route. Nicely done, Becca thought, and she watched her mother's features dissolve into a wild, thwarted fury for only an instant before she wiped them clean again.

By the time they climbed out of the patrol vehicle and headed toward Monica in the cold December air, her mother had turned on what Becca always considered her Distressed Maiden persona.

She was very good at what she did. It was always a bit of a surprise to watch the transformation. In the thirty seconds it took them to exit Trace's patrol vehicle, Monica had somehow managed to mess her hair a little like someone flustered and mussed, and transform her features so she looked somehow older, frightened.

"Officer. I'm so glad you're here. You must help me."

Trace raised an eyebrow, looking singularly unmoved. "Must I?"

"Yes. My child is being held here against her will." Her fingers trembled slightly as she pointed at Becca. "She took her away from me and ran off with her. You wouldn't believe how frantic I've been."

"No doubt."

"I've been looking for her for months and now I've finally found her. I've just been waiting for my chance to take her."

"How terrifying for you."

She studied him, apparently trying to decide if he was sarcastic or not but Trace wore no expression.

"Yes, well, I've found her now. We're together again." She offered up a quivery sort of smile. "I don't want to press charges or anything. I just want to take my child and leave your lovely little town."

"Why?"

That single word seemed to stymie Monica. She stared at him for a moment. "Why?"

"Yes. Why? We police types tend to look for motive. It's a bad habit." He gave a self-deprecating little smile that still sent chills down Becca's spine.

In official cop mode, Trace was nothing short of terrifying. Who would have expected the nice man he seemed to be most of the time to be able to come off as such a badass?

"What reason would Ms. Parsons have to take your daughter away from you and move here to Pine Gulch?"

"Spite. Vengeance. She was angry at me because of…some unfortunate real-estate investments and she struck out at me the one way she knew would hurt the most, by keeping my child away from me."

Trace nodded as if he sympathized with her, even accepted the hypothesis. For an instant, Becca felt a clutch of fear. What if he bought Monica's lies? She was extraordinarily good at the con.

No. She reined in the panic. Trace *knew* her. They were friends—and possibly more. He would never believe she would take Gabi out of spite. She had to trust him.

"Why don't we all go inside out of the cold and talk about this?" Trace spoke in a calm-the-situation voice. "Where is Gabi now?"

"Inside packing her things. She can't wait to leave."

Becca stared at her mother, shocked at such a fervent and blatant lie that would be ridiculously easy to disprove simply by asking Gabi. It was not the sort of mistake Monica would normally make, unless she was completely certain Gabi would back up her story. She wouldn't, would she? Gabi had called her, begging her to prevent Monica from taking her.

When they walked inside the house, Gabi was sitting on the floor next to the Christmas tree Trace had brought them. Though it was only midmorning, all the lights on the tree were blazing here in the overcast gloom. Her sister's gaze instantly found Becca's. Instead of her usual cool reserve, Gabi looked frightened.

Becca instantly went to her and pulled her into a hug. This was one of those cherished moments when Gabi didn't resist; she just threw her arms around her sister.

"Doesn't look to me as if she can't wait to leave," Trace commented.

A hint of fury sparked in Monica's eyes again but she maintained her Distressed Maiden act. "Tell the police officer, Gabrielle. How Rebecca took you away from me and I couldn't find you for months. She brought you here and you've been miserable and can't wait to leave. You called me and begged me to come rescue you. Go ahead and tell him."

Becca felt her sister's withdrawal. Gabi sat up and moved away from her, her thin features pinched. "I called her," she whispered.

Her heart sank. What hold did Monica have on Gabi, beyond the helpless love of a child for her mother? *Oh, sweetheart.*

Trace didn't reveal a hint of his thoughts in his eyes or his expression and she felt that clutch of fear again. With Gabi's apparent corroboration, would he believe that she had taken her sister without Monica's permission?

"Gabi, this is important. I need to know the truth. Do you want to go with your mother?" Trace asked.

The girl's gaze flickered from him to their homespun Christmas tree then to her mother. She completely avoided looking at Becca. She didn't speak, however, merely gave a tiny nod that seared through Becca like acid.

Monica must have convinced her to lie somehow. She remembered Gabi's frightened voice on the phone. *I don't want to go, Becca. I like it here with you.*

Triumph flashed in Monica's perfectly made-up eyes. She smiled at Gabi, who looked even more frightened. "See? I told you! She's been miserable here. Poor thing. It's been a nightmare for the girl. She can't wait to leave!"

She turned on Becca. "I hope you're ashamed of yourself, trying to keep a child away from her loving mother. I can't imagine how a child I raised could possibly be so heartless. Now if you don't mind moving your vehicle, sir, we'll just be on our way. We've got a long drive ahead of us. I'm sure you understand."

"I do. I believe I understand perfectly." He smiled and those chills skittered down Becca's spine again. "I'm afraid I can't allow you to leave town just yet. I need to make a few phone calls first. I'm sure you understand. Just procedure."

Monica shifted and her careful mask began to slip. "I don't understand. What sort of phone calls?"

"Just technicalities. There's still the matter of your abandonment of your daughter in Arizona."

"Abandonment? I didn't abandon anyone. *She* took her and left town. How was I supposed to find her?"

"You'll have to forgive me but that's the point I'm unclear about. Gabi, how long were you with your sister in Phoenix before you moved here?"

Gabi frowned in confusion. "I don't know. A month, maybe."

"A month. I see. And where was your mother during that time?"

Gabi looked at Becca then at Monica before meeting Trace's gaze. "I don't know. She didn't say. We were staying with Becca in Arizona. And one morning when I woke up, my mom wasn't there. She didn't say anything to me before she left. I waited and waited for her to come back but she never did."

Her sister sounded forlorn, abject. Becca might have thought it was an act, just another masquerade, but she remembered how torn up Gabi had been after Monica left.

"And Becca." Trace directed his attention to her.

"Did you have any idea where your mother was during that time?"

She felt a tiny glimmer of hope, like a pale sunbeam just barely piercing through clouds. She understood exactly where he was going with this and she couldn't see at all how Monica could wriggle out. "None whatsoever," she said firmly. "She didn't leave a note or email or try to contact us in any way. The only thing she left was a mountain of debts I ended up having to pay. It took me a month to sell my town house and liquidate what was left of my assets in order for us to move here to the house my grandfather gave me."

Trace gave Monica a long, slow look of appraisal. "Sounds like a fairly cut-and-dried case of child abandonment to me."

Shock held Monica speechless for a long moment. She looked at the three of them as if trying to figure out just where the game had gone wrong. When she spoke, Distressed Maiden had been kicked to the curb. Monica's voice was hard, angry. "Well, I'm here now and I want my child. She said herself she wants to go with me."

"With apologies to Gabi here, I'm afraid it doesn't work that way, ma'am. I'm going to have to take you down to the station with me. We don't deal with this sort of thing very often, so I'm going to have to contact the authorities in Arizona about their particular laws and ordinances. With it being Christmas Eve, that might take longer than normal." He shrugged, just a Good Old Boy frustrated with the system. Apparently the Parsons women weren't the only con artists around.

"It's all going to take time," Trace went on, "but I'm

sure you don't mind. You probably don't have anywhere to be for a few days anyway, do you?"

In that moment, Becca realized with startling, joyful clarity that she was fiercely, crazily in love with Trace Bowman. She wanted to run to him and hug him until her arms ached, to tell him just how perfectly he had handled things from the moment they pulled in.

Gabi had sidled closer to her and reached out to grip her knee. Her sister was afraid to hope, she realized. She knew exactly what that felt like. She covered Gabi's fingers with hers and gave a comforting squeeze.

Monica had apparently decided to try on Angry Power-Broker for size. Her eyes were hard, glittery, her shoulders thrown back. "You are making a serious mistake. You have no idea how much of one. You're crazy if you think I'm going to let some two-bit cop railroad me into some half-assed child abandonment charge that won't stick, anyway. I have an excellent attorney and he'll have your badge before we're done with this."

Trace merely gazed back, unfazed. "I look forward to it, ma'am. I truly do. Now would you please put your hands behind your back?"

"You are not going to arrest me."

His smile was lethally sharp. "Watch me."

Much to Becca's shock, he moved behind Monica and grabbed one arm. The metallic clink of his handcuffs sliding on pinged through the room. Gabi made a little sound of distress that caught Trace's attention. He gazed at her younger sister for a long moment, pausing before sliding the other cuff on, then turned back to Monica.

"You know, now that I think about it, there is one more alternative."

"What?" Monica seized on the possibility.

"You sign a legal document giving Becca guardianship of Gabi."

"Forget it!"

He reached for her other arm, handcuff at the ready. "Fine. This way means a lot more paperwork, but it's better than being out in the snow on Christmas Eve, anyway. Like I said, it might be a couple of days before I can reach anyone in Arizona but we'll get this straightened out eventually. We might have a few open cases around here we can talk to you about. Oh, say, something that happened ten years ago right around this time of year."

Monica's mouth turned white and she aimed another vicious glare at Becca, looking suddenly years older than her very well-maintained fifty. "I didn't do anything."

"Then you've got nothing to worry about." He sounded cheerful. "We'll sort all that out eventually."

"This isn't right. Trying to take a child from her mother."

He glanced toward the couch, where Becca now sat holding Gabi's hand. "You know, you're absolutely right. Funny thing is, that's exactly what we're trying to avoid here. A woman doesn't necessarily have to give birth to be just the person for the job."

Tears burned in Becca's eyes and she held Gabi's hand more tightly.

The mantel clock chimed ten o'clock. Not even noon and Becca felt as if she'd lived a lifetime since she awoke filled with anticipation for Christmas Eve.

Monica looked at the clock, a hint of panic in her eyes, then she gazed at the sofa at her two daughters.

After a long pause, during which Becca could practically see her spinning all the angles, Monica finally released a heavy sigh.

"You're not going to give me a choice, are you?"

"I believe I gave you a choice," Trace said calmly. "Child abandonment charges—and whatever else I can find—or you sign custody over to Becca and leave Pine Gulch."

They all waited, the moments ticking past, until Monica finally frowned. "How am I supposed to sign anything with these stupid cuffs on?"

Gabi hitched in a little breath beside her, her gamine little features a strangely poignant mix of relief and sadness.

"No problem. They weren't locked, anyway." He pulled the cuffs off and hooked them on his belt again.

"Becca, you're the attorney. Write up something legally binding that will stand up in court, will you? I can witness as an officer of the court. We still might need to do some maneuvering to dot all the *i*'s, but I have friends on the bench."

Monica looked even more furious at this—probably expecting she eventually could figure out a way to wrangle out of any hasty agreement.

"Let's get this over with, then. I've got places to go."

Fifteen minutes later, it was done. Her quickly composed guardianship transfer was as legally sound as she could make it. Monica signed with short, bitter strokes, then Trace and Gabi unloaded her trunk and backseat. Her mother gave Gabi a tearful hug goodbye, promising to visit as soon as she could. To Becca, Monica only delivered a deep, angry glare, which bothered her not one bit.

Trace backed his patrol car out of the driveway and Monica drove off through the murky December sunlight.

To Becca's surprise, Trace pulled back into the driveway and climbed out.

"You okay, kiddo?" he asked Gabi, whose chin still tended to wobble as she watched her mother drive away. "You didn't mean what you said about wanting to go with her, did you?"

"I only said that because she said she would have Becca put in jail for taking me if I didn't. She's my mom. I love her, even though sometimes it's hard. But things have been better since we've been here. I like going to school and making friends and having my own bedroom." She paused, her features uncertain as she looked at Becca. "Are you sure you want me to stay, though? I've caused a lot of trouble."

"Oh, absolutely, my dear." She hugged her sister close, thinking about how very much her life had changed in a few months. Trace's words seemed to ring through her head. *A woman doesn't necessarily have to give birth to be just the person for the job.*

She hadn't wanted to be a mother before Gabi came into her life. Now she couldn't imagine her world without her funny, clever, challenging little sister.

"I'm going to start putting my things away," Gabi said. "Do you think maybe I could get some posters to hang on the wall?"

Becca fought tears. Gabi wanted to decorate her room, finally, after nearly a month here. "I think that would be just perfect."

With the resiliency of the young, Gabi hurried up

the stairs, leaving Trace and Becca alone in her grand-father's living room.

She was suddenly fiercely aware of him, his solid strength and comfort. She remembered the heat of his mouth on hers and the sweet peace she found in his arms.

She swallowed, choosing to focus on the events of the morning instead of those handful of dangerous moments she replayed over and over in her mind.

"Thank you for everything. I can't believe you just let Monica leave like that, without arresting her. What about the old case?"

"The whole point was to convince her to sign the guardianship papers, not to pursue a hazy link to a ten-year-old crime she probably could never be prosecuted for. I would have liked to question her to see if she could lead us to someone else involved, but maybe I can still eventually pursue that."

She stared at him, the pieces falling together finally. Ten years. Pine Gulch. Christmas. A job that went violently wrong. "Your parents. Oh, dear heavens. Do you think she might have been involved with your parents' murders?"

He looked more distant than he had all morning. "Possibly. A woman claiming to be an art student showed up at the house out of the blue a few days before the murders, asking to see the collection. My mother was the only one home. Caidy said my mother told her about it and said she felt sorry for the woman because she was quite pregnant, without a ring on her finger, and seemed tired and down. That's the sort of thing my mother would have worried about. She thought the artwork would cheer her up, so she let her inside to see the collection and take pictures. My mother told Caidy she was quite charming."

Nausea churned in her stomach. "You think that might have been Monica?"

"I don't know. Maybe."

"All the more reason you should have arrested her!"

"I have no proof. Nothing to definitely connect her except a ten-year-old hearsay account of an encounter that may or may not have taken place. It's a starting point, though. A lead I didn't have yesterday."

"I'm so sorry."

"It's not your fault," he said firmly. "You're not responsible for something your mother may or may not have done."

He was absolutely right. She had spent far too much time in her life apologizing for Monica. In Phoenix, she had basically cleaned out her assets to pay Monica's debts. Someone else might have walked away and left the victims to suffer, but that wasn't in her nature. She might not have committed the crimes, but Monica had used Becca's connections in the real-estate world, which left her tangentially responsible.

Trace glanced at the mantel clock. "I should go. We're shorthanded from the holidays and I should be out on patrol."

"Of course. Thank you, again. You've given me a precious gift for Christmas. Peace of mind is better than anything else I could find under the tree."

"I'm glad." He smiled, and for a moment she was lost in the green of his eyes, like new leaves unfurling in the springtime....

She jerked herself back to reality. "I hate to ask but I wondered if I could have one more favor."

"Absolutely."

His immediate willingness sent more warmth to nestle near her heart. "Are you still serious about finding another home for your dog?"

He blinked. "I don't want to give him away," he said slowly. "But I have to think he would be happier where he's not alone all the time."

Wouldn't we all? she thought. "In that case, I think Gabi would love to add Grunt to our family. She's never had a pet before."

"Great! I think you're going to make a dog very happy. And a girl, for that matter. Do you want me to bring him over later so you can give him to her for Christmas morning?"

"What a wonderful idea! I never thought of that."

"I'm on until eleven. Would it be too late for me to bring him over after my shift?"

"Not at all. Are you sure you're okay with giving him away?"

"It will be better for Grunt. He'll be happy to be back here, the place that was the only home he knew. I'll miss his ugly little face but I can always visit, right?"

For some ridiculous reason, she could feel herself blush. "Yes. Anytime you'd like."

"Good to know." He smiled warmly and her blush spread.

"Merry Christmas. I'll stop by later tonight with Grunt."

She nodded and held the door open. Because of him, her Christmas suddenly seemed wonderfully bright—in no small part because she knew she would see him again in a few hours.

Chapter 13

"I know it's cold. Hang on, little dude. We'll be there in a minute."

Grunt tugged against his leash, his squat legs waddling through snow that reached his barrel chest. The dog seemed to sense he was heading back to his former home as they walked through the moonlit Christmas Eve. He showed more energy and enthusiasm than he had in a long time. Trace had to hurry to keep up, juggling his bundle of blankets and the bag full of food, toys, a water dish.

He had to admit that he was just as eager to reach Becca's house, but he forced himself to take his time and enjoy the cold air, the glitter of stars overhead, the reflection of his neighbors' colored lights gleaming through snow.

All day and evening as he had worked the inevitable fender-benders, grim domestic-disturbance calls, a small kitchen fire at old Mrs. McPurdy's that had resulted in a quick change of venue for her family's annual Christmas Eve bash, he had been aware of a low thrum of anticipation, knowing he would see Becca again.

He hadn't been able to shake the memory of the joy on her face while their mother drove away. Somehow he sensed those moments of sheer relieved joy had been rare in her life and he wanted to give her more.

Yeah, he had it bad.

He sighed, hoping he wasn't jumping ahead of himself here, like Grunt leaping into snowdrifts he couldn't find his way out of again.

The dog gave an excited huff as they reached old Wally Taylor's sidewalk and he started a sideways little dance that made Trace smile. Yes, this would be good for the dog and, he hoped, for Gabi.

The curtains were open again and he could see the Christmas tree he'd brought over a lifetime ago glowing against the winter's night. The scene inside looked bright and warm and infinitely inviting.

He knocked softly on the door, not wanting to wake up Gabi on this night where children found sleep so very difficult.

Becca opened it almost instantly, as if she had been waiting there for him. Her features were soft and welcoming and he wanted to stand on this cold porch all night and just soak her in.

"Hi."

"Hi." He couldn't think what else to say, so he only held up the leash and Grunt pranced through the doorway, the squat, ugly little lord of the manor.

Becca smiled, her eyes bright and happy as she knelt down to scratch Grunt's chin. The little French bulldog gazed at her with complete adoration. "Thank you for bringing him over. Gabi will be so thrilled tomorrow morning when she finds him under the tree."

"He's not the most attractive dog in the world for a nine-year-old girl."

"He's adorably ugly. Trust me, she's going to love him."

Trace reached down to unhook his leash and Grunt trotted around the room, sniffing all the corners and the Christmas tree. At least he no longer looked as if he expected to see Wally around every corner.

"Do you want to come in?" she asked.

Yes. With a ferocity that unsettled him. He managed a calm smile. "Sure. Thank you."

She closed the door behind him and he was immediately enveloped in the warmth from the fire and the sweet Christmas smells of pine boughs and cinnamon sugar.

"Let me take your coat," she said.

He shrugged out of it and handed it over to her. Their hands brushed, a tiny spark dancing between them, and he wanted to kiss her with a hunger that bordered on insatiable. She had pushed him away the last time. Would she again?

She hung his coat on the hook by the door. "Can I get you something? Cocoa or tea or something? I'm afraid I don't have anything stronger right now. I should have bought something but I didn't think about it."

"I'm good. Thanks."

They stood in a slightly awkward silence. She was

the first to break it, blurting out as if she'd rehearsed it, "I have to say this again. I'm so sorry again about… my mother and Gabi and everything. I feel horrible that I lied to you."

He shook his head. "Please, don't worry about it. I understand why you did. I only wish you had trusted me to help you."

"I should have." She sighed. "From the very first day we met, you've been nothing but…kind to me and to Gabi."

"Kindness has nothing to do with it."

His words sounded harsh, even to his ears. She flashed a quick look at him and he saw awareness bloom there. A fine and delicate tension suddenly seethed between them, and with a low sigh he finally reached for her and kissed her.

After a surprised moment, her mouth softened under his and he felt the brush of her arms at his sides as she wrapped them around him. She fit against him perfectly, her curves in exactly the right places, and she tasted sweet and enticing, a hint of chocolate, a hint of peppermint.

They kissed for a long time and he had the strange sense of familiarity, as if he'd been waiting for just this moment his entire life.

She made a tiny sound of pleasure that slid down his spine as if she'd trailed her fingers there, and her arms tightened around him, pressing her curves against him.

When he lifted his head some time later, her eyes were dazed, her mouth full and so lush he wanted to start all over again at the beginning. He tried to speak and had to clear his throat twice to make any words come out. "I have to know, Becca," he said gruffly. "The last time we were here in this particular place, you told me you weren't interested in a relationship. Does that statement still stand?"

She gazed at him, her eyes a huge, lash-fringed blue. She didn't say anything for several seconds, as if trying to come to a decision, and then she shook her head with a soft smile and stood on tiptoe to kiss him again.

Joy exploded through him and he laughed a little against her mouth, yanking her more tightly toward him. He kissed her hard, fiercely. She responded with a heat and passion that scorched through him, made him want to lower her to the floor right now and forget the world....

He drew in a breath, fighting for control. It was too much, too fast. He wanted to slow things down and savor every moment of this magical heat between them.

With supreme effort, he slid his mouth away, his breathing ragged. They were still standing in her entryway, he realized with some vague sense of surprise. He tugged her with him to the sofa, where he sat down and pulled her alongside him, absorbing her sweetness and her strength and all the things about this particular woman that called so strongly to him.

"It was never about you," she admitted after a moment, wrapped in his arms on the sofa while the fire glowed and the Christmas tree lights flickered.

He was aware of a vast feeling of contentment seeping through him, warming all the cold, empty places he tried not to notice most of the time.

"If you want the truth, I was afraid to let you too close. I sensed, even that first day, that you were a man I could count on, but I just...haven't had very many of those in my life."

He kissed her gently, thinking of how she had walked such a long, difficult road by herself. He hated imagining her as a girl of sixteen trying to make her way alone in a world that usually wasn't very kind.

By her own strength and force of will, she had carved out a life for herself. Had studied and worked and become an attorney, then had forced herself to give it all up to start over again because of her innate sense of right and wrong.

"I'm here now," he murmured. "And if it's okay with you, I don't plan on going anywhere."

He paused, the words he'd never said to another woman hovering on his tongue. Though some part of him warned caution, he disregarded it. She was the bravest woman he knew. He could at least show a little of that courage. "I might as well get this out there while we're laying our cards on the table. I'm in love with you, Becca."

The echo of his words seemed to hang in the air between them as she stared at him silently for a moment that seemed to drag on forever. Just as he was beginning to think he had spoken too soon, her features seemed to light up from the inside like the sparkle of Christmas lights gleaming under snow—a brilliant, beautiful smile unclouded by worry or stress.

She took his breath away, this woman who had become so vitally important to him.

"That's good," she murmured. "That's, um, really great, since I feel the same way about you."

She kissed him again and he tightened his arms around her, wanting to stay right here for the next, oh, fifty or sixty years. For a start.

* * *

She had never dreamed she could be so happy. Joy seemed to pulse through her like her heartbeat, strong and insistent, a beautiful comfort. Monica was gone, she was much closer to official guardianship of Gabi than she would have imagined, and this strong, wonderful man was holding her as if he never wanted to let her go.

Happy didn't begin to cover it.

The old clock on the mantel chimed softly, a gentle sound in the quiet hush of the house. Oddly, she imagined she felt her grandfather's presence and she wished again that she'd had the chance to know him. A long, twisting road had led her to this moment, she thought, but right now she wouldn't have changed any step on that journey.

The chimes stopped and she looked out the window at the snowflakes drifting down through a moonbeam that must be shining through the clouds.

"It's midnight," she whispered. "Merry Christmas."

He kissed her again, his body warm and solid against hers. Perfect.

"I should go," he said after more long, delicious moments. "You need some sleep."

"Don't go."

He raised an eyebrow and she could feel herself blush. "That's not what I meant. Well, it's what I want, just not quite yet. I mean…"

He laughed and kissed her forehead. "I know what you mean."

"I still have to play Santa Claus and set out the presents I bought for Gabi. I want everything to be perfect. Her first real Christmas. I know how you feel about

Christmas and I don't blame you a bit, but...would you stay and help me?"

"I can't think of anything else I'd like to do more." He gave a slightly wicked smile. "Well, okay, I can think of a *few* things. But this will do for now."

He helped her carry the presents up from the corner of the dirt-floor cellar where she'd hidden them inside boxes. It took more trips than she had expected and she was surprised by the pile of presents that had collected over the past few weeks.

As they laughed and joked, setting things around the tree, she fell further and further in love with him. Just when she thought she couldn't be filled with more happiness, somehow she managed to find a little extra room inside.

When they finished the last trip, she stood back and looked beneath the tree, full from floor to bottom branches with presents.

"I'm afraid I might have gotten a bit carried away," she admitted. "I wrapped things as I bought them and I didn't catch the full impact until now, when I see them all together like this. Do you think it's too much?"

"I think it's just right. Gabi will be thrilled."

Grunt waddled over in front of the presents and plopped his hindquarters down, gazing at them both with an expectant sort of look.

Becca laughed. "Now, if only he would stay right there for the next five hours or so until she wakes up."

"Probably not much chance of that," he said with a smile of his own. "You're really into this, aren't you?"

"I never have been before. Christmas has always been just another day to get through. This year is different."

She paused, and for some ridiculous reason, she felt tears swell in her throat. "It's wonderful. The most perfect Christmas ever."

"I completely agree," he murmured, and kissed her again while the tree lights twinkled around them and the snow drifted down lightly outside and the ugly little dog looked on with an approving sort of smile.

* * * * *

YOU HAVE
JUST READ A
HARLEQUIN®
SPECIAL
EDITION
BOOK.

Discover more heartfelt tales of **family, friendship** and **love** from the Harlequin Special Edition series. Be sure to look for all six Harlequin® Special Edition books every month.

❖HARLEQUIN®

SPECIAL EDITION

Ben figured it was only a matter of time before the security guards came to check that he'd exited. But having gotten what he'd come for, he had no reason to stay.

He went out the door and it closed automatically behind him. When he tested it out of curiosity, it was locked.

"Crazy old bat," he muttered under his breath.

But he didn't really believe it.

Kate Fortune was many things. Of that he was certain.

But crazy wasn't one of them.

He looked around, getting his bearings before setting off to his left. It was dark, only a few lights situated here and there to show off some landscape feature. But he soon made his way around the side of the enormous house and to the front, which was not just well lit, but magnificently so. He stopped at the valet and handed over his ticket to a skinny kid in a black shirt and trousers.

He tried to imagine Ella dashing off the way this kid was to retrieve his car, parked somewhere on the vast property. He couldn't quite picture it.

But in his head, he could picture *her* quite clearly.

Not the red hair. That just reminded him of Stephanie. But the faint gap in her toothy smile and the clear light shining from her pretty eyes.

That was all Ella.

A moment later, when the valet returned with his Porsche, Ben got in and drove away.

Don't miss
FORTUNE'S SECRET HEIR
by New York Times *bestselling author Allison Leigh,*
available January 2016 wherever
Harlequin® Special Edition books and ebooks are sold.

www.Harlequin.com

HSEEXP1215